Echo
and the Sea

Matthew Phillion

Echo and the Sea
Lost Continuity Press
Contact:
theindestructiblesbook@gmail.com
www.theindestructiblesbook.com
2nd Edition
June 2017
Printed in the United States of America
© 2017 Matthew Phillion
First Edition: © Matthew Phillion / Lost Continuity Press
ISBN-13: 978-0-9979165-0-8
Cover Design by Sterling Arts and Design:
http://www.sterlingartsanddesign.com
"Echo and the Sea Silhouette" art by Matthew Phillion

To Stephanie
Who keeps this lost ship on course.

Acknowledgments

It started out as a joke, really, very on while working on the Indestructibles series. The topic came up that it seems like, in every superhero-y world, there's always an Atlantis. And we talked about how the Atlanteans are always presented as incredibly powerful, but often forgotten (and of course the inevitable "he talks to fish" jokes). It got me thinking: what would Atlantis look like in the Indestructibles universe? Who would their heroes be? Would the rest of the world know about them?

I grew near the ocean. Even had dreams of being a marine biologist as a kid (what kid who grows up around the water doesn't have that dream at some point though, right?). I have *Jaws* practically memorized. I have a strong environmentalist slant in my personal beliefs. All of this started coming together to tell a story about an Atlantis, afraid for their own survival, lashing out at the surface world, and trapped in between would be this human/Atlantean young woman who would have to try to stop the two worlds she was a part of from colliding.
And that's how Echo was born.

From there, I started picking away at the mythic aspect of Atlantis. I was as much a mythology buff as I was a fanatic of whales and sharks as a kid—maybe even more so—and so I knew mythological creatures, from mermaids to minotaurs to sea monsters, would all need to play a part in this. Atlantis, I think, is tied forever to myth and magic, but cannot exist in a modern story without addressing humanity's impact on the oceans, and where the future lies for all of us.

I hope that Echo's story, and that of her friends Yuri, Barnabas, and Artem, are a swashbuckling adventure with a heart. They exist in the same universe as the Indestructibles—long-time readers will see some cameos here and there—but they have a very different world to save, one that exists outside human society, on the fringes of the fantastical and mystical parts of the Indestructiverse.

If you're an Indestructibles reader, thank you for taking a chance on Echo and her crew and allowing me the chance to explore a different part of the Indestructiverse for a while. And if you're new to this shared universe, have no fear—it's a story that runs alongside the Indestructibles series but is very much its own tale. Timeline-wise, *Echo and the Sea* takes place right around the time the first Indestructibles story happens, give or take a few months.

This story couldn't have happened without the support of those who have helped me all along: Stephanie Buck for being my ever-present lifeline through the process. Fellow writers and test subjects Colin Carlton and Christian Hegg, who let me bounce idea after idea off them all day (sorry guys). Christine Geiger, who has been a life-saver of an editor for this book. (Thank you for spotting the inadvertent Pokémon joke.) Sterling Arts & Design, who as always has done a marvelous job creating the cover. My family, for supporting my weirdness, and the fact that over the past few years more and more of my wardrobe has been made up of comic book tee shirts.

And to you, my fellow explorers of the Indestructiverse. Thanks for taking the plunge into Atlantis with me. Let's set sail together and see what we find.

Matthew Phillion
Salem, Massachusetts
June 2017

Prologue: A love story

The shoreline was nearly empty at dawn, a barren stretch of pale sand, palm trees swaying just beyond the beach. Meredith bobbed on her surfboard, the sky pink as new skin above her, her feet dangling. Cool water lapped at her bare legs, as she waited for the next crest, soaking in the emptiness of it all.

I'll miss this place, she thought. Hawaii had treated her well in her years here. She was a New England girl at heart, and she knew this, she could not fight it, but the energy here, the warmth, it was addictive. A different kind of beautiful. And to surf in a bikini instead of a heavy wetsuit, to look in to crystal-clear waters and see the soft sand below instead of the impenetrable darkness in the Atlantic—these things made her wish she could stay.

Meredith had always been a woman of the ocean, but this place changed her. The ocean wasn't always angry here the way it was back home. It wasn't always cold, it wasn't always bitter in its beauty. Sometimes, the ocean welcomed you with warm, enfolding arms.

She felt the sea swell below her and she readied herself, caught the incoming wave, planted her feet, and let her limbs fall loose. The world turned slow and languid when she surfed. Time stood still. Just a woman and the ocean, the surface of the board warm where her body had been resting seconds before, cool where the water enveloped it.

The wave wasn't particularly strong, and the morning approached quickly, so she let herself fall into the water close to shore. She still had work to do, things to see to before she went home for the funeral. So many funerals for the men and women of the sea back home. The ocean always takes its due.

When Meredith surfaced, she saw a man sitting on the beach, peacefully observing the waves. She watched him for a moment, a long-bodied stranger with a mop of curls leaning back on his hands, staring out at the sea. Curiosity overtook her. Meredith paddled in, close enough to feel the sand skim the tips of her fingers, and as she climbed from her board the weight of the world came crashing down on her. Gravity pushed on her shoulders in that strange weight she always felt as she left the ocean.

The man saw her and smiled. He had such perfect white teeth, Meredith thought, the sort of radiant smile that stopped hearts, almost unfair in its beauty. Some people can sway the world with their smiles, she thought.

"Hey," Meredith said.

"Hello," the man said.

"You waiting for someone?"

"No," the man said. He turned pale eyes out across the sea again. "I just wanted to take it all in. I never get to see the ocean from this perspective. It makes it all feel so... simple."

"I think so," Meredith said. There was a calmness to the man, a quiet contemplation that drew her in. She found herself sitting down beside him almost without intending to, setting her surfboard in the sand.

"You do?"

"I do," she said. "It's why I surf at this time of day. For the peace. I feel like it's just me and the ocean. I'm part of it. It's part of me."

4

"It is," the man said. "It's part of all of us. It's where we all come from."

"What are you, a philosophy major?" Meredith said.

"A what?"

Meredith laughed. She liked her laugh. She knew it disarmed people. She found herself hoping, vaguely, that it might disarm this beautiful man watching the waves.

"Maybe not, then," she said. "A poet? An oceanographer? What's you're deal?"

The man turned his pale eyes on her. There was a strange serenity there, and an agelessness, as if he were from another time, another world. Meredith felt strangely self-conscious as he looked at her.

"There are days I wish I could stay here forever," the man said.

"On the beach?"

"So to speak."

"Me too," Meredith said. "I have to fly home soon. Funeral for an old friend. He died at sea."

"Died at sea?"

"Yeah," Meredith said. "It's so awful. You'd think, after all this time, we'd find a way, but… the ocean always takes what it wants, doesn't it?"

"You have no idea," the man said.

Meredith stared at him. The silver flecked in his beard, his strange eyes, the way his body looked almost serpentine, as if he spent his entire life swimming. He barely looked human, in some ways. In others, he looked perfect.

"I'm Meredith," she offered.

"Hello, Meredith," the man said, his eyes looking so intently in hers she felt as if there were no other people in the entire world. "I'm Rhegis."

I suppose this is what love feels like, Meredith thought. I hope it never ends.

Chapter 1: The young woman and the sea

Echo had always felt at home in the water.

Not simply living near it, which she had, her entire life; but submerged in it, surrounded by it, seeing a darkened world through the light filtered through uneven waves; the cool, distant thrum of noises carried across the depths. The waters off the coast of Massachusetts were not known for their forgiving warmth, but the cool temperatures had never bothered Echo.

Below the surface, she felt at home.

She'd swim laps in the harbor, following the shoreline, an activity that made even the strongest swimmers she knew nervous. The undertow, they'd say, or occasionally "sharks," though anyone who grew up by the sea knew that the former was far more frequent a threat than the latter. But Echo never worried. She had no fear of the sea.

That scared her mother sometimes.

Meredith had an almost superstitious reverence for the ocean. Not religious, exactly; more what Echo called her mother's "hippie moments," when she'd talk about feeling as though the ocean had a spiritual element to it, something that called out to her. Echo always assumed that was just her mother's inner surfer speaking.

She'd been a brilliant surfer in her youth, and still was, when she allowed herself the time away from work at the icehouse their family had owned for generations. Meredith was the only heir from her generation, and Echo was Meredith's only child, so, she supposed, the icehouse would someday be hers as well.

At least it would keep her by the water.

Echo finished her laps and dragged herself back to shore, her body heavy in that way it always was when she left the ocean's cool embrace, as though the world wanted to push her back in. She shoved her hair back from her face—hair she'd dyed sea-foam green and kept shaved almost to the scalp along the left side, a look her mother said made Echo look like a broken piece of coral.

She'd left a towel and flip-flops on the shore, confident no one this early in the morning—or ever, really—would care enough to steal them. She dried off, trying in vain to kick the sand from her feet as it stuck to her skin. She found herself staring out across the harbor, watching the near-black ocean meet the near-pink skyline. It's like it goes on forever, she thought. As if I'm standing at the foot of a colossus.

She felt lost for a moment, cut adrift, as if she were not where she was meant to be. The sensation quickly faded, though, as her reverie was interrupted by a familiar voice.

"Hey! Hey, Echo!"

Yuri Rodriguez came barreling across the beach, sneakers kicking up sand behind him.

Yuri was a lot of things to Echo. Coworker at the icehouse, yes, and housemate, because Yuri had come to live with Echo and her mom when his own mother died six years ago. Best friend, in many ways, because when you live together and work together and when someone shares your mom with you, the options are best friends or worst enemies, and it was hard to not love Yuri. A big, affable guy, with a round face framed by a beard he couldn't quite fill in properly and a cheap pair of glasses, when Yuri found something funny, everyone found that something funny. And clearly right now he found something very funny. The growing grin on his face right now was infectious.

"Echo, you gotta see this," Yuri said. His face was flushed from running—he was a strong kid, but sprinting would never be his strong suit. His rested his hands on his knees and wheezed. "You're not going to believe who's docked out back."

"Okay, okay, I'm coming," Echo said. They did tend to share similar views on comedy.

They shared more than work and home, though, Echo knew, a thought they rarely spoke about but both often had. They'd both lost their fathers to the sea. It was a common theme in this town, and why Yuri's mom had asked Echo's to offer Yuri a job at the icehouse when he was old enough. His mother wanted to make sure she wouldn't lose her son the way she'd lost her husband.

Echo gave up on her flip-flops and ran barefoot for the icehouse, tying her towel around her waist as she jogged. She had to slow her pace a bit to let Yuri keep up. He often teased her about her untapped athletic ability—if he were half as fast as she was, he said, he'd have run track at school or been a running back or something. The fact that she could easily keep up with him hauling ice at work was a long-standing joke, too, given Yuri was nearly twice her size.

Then she saw the man that had Yuri in a lather.

"Okay, you're right. I don't believe it," Echo said.

Her mother stood with a stranger on that stranger's craft, a long, narrow ship that seemed more like an oversized skiff. The vessel was hard to look at somehow, as if it were designed to deceive the viewer about its size and shape. It had a single mast and an elegant prow. Nothing about the watercraft looked real, though—it seemed like something from an artist's imagination, something that made for beautiful art but would never survive at sea.

The man himself was even stranger. He wore a salt-stained leather duster, marked all along the edges with symbols Echo had never seen before. They somehow felt familiar, though, she thought, following the patterns along the man's jacket. More of these symbols dotted the man's visible skin, the backs of his hands, the side of his neck, even along his scalp, which had been shorn down to a faded stubble. He had a wild, sun-faded beard that looked like something a caveman would grow, and a silly gold hoop in his ear. A decrepit leather satchel was slung over his shoulder and, no joke, he had a sword hanging on his belt.

"Is that a sword?" Echo said out loud involuntarily.

"That is definitely a sword," Yuri answered. "He looks like Jack Sparrow's uglier, balder cousin."

"Who carries a sword?" Echo asked.

"Pirates? *Game of Thrones* cosplayers?"

The man turned his sunburned gaze on them and stared. Ordinarily it was the sort of long look that would have grossed Echo out, usually reserved for men downtown or sometimes crew on the fishing vessels who docked here for ice, but there was something different about the stare. It wasn't lascivious. It felt more curious than threatening.

He turned his attention back to Meredith. They shook hands, and Echo's mother leaned in and kissed the strange man lightly on the cheek. He smiled and his whole face brightened. Meredith disembarked with casual skill and before Echo or Yuri could get close enough to ask any questions, the little ship was drifting away.

"Wait!" Yuri said. "I had so many questions! Do you work at Disneyworld? Who makes your costumes?"

"You be nice, Yuri," Meredith said. "That was an old friend."

"Figured as much by the casual kiss on the cheek, mom," Echo said.

Meredith let out a boisterous belly laugh.

"Oh, stop that noise right there, darling daughter," she said. "Barnabas has done some good things for our business over the years. He doesn't come by much. I was just happy to see him." "Wait, wait hang on wait," Yuri said. "Barnabas?"

"I see you're having a lot of trouble processing this," Meredith said. "I propose we have breakfast so I can replace the nosey questions in your mouth with pancakes. Echo's cooking."

"I am?" Echo said.

"You are," Meredith said

"Why?" Echo said.

"Because I know for a fact you can't cook and talk at the same time," Meredith said.

"Foiled again. You know me too well," Echo said.

"Well," her mother grinned. "I am your mother after all."

Chapter 2: The oil rig

Carl Goggins never figured this was where he'd end up in life. If he was in an honest mood, he'd tell you he lucked into it—a directionless kid offered a steady paycheck working on an offshore oil rig, a chance encounter with someone who took a liking to him and put in a good word. Twenty years later, he still worked on oil rigs, and the entire environment—the noise, the rough humor of his coworkers, the wonderfully heavy dinners at the end of long, hard days—had become home to him.

He worked two weeks on, two weeks off, same as the other guys, but he didn't have much to go home to—again, something he'd tell you in a particularly honest mood. There was a wife a long time ago who left him, a brother who moved to California he talked to a few times a year. Parents gone, no kids. Just work. Maybe this is the sort of life he was born to do, he wondered, the kind of lonely business for a guy who didn't have anyone waiting for him at home.

The workers here were kind of like family, though, Carl thought. You had to be, given how tight the environment was, the dormitory-style sleeping arrangements, the fact there truly was nowhere to go to get away from everyone else.

He'd worked the day shift but a backache kept him restless and he couldn't sleep, so Carl wandered up onto one of the high walkways to look at the ocean. You get to the point, he realized, that you don't see it anymore, the water. You're out here, surrounded by it, no land in sight, and you think it'd impact you more. That it might even scare you a little. But like anything, familiarity breeds contempt, and the ocean was the proverbial lawn outside their office building. Just something your eyes don't even notice anymore after a while.

Tonight though, and he couldn't tell you why, his eye was drawn to it. He leaned on the railing and watched moonlight break across the surface. The darkness of it, the vastness, gave Carl a feeling of vertigo, as if his mind had trouble processing just how much of it there was.

The unpleasant fluttering in his stomach started to subside. He took comfort in the things he'd come to count on: the smell of machinery and fuel; the solidity of the frame beneath him; the cool air blowing in off the water. Familiar things. Sensations he'd known his entire adult life. The noise of the place, he thought, so much noise, but that noise meant you were never alone. The rig was filled with life, and the rig itself was alive in a way, a great beast of a thing, standing so tall the ocean was just a wading pool for it.

But then he noticed the quiet.

The usual hum of activity was gone. The clank and rumble of automated machinery, yes, but the voices—the yelling, the laughing, the cursing, the general babble of humanity—had fallen silent.

Carl looked out at the water and listened.

I've never felt this alone in my entire life, he thought.

He started back town the metal stairs, heading deeper into the rig. He wanted to start yelling to see if anyone would answer back, but something instinctual, some gut-level impetus, told him to stay quiet.

He placed his hand against the railing as he reached the bottom of the staircase. His palm came away wet. Ordinarily, this shouldn't come as any surprise—even this high up the sea would kick off mists, and the heat of the day would turn to condensation as the air grew cold.

Again, his instincts cried out to him. He turned his hand over so he could look at his palm. His skin was bright red with blood.

"No," he muttered. No, this can't be blood. It's a something else. Something benign. It just looks red in the dark.

He tried then to call out to his coworkers, to ask if they were playing a joke on him. This wasn't fair. It wasn't funny at all. You can't joke around out here, he thought. The rig could kill you so fast if you weren't careful. Practical jokes were a liability here.

But his voice wouldn't work. The words became a croaking sound. His tongue felt dry.

And then he felt a thump in his chest, followed by searing pain. It happened so fast he barely registered it at all—one moment he was terrified, and the next, he couldn't draw a breath.

He looked down. The shaft of an ornate spear jutted out of his chest. This should hurt more, he found himself thinking, his body growing cold, has panic fading. This doesn't feel real.

He saw the creature's eyes first, stepping up out of the bowels of the rig from where the spear had launched. Not a creature, Carl thought, his body growing cold and numb. A man, in a mask, some half-helmet carved like an ocean predator, with pointed angles and sweeping fins. The attacker calmly took hold of the spear, twisting it a bit, sending waves of pain through Carl's entire body.

Again, Carl's words left him. His thoughts grew more incoherent. All these years, he had worried he'd die on an oil rig, in an accident, in an explosion. Some slip of attention or safety violation.

Not like this, Carl thought. Not like this.

The man in the mask choked up on his grip on the spear with one hand and pushed Carl backward with the other, shoving him off the hooked, tri-bladed end. Carl dropped over the railing, plummeting into the ocean. As he fell, his world rotated, oil rig, sky, and waves. Oil rig, sky, and waves.

The waves enveloped him, and they welcomed him home.

Chapter 3: The icehouse

Life, Echo thought, could be amazingly mundane.

Aside from encountering the guy who they thought was a pirate in the morning, the day was extraordinarily quiet. Orders were taken, delivery trucks loaded up. Yuri and Echo competed, as they sometimes did, with moving huge blocks of ice using long, hooked metal poles, with Yuri, as usual, feigning shock at how strong she was.

"They need a name for what you can do," Yuri said. "You must have super-strength or something."

"Maybe you're just weaker than you look," she taunted back. Yuri flexed playfully.

"Maybe I let you win," he said. But his breathlessness and red face told another story.

Echo wandered down to the office late in the day, leaving Yuri to finish up in the warehouse. She cut through reception, where the aging television mounted high on the wall played a twenty-four hour news station. The sound had been turned down low, but she could still pick up what was being said. Echo grabbed the remote from beneath the front desk and raised the volume.

"—dozens of oil rig workers disappeared in the night in what officials are simply calling an ongoing investigation," the too-blonde reporter said, reading from a script. "Unverified accounts have reported blood on the rig, but not a single employee remained on board. Search and rescue teams are on the scene…"

Echo grimaced. She had an environmentalist's heart, like her mother. The idea of drilling for oil in the ocean turned her stomach. But she knew plenty of people who worked hard at jobs she didn't agree with. Nobody deserved to meet a bad end just trying to make a living. The news footage indicated it was a jack-up rig—she'd read somewhere those could have more than fifty workers on-site.

Where do fifty people go in the middle of the night? Echo thought about the weird pirate this morning, and how he looked nothing like what modern pirates looked like with their machine guns and fast little ships. Maybe someone attacked the rig in the dark. An ambush.

In the end, she shrugged it off. Nothing she could do about it, Echo thought. Still, she liked a mystery, especially if it happened at sea. She hoped the workers were okay, though part of her hoped the rig itself would not reopen. Reading stories of oil spills kept her up at night the way regular people had nightmares about serial killers.

She walked into the office, situated behind the lobby with windows looking out at the front desk, and found her mother reviewing invoices.

Meredith looked up at her and smiled broadly.

"And all of this, my sweet child, will someday be yours," she said.

"Do I have to?" Echo said.

Meredith shrugged.

"Believe me, there have been whole entire years I've thought about selling it," she said. "I wanted to move to Hawaii, you know."

"Oh, I've heard that story a few times," Echo said. "Why didn't you?"

"And leave all this behind?"

"Seriously, mom. I know you're not unhappy here, but running the family business wasn't what you wanted," Echo said.

"I can't help but wonder if you're feeling me out for how I'd respond if you bailed on the family business," Meredith said.

Echo shrugged.

"I just don't want—okay, you went away for a while, right? You lived other places."

"I did," Meredith said.

"I don't want to be the girl who never left home," Echo said.

"I would be sorely disappointed in you if you never left home, Echo," her mom said.

"No, seriously," Echo said.

"Seriously," Meredith said. "I would be furious with you if you never went out and saw the world. You know why I've stuck it out here this long? Because I want to make sure I can help you do that."

"Mom."

"Daughter."

Echo laughed.

"Look," Meredith said. "I didn't have a daughter so she could be my little mini-me and do all the things I did in the exact same way. I want you to do what you need to do to be happy, and I will always have your back, whatever you choose."

"You know you're the best mom, right?"

"Oh, I know I'm the best mom. I checked. Ranked first in the world."

This time they both chuckled. Meredith tidied up a stack of invoices and set them aside.

"So that dude this morning," Echo said. "I have another question."

"Barnabas. You worried I'm going to sail away with the crazy guy with the sword?"

"Okay seriously, I wasn't going to bring it up, but he had a sword, mom. What kind of person walks around wearing a sword?

Also, he didn't have any crew I could see. That was too much boat for one guy, unless he's some sort of world-class sailor."

"Barnabas is a weird creature," Meredith said. "But he's been a friend to our business, and a friend to me. I told you I hadn't seen him for a few years until yesterday. If I'd known he was going to come here, I would've made sure you were around to meet him."

"He didn't seem interested in meeting me, the way he left," Echo said.

Meredith smirked.

"Maybe it was the way you and Yuri were staring at him," Meredith said.

Echo bobbed her head back and forth noncommittally. She had a point.

"Anyway," Echo said. "You hear about the oil rig?"

"Yeah," Meredith said. The smile faded from her face. "It's sad. But that's the thing we always forget. We think we're the masters of this world, but… the sea always takes its due. It's one of the inevitabilities of life."

"There you go, being hippie mom again," Echo said.

"But I'm the *best* hippie mom," Meredith said. "And don't you forget it."

Chapter 4: The predators

A man sat alone on a rocky outcropping in the middle of the empty ocean. The outcropping had delusions of being an island, but in truth, it existed as little more than a clawed finger jutting out of the sea, a thing for ships to run into in the dark. The ocean was littered with tiny deathtraps like this, the man knew. They'd kept sailors from returning to their families in time immemorial.

The man was himself equally unassuming, in a way. Soft-spoken, he had the sort of handsome face that would leave people struggling to remember where they'd met him before, just interesting enough to be attractive, but without anything truly distinguishing to make him memorable. He wore his hair, the sort of black so dark it looked almost blue in certain lights, brushed back smoothly from his forehead. If he had one characteristic that stood out it was the expressiveness of his eyebrows. He said little with his voice, but could hold an entire conversation with a look.

The man was known as the Barracuda. A dramatic name for an unremarkable person, the moniker was something he'd resented for a long time, a joke about his blade-thin body, of course, but also about his profession.

Where Barracuda was born, to be named after an ocean creature meant one of two things. For some it was intended as a grotesque insult. And for others, it was a mark of a certain brotherhood, a profession among his people. Those who were named after ocean predators were men who had given up their names in the service of their lords, and that service was murder.

Barracuda was an assassin. And he was very good at his job.

Today, though, the task was not killing. Not directly, at least. He'd been sent here as a middle-man, for the distasteful task of hiring muscle to do a nasty deed. The sort of nasty deed a professional killer would be overqualified for, for one; but also, a deed where plausible deniability would be required.

The hired help arrived in the form of a dozen men, rising out of the ocean wearing rags. For anyone else, the sight might have been terrifying. The men were all sizable fellows, broad-shouldered with thick, powerful limbs. Many of them were misshapen in some way—their mouths too wide, their teeth too big, their eyes too wide-set, their noses too small. This characteristic was far more prominent on some than others. The leader, who wore his graying hair in a mohawk that had flopped to one side, soaked with water, looked more keenly human than the others. He might pass among ordinary company, if he kept his mouth shut.

"We got your message, assassin," the leader said. His voice had a roughness to it, as if he rarely spoke. Even the words seemed malformed, tongue and teeth turning over the syllables with unfamiliarity.

"Good," Barracuda said. He stood up and unfurled a hand-drawn map, which he placed on the ground for all to see. He gestured to a location on that map, a harbor along a nearby coastline.

"I have more details about the location for you," Barracuda said. "The targets will be here. You are to fetch them for me."

"Fetch," the leader said. He looked at Barracuda as if he'd never heard the word before.

"Capture," Barracuda said. "Alive."

"That's not our usual role," the man said.

"I don't care. I know you've engaged in kidnapping before.

You're going to do so again," he said. "You're not to kill them, but you are to scare the living hell out of them. I'd like you to wear your… other faces when you take them."

"We hate these faces," the man said. "Our other faces are more true."

"Then you'll give me no argument over using them," Barracuda said. The leader nodded, his men behind him bobbing in agreement. "No harm is to befall either target. Is that understood."

"Accidents," the leader said. "They happen."

"If they happen I will exact such a price that you will very much regret it," Barracuda said.

The men outnumbered him six to one. Each one of them outweighed him by a hundred pounds, at least. They bristled at his threatening words. The leader took encouragement from the rumble of discontent from his men and leaned in. His breath smelled like spoiled meat. These creatures always smelled like dead flesh, Barracuda thought. He found them all distasteful. But his employer had asked specifically for this breed for the task.

"You think you can scare us?" the leader said.

"I believe you know well enough to fear me," Barracuda said.

"You think too much of your reputation," the leader said. He shot a hand out to grab Barracuda by the throat.

Two of the man's fingers landed on the rocky ground beneath them.

Blood spurted from his hand for a moment, but stopped with supernatural speed. The leader held his hand, staunching the blood flow. He stared at the blade that has appeared as if from nothing in Barracuda's hand, a dagger made of bone.

The leader took an involuntary step back. He removed his grip from his hand. The stumps of his fingers were already starting to grow back. Barracuda knew this would happen. It was one of the reasons these men were so useful.

"Touch me again and I'll use a blade of iron," Barracuda said. "Do not push me."

The leader looked back at his men. None would make eye

contact with him. He turned back to Barracuda.

"Payment," the man said, still absently rubbing the stumps where his fingers had been just a moment before.

Barracuda kicked a leather sack on the ground next to him.

"You'll find this sufficient. And I'll double it when you bring your captives to me," he said.

"It will be done," the man said.

He scooped up the satchel and slung it over his shoulder. He and his men walked back into the ocean, disappearing beneath the waves, no ship in sight.

When they'd gone, Barracuda kicked the stray fingers into the ocean, tucking the bone-knife back into his belt. It was a simple thing, the task his master wanted these creatures to perform.

But Barracuda learned long ago that having faith in monsters was a losing proposition. He hoped, this time, that his master's faith was deserved.

Chapter 5: The heartbeat of the world

Echo returned to the beach that evening, as she often did, swimming more laps before the sun dropped too low in the sky. She liked the ocean at this time of day; the way the water held onto some of the warmth of the sun, far longer than the air did, so diving in felt like a blanket enveloping her as she took the plunge.

Sometimes people would ask her—strangers, mostly, seeing her swimming along the shore so late in the day—if the ocean scared her, if not knowing what resided beneath her there in the dark New England waters ever moved her to fear.

Maybe it should, she thought. Maybe I have too much faith in the ocean. But wrapped in salt water, her arms and legs moving with power and grace to propel her forward, the ocean felt like home. She felt welcomed by it, as if this were always and forever exactly where she belonged.

She finished her circuit and swam back to shore, but she didn't pull herself from the water right away. She let herself drift in a few feet of water, just her face above the surface, and closed her eyes. She felt like she could hear for miles like this. Echo knew that it couldn't be real, not truly. But she imagined she could catch snippets of whale songs in the distance, the rumble of waves unseen, rocks clinking together along the ocean floor knocked about by tidal movement.

The surface world faded away as she floated, her life, the troubles, and tribulations an eternity away. She could hear the heartbeat of the world.

Or she could until Yuri interrupted her.

"Hey, Ariel. Gonna grow some legs and come to dinner?"

Echo sat up in the water, brushing the hair from her face. She sat in the shallows for a moment, unwilling to meet the cooling evening air.

"Depends. You cooking?"

"Your mom and I had a long discussion about our culinary options and we decided to pursue the path of laziness and order pizza," Yuri said.

"As long as you're not cooking, I'll join you," Echo said.

"You like my cooking."

"I'm polite."

"Your mom likes my cooking," Yuri said.

"My mom is polite too."

Yuri's relationship with Meredith was a source of infinite amusement for Echo. She never had any siblings, but Yuri had joined the family with almost preternatural smoothness, as if this lost young man was the missing piece in their household. His father was a fisherman, lost at sea during a tragic accident when Yuri was very young. Because of that loss, Yuri's mother had forced him to work at the icehouse instead of following in his father's footsteps. It was a bit of motherly manipulation Yuri resented at first. But he'd come to consider the icehouse a second home eventually, and Meredith and Echo a part of his family. So, when his mother passed away suddenly, and Yuri found himself with nowhere to go… he came here and never left.

Despite everything he'd been through, Echo admired Yuri's buoyant optimism. For all the tragedy he'd faced, he smiled more easily than anyone she knew, and he could get Meredith laughing with a casual joke or observation. He worked hard, and he cared about the icehouse, maybe even more than Echo did. In a way,

Echo hoped her mom would turn the place over to Yuri when she was ready to retire, instead of to Echo herself. He'd be a better steward for the icehouse. He loved it in ways she didn't.

"Why you looking at me like that," Yuri said, shaking Echo out of her memories.

"You have something on your face," Echo said, jumping, as usual, immediately to sarcasm to cover her maudlin moment.

"Do yourself a favor, Echo, and never go into insult comedy," Yuri said. "You're not quick-witted enough for it."

"Now you're getting personal."

"Actually, I'm just getting hungry," Yuri said. "I suggest you hurry up and get to the kitchen before Meredith and I eat all the mushroom and green pepper slices."

"You wouldn't dare," Echo said

Yuri spun on his heel and started running.

"Try and stop me!"

And he was off. Echo jumped out of the water and started running as well, grabbing her towel and sandals as she ran.

For just a moment, though, the ocean called to her, a tickle at the back of her mind. Echo turned around, looking back at the waves. The sun was low, the sky burnt orange, the water itself a deep and angry gray.

The ocean has moods, she thought. And she didn't like the mood it seemed to be in tonight.

Chapter 6: The hunt begins

Creatures swam below the surface, silent and agile despite their bulk. Their bodies were almost human, though their musculature was more designed for a life aquatic than land-bound. They had head like sharks, wedge-shaped mostly, though one of their number bore the signature countenance of a hammerhead, their eyes black pearls, their skin sandpaper.

Dorsal fins jutted from between their shoulder blades. Their shark-like appearance was supplemented with tails, functional and powerful. Their calves and forearms were decorated with fins as well, their hands and feet webbed and tipped with sharp points of bone.

Just hours before, these creatures had walked the surface like men. For some, this had been a more painful experience than others. While a few, like their leader, were born in the world of men, others began life below the surface, and emerging into the light above was like torture. Their bodies did not move comfortably in that world, the shapes their human forms took on appeared not quite right, unpleasing to human eyes, the rough approximation of a land-dweller.

This is why they followed their leader, the one who called himself Maw, despite the fact that Maw had lived for years among ordinary men before abandoning that life for the ocean. Maw spoke like a man, he knew the dealings of humans. He could navigate both worlds in ways those born like the sharks they shared so many characteristics with never could. Those of their kind born at sea fell prey to their baser instincts more readily than their land-born kin. Though Maw and his brothers were more than capable of baser deeds. He earned the name he wore through acts of tooth and claw, after all.

Acts such as the one the killer called Barracuda had paid them to do tonight. They'd accepted his payment, shed their human forms, and slithered into the sea like the predators they all were—bodies fading to white, silver, and blue, minds dulling to thoughts of hunting and feeding. These creatures were feared throughout the all the oceans of the world, though their numbers were few, and growing fewer each year. They were a dying breed of monster, born of legends even sailors have long forgotten.

Their blood money came in the form of the sort of things one could trade among the myths and monsters who inhabited the seas; currency based on rarity and usefulness, the glamorous and the mysterious. These creatures, these lycanthropic shark-men, could be easily bought with baubles, or such things that would aid them in a hunt.

For most of their kind, the hunt was their entire existence. It served them well, and it kept them alive.

And tonight, they hunted.

Chapter 7: The long night

A storm rolled in after dinner and never let up. Echo and her family watched it shamble toward them like an angry god, thick black clouds spitting lightning in the distance, bringing an early end to what had been a beautiful day. The wind whistled through the screen windows as Echo and Meredith rushed to seal up the house. Yuri ran across the street to make sure the windows in the office at the ice house were shut tight.

Echo loved ocean storms. She knew they scared people with their fury and power, but to her, these storms were nature incarnate, everything beautiful and dangerous the natural world could be.

Rain came without warning, the sort of sheets that kicked back up off the pavement like miniature geysers. She laughed as she watched Yuri run back, soaked through, holding his jacket up over his head in a pointless effort to stay dry.

He got her back, quickly pulling off his jacket and squeezing it over her head. Cold rainwater poured down her scalp and the back of her shirt.

"Oh, come on!" Echo yelled.

"You're mad at *me*? I just watched you laugh at me the whole way back!"

"Don't deny me life's little joys, Yuri."

"Whatever," he said, feigning anger. "I'm going to change my shoes."

The lights flickered a few times, and Meredith gave up watching television—"I don't want to get absorbed in something and have the power go out," she said, retiring to her room. Never a night owl, Yuri fell asleep sitting up on the couch and eventually roused himself enough to find his way to bed. Echo locked up and took a book to her room. Eventually sleep found her as well, curled up like a cat in her bed, still dressed from the day.

She woke up in the middle of the night, unsure what disrupted her sleep. She laid in bed for a moment, staring at the ceiling, eyes adjusting to the light she'd left on, her face numb from where she'd pressed it into the sheets.

She heard a thump downstairs and sat up quickly, listening. Yuri was a big guy, and he didn't have the best eyesight, so he did have a tendency to walk into furniture in the night if he got up for a midnight snack. But something in her gut told her to pay attention. She heard floorboards creak. Not in just one part of the house, either. Were her mother and Yuri both up? Her mom slept like a hibernating bear. She never got up in the night. Was someone sick?

She sniffed at the air. Seawater. The house smelled like seawater. Echo wrinkled her nose. It made no sense. Maybe I'm still dreaming, she thought. Maybe this is all in my head. I'll wake up and be angry I lost my page in the book.

Then she heard footsteps outside her door.

Instinct sent her to her nightstand, where, inside her top drawer, she kept a dive knife for when she went skin diving in the warmer months. She pulled the knife from its sheath and reversed her grip on it. She crept to her door and stood alongside the frame, listening.

The doorknob turned. She knew, instantly, that something was truly wrong. Her mother always knocked; and Yuri, ever respectful of her space, would announce himself from the hallway. Only a stranger would open her door in the night.

She readied herself to attack, expecting a thief, or worse. But what entered her room that night was the stuff of nightmares.

The smell hit her first, seawater and rotten meat, an alien tang that was almost overwhelming. Next came the bulk, the sheer size of the thing, bigger than a man, and shaped all wrong. Its head entered before the rest of its body, and the sight was so absurd Echo almost laughed—a full-sized shark's head, the triangular nose, the button-black eyes, the rows of teeth in a wicked smile. But it had arms like a man, muscular and grayish white, and hands twice the size any human's hands should be.

This can't be happening, she thought.

And then it saw her.

She did the first thing her body told her to do and drove her dive knife into the creature's right eye, connecting perfectly, blood and ichor spurting out onto her enclosed fist. The sound the creature made was inhuman, a wheezing bellow so loud it took her breath away. But Echo plunged the knife down, over and over, more times than she could remember, the surface of the creature's head and shoulder so wide she couldn't miss.

The creature swung at Echo with an apelike arm, battering her aside. It tried to scoop her up in its oversized hands, but she jammed her dive knife through its palm, evoking another scream of pain. She scurried away, slipping as her bare feet connected with its blood, and the creature ran at her, feet like those a dinosaur would have chipping and breaking the wooden floor.

Without thinking, Echo put her feet up. They connected with the creature's belly, but its momentum carried it forward, up, and over, smashing through her bedroom window, the mass of the beast breaking through glass and plaster and wood, sending it spiraling down to the street a story below.

She bolted upright, her legs wobbly, her heart pounding. And then she heard her mother scream.

Echo ran into the hallway, barefoot and unarmed. She made it just a few steps before another one of the shark-men stomped up the stairs, blocking her path. He didn't speak, just stared at her with his blank, emotionless eyes and wide, grinning mouth. He stepped toward her, hands outstretched.

Then Echo heard a metallic thump, a brutal sound, and the creature wobbled on its feet. Another thump accompanied by the grotesque sound of flesh ripping; the shark creature fell to its knees. Behind him, Yuri stood with one of the long metal ice picks he and Echo used to drag and push the cakes of ice around the floor at the icehouse. He held it like a battle-axe, dropping it again on the monster's head.

Yuri looked down at the fallen creature, which still stirred with life. Echo jumped over him as best she could, headed for the stairs.

"My mom!" she yelled.

Yuri hesitated a split second, looking at the blood on his ice pick.

"What are these things?" he asked, mostly to himself.

Echo ignored him, barreling down the stairs. She could hear Yuri running to catch up to her. At the foot of the stairs, another shark-man waited, and Echo, with no weapon, no way to defend herself, just charged at him, throwing a haymaker at his face. She expected her fist to just bounce off, as effective as punching a wall; but the creature's pointed snout crumpled under her fist so badly she heard cartilage snapping, and the shark-man lost his footing, falling into the wall.

Echo left him there, hearing but not looking back as Yuri planted his ice pick between the creature's eyes. Echo kept going, though, running into the kitchen to find one of the monsters standing over her mother, looking at her with a strange mixture of hunger and curiosity. A bread knife stuck out of the shark-man's head, a comical decoration to the beastly countenance; a chef's knife stuck out of the creature's side, dripping with blood.

But her mother held her own abdomen, as if trying to stop her own life from spilling out. Blood covered the floor beneath her.

"No!" Echo yelled. Without thinking, she ran at the shark-man. The creature seemed too confused to know what to do as this diminutive ran at him with unleashed fury. Echo heard Yuri behind her, yelling incoherently, something between fear and grief, but she was too far gone, to angry, and she grabbed hold of the monster, her fingers digging into the gills on his oversized throat, and she yanked him away from her mother, spinning and throwing him at the glass doors leading out to their back deck. Glass exploded all around them; the foundation of the house shook, and then, silence.

Yuri was trying to talk to her. Echo couldn't hear him. Not through her anger. She ran to her mother, dropping to her knees to hold her in her arms like a baby.

"Momma," Echo said.

Meredith looked up at her, a thin trickle of blood running from the corner of her mouth.

"My beautiful girl," she said. Her hand, slick with blood, took Echo's, and she squeezed with a frighteningly weak grip.

"No," Echo said.

"There's so many things I should have told you," her mother said. Echo gasped as her mother's eyes became unclear; she seemed to star as much into eternity as into Echo's face.

"You still have time, momma," Echo said.

"We kept a whole world from you," Meredith said. "That was such a mistake. We made so many mistakes."

"What do you mean?" Echo said. She held her mother tighter. "What are you talking about? Yuri! Yuri, call an ambulance!"

Out of the corner of her eye she saw Yuri pacing, his ice pick in one hand, a cell phone in the other, his body language like that of someone who had just witnessed an explosion, confused, anxious, fearful, lost. Echo couldn't make out his words, but they were full of panic.

"I'm sorry baby," Meredith said. "I'm sorry for leaving you. This is all my fault."

"No!" Echo said. "You're not leaving. Yuri! Yuri help! Momma you can't leave. You can't leave me."

The monsters, the nightmare, it all faded away; the only thing real in the entire world was her mother, dying in her arms, staring distantly into her daughter's eyes.

Echo felt Yuri's warmth as he knelt beside them, his big hand helping Meredith stanch the blood pouring out of her belly. Meredith looked up at Yuri and smiled at him softly.

"Look out for my baby," she said.

"No," Yuri said, fear rising in his voice. "No, you're going to look out for her yourself, don't you dare tell me…"

"I love you both so much," Meredith said. She smiled and looked at a point in the distance no one else could see. "I'm so happy I could say goodbye. Not everyone says goodbye."

And then she exhaled, and drew no more breath.

"No!" Echo yelled again, burying her face in her mother's hair. She sensed movement behind her, but she didn't care—this was a nightmare, she thought, this was all a terrible dream, these monsters, her mother, she'd wake up tomorrow and everything would be the way it was supposed to be.

Yuri stood up fast, his ice pick scraping against the floor. He held it like a baseball bat. Echo glanced over her shoulder. Two of the shark creatures had returned, one viciously scarred, bigger than the others; the second with a skull like a hammerhead shark. They pressed into the house, slowly, as if not to startle the humans.

"Echo…" Yuri said.

And then there was a bright flash of blue, and an explosive bang, once, twice, the room lighting up, filling up with the smell of electricity. The shark-creatures shuddered, their bodies collapsing, writhing. Echo could see the face of the scarred one; a gaping wound had replaced where its eye had been.

Striding through the shattered glass doors was the pirate from that morning. Barnabas. Her mother's friend. He walked calmly, that insane sword in one hand, an old-fashioned gun in the other. The gun glowed blue as if it burned with an inner power. He aimed it at the hammerhead shark-man and fired again, then holstered the weapon.

"We've got to get you out of here," Barnabas said, extending a hand to Echo. She just stared at him.

"My mother," Echo said.

Barnabas looked at Meredith's body, and his ugly, tattooed,

scarred face softened. For just a moment, he looked as if he might cry. But like heated clay, that face hardened again.

"We can't stay here. Come on," Barnabas said.

"Why should we go with you?" Echo said.

"Because it's what Meredith would have wanted. Because I made her a promise," Barnabas said. "Now come on before I have to knock you out and drag you to my ship."

Yuri stepped between them, ice pick in hand.

"You're not taking her anywhere," he said.

"Oh, for the love of all the gods—these things aren't dead. Move."

"I'm not letting you take her," Yuri said.

"I'm not leaving Yuri here with these things," Echo said.

Barnabas sighed, looking at the shark-men, back and forth. He pulled his gun out and shot the scarred one in the head again.

"This won't work forever," he said. "Fine. The boy can come. Move it. "

"We can't just leave like this," Yuri said. "The police…"

"Can't help you. Now."

"My mother," Echo said. "We can't just…"

Again, Barnabas' harsh gaze softened. He pointed at Yuri.

"You have to carry her," he said.

Yuri looked about to argue, but changed his mind, looping his ice pick into his belt and kneeling beside Meredith's body. He scooped her up easily, holding her like a sleeping child. Echo knew, at that moment, she'd never forget the tenderness her friend was capable of.

Barnabas stepped back outside, and Echo saw his gun flash again, the thump of a massive body shaking the frame of the house. She followed, bare feet covered in blood, looking over her shoulder to make sure Yuri was close by. Together, the trio ran for Barnabas' ship, waiting at the dock behind the icehouse. Before they were even on board, the ship began to pull away, as if of its own volition. Barnabas took Meredith's body from Yuri and laid her down on the deck. With shocking gentleness, he reached down and closed her eyes with his index finger and thumb.

"I'm sorry, my old friend. I got here as fast as I could," he said in almost a whisper.

He stood up, making no move to steer or control the ship, letting the craft do whatever it appeared to want to do of its own free will. He pulled out his pistol again and whispered something to it, muttering in a spidery language Echo couldn't identify. He pointed it at their home, growing small and lonely in the distance. Barnabas pulled the trigger. Instead of blue light, a burst of orange flame erupted from the gun instead.

That light struck the house. The entire building erupted in flames.

"What are you doing?" Echo screamed.

"Buying us time," Barnabas said. Then he spoke to no one at all, yelling into the night air. "Gentlemen! Get us out of here. Where? East. I don't care the specifics. Just put as much distance as you can between us and those psychopathic lycanthropes."

"We've been kidnapped by a crazy person," Yuri said. He sat alone in the prow of the ship, looking at the blood drying on his ice pick.

Barnabas left them, stomping up toward the helm, which seemed to be steering them just fine on its own.

"This is a nightmare," Echo said, numbness setting in. "Tell me this is a nightmare, Yuri."

"I hope it's a nightmare, Echo," Yuri said. "I have to believe that."

Chapter 8: Derelict

Jeremy Kiper had dedicated his life to stopping whaling. His parents always wished he'd used his brains for something more productive—his mother was fond of saying he could've been a doctor if he wanted to save the world—but Jeremy had always been a dreamer and an idealist, and the idea of a world where humans kept killing off species of animals for profit was abhorrent to him.

He'd spent most of his adult life roaming the planet, engaging in what most rational people would consider near-suicidal tactics to stop whaling ships from hunting their targets.

But he'd never seen anything like the sight of the whaling vessel *Three Brothers* in front of him right now.

The ship, a mid-sized commercial whaling vessel that had for years worked under the deceitful terminology of "scientific whaling," listed to one side drunkenly. Lights onboard flickered as if on the fritz. Its engines were silent, and so was its crew. It looked, from two hundred meters away, like a ghost ship.

"Get us in closer," Jeremy said. His own team brought their inflatable Zodiac boat around the side of the whaler. The half-dozen activists onboard exchanged fearful looks. They usually only got this close if they tried to get between a whaler and a whale, putting their own lives at risk to act as a human shield. No one cursed them out from the deck of the ship. No death threats in foreign tongues lashed out at them. Just silence.

"I'm going on board," Jeremy said. Sven, the Zodiac's pilot, shook his head vigorously.

"You're nuts," he said. "They'll kill you. You know they'll kill you."

Jeremy stared up at the massive, silent vessel.

"I don't think they will," he said.

"I'll go with you," Camila, an activist from Colombia, said, tying her hair back and rolling up her sleeves.

"Me too," said James, an aging Brit who'd been at this game so long his long hair had turned completely gray.

"Okay," Jeremy said. He turned to Sven. "If anything happens, you take the rest of the crew and go, okay? Leave us. We'll work it out."

"I'm not just abandoning you," Sven said.

"You have to, mate," James said. "Need someone to go get the ransom money and the lawyers."

Sven nodded slightly, unhappy but understanding.

Jeremy, Camila, and James hauled themselves up over the rail onto the deck of the whaling ship. They were unarmed, though James had a heavy-duty flashlight that could act—and had acted—as a club in a pinch. They walked slowly, quietly, toward the stern of the ship.

The decks were stained and grimy. This was an older vessel, an ancient killing machine. Jeremy wanted to set it on fire and go. But the silence scared him. What happened here? Did they abandon ship?

"Jeremy," Camila said softly. She pointed. James turned on his flashlight and followed her gesture with the beam.

"It's a body," Jeremy said. One of the crewmen was on his back, throat cut, blood staining the wooden deck below him.

"Oh, my God," Camila said.

"Don't touch anything," James warned. "They'll blame us for

this if they catch us."

"Wait," Jeremy said. He reached over and took James' wrist, aiming his flashlight inside a nearby doorway. Another crewman, sitting on the floor, slouched over, his head tilted at an impossible angle.

"Was there a mutiny?" Camila said.

"Come on," Jeremy said, heading toward the back of the ship where the bulk of the whaling machinery would be. Was Camila right? Was this a mutiny? Pirates? Was there some other activist group that had gone too far? His stomach felt loose and hot. He'd been afraid before—driving an inflatable dinghy at a huge commercial vessel felt like rolling the dice on suicide—but not like this. This wasn't protest violence. This was murder.

And there they found the rest of the crew.

A common nightmarish sight for the activists had always been dead whales hung by their tails; whalers would often transport them like this, majestic creatures reduced to all the beauty of a wet sock hanging from a rack. Whoever attacked the *Three Brothers* had a grim sense of humor. The rest of the crew had been strung up in a grotesque parody of their whale victims, feet lashed together and bodies hung upside down by their ankles.

Camila started swearing in Spanish. James wretched. Jeremy felt his head spinning. This was something out of a horror movie, he thought. This can't be real.

"We're going," James said. "We… we're leaving. We can't stay here."

"We have to call it in," Camila said. "We can't just leave this ship here."

"We call it in they're going to assume we did it," James said. "It'll destroy us. We can't."

"What if these people are out there hunting other ships!" Camila yelled.

"Then good!" James said. "Who cares! These bastards have been murdering innocent creatures for money. Maybe this is karma!"

"We're not calling it in from here," Jeremy said. "Don't touch anything. We're going to go back to our boat and we'll call it in from somewhere safer."

"Safer?" Camila said.

"Whoever did this might still be on board," Jeremy said.

That got the trio of activists moving—it was all they could do to resist sprinting back to their boat. Jeremy almost burst into tears when he saw their companions were still there, Sven and the others looking up at them expectantly. He waited for Camila and James to disembark before climbing over the railing as well, careful not to touch the railing with his bare hands, afraid of leaving fingerprints.

But as he threw his leg over to climb down, something caught his eye. A knife unlike anything he'd seen before, with a blade almost white, like bone, its handle carved from right pink coral. Dried rivulets of blood stained the edge.

"No," Jeremy said. He didn't want to know. He never wanted to meet the sort of people who could do something like this.

The sky darkened as the Zodiac zipped away. Jeremy could hear James on the radio calling for help. Jeremy watched as the whaling vessel grew smaller in the distance, a derelict ship full of dead men.

Chapter 9: Who you are

At some point during the night, Barnabas had draped a blanket over Meredith's body. Echo watched him do it; it was a strangely delicate act, the rough, ragged man gently wrapping the blanket around her, as if afraid to disturb her. He said nothing to Echo, returning to the helm instead.

He never took control of the ship. It seemed, for all intents and purposes, to sail itself. Any other day, this would have been a source of endless fascination for Echo. But today, sitting ten feet from her mother's body… today none of it mattered.

Yuri seemed to have an even harder time with what was going on around them. He kept muttering to himself that none of this was real.

"This didn't really happen. It's a nightmare. Right? It has to be a nightmare," Yuri said. "I'm going to wake up and have to tell you all about my nightmare and you aren't going to believe any of it."

Echo had no answer for him. She just let him ramble.

"I'm not even wearing pants," Yuri said. He looked down at his bare legs sticking out from a pair of boxers with anchors on them. "I'm not wearing pants. That always means you're dreaming."

"It's real, Yuri," Echo said. She looked up at Barnabas, leaning against a rail, the sun growing pink and new in the sky behind him.

"And I'm going to get some answers. Come on."

She stood up, the wooden deck cool beneath her bare feet. Barnabas watched her climb the stairs to join him, Yuri following behind her like a hesitant shadow.

"What the hell is going on," Echo said. She folded her arms across her chest.

Barnabas rubbed his lined eyes with the base of his palms and ran his fingers across the stubble of his scalp. He tried to smile, but there was no joy there.

"I'm sorry for your loss," he said.

"I…" Echo started, but her voice caught in her throat. Her mother was gone. She kept repeating that thought in her head: my mother is gone. My mother is gone. My mother is gone.

She cleared her throat.

"Tell me why this happened," she said.

Barnabas sighed.

"Where to begin," he said. "Meredith never told you anything, did she? Dammit, I asked her. All this time. I offered to do it but she thought you'd be safer not knowing. I wish she'd let us meet sooner."

"What do you mean, never told me anything?" His tone had not been cruel, but the accusation the stranger leveled at her mother burned in her chest. She found herself grinding her teeth. How dare he.

"Did she… did she ever tell you anything about your father?" Barnabas said.

Echo looked over her shoulder at Yuri, but the big man looked shell-shocked. He was no help.

"She said he died at sea," Echo said.

Barnabas rubbed his eyes again.

"Look," Barnabas said. "I'll tell you what I know. You need to promise you'll listen. You can be angry later, but I need you to listen."

"I'll listen," Echo said.

"Your father is alive," Barnabas said. "And he's not human."

"This is so totally a dream," Yuri said. "Okay, I can wake up now. Now it's getting weird."

"Don't mess with my head," Echo said. "My mother is dead down there. I'm not here to listen to you lie and make up stories."

"I'm not lying," Barnabas said. "Your mother... okay, look, 'lost at sea' isn't such a stretch. Your father couldn't come back. His people aren't supposed to meet with humans at all. He made a mistake."

"He made a mistake? I'm a mistake?"

"No!" Barnabas said. "I told you that you need to listen first, and get angry later. This isn't my job. This wasn't supposed to be my job."

"And what was your job then?" Echo said.

"I was paid to keep an eye on you and your mother. To be a lookout. To not interfere. I was just here to watch."

"Who paid you?" Echo said. "My father? Do you know who he is?"

Barnabas shook his head.

"I was hired through an emissary, someone who worked for your father. I don't even know his identity, not that it much matters to us up here on the surface. Your mother might not have even known exactly who he really is. He's someone important, though, to have the means to hire someone like me to watch over you, but I never found out his name," Barnabas said. "And I wasn't the first. There was someone like me before me, too."

"Someone like you," Echo said.

"What are you, anyway?" Yuri muttered. "You look like you walked off the set of the *Pirates of the Caribbean*."

"What I am isn't important," Barnabas said.

"You just abducted us from our home in a boat that sails itself," Echo said. "Who you are is very important to me right now."

"I'm a... Look. I have skills that could be used to protect you. And to watch out in case someone ever found you."

"Who!" Echo said. "Who would want to find me? Why? Why won't you give me a simple answer!"

Barnabas held up both hands. Echo could see scars there mixed in with his tattoos.

"What do you know about Atlantis," Barnabas said.

"No," Echo said. "I said answers, not fairy tales."

"I wonder what I ate before I went to sleep to give me dreams like this," Yuri said. "I thought pepperoni pizza was a safe choice. This is not good."

Barnabas spoke sharply.

"*You* are a fairy tale," Barnabas said. "I am a fairy tale. This world is full of fairy tales. I have some terrible, terrible news for you, Echo. Fairy tales are real. And they're dangerous. And you're a part of them now, and despite the fact that it would be in my best interests to not do so, I'm going to try to help keep those fairy tales from destroying you. Okay?"

The trio stood in silence, Echo and Barnabas glaring at each other in frustration and anger, Yuri still dazed, watching the stare-down with absent-minded curiosity.

"Atlantis," Echo said. Her skin burned with anger.

"It's real," Barnabas said. Softer now. His voice was gravelly, but his tone kind. "It's a place. It's a kingdom. It's a kingdom in decline, if I'm being honest with you. It's not what it once was. But your father is Atlantean. Probably someone high up in society. A noble or something. And he did something terrible. He fell in love with a woman on the surface."

"My mother," Echo said.

"I don't know the whole story," Barnabas said. "But I know Atlanteans. He couldn't take her back with him. And they would have dragged him home if he stayed. There aren't enough of them left to let their people run away from home. Especially if he's important enough to have the pull to hire a protector for you."

Echo stole a glance at the blanket on the deck where her mother's body lay.

"Did he... Did he ever ask about us?"

Barnabas almost smiled just then. A hint of light in his eyes. He blinked a few times.

"That was my other job," he said. "And that's why your mother knew who I was. Because I sent stories home. You're not the only accidental child on the surface, Echo, but most people like you are abandoned. Their Atlantean parents simply disappear. Someone out there loved you and your mother very much."

Echo looked at her hands. Long fingers, tanned from the sun, strong from moving blocks of ice. The icehouse. I don't think we're ever going home again, she thought. I'll never see my home again.

"Does this mean I'm... what, half-mermaid?"

Yuri started humming "Part of that World" under his breath. Echo's bafflement almost disappeared under a powerful desire to shout at him, but one look at his face saw the boy was very much in shock.

"Atlanteans aren't mermaids," Barnabas said. "Mermaids are real though, they're just... something different entirely. Atlanteans are people, more or less. But strange things happen when Atlanteans and surfacers meet. Was that you I saw who threw the were-shark through the wall?"

"Wait, were-shark?" Yuri said. "Like... these were werewolf sharks? Are you serious?"

Echo and Barnabas both waved their hands at Yuri to shush him.

"I—that was me," Echo said. "I hit one really hard, too. I didn't know I could do something like that."

"You've probably got enhanced strength," Barnabas said. "That wouldn't surprise me. I'm almost positive you can breathe underwater too, but I bet you've never tested that out."

"I got caught in an undertow when I was little," Echo said. "I should've drowned, they said. I should have..."

"We'll figure these things out," Barnabas said. "Take a deep breath. We'll work it all out."

He sighed. Echo raised an eyebrow.

"What," Echo said.

"Your mother was always so kind to me," Barnabas said. "She

looked out for me in some ways, too. She always thought I was a little lost myself. She'd send food along with me when I'd visit. So, I hate saying this. But you... You should have known. I'm sorry this is how you're finding this all out. This is unfair."

Echo looked at Meredith's body one more time.

"I'm sure she had a reason," she said.

Barnabas nodded. Echo rubbed the stubble on the side of her scalp absently, the scratchy sensation strangely soothing beneath her fingertips.

"What happens next," Echo said.

Barnabas looked out over the horizon. The sky had brightened to gold and orange. A new day. A new life.

"We're going to get some answers," he said.

"To what questions," Echo said. She took a deep breath. Her belly was full of fear, but her heart raced, her muscles felt ready to spring. Forward, she thought. We're moving forward.

"We're going to find out why someone tried to kill you, so I know what we have to do make sure that doesn't happen again," Barnabas said.

"No," Echo said. Barnabas raised an eyebrow at her quizzically. "No. We're going to find out who killed my mother. And we're going to find out who my father is. And there is going to be a reckoning for what happened last night."

Barnabas stared at her a moment, as if he might try to change her mind. His mouth twitched, almost smiling.

"I think we can get you those answers," he said.

"Where?"

"From someone I haven't seen in a very long time," Barnabas said.

"Who is that?"

Barnabas let out a long sigh, loaded heavily with the weight of anxiety.

"My mother."

Chapter 10: Failure

Barracuda met his minions on the same small island at mid-day, when he knew the sun would sap much of their strength above water. The sharks that walked like men crawled out of the ocean looking worse for wear, still sporting bruises and burns that would heal with supernatural speed. They were short one man, and nowhere among their number were the two women they were supposed to obtain.

Barracuda did not let his anger show. Anger was a pointless emotion, in his view. People behaved irrationally when they were angry.

Instead, he simply stated the obvious.

"You failed," he said, directing his attention to the leader of the rabble, the were-shark called Maw.

"We ran into problems," Maw said.

"Life is a series of problems. It's what you do about them that defines you," Barracuda said.

"What?" Maw said, his expression dull.

Barracuda had profoundly disapproved of his employer's request to use monsters to handle this task. Barracuda knew that his master had wanted the women terrified, and that were-sharks were, inherently, horrifying to anyone who has never seen them before, and unsettling at best even among those who had. But Barracuda had recommended precision. Trustworthy soldiers from his master's own forces. Plausible deniability and terror won out, though. That is how you fail, Barracuda thought, shaking his head, through rigid adherence to a flawed plan.

"Where have they gone, then," Barracuda asked. "I assume they escaped, though the gods know how you could have let two land-dwellers best you."

"The girl had unnatural strength," Maw said. "You should have told us to prepare for her to possess some sort of superhuman powers."

Barracuda frowned. He had to concede that one point to these halfwits. If the girl was enhanced in any way, that was intelligence he should have been provided, and he should have passed on to these monsters.

"That's useful to know," Barracuda said. "So, this wasn't a complete waste of time."

"And an interloper interfered in the end. That annoying little ship's mage, Barnabas Coy."

Barracuda let his surprise show this time. Barnabas Coy was one of those figures men in his circle know about; a low-level magician, a brawler and thief, a sometimes smuggler and treasurer hunter, the sort of character who adds color to the pastiche of the region without adding much else. Not someone Barracuda would call a hero, by any stretch.

"I imagine he was paid for that interference," Barracuda said. "Coy's not known for altruism."

Maw looked back over his shoulder at his men, then back at Barracuda. Barracuda didn't speak, simply staring until Maw spoke again.

"The older woman is dead," Maw said.

Barracuda went very still. No party of him moved, not even his eyes. He waited a moment, the distance of a single breath, and spoke.

"Dead."

"This wasn't the job you signed us up for, assassin," Maw said.

"You killed an unarmed and untrained woman because she… defended herself."

"We didn't—"

"Who killed her?" Barracuda asked.

"What?"

"Which one of you is responsible?"

Maw took a step forward.

"She got herself killed. If she'd just stopped—"

"Which one of you."

One of the less malformed were-sharks stepped forward. In his human guise, he had short blond hair, wide-set eyes, a thick jaw with a wide, thin-lipped mouth.

"I didn't kill nobody," the blond were-shark said. "She pushed me, I pushed back. Not my fault. I—"

Barracuda was on him before any of his pack-mates could speak. The knife appeared in his hand so fast it was as if he conjured it with magic; the dark metal blade slide up through the were-shark's gut like a razor. One slash up, from navel to sternum; one across his throat; and a third side to side across his lower belly, opening him up like a curtain. The were-shark collapsed to his knees, arms feebly trying to push his intestines back inside, a look of surprise rather than pain on his face.

"No!" Maw yelled, transforming to his true self in fluid shimmer of motion accompanied by the sound of bones bending and muscle stretching, his massive, triangular head becoming alien and monstrous. The others followed suit, surrounding Barracuda in a wall of teeth and sharkskin.

Barracuda pulled a second knife from his belt, holding each blade out, arms extended, moving in a slow semi-circle.

"Cold iron," he said. The corner of his mouth quirked into a smile he had to fight to tamp down. The violence got his blood up. Don't lose focus, old boy, he thought to himself. Now's not the time for slaughter. You still need these beasts. "I know what kills your kind, Maw. You knew there had to be a price for this kind of failure. Don't make me take more."

The sharks stopped encroaching upon him, though all four remained in their beastly forms. Maw broke the standoff.

"This is an insult we won't forget, Barracuda."

"And you still have a job to do," Barracuda said. "You have a new assignment. You want the other half of your payment? Find the girl. Do not engage her. You'll find her, and you'll tell me where she is, and I'll get her my bloody self. Do you approve alteration of the contract?"

Maw's black eyes darted back and forth between his men, then back to Barracuda.

"We'll find her."

"Do not touch her," Barracuda said.

"We'll find her," Maw repeated.

"Then go," Barracuda said. "You have money to earn, and I have no desire to kill the lot of you."

Chapter 11: Magic wands and ghost ships

Echo wandered the ship, pacing, unable to shake the feeling of being trapped. She found herself staring into the water, as if expecting one of the monsters she'd fought to rise from the depths and attack again. Over and over again she found her eyes drawn to the blanket shrouding her mother's body. Finally, she marched back up the stairs to Barnabas. Yuri followed her.

"What are we doing," Yuri asked.

"I'm going to ask a question," she said.

"Okay, good. I have some questions too."

I'm sure you do, Echo thought. She stopped a few paces from Barnabas.

"You need to tell me what we're going to do about my mom," Echo said. "I can't do this. I can't sit here not knowing."

"What do you want to do?" Barnabas said. "What would she want? We can't go back. It's not safe."

"I understand that," Echo said.

"We could have a proper burial when we get to our destination," Barnabas said. Echo could sense from his tone that he left something unsaid. It didn't matter.

"She always told me she wanted her ashes spread into the ocean," Echo said. A weight wrapped around her heart and squeezed. My mother is gone, she thought. This isn't a nightmare. My mother is gone.

"Ashes," Barnabas said. "Yeah. Yeah, I think we can do something about that. If that's what you want."

"It's what she wanted. So, it's what I want."

"Of course," Barnabas said.

He locked eyes with her. Echo nodded, unsure what else to say. This is my life preserver? She thought. This bizarre man is who I'm relying on to make sense of everything?

"I have some questions," Yuri said unexpectedly.

Echo spun around to look at him. Barnabas just blinked.

"No," Barnabas said.

"Why not? You don't even know what my question is."

"You look like the type of kid who asks questions that shouldn't be answered," Barnabas said.

"Try me."

After a moment, Barnabas gestured. Go on.

"How does your gun shoot fire," Yuri said.

Echo's mouth dropped open. He really must be in shock, she thought. He's asking this right now? But then again—after Yuri asked the question, Echo suddenly realized she was curious herself.

"It's not a gun," Barnabas said.

"It looks like a gun," Yuri said. "I mean it looks like a gun you'd find in a museum, but it looks like a gun."

"It's not a gun," Barnabas repeated. "It's an artifact."

"It's an old gun," Yuri said.

Barnabas opened his mouth, closed it, then shook his head in frustration.

"Fine. It's a gun, but it's not. It's—look, this is hard to explain. Artifacts are objects that help you focus spells in specific ways."

"Spells," Yuri said.

"Spells," Barnabas said. "Magic."

"You're a wizard," Yuri said. Echo found herself bouncing back and forth looking at the two men, unable to believe the conversation was real.

"I know some spells," Barnabas said. "That doesn't make me a wizard."

"Okay, Gandalf. You have a magic gun that isn't a gun that shoots fire."

"It… think of it as a magic wand," Barnabas said.

"Dumbledore then. Not Gandalf."

"You're taking this really well for someone who has never seen magic before," Barnabas said.

"I'm still convinced none of this is real," Yuri said. He turned to Echo. "I'm going to try really hard to tell you about this nightmare when we wake up. I apologize in advance."

"Yuri," Echo said. "Stop it."

"Okay, David Copperfield," Yuri said. "Do all magic wands look like guns?"

"Short answer: no," Barnabas said. "Different artifacts do different things. This is an offensive artifact. A magic weapon."

"Are magic wands real," Yuri said.

"Stop it, Yuri," Echo said, anger rising in her tone. She couldn't tell if he was truly in shock or not.

"Next question," Yuri said. "You haven't done a single thing to make this ship move, and yet we're sailing away. How."

Barnabas glanced at Echo. Echo frowned at him but shrugged. Yuri was asking good questions; and somehow, they were distracting her from her grief, if only for a moment. I don't want to be distracted, she thought. I want to feel this grief. I want to be angry.

But maybe knowing more would shake Yuri out of whatever was happening to him, Echo thought.

Barnabas rubbed his stubbly, scarred head with his palm.

"I'm not sailing this ship," he said. "They are."

"We're the only three people on this boat," Yuri said.

Barnabas spoke to Echo rather than Yuri next.

"No, we're not," he said. "You can sense them, can't you?"

Echo wrinkled her nose at him, confused. But she could feel it, all around her, a strange coolness in the air, a lack of stillness. It didn't feel like life, though; it felt like… like movement, like presence.

"What is that?" she asked.

"What is what?" Yuri said.

"Them," Barnabas said, and he waved his hand in the air. His palm glowed pale white.

And then Echo saw them.

There were men and women all around, pale reflections of life, bustling about, a complete compliment of crewmen. They were dressed strangely, each and every one—some wore old mariners' clothing; others wore naval uniforms long retired. A dashing young man in a fitted polo and shorts cut in a style that were popular when Echo's grandfather was young adjusted the sails.

Echo caught Yuri flinching out of the corner of her eye, looking around in disbelief. Echo, though, found herself unexpectedly smiling.

"Who are they?" she asked.

"Ghosts," Barnabas said

"What?" Yuri said, just a little too loud.

"This is the *Endless*. It's a ghost ship," Barnabas said. "And these are the ghosts of men and women who died at sea but weren't ready to stop sailing yet. This ship is manned by souls who would rather stay and ride the seven seas than move on."

"I think I'm going to be sick," Yuri said.

"And you're the captain?" Echo said.

Barnabas shook his head.

"I just provide a little direction. All these men and women want is a place to sail to."

"What if they don't want to go where you tell them?" Echo asked.

"I guess I'll have to tell you that when I find out. Hasn't happened yet."

"I'm literally going to be sick. I'll be right back," Yuri said, marching back downstairs toward the rail. "Magic wands and ghost ships. This has got to be real. I don't have enough of an imagination to think this up on my own."

As Yuri stomped away, Echo spoke softly to Barnabas.

"This is really happening, isn't it," she said.

Barnabas grimaced, then smiled.

"This world is far more magical and horrible than you've ever known, Echo," Barnabas said. "And it's only going to get stranger from here."

Chapter 12: The Lost Kingdom

The graveyards of Atlantis were hidden among the spires of a coral forest, deep below the surface. Atlanteans didn't bury their dead. The sea, as a rule, would be allowed to reclaim those who belonged to it.

But certain Atlanteans were exceptions to the rule. Kings and queens were among those exceptions.

The reef beneath which the royal tombs of Atlantis were hidden was a massive structure, twisted in ways requiring as much nurture as nature, the caretakers of Atlantis cultivating this place as a living sculpture to honor the dead. Few visited these tombs. Atlanteans were not sentimental creatures by nature, and the last resting places of kings were not welcoming.

Reina knew she would find one visitor tonight, though. She wrapped a cloak the color of seaweed tighter around her shoulders and drifted down among the spires of the reef until she found her brother.

Rhegis still dressed for mourning, form-fitting Atlantean garb tinted bluish-black, accented with coppery metal highlights. His back to her, Rhegis stood with his head bowed in front of their father's sepulcher. His softly curling hair drifted on the current, lit dramatically by the enchanted globes that dotted the reef like torches.

"Come to pay your respects, sister?" Rhegis said, never turning away from the tomb.

Their father, the late King Seidon, had passed away peacefully in his sleep a week before. No warrior's death for our father, Reina thought. But exactly how he would have wanted it. Quietly, without drama, a whispering wave against the shores of time. He died as he lived. It was a life that had galled Reina, too passive, too cowardly, but still, standing behind her twin brother and looking up on her father's tomb, she missed him. He was a coward in her eyes, but he was not a terrible man, even if he had been a terrible king.

Unfortunately, there was too much of their father in her brother.

"I came here to find you," Reina said. "I want to talk."

"About what happens next," Rhegis said.

"About where we're going to lead our people," Reina said. "Our father was too—"

"Really," Rhegis said, turning to face her at last. "You're going to demean his legacy here. In front of his own grave. I know you have trouble holding your tongue, Reina, but this is beneath you."

"If not here then when?" she asked. "In front of the council? We need to act."

"And we will," Rhegis said. "It was our father's will that we rule together, and we shall, but what is the rush to action? His body is barely cold and what, you want to go to war?"

"He let the land-dwellers defecate all over our kingdom, Rhegis," Reina said. "He sat idly by as they destroyed our waters, killed the creatures we were sworn to protect, irradiated our farmlands, dredged up poison from beneath the ocean floor. They are a menace and he let them run rampant for almost a century. We don't have much time to save what's left of our world."

"We are not going to war with the surface, Reina. We've talked about this. They are not the society they were when father was young," Rhegis said. "They are not a dragon we want to awaken."

"We have far more power at our disposal than them. We've been too afraid to use it."

Rhegis' face flushed.

"What are you suggesting? Annihilation? Genocide?"

"I'd prefer subjugation," Reina said. "But that's beneath us. Simply demonstrating the scythe we have positioned over their necks and showing them who truly rules the oceans would be sufficient."

"You'll get us all killed," Rhegis said.

"Only if we lose. Which we won't," Reina said. "You'll destroy us in small increments. Just like father did."

Rhegis fumed. He even looks more like our father, she thought. Reina favored their mother's aspect, with darker hair, sharper features. Light and dark. We've always been light and dark, she thought.

"You never did forgive him," Rhegis said.

"I can't believe you did," Reina said. It was an unspoken thing between them, the surface-dwellers who killed their mother. There had been calls for war at the time, and they went on for year. For some in Atlantis, those cries had never silenced. But Seidon called it an accident, a misunderstanding between individuals, not an act of war, and he preferred they stay silent and hidden beneath the waves, to grieve.

Reina waited her entire life to take control of Atlantis and seek out her revenge. Her father had always stood in the way. And now, it seems, her twin brother would follow in his footsteps.

"We need to stop them before they destroy this world and take us with it," Reina said.

"You want blood. Don't pretend this is about saving the world," Rhegis said.

"Don't you dare belittle this," Reina said. "Do I want to avenge our mother? Of course. But she's been dead decades, Rhegis. I've long let my anger cool. What I want is a world for Atlantis to prosper in before they ruin it."

Rhegis sighed. He looked over his shoulder at their father's tomb.

"I thought you might grow more reasonable with age," he said.

"I'm tired of arguing about this on top of our father's corpse."

He darted upward, swimming with the supernatural grace all Atlanteans possessed, disappearing before Reina could get in the last word. She just shook her head at him. *I'd wished I wouldn't have to resort to the things I'm going to have to do,* she thought. *But I won't let them destroy this world. And I'm tired of sitting on my hands while they do it.*

"He'll never change his mind," a lyrical voice said behind her.

"This is an inappropriate place for you to find me, Barracuda," Reina said. "My brother might have seen you."

"Your brother would *not* have seen me, and you know that," Barracuda said. The assassin drifted out of the shadows like his namesake, lean and sharp.

"Is it done, then?" she asked him. "Do you have the woman and the girl?"

"There has been a complication," Barracuda said. "The mother is dead."

Reina felt as if a cold hand grasped her stomach and squeezed. She fought hard to not raise her voice.

"Dead? How?"

"I warned you against sending those creatures," Barracuda said. His voice was a soft purr. "My recommendation was to send some of your personal guard to do the job."

"I can't have anyone from the city involved," Reina said. "No matter how loyal my bodyguards are, they might make a mistake. We needed discretion. And I wanted them scared, Barracuda. Scared, not dead."

"You sent dimwitted hunters on a surgical strike," Barracuda said.

"No, you sent them."

"I was doing as instructed. This was your choice."

"Watch your tone, assassin."

"You don't pay me to watch my tone," Barracuda said. "You hired me for my advice and you ignored it."

Reina gritted her teeth. Barracuda had some roots in Atlantis, but he had lived apart from it, a mercenary of rare talent. In putting her plans into motion, he had been invaluable. But his suggestion to use Atlanteans in the kidnapping terrified her.

"Very well then," she said. "The woman is dead. Is the girl in your custody?"

"She escaped."

"Escaped? I suppose you'll blame the were-sharks for this as well?"

"She had help," Barracuda said. "Your brother is soft, but he's no fool. He had someone watching them."

"Who? One of ours?" Reina felt the hint of fear slip along her spine. If the attempted kidnapping had been seen and reported back to Rhegis, he'd suspect her instantly. Not the murder—no matter what, Rhegis wouldn't expect cold-blooded killing from her, not yet—but he knew...

"A smuggler and wanderer. Someone known to us. I suspect someone advised your brother how best to protect them, and he listened."

"You are treading dangerously close to a level of impertinence I cannot tolerate, Barracuda."

"My apologies, Regent," Barracuda said. "But the girl is on the run. I am tracking her, and she will be captured—alive—as the plan dictates."

"We needed them both for insurance," Reina said.

"One will do."

Reina frowned. They could work with this. Her brother would be furious, but if they had one of the women, they had what they needed.

"And our other operations?"

"Going as planned," Barracuda said. "Has your brother found out yet?"

"I don't believe so," she said.

"He will. I know there are double agents among the Atlanteans we've involved who will report back to his people."

Reina grimaced. She had longed for war against the surface her entire life. She looked forward to the battle. But the cloak and dagger gamesmanship leading up to it left her feeling greasy and angry.

"Let me know the moment you have her," Reina said.

Barracuda bowed curtly and jetted away, the opposite direction her brother had taken. She swam up to her father's tomb and put her hand on the coral wall.

"If only you'd been braver," she said. "None of this would be necessary if you'd had more courage to do what needs to be done."

Chapter 13: Inclined to impulsivity

Echo didn't sleep.

The journey took all day, but something about the journey itself—not the ghost sailors she kept catching glimpses of out of the corner of her eye, not the ever-present sense of pending doom—but the way the ship cut through the water made her feel uneasy, as if time itself did not follow all the rules here.

Barnabas said little. He watched the horizon, looking over his shoulder from where they came, checking a compass he kept pulling from his pocket. Yuri, mercifully, napped. His anxiety had maxed out, and the big man nodded off, wrapped in a blanket he found below deck, muttering in his sleep.

Eventually, a spot of green rose from the ocean ahead, a small island covered in foliage. Echo hopped to her feet and joined Barnabas, who watched the island grow closer with a visible sense of unease.

"This doesn't feel right," Echo said.

"How so," Barnabas asked. Echo shot him a dirty look. "Honest question. Tell me what you see."

"It's the wrong sort of island," Echo said. "It doesn't feel like it belongs so close to where we lived. It looks almost tropical. That can't be right."

"Good," Barnabas said.

"Good?"

"You're learning not to trust your eyes," he said. "First rule of surviving the hidden world. A healthy measure of distrust is important."

"And this is where your mother lives," Echo said.

"Unfortunately," he said. "Let's get your friend up." Barnabas swooped to the rail to hell down at Yuri on the deck below.

"Hey! Boy! Person. You! Wake up!"

"What?" Yuri said, rubbing his eyes. He'd removed his glasses earlier, and delicately replaced them on his face. "Boy-person?"

"I don't know your name," Barnabas said. He looked at Echo. "What's his name?"

"Yuri."

"My name is Yuri Rodriguez, you Jack Sparrow wannabe," Yuri said. Then he noticed the island. "Oh. Oh, wow."

"We're here," Echo said.

"We're going to Gilligan's Island," Yuri said.

"We are," Barnabas said. "You're not."

"Excuse me, what?" Yuri said.

"You're staying with the ship," Barnabas said.

"Pardon me?"

"You're staying here, and you have very specific instructions for while we're gone."

Barnabas hopped the rail and dropped to the deck below. Echo took the stairs.

"One," Barnabas said. "You are to stay with the ship. *With* the ship. Not near the ship, not around the ship. With it. On it. Do not leave."

"You're just going to take my friend to some deserted island and leave me on the boat?" Yuri yelled.

"Two," Barnabas said. "You will remain below."

Yuri said a vulgar equivalent of "I will not do that." Echo winced.

"Three, you will not speak to anyone or anything until we return," Barnabas said. "Is that clear?"

"It's clearly stupid," Yuri said. "I'm not doing any of those things."

Yuri looked at Echo for help. She folded her arms across her chest.

"You can't just tell him to do all of this without reason," Echo said. "We need answers."

"Also, there are ghosts on this ship!" Yuri said. "You want me to stay, on the haunted ship, in the haunted ship's creepy basement…"

"Ships don't have basements," Barnabas said.

"In the equivalent of this ship's creepy basement," Yuri said, "and you're not going to tell me why?"

Barnabas rubbed his forehead with his tattooed hands.

"Boy," Barnabas said.

"Yuri," Yuri said.

"Yuri," Barnabas said. "This island is home to many things you've heard of only in stories."

"Like shark-men," Echo said.

"Other things," Barnabas said. "Creatures who lure men into the sea and never let them return."

"Like sirens," Echo said.

"Not like sirens. Literally sirens. Sirens are real," Barnabas said. "And other things. Darker creatures. The world has little room for them anymore, and so they find places like this, where they hide, and they sing, and they wait."

"This is an island of… sea nymphs?" Echo said.

Barnabas smiled at her, the warm smile he's shown glimpses of earlier.

"Nereids and sylphs and mermaids and sirens," Barnabas said. "They all hate to be alone. And as the world grows smaller and darker, they huddle together, in places like this. To hide."

"We're on an island full of mythological women and you want me to hide," Yuri said. "This sounds awesome."

"You strike me as the type of man who is inclined to impulsivity," Barnabas said. Yuri started to protest, but Echo cut him off.

"Oh, don't argue that point, Yuri," Echo said. "You know you're impulsive."

"Impulsive is getting fast food at one in the morning," Yuri said. "Not... whatever he's hinting at."

"Yuri," Barnabas said.

"My name is Yuri—oh, wait. What," Yuri said.

"I can't protect you if I'm not here," Barnabas said. "And I'm not sure I can keep you safe at all if you set foot on this island. You will stay here, so you will not die. Am I making myself clear?"

Yuri glanced at Echo again.

"Yuri, dude, shark-men tried to kill us last night," she said. "At this point I'm believing everything until proven otherwise. Please stay below. You're my best friend. I don't want you to get eaten by a mermaid."

"Oh, but what a way to go," Yuri said.

"It's a terrible way to go," Barnabas snapped.

"Mermaids eat people?" Echo said, but Barnabas ignored her.

"This feels really sexist," Yuri said. "Why don't they try to murder women, too?"

"Historical evidence has proven men make much worse decisions than women on a daily basis," Barnabas said. "I like to think they chose their prey because men are easier targets."

Yuri blinked a few times then shrugged as if to indicate he had no argument with that logic.

"Hey," Yuri said. "Wait. Why don't they try to eat you when you set foot on this island?"

"Because," Barnabas said. "I'm family."

Chapter 14: All the greatest mistakes in the world are made out of love

Echo and Barnabas took a dinghy to the shore, leaving Yuri behind. Yuri watched them from the deck, and Echo made vehement motions for him to go below. Now.

"I give fifty-fifty odds your friend is alive when we get back, and he has no one to blame but himself," Barnabas said as he dragged the dinghy onto the sand.

"He'll be fine," Echo said. "It's all an act with him. Well, not all. Mostly an act."

Echo kept the sea at her back, scanning the forest before them. Palm trees dotted the coast but the foliage grew denser and less identifiable just beyond. Barnabas began walking to a break in the trees. Echo followed.

The sand was cool beneath her feet. She had left her shoes back at the house, with her old life. It felt strangely symbolic to walk barefoot in this strange place, this impossible island. As sand and earth mixed between her toes, she had a sense of connection to this place. It felt almost familiar. Like she'd been here once in a dream.

Barnabas moved with a purpose, shoving massive leaves and branches aside as they walked. Eventually, they came upon a waterfall. He worked his way around it like one approaches a wild animal.

"You look scared," Echo said.

"I am," Barnabas said.

"I thought you said you were family."

"I did. But that doesn't mean they want me here. Creatures like me—creatures like both of us, Echo—we remind the people who made us of their own frailty. Nobody likes reminders of what they think is their weakness."

"Your mother—she'll be willing to help us?"

"If her sisters don't tear us apart first," Barnabas said. He reached inside his jacket and pulled out a long, curved knife. He handed it to her. "Take this."

"I don't know how to use this," Echo said.

"It was you who put that dive knife through the nose of one of the were-sharks, yeah?" he said.

"Yeah."

"Then you know how to use this," he said. "But just… wait 'til I stab something first. Just to be sure we're stabbing the right people."

He led them closer to the waterfall, almost crawling, staying low to the ground. Echo followed his lead. She felt an energy rushing through her, adrenaline or something like it, and strength in her limbs she'd never been aware of before. Have I always been this strong? She wondered. What else can I do that I've never noticed before?

Echo heard splashing below. Barnabas sighed heavily and stood up.

"Hello," he said, hesitatingly.

"Intruder," a musical voice said.

"Outsider," said another.

"You do not belong here," said a third.

"You don't recognize me?" Barnabas said. "I'm your little nephew."

"We know you, Barnabas Coy," one of the voices said. "You are not welcome here."

Echo crept closer to the edge to glance over. Three women drifted lazily around the pool below, just beyond the reach of the waterfall. Their skin was like pearl, their hair dark and wet. They wore thin frocks. From this distance, Echo thought they were siblings.

"I'd like to speak to my mother, please," Barnabas said.

"We'd like to tear you limb from limb," one of the women said. She said it in such a mellifluous tone it almost sounded like a joke. "But we can't all have what we want."

"Who do you have with you, Barnabas Coy?" another asked. "Let's see her now. She smells like an Atlantean."

Echo stood up to her full height and joined Barnabas by the edge. Her hands balled into fists. What does an Atlantean smell like? She thought. Is this just some sort of petty insult? One of the nymphs below solved that riddle.

"And she looks the part, too," she said. "What business do you have with one of those old dictators, Barnabas Coy? No good ever comes from deals with them. You know that."

"This girl's under my protection… more or less," he said. "I'm trying to…"

"You want to unlock her mystery," a new voice said. This one was less sing-songy than the others. More mature. Deeper. Echo saw a fourth woman emerging from the waterfall. Her skin glimmered like a snake's—not scaled, but patterned, almost metallic, and pale, pale like the others. Unearthly. Inhuman. But everything else about her was human, her face, her shape. And the way she looked at Barnabas.

"My boy," the woman said. Even at from across the pool, Echo could see love in her eyes. She's so young, Echo thought. She looks as young as me. But no, not with that voice, not with that commanding presence. However young she looked, this being was something much more ancient than she appeared to be.

"It's good to see you, mum," Barnabas said. His tone had changed as well. Gentler than before.

"I saw your visit in a dream," the woman said. "What have you got yourself mixed up in, my son? What have you done now?"

***

"Call me Galatea," the woman said, leading Echo and Barnabas into the caverns behind the waterfall. They were both soaked through gaining entry; the other nereids, Galatea's sisters, had mocked them as they climbed the rocks, slipping on smooth stone and moss.

The caves were lit by thin veins of a kind of phosphorescent stone, casting them in a blue-green light. The glow made Galatea's skin gleam like a sea creature's. Echo brushed her hair out of her face and wrung out her tee shirt, shivering with the chill of the cave.

"I'm Echo," she said, trying to keep her teeth from chattering.

"I knew your namesake," Galatea said.

"The myth?" Echo said.

Galatea laughed.

"You'll find a lot of myths are more than stories," Galatea said. "But yes. The nymph named Echo. That poor girl. The things we suffer at the hands of the gods. They are the worst of us made flesh and blood."

Barnabas said nothing, taking in the cave as if he'd never been there before, eyes roaming the walls and shadows.

"So, this is the little one you've been watching over all these years," Galatea said. "I never liked you taking Atlantean coin, Barnabas."

"I never liked taking it, but a man has to make a living, mother," he said.

"There are better ways."

"If only I hadn't been cast out of my own home," he said. The words were harsh, but his tone was almost playful.

"You know I couldn't keep you here," Galatea said. "I would have, if I could."

"You had to give your son away?" Echo asked.

Galatea paused. She did not turn to look at them.

"I made one terrible mistake," she said softly. "A mistake, I suspect, similar to the circumstance of your own birth, little one."

"What was his name?" Echo said.

Now Galatea faced her.

"You're a clever little thing, aren't you," she said. "Samuel. His name was Samuel. And that's all you'll get from me this night, clever girl."

"Did you love him very much?" Echo asked, pressing.

Galatea's eyes glistened. Echo couldn't tell if it was from tears or just the moisture in the air.

"All the greatest mistakes in the world are made out of love," Galatea said. "There is no more powerful force, no greater device for blinding one to reality or common sense than love. You'd do well to remember that, clever girl."

At last, they came upon a chamber, an opening in the cave. Echo looked up and saw the sky through a small gap in the ceiling above. The room itself revolved around a basin of water that seemed to writhe and dance with a life of its own.

"It's been a long time since I've seen this place," Barnabas said.

"The less you see of this place the better," Galatea said. Along the back wall of the cave, rows of vials stood, each filled with some sort of potion, each a different color or shade. Galatea chose one—almost at random, Echo thought—and uncorked it.

The nymph looked Echo in the eyes.

"Shall we find out who you really are?" Galatea said.

"I don't know that I want that answer," Echo said.

Galatea nodded.

"I understand," she said. "You lost your mother last night."

"Yes." Echo felt a roiling in her stomach, anger and rage and grief feeding on each other like sharks.

"We could let her secrets die with her," Galatea said. "There's honor in that. It would be a just end."

"But they'll just keep coming after us, won't they," Echo said.

"The things that killed her. Or other things. Worse things. Something wants me because of what I am."

"This is what my son thinks," Galatea said. "I don't know for sure."

Echo pursed her lips and flexed her hands.

"Your sisters said they could tell I'm an Atlantean," she said. "What does that mean?"

"It's an insult, little one," Galatea said. "All the creatures of the sea, from selkies to krakens… we all know that Atlanteans mean trouble. And you, standing there by my son—whom my sisters have no real love for, if you must know… you are trouble incarnate."

"But we don't know for sure," Echo said.

"And we may not, even if I do a bit of scrying for you," Galatea said. "Magic makes no promises. It's a fickle thing."

Echo studied Barnabas as he listened quietly. He seemed tired. His shoulders slumped. How much did this visit cost him, she wondered? What did it feel like, returning to place where you are some unwanted thing, where your own family looks at you like a stray dog?

"Tell me," Echo said.

Galatea nodded. She reached out and plucked a hair from Echo's head. Echo cried out.

"Why did you do that?" Echo said.

"DNA," Galatea said.

Echo was taken aback. Her expression gave her away.

"Oh, don't look at me like that. Magic was science before science was science," Galatea said. She pointed at Barnabas. "This one has a lot to learn, Barnabas."

"We'll work on that," he said.

Galatea dropped Echo's hair into the pool, then drank half the contents of the vial in her hand, emptying the rest into the pool as well. The water shimmered with light, dancing and playing.

Galatea gripped either side of the pool and leaned forward. Images began to appear. Echo saw her mother, but young, so young, on a beach she didn't recognize. She saw a beautiful man, unlike anyone she'd ever seen before, the evening sun turning his hair into a halo—no, not a halo. A crown. She saw a city beneath the sea, glowing gold and silver from within. She saw blood in the water, flashing teeth. A woman she'd never seen before, and yet—a stranger who looks like me, Echo thought, she has my eyes, she has my mouth. She heard a rumbling, the fog of war, she heard men dying in the darkness…

Galatea gasped, pulling herself away from the pool. The spell was broken. The room so silent. The rumble of the waterfall was deafening.

Echo looked up at Barnabas. He stared into the pool, his expression blank, his eyes glassy.

"What have you got yourself tangled up in, my dear, dear boy," Galatea said. She spared a glance at Echo. "You poor thing. You don't even know what this world has done to you. This is an unfair life you will be forced to lead."

"What did that all mean?" Echo said. "Who were those people? What was that? Was that the future? The past?"

"Barnabas," Galatea said. "She can't stay here."

Barnabas stared wordlessly at his mother.

"You know this. You know what they'll do," she said.

"I know," Barnabas said, his throat tight.

"Was that my father?" Echo said, ignoring the conversation.

"Yes, it was," Galatea answered. "Barnabas, you know what is happening below."

"I'd heard Seidon's dead."

"And war is brewing. If this is Rhegis's daughter…"

"I don't know what any of this means," Echo said. "Will one of you stop talking in Tolkeinese and explain to me what's going on?"

"I'll explain on the *Endless*," Barnabas said. "I'm sorry we came here, mother."

"You didn't know," Galatea said. She reached up and touched her son's cheek. "It was good to see your face again."

"Where should we go?" Barnabas said.

"You know where to go," Galatea said. "You need to bring her somewhere she'll be safe, and where she can learn the things she needs to survive."

Barnabas' gaze darkened.

"I know the place," he said.

"It kept you safe when I couldn't," Galatea said. "Maybe it can do the same for her."

"I'm getting really tired of not knowing what's going on," Echo said. "Barnabas. Please."

"I'll explain on the ship," he said. "We need to leave."

He reached out and placed a hand on his mother's shoulder.

"You could come with us. I'll keep you safe."

"No," Galatea said. "I think you know that as long as you're with this girl, you'll never be safe."

Barnabas broke into a sad, lost smile and kissed his mother on the forehead.

"I love you, mother," Barnabas said.

"I love you too, my favorite mistake," Galatea said. "Now go. Be swift."

Chapter 15: Not the little mermaid

Yuri was positive he could hear the ghosts all around him.

He couldn't see them, though whether that was because they didn't want to be seen or if Barnabas needed to cast some sort of spell to make them visible, but he knew, he knew, he knew he could hear them. The creaking of the deck above, the sound of ropes tightening, feint laughter or cursing...

They're all around me, he thought.

If not for the ghosts, below deck was fairly pleasant, he thought. Barnabas wasn't what you'd call tidy, but it was warm, and Yuri even found a crate full of old clothes where he helped himself to a pair of pants—huge, oversized pirate pants, striped black and white, with billowy openings at the ankles. He found a stash of rum that would make a bar owner blush, which he had planned on partaking from, when he heard a woman singing.

"This is the weirdest dream I've ever had," Yuri said out loud. "You hear that, ghosts? I know you're not real. You're just figments of my pepperoni pizza-fueled night terrors."

Still, best to investigate, he thought.

"Oh, but Barnabas said stay below," Yuri said. "It's dangerous here, sure, sure, sure. Whatever dude. Maybe she'll be the love of my life. Or at least make this more like one of my usual dreams."

Yuri strode confidently upstairs and out onto the deck. A gust of sea air splashed against his face, wet with mist. It feels so real, he thought. But no. I refuse to believe any of this has really happened. Shark men. Pirate magicians. It's all a horrible dream.

"Hello?" he said.

No answer came. Just more singing. She had a beautiful voice, whoever she was, and spoke in a language Yuri had never heard.

"Is that Russian?" he asked. "Wait. No. I bet it's Greek. Right? That would be right in line with this nightmare."

Yuri meandered up to the rail and looked over. A face looked back at him: a smiling face, framed in coppery hair, pale eyes shining with intrigue.

"Ariel?"

The woman reached up to him, long, pale fingers outstretched. She smiled at him, and he felt his heart skip a beat, pulse racing. This can't be real either, he thought. Why would it be real? Just the Little Mermaid hanging out next to the boat, and she wants to hold my hand.

Yuri reached down and took her hand. Her skin was cold to the touch, and her grip surprisingly strong.

"Do you want to come up here—" he started to say, but before he could finish, he was airborne, yanked from the ship and into the water, unable to break her powerful grasp on his hand.

He hit the water with a painful slap, pulled under before he could take a breath. Bubbles tickled his face and neck, but the burning in his lungs took precedent, salt water flooding his mouth, choking him. He flailed, unable to see, unable to free his hand, throwing his legs and one free arm around trying to dislodge himself.

He felt a hand touch his face, and with it all panic disappeared. The singer was with him, smiling at him in the blue emptiness of the water, fingers on his cheek tenderly.

I can't breathe, he thought. I'm going to die here. But...

He stared into the welcoming eyes of this being, only just now noticing the diaphanous fins on her forearms, the powerful silvery tail she had instead of legs. She's going to kill me, Yuri thought. Why am I not afraid? Why does this feel like where I was always meant to be?

The water erupted again, a streak of bubbles rushing past. The singing creature pulled away so fast his shoulder felt as if it might dislocate, but her grip loosened and finally let go. His palm felt strangely cold as water touched it directly, unprotected by her grasp. He felt strong hands grab him, dragging him to the surface. No, he thought, I'm not ready to go back, I want to stay down here forever…

The air hit him like a smack to the face. He gasped, then hacked, water spurting up from his belly and lungs violently. He looked at who had grabbed him. Echo. Her sea foam green hair was plastered to her face as she dragged him toward the ship. Out of the corner of his eye, he saw Barnabas standing in the dinghy, his hands surrounded by ornate halos of blue-white light. The magician was shouting and so was Echo, cursing at him. Even in his state of shock, Yuri was surprised at how easily Echo hoisted him up the rope ladder onto the ship, dumping him unceremoniously on the deck, both pouring water from their clothes.

Yuri could finally make out what Barnabas shouted—it wasn't magic, not some spell, but simple chastisement.

"Get out of here, you greedy little creature!" Barnabas said. "Get lost! He's not yours!"

The singing girl shouted back at him in another language, the same language she'd been singing in. Barnabas clearly understood it, but didn't bother to translate.

"I don't care if you found him! He's my crew, and you can't have him!" Barnabas yelled. More melodic shouting. "Yeah? Fine. Go tell your sisters. Go on."

There was a petulant splash, and then quiet.

Yuri listened anxiously as Barnabas climbed his way up the rope ladder. He was soaked as well, his face grim.

"We need to leave," Barnabas said.

"Her sisters?" Echo said.

"We're about to have our ship surrounded by dozens of angry mermaids. This is not a good scenario," Barnabas said. He pointed at Yuri. "You! I gave you one job!"

Yuri coughed. He wiped his nose.

"Hey Echo," he said.

"What, Yuri," Echo said.

"I don't think this is a dream anymore," he said.

"It's not, Yuri."

"I want to go home," he said.

Echo brushed rivulets of water from his face and looked him in the eyes.

"I know," she said. "I wish we could."

Chapter 16: Heavy hangs the head

Rhegis found his thoughts drifting to the surface world tonight. Not the world full of people his sister despised so much, but rather one place, two people, a home he'd never seen, a child he'd never met.

All these years, and he rarely thought of them. Not because he did not love them, because he had always loved Meredith, with the sort of love you never get over; and he had the sort of love a parent has for a child they could not be with, a wishful love, full of hope for what she'd become, who she had grown up to be.

He forced himself to not think of them often by choice, an exercise against melancholy he'd learned as a younger man. Don't think long on what you've lost, he believed. You can't have it back, and you can't move forward.

There was much moving forward in Atlantis these days. And, if his sister had her way, much sliding backward as well.

"My lord."

His best counselor, Grimmin, cleared his throat politely, drawing him back into the conversation. They met, as they always did, in Rhegis's private chambers, a vast room of gold and pearl-like stone with giant windows holding the ocean at bay. Atlantis itself was a strange combination of submerged landscape and pockets of air, maintained with magic alongside technology so nuanced it might as well be magic. Whole castles were filled with breathable air. Homes, cottages, keeps, stables, and factories, all resting on the bottom of the sea. His people could breathe both air and water, and for some reason, eons ago, they chose to build a world below the surface allowing them to do both whenever they wished to. Rhegis preferred the airtight chamber for his meetings with Grimmin. Water carried sound, and tonight they spoke of secrets.

Grimmin was an older man, white of beard and bald. What little hair he had left on top of his head he gathered in a gloriously maintained ponytail cascading down his back. He'd been a soldier in his youth, and a spy for much of his adult life—Atlanteans loved their spies, their games of espionage—a trait his people possessed that Rhegis despised, but considered a necessary evil. Since Rhegis reached an age in which he needed his own advisors and agents, Grimmin had been his man. Listening for secrets and keeping them, fighting the hidden war of words and whispers his sister and her cadre of allies had forced him to participate in.

The ocean is unsubtle, Rhegis thought. Unpredictable, unreliable, capable of surprise or deceit, but it was not an environment for spycraft. Where did we learn this nonsense?

"I'm sorry, Grimmin," Rhegis said. He made a vague gesture beside his head. "My mind…"

"Worry can make the mind wander, my lord. I understand."

Rhegis could see concern in Grimmin's eyes, too. For a man of whispers, he could be strangely honest. Perhaps this is why we've worked so well together all these years, he thought.

"Tell me about the attacks," Rhegis said.

"They're varied, and they're scattered," Grimmin said. He had a map spread out on a table between them, drawn on paper made of pale seaweed plucked from the depths of the sea. The plant gave the paper a textured quality, as if every inch of the map were covered with tiny, raised waves. "The targets are inconsistent, so it's hard to see a pattern, unless you look for the very biggest picture possible."

"To simply strike out at the surface world," Rhegis said.

"That's it," Grimmin said. "The attacks do nothing except break the land-dwellers' toys."

"And you know it's our people," Rhegis said.

"I recognize their tactics, sir."

"You're sure?"

Grimmin almost smiled.

"I helped develop many of those guerrilla tactics, my lord," he said. "I'd be willing to bet I trained some of the soldiers participating in the attacks."

"I assume my sister has something to do with all of this," Rhegis said. Her damned war. She's going to get it somehow, he thought. He silently cursed his father's indecisiveness. He thought we could work out our differences and rule together, but all he's done is given Atlantis two rulers with diametrically opposed viewpoints. And one of us is going to get us all killed.

"If the surface folk realize it's us..." he said.

"We have one advantage: they don't truly know we exist," Grimmin said. "And that means they don't know our capabilities, they don't know our tactics, they don't know our numbers."

"There's a but, isn't there."

"But if there's one thing they've excelled at in their evolution, it's creating weapons of war. All they have to do is find us and drop them," Grimmin said. "I know you've a soft spot for the surfacers, my lord, but they can be a nasty piece of work when provoked."

"So can we, unfortunately," Rhegis said. "What do you recommend?"

"We nip these bloody attacks in the bud, sir," Grimmin said. "Before we start dying."

Rhegis nodded and ran a hand through his graying hair.

"I'm going to have to do something about my sister," he said.

"My lord," Grimmin said. His tone changed. He sounded hesitant.

"Go ahead."

"We need to do something about your sister before she does something about you," Grimmin said.

Rhegis wanted to be angry at the suggestion. To be disgusted that anyone could think his sister capable of betraying him. But she was his twin. He had never existed without her. He knew her heartbeat. And he knew her rage.

"I'll talk to her," Rhegis said.

"Here, in the palace, with guards present," Grimmin said. "I'd like to be there myself, if you'd allow it."

"I don't know that having my spymaster present will help persuade her," Rhegis said. "But I'll take it under consideration."

Grimmin nodded and started to roll up the map.

"Grimmin?" Rhegis said. The old spy nodded. "Have you heard from your man on the surface lately?"

"I wouldn't call him my man, sir. The freelancer hasn't checked in, but he's often gone a spell. He wanders. It's better he isn't always there. Less conspicuous."

"Do me a favor, would you?"

"You're my king. There are no favors. I'm at your command."

"Humor me, then. Check in with your wandering mage. Make sure my… make sure his charges are safe."

Grimmin frowned, his white eyebrows drawing together ridiculously.

"You heard something?" There was real concern in his tone; Grimmin did not like to be out of the loop on anything.

"Don't worry, you old snoop. You haven't missed anything. Just a feeling, nothing more."

Grimmin saluted him. It was an unnecessary gesture, but Rhegis allowed it. It made Grimmin feel better.

"I'll check with him immediately."

"Be safe, Grimmin."

The old spy stuffed his map roughly into a protective tube and sealed it.

"You as well, my lord. I beg you, be safe."

Chapter 17: Viking funeral

They'd been sailing east for several hours before Barnabas
loosened up enough to talk to either of them. Echo rotated
between trying not to be angry with Yuri for almost dying, and
replaying all the things Galatea had said to her.

A day ago, I hauled ice for a living, she thought. And today I'm
supposed to be the hidden daughter of the king of the sea. It felt
like a fairy tale, she thought—a real one, not the saccharine
versions fed to kids to make them feel safe, but the truest ones, the
Brothers Grimm, full of death and blood, of tragedy and terror.
And I am terrified, she thought. This isn't the life I wanted.
I didn't want the life at the icehouse either, she thought. I wanted
to be someone. To go places. To see things. But not like this. I
don't want to be scared the rest of my life.

"I want my mom," she said out loud. She thought of the body,
moved below by the ghosts who manned this strange ship,
wrapped so carefully and respectfully by Barnabas in some old
tradition Echo had never heard of. My mother's gone. And I don't
know what to do about that.

"Echo," Barnabas said. He's been so quiet approaching her she
hadn't noticed him standing there. The sun was low in the sky, and
the gold hues highlighted the shadows in his face. He's had a hard

life, she realized. And it shows. Every inch of him is lived in. The scars and tattoos, the lines around his face. But he's not as old as he looks. Experience doesn't require years. She'd been relying on him for guidance without thinking about the things he'd had to see and go through to know so much.

"So, your mother is a sea nymph," Echo said, trying to smile.

"And a seer, and a crazy old woman," Barnabas said.

"She loves you very much," Echo said.

"And that will always be her downfall," Barnabas said. "Your mother loved you very much too, Echo."

"I know. I always knew."

"You're lucky to have that," Barnabas said. "I know it's no comfort now, not with what you've been through, but... where we're going. It's a place for forgotten things. Abandoned things. Unwanted. Unloved."

"She sent you there, didn't she," Echo said.

"She did. And among the unwanted things I felt unwanted. There's a beauty to it, you know. The brotherhood of thinking you're unloved."

"She told me every day," Echo said. "She told me she loved me every day."

"You should remember that."

"I will."

Barnabas looked out across the water. The ship was slowing. Echo gave him a worried look.

"We're stopping," she said.

"We are," he said. "It's time to say goodbye."

Echo's heart leapt into her throat.

"You can't leave us," she said. "We'll be too lost—"

"Not to me. To her."

Barnabas waved his hands as if finger-painting. Wherever he gestured, Echo could see the spirits of this ghost ship. They were busy, strapping together lengths of wood into a makeshift raft. Their hands were pale greenish white, and she watched as they moved so deftly, so delicately. The dead building something from nothing.

Yuri rose out of the belly of the ship, gently carrying Meredith's body in his arms. Tears streamed openly down his face. He locked eyes with Echo as he placed the body onto the raft the ghosts had built. He stepped back, and the ghosts—a man from the British Navy during the Revolutionary War, World War II U.S. sailor, a girl dressed for yachting in khaki shorts and a deep blue polo, they worked together to delicately tie the shrouded body to the raft.

"She wanted to become ashes, you said," Barnabas said.

"She did."

"Then ashes she shall become," he said.

"A Viking funeral," Echo said.

"It's something a lot of cultures who live and die by the sea have done."

Echo's eyes welled up. She wiped the tears away, and allowed herself to smile.

"A Viking funeral. She would have loved this," she said.

Yuri joined them, putting one burly arm around Echo's shoulders. Instead of comforting her though, he buried his face in her shoulder and sobbed, one deep, soul-crushing gasp, and Echo could feel his tears soaking her shirt. He's lost his mom twice, Echo thought. Look at the three of us. A bunch of orphans, surrounded by ghosts, lost at sea.

Echo kissed Yuri on top of his head and walked over to the raft. She knelt beside the body, trying to make out the shape of her mother's face beneath the shroud. I'll never see you again, she thought. My best friend. We should have had so much more time together.

"I miss you, mom," she whispered. "I'll make you proud."

She stood up and turned to Barnabas for help. He gestured to the ghosts still visible around Echo, and the spirits, four of them, lifted the raft and carried it to the edge of the ship. She noticed they'd prepared ropes to lower it to the water, and they did, the dead caring for the dead. Echo wondered if this sacred duty meant more to those who had once been alive, who had been lost at sea, who never got to say the goodbyes they'd wished to say.

The raft drifted on the water, rocking gently. The current drew it away, ten feet, twenty, fifty. Barnabas took Echo's hand and placed something in it. His pistol. The artifact. The magic wand that looked like a gun.

"Light the fire when you're ready," he said.

"What if I miss," she asked.

"You won't," Barnabas said. "I promise."

She held the old flintlock pistol out in front of her. It felt alien in her hand, too heavy, too strange. Her hand shook. She closed her eyes and pulled the trigger. When she opened them, she could see a comet of flame fall gently onto the raft. As it struck, the raft was consumed, burning bright as the sun, gold and red and white, the pink and orange sunset just above, the deep blue-black of the sea below.

Echo wiped her eyes with her free hand and held the pistol out to her side, feeling Barnabas take it from her without looking. She watched the funeral pyre blaze for a long time.

At last, she spoke.

"We have a lot of work to do," she said. "Let's begin."

Chapter 18: The timetable

Reina didn't consider herself a magician. She was a dabbler, much like her mother, with her mother's innate talents, but the magic arts had never been something she wanted to fully invest in. Still, just like her mother, she could weave a spell or two, and had a skill for scrying, for stealing thoughts, for viewing things from afar.

Tonight, she stood over a pool of water in her airtight chambers, watching. She swirled the basin with her finger, and sparkles of light drifted in its wake. Images appeared, swimming into existence. A great leviathan making its way through the deep. No living thing, this beast. Rather a great and mighty machine, a weapon of war born on the surface, controlled by the men above. An undersea warship.

Her chambers were dark, lit only by the glow of the basin and the broken light filtering in from outside. She wore black, still giving the impression of mourning, though she had long since moved on from her father's death.

She sensed her brother's approach before she heard him, banging on her door. She ran her hand through the waters in the basin again, shattering the image, leaving only an unsettled pool.

Rhegis entered, alone, surprisingly. No guards. No advisors. Just him. He still trusts me, she thought. Maybe not on all things, but he honestly believes I won't hurt him. He's too good a person to rule a kingdom.

"Brother," she said.

"You need to call off your agents," he said without preamble.

"I have no idea what you're talking about," she said. "What do you think you're doing? I know you're behind the attacks on the surface."

Reina gave her most sincere look of offended innocence.

"How could you even suspect me of such a thing? You know I'd never—"

"Reina," Rhegis said. His eyes were lined and tired. Always the worrier, her brother. "We cannot survive a war with the surface."

"We cannot survive without one, if they keep destroying our kingdom," Reina said. "But I assure you, I am not doing whatever you think I'm doing."

Rhegis laid an unblinking gaze on her. She sighed.

"Look. Perhaps it's someone in my circle. You know my friends and allies are restless. I'll look into it."

"Don't play games with me, Reina."

"None of it is games, brother. It's all deadly serious," she said. "Our people, our kingdom, our seas. All at risk. But I will investigate. For you."

"Don't make me have to do something I'll regret, sister," Rhegis said. Reina barked out a bitter laugh.

"Something you'll regret?" she said. "We rule as equals, Rhegis. You have no more power over me than I have over you. That's how we got to this point in the first place."

"He wanted us to be foils for each other, not enemies," Rhegis said.

"Well perhaps someday we'll get there," Reina said. She rolled her eyes as Rhegis continued to glower. "Relax. I'll get you answers."

Rhegis held her gaze a moment longer, then turned to leave, his long black mourning cloak trailing behind him.

"We need the girl, assassin," Reina said, knowing Barracuda had witnessed the conversation from the shadows. The slender mercenary emerged from the darkness.

"We'll have her soon," he said.

"What of our other acquisitions," Reina said.

"Our teams are prepared. They'll move on your word."

"Find the girl, Barracuda," Reina said. "I need something to leash my brother with before we begin the next step."

"There's something else, Regent," Barracuda said.

Reina nodded at him to continue.

"Your brother's spymaster is preparing to depart. It's been a long while since he's headed for the surface. I suspect Rhegis is sending him to check on the girl and her mother," Barracuda said.

"Deal with him," Reina said.

"How permanent would you like the solution?" Barracuda said.

"Make it look like an accident," Reina said. "There are many dangers for an Atlantean traveling the open seas alone."

Barracuda tilted his head in acknowledgement and began to leave.

"And assassin," Reina said. Barracuda stopped and waited. "If he is checking on the girl, then Rhegis suspects something. This moves our timetable up. Plan accordingly."

Barracuda nodded again and disappeared into the shadows.

Reina stirred the water in the basin again, wishing, for the first time, her brother had introduced her to the family he left on the surface. Perhaps if she'd met this little half-made thing, she'd see her in the mirrored waters of the bowl.

Instead, she simply had to wait.

Chapter 19: The Island of Unwanted Things

Echo watched the island grow bigger in the distance, details coming into focus one at a time: a row of stone statues, watching them with courageous stances and grim faces; marble structures, like one would find in Ancient Greece; palm trees swaying in the warm breeze; small wooden houses set back just slightly from the sand; the remnants of a sailing vessel, cracked open like an egg on the shore.

This is where we'll hide, she thought. Among all the unwanted things.

She snapped out of her reverie when she heard Yuri let loose a high-pitched scream.

"What was that!" Yuri yelled. Echo spun around to see Yuri holding his ear, his face flushed with anger or pain, Barnabas standing over him looking vaguely self-satisfied.

"Don't be a weakling," Barnabas said. "It couldn't have hurt that much."

"What did you do, stab me in the ear?" Yuri said. Echo walked over quickly and pulled Yuri's hand away from his ear. Barnabas had, in fact, literally pierced Yuri's ear.

"It's a pearl earring," Echo said. "It looks good on you."

"Don't tease me," Yuri said.

"I think this is your style," Echo said.

"Echo, you betray me," Yuri said. "Seriously, dude, why did you do that."

"That, my impulsive friend, is an artifact," Barnabas said.

"It's an earring," Yuri said. "Echo said it's an earring."

"It's an earring that is an artifact," Barnabas said.

"You get an artifact and it looks like a flintlock pistol, I get an artifact and it's a shiny earring," Yuri said. "I like you less and less every time we interact."

"Don't hold a grudge just yet," Barnabas said. "That artifact will save your life someday."

"Because it makes me so pretty?"

"Because as long as you're wearing it, you can breathe underwater," Barnabas said.

Yuri gave Barnabas a dead-eyed stare.

"I let one mermaid almost drown me one time, and now you think you can just piece my ear whenever you feel like it," Yuri said.

Echo petted Yuri on the head as if to comfort him. Yuri raised an eyebrow at her indicating he felt the gesture was hollow.

"What about me," Echo said. "You going to pierce my ear when I'm not looking?"

Barnabas shook his head.

"You're Atlantean," he said. "You don't need one. You said you've been in a situation when you should have drowned, but didn't?"

Echo nodded. When she was thirteen, she went surfing, against her mother's advice, when New England was feeling the effects of a tropical storm further south. The waves were killer, both literally and figuratively. Echo had been torn from her board by a powerful wave and became tangled up in her own leash. She'd clawed her way to the surface, but she was under for a long time, long enough to have sucked a lot of water into her lungs. But when she dragged herself onto the beach, she was tired, bruised, and scared... but otherwise, fine. And as Barnabas put the question to her, Echo realized there had been more than one time when, if nothing else, she should have been throwing water up after being pulled under.

"You mean I've been able to breathe underwater my whole life and I've never known," Echo said.

"We'll test it out safely, but I've never known anyone related to Atlantis who wasn't born amphibious," Barnabas said. "I'm the same, by the way—one of the few fortunate gifts of being born the son of a nereid. I found that out the hard way. And I learned it here."

"On this island," Echo said. The ship slowed, and she heard the clank of dropping anchor.

"On this island," Barnabas said softly. "Among other things."

***

Yuri complained most of the way to the shore. Barnabas seemed to almost, almost feel bad about the ambush on the ship, because he rowed the dinghy in himself the entire way. He did try to force Yuri to get out of the little boat and drag them to shore when they were close enough, which kicked off another argument. Echo, tired of the fighting, jumped out and dragged the dinghy easily one-handed to the beach, enjoying the looks of surprise on both men's faces.

I could get used to super-strength, she thought, almost smiling.

They were not alone when they arrived, though. Two men stood on the shore, waiting. Both were striking in their own way. One was older, short, and built like a human boulder, scalp shaved down to the skin so it gleamed in the sun. He smiled at them with brilliantly white teeth, and wore some sort of kilt or wrap and a sword belt and little else.

The younger man, Echo thought, was possibly the most beautiful human being she'd ever seen, man or woman, in her entire life. He had a face like an eagle, high cheeks, royal nose, dark eyes, his long hair so dark it seemed to absorb the light. He wore it tied up in a messy topknot. Tall and lean, he was dressed similarly to the older man, though he had a metal shield strapped to his back and wore high sandals, like something out of a gladiator movie.

"Barnabas Coy," the older man said. He sounded threatening at first, but then he burst into laughter. "I guess it's true what they say about the good dying young. I'd heard rumors you'd been killed by the sons of Polyphemus a few years back."

"It was a misunderstanding," Barnabas said. "Rule to live by: never use the phrase 'see eye to eye' when dealing with a cyclops."

"Still spinning tales," the older man said. Finally, he strode right up to Barnabas and wrapped him in a rib-cracking hug. "It's good to see you, old friend. You've been away too long."

"The world keeps us busy," Barnabas said.

"And what have you brought us," the older man said. "More lost puppies?"

"Do we bring anyone else here?" Barnabas said. "Merrick, this is Echo."

Merrick, the older man, looked her over—not in a creepy way, Echo thought, but in an appraising way, like one does before entering a fight.

"Echo," Merrick said. "There's a name with some history. You're Atlantean."

"How does everyone know that?" Echo said, exasperated.

"It's the eyebrows," the younger man said.

Echo shot a look at him.

"What's wrong with my eyebrows," she said.

The young man smirked. Echo smoothed her eyebrows back self-consciously.

"Who are you, anyway," Echo said.

"Barnabas, you remember Artem," Merrick said.

"Of course," Barnabas said. "You've got your mother's look."

Artem looked at the ground, then back up again.

"I'll take that as both a compliment and in insult," Artem said.

Echo watched the exchange with curiosity, trying to read the subtext between the men. Parentage seemed to be an important thing here—not for status, but simply for knowing how to assess each other.

"So, Barnabas is the son of a sea nymph, and clearly he looks like his dad," Echo said.

"Again, compliment and insult at the same time," Barnabas said.

"And you both knew I was an Atlantean's daughter as soon as you saw me," Echo said. "Do I get to know what sort of... whatever you are?"

"Mine's a bit boring," Merrick said. "But Artem here..."

"I'm an Amazon," he said.

Echo opened her mouth to speak, but Artem cut her off.

"And what in the seven seas is he?" Artem said, pointing at Yuri.

"Angry and hungry," Yuri said. "Got anything to eat?"

***

Merrick and Artem were not alone on the island, they discovered as they sat down to dinner of cooked white fish and island fruit.

Once Merrick had given some signal that their visitors were safe, others came out of the forest. Children, many of them, maybe a dozen, and men and women as well of all ages, each with something unworldly about them. Some were exceptionally tall, or wide. One man had three eyes, another an extra set of arms. Other oddities were less immediately noticeable. Pointed ears or strangely-colored eyes, a forked tongue, or feet like a bird's.

"The Island of Unwanted Things," Echo said.

She as nearly positive that Yuri had not blinked since dinner was served, staring wide-eyed as a woman whose lower body was that of a giant snake slithered in, a string of fish hanging from hooks over her shoulder.

"It's like Mos Eisley around here," Yuri said.

"Nobody here is unwanted," Merrick said. He eyed Barnabas when he said it. "That's why this place exists. The sea is a strange place. It is full of wonder, but sometimes... sometimes it doesn't like when things are out of place. And so, for many who are themselves out of place, this island becomes home."

Barnabas leaned in, speaking in a hushed tone.

"That's why we're here, Merrick," Barnabas said. "Echo isn't unwanted. She's wanted by the wrong people."

Artem leaned back in his chair and crossed his arms.

"We're not here to protect every stray that comes running to us," he said. "This is supposed to be a place for the lost, not the pursued. There's a difference."

Merrick wrinkled his nose at the younger man's statement, but nodded.

"We're not made to hide people, Barnabas. If someone wants to find her here, they'll find her. And I can't put the others at risk."

"I know," Barnabas said. "But she needs a teacher if she's going to survive out there. And you're the best I know."

Merrick shook his head despite the gleaming smile growing across his face.

"Not anymore I'm not," he said. He pointed at Artem. "This one's like nothing I've ever seen."

"Genetics," Artem said. "You know genetics plays into that."

"Some," Merrick said. "But there are things that can't be explained by genetics and can't be explained by luck. Have you ever fought before, girl?"

Echo leaned back, not expecting to be drawn into the conversation. She had resigned herself to the unpleasant thought of being talked about, rather than talked with.

"I mean I can throw a punch," she said. "But you mean, like martial arts?"

"Anything," Merrick said. "From what I remember, Barnabas has no talent for any sort of martial arts, but he's good in a bar brawl."

"I have my uses," Barnabas said.

"Well, we'll get you fed," Merrick said. "And get you some gear. Then we'll put you in the ring with our Artem over here and see what you can do."

"I do not like this idea at all," Echo said. "At all."

Artem laughed. It was so unexpected, so surprising from the sullen young man, that everyone, even Merrick, pulled back for a moment. Echo just watched though. Artem's face completely changed, a radiant smile breaking the sullen expression he'd worn since they arrived. His eyes glittered with a different kind of light and life.

"Don't worry," he said. "I think you'll know more already than you even realize. You'll be safe with me."

Echo smiled back at him.
"What makes you say that?"

"I know a fighter when I see one," he said.

Yuri, who had remained almost entirely silent through the whole exchange, chimed in, an edge to his voice.

"What about me?" he said.

"What about you?" Barnabas said.

"Oh, don't you start on me, Jack Sparrow," Yuri said. "Echo's going to be trained to be some kind of sea-ninja or something and I'm gonna what, hang out on the ship? What am I, her sidekick?" Echo shot a sympathetic look at Artem, then at Merrick, and finally at Barnabas. Barnabas sighed dramatically.

"Okay, okay," he said. "You should probably know how to avoid getting yourself killed too, as much as I don't particularly care one way or another."

"You do care," Echo said. "You gave him an artifact so he wouldn't drown. Don't pretend you're a jerk."

"Don't go telling people that," Barnabas said. "I have a reputation to maintain. What do you say, Merrick? Think there's anyone who could show Yuri how which end of a sword is the sharp end?"

"I think we can manage," Merrick said. "Let it never be said we've turned away a lost cause."

Chapter 20: The hunted

Grimmin knew he was being followed almost immediately. He'd spent too many years being the keeper of secrets to not be paranoid enough to notice. Still, as he made his way from Atlantis to the surface—alone, and swimming, the Atlantean version of "on foot"—he kept moving forward, cautious but swift.

The open ocean, even for someone with his experience, was a terrible place for combat. Too open, too uncontrolled. Danger could come at you from any direction. He needed a surface, a wall, something to put his back against for defense.

So, he kept moving.

Hunting and tracking in the open ocean was not all that different from doing so on land, he thought. You use different senses—hearing, touch, and for those capable, scent—to make up for not being able to look for tracks or spoor, other evidence of hunter and hunted. He could feel the subtle changes in the water around him, that innate sixth sense aquatic creatures possessed that teetered on paranoia, the ability to know something was amiss.

It wasn't an Atlantean assassin, he knew. Their tactics were so familiar to him he'd recognize their tricks in a heartbeat. Some sort of beast? He thought. A hunting animal. A trained shark, maybe. The men of the surface found most sea creatures untrainable, but

Atlanteans had learned to make the most of their symbiotic relationships with ocean beasts over centuries. If it had a brain, if it had instincts, they knew how to manipulate it.

He carried his trident openly, the long, silvery weapon held out in front of him like an arrowhead. He kept a long knife at the ready, too. The water was clear, but at this depth, visibility was not perfect, so he changed course, heading more directly for the surface. Whatever followed him was at ease in the water—perhaps if he could make his way on land, he could turn having legs to an advantage.

Stupid old man, he thought. Stupid to travel alone. Stupid to isolate myself. I've set myself up for this. I'm losing my edge.

He felt pressure in the water around him and drew his knife, but it was too late—the hunter was upon him, the seawater turning to foam in its violent wake. It's big, he thought, unable to get a full look at it beyond its dark, speckled skin. Grimmin was appalled it had got so close without him seeing, but it must be fast, he thought, so fast. It pounced with the ruthlessness of a top-tier predator, using its bulk to stun him, and then he felt a piercing pain in his side. The water around him turned red with blood. My blood, the old spy thought.

This is not how I want to die, Grimmin thought. He gave up on his trident, too bulky for close combat, and instead lashed out with his knife, feeling it bite through skin and sinew. He turned it again, unsure what part of the creature he'd struck, but he dragged that blade as far as he could, more than an arm's length, a vicious gouge through muscle, scraping against bone.

Something hit him hard—the tail, he realized, it's got a tail—and Grimmin's guts clenched up as his body reacted with fear and pain. The beast was above him now, blocking his escape to the surface. He saw it turn on him, a giant wedge-shaped head and massive jaws splitting, long, yellowed teeth snapping. It plunged down, snout slamming into Grimmin's chest, and together, they plummeted down, down, down into the depths, and into the darkness below.

Chapter 21: The life and times of Barnabas Coy

The sea moved tirelessly beneath the *Endless*, just as Barnabas Coy moved tirelessly aboard the ship. Born of the sea, he thought. I've never been able to stay still. He leaned against the railing as the sun dropped from the sky like a hot coal. He'd left Echo and Yuri on land, but the proximity of the place, with all its memories, had proven too much for him.

This is where I was truly born, he thought. Not in that shrouded place filled with sea nymphs and their kin. That was where I entered this world, but the person I am, the person I became, he was born here, no matter how far away I traveled to escape it.

All these miles, all these oceans, traveling the world to places mankind had forgotten ever existed, walking on sandy shores no human foot had tread... All these years, and still I end up back here. The Island of Unwanted Things.

It hadn't changed much, he thought, not in any meaningful way, not since he arrived here as a child. The huts had been updated and repaired a little, the trees grew or fell, but still. The sea never stopped moving, but it also never really changed. That is the way of all immortal things, though, isn't it, Barnabas thought. Restlessness and immutability. When you have forever, change happens in the falling of grains of sand.

I was so little when she sent me here, he thought. Maybe it was better that way. Everything strange, all the other misfits… when you're young, everything is unfamiliar, so nothing is alien. Boys with lobster claws for hands or women with eyes that blinked sideways, men made of coral whose skin was barbed with barnacles. None of it scared him. Or all of it did. Probably both, he thought, but then again, look where I was born—surrounded by creatures who looked like women, sometimes, who saw him as an abomination, who hated his mother for not drowning him. That was how his mother learned for certain he could breathe seawater, when one of her sisters held his little head under to put him out of his misery. But he'd survived, and his mother knew it was only a matter of time before it happened again, only worse, something more permanent, deadlier, bloodier.

He remembered the drowning like a dream. He asked his mother about it once, if it had been real or not, and Galatea warned him that some of her sisters were not to be trusted.

"They aren't evil, my little pearl," she said. "My kind, we have too much of the sea in us. We can be dangerous, and feral, and wild. And the other creatures who live with us are so much worse. But it is just their nature, my love. It's just their nature."
He traveled the world for many years, and if he learned anything at all, it's that no creature that speaks and reasons does evil because of its nature. Evil is a choice. Cruelty is a choice. And he knew where he was not wanted.

And so, she left him here. He remembered the way a young Merrick looked at Galatea on that shore, wary but kind.

"You're not the first of your people to fall in love with a sailor," he said. "He won't be the first boy like him we've had to take in."

Right there, Barnabas thought. He could see the spot on the beach where he'd first met Merrick, standing side by side with his partner Theo—pronounced with a hard T, Barnabas later learned, when that same man taught him how to read. Merrick put a sword in Barnabas' hand, but Merrick's lover put a book in the other. And they made something out of nothing.

The island is so quiet, Barnabas thought. Quiet and lovely. You'd almost think it safe. But there are things here, as there are in every hidden place like this, where monsters sleep. Barnabas knew where the monsters were, too. He found one, as a boy, an old serpent with milky eyes and a soft voice. The creature should have eaten him, swallowed him whole for his foolishness and indiscretion, but instead the monster whispered in his ear. Because, you see, that serpent had seen the world before it went blind, and it wanted an audience. Serpents are always performers, Barnabas knew. He learned that early, and he proved it true through all his travels.

He visited the monster many times. No one ever knew, not even Merrick and Theo, though the old scholar may have suspected.

The serpent told him so many things in those whispers. And Barnabas learned that the world was very big, and this island was very small, and he could not be satisfied living here forever.

On the boy's fourteenth birthday the snake passed away, leaving behind a cavern full of old secrets, artifacts and books collected over centuries from men he'd killed. Barnabas wondered, briefly, if he might have been one of the serpent's victims himself if he'd had anything to offer; or if, instead, the old monster wanted to leave all this knowledge behind for someone rather than rot in a cave on some forgotten island. And so, Barnabas continued to come here, day after day, even as the monster's corpse mummified and turned to dust, a grim and morbid guardian.

Among the cluttered and disorganized piles of ill-gotten loot Barnabas found spell books and weapons; gold and gems; but most importantly he found maps. So many maps. It was these he busied himself most, though the books of magic he scoured for practical use.

And then one day he told Merrick and Theo he wanted to leave this island.

"The world is strange and full of wonder. I want to see it," he told them. Both men looked displeased, but it was Theo, wrapped as he often was in a heavy red blanket against the night air as they talked after dinner, who finally understood.

"None of you are really meant to stay here forever, you know. We do the best we can with all you foundlings, but in the end…" Theo said. "In the end, you have to go where fate calls you. Just like fate called us here."

Barnabas left with the next merchant vessel—odd traders often stopped by the island to trade goods for fresh water or fruit, and the island had a reputation for fearsome warriors, so none ever gave them trouble.

His sailing skills were terrible, but one of the books he took from the serpent's cave had taught him how to call the wind, and he made sure that vessel sailed straight and true to its next port. He could turn salt water to fresh, call up minor elementals from the deep water. Looking back, Barnabas knew now, it was all very dangerous. Incredibly stupid. The spirits he yoked were vengeful and angry. But at the time, he was young, and the world was, he knew, strange and full of wonder, and so big, bigger than anyone map could show you.

He was free. Free of the evil spite of the sea nymphs, of his mother's abandonment, of the responsible gaze of Theo and Merrick, free of his fellow unwanted things. He'd return to the island sometimes, with traders, or eventually on his own, each time looking even stranger, covering himself in tattoos to ward off angry spirits or warn him of danger or protect him from harm. Spells pierced into his skin with ink and blood.

He was not there when Theo died, and he didn't return much after that. As much as he owed to Merrick, it had been Theo who Barnabas saw as a father figure, and without him, the island left him little to return to. His adventures took him very far away, and the place where he'd grown up had itself grown different.

Here, now, staring at the shoreline, so mystifyingly unchanged all these years from the outside, so unfamiliar up close… it gave him vertigo. It made him homesick for a place just a hundred yards away from him. And it made him realize that he had seen the strange and wonderful world, but he had done so alone, on a ship filled with ghosts, and he had truly become a man with no home.

The old serpent died alone with a belly full of knowledge. Maybe that's the fate he hoped for me, Barnabas thought.

Maybe that was why he let me live. To pass his curse on to me.

The night grew cold, with icy stars watching him from a black sky. Barnabas remained on deck until the last of the fires on the island burned out, and only then he wrapped his coat tightly around himself and went below, to sleep and to dream.

Chapter 22: The Natural

They spent the night in one of the simple shacks along the shore; Echo choosing a hammock made of net and Yuri what looked like a hand-made sleeping bag. Barnabas didn't remain with them; he said he need to go back to the ship, but Echo picked up on a strange tone in his voice, as if being on the island made him uncomfortable.

Artem woke Echo early the next morning, the sun splitting the horizon in shades of gold and black.

"Come," he said. He had a set of clothes draped over one arm, multiple weapons gripped casually in the other.

He gave her time to change into the clothing he'd brought her—she worried it would be the ridiculous gladiatorial get-up Artem and Merrick both wore, but it turned out to be a fabric not dissimilar to a wetsuit, with ankle-length pants in a mottled blue-gray pattern, a tank-top of the same material.

"No shoes, I take it," she asked, stepping outside to find him waiting, watching the sunrise.

"It'll be better for you to feel the sand beneath your feet," he said.

He led her down to the water and tossed her one of the weapons, a long, three-pronged spear. A trident, she thought. Of course it's a trident. I'm a stereotype.

"You know, back where I come from, we have, like, guns and stuff," she said.

"Which will work fantastic underwater," Artem said. "I know it seems ridiculous, but the people who will be coming after you… these old weapons of war will work best. And they'll help us trigger your innate abilities better."

"Trigger my innate abilities," Echo said, her voice lilting with humor. "You keep saying that. I have trouble believing—"

Without warning, Artem attacked her with a trident of his own. It was an unsubtle attack, overhead and aggressive, and Echo got her own weapon up fast, catching his strike with the shaft of her trident. Without thinking, she kicked him in the chest, hammering at him like a horse-kick. Artem bounced back and out of range easily, laughing as he did.

"What the hell!" Echo said.

"Look what you just did," he said.

Echo paused, realizing that she'd taken on a fighter's stance, legs at the ready, turned sideways to create a narrower target. The trident felt perfectly natural in her hands, held lightly with her fingers.

And as soon as she noticed this, the entire thing fell apart. She felt silly and awkward. The trident became heavy and alien.

"Maybe I saw it in a movie or something," she said.

Artem shook his head, smiling.

"Atlanteans have as much of the old magic in their veins as they do blood," he said. "For millennia, your people tinkered with their genes, with magic, with technology. Mother sea lions don't have to teach their babies how to swim the way human mothers must teach their children. You know this, right? Or how land-dwelling animals know how to walk as soon as they're born, rather than needing to practice."

"It's instinct," Echo said. "But you know baby humans can't walk because we're born not fully developed because our brains are so big though, right? It's a tradeoff for a different genetic advantage."

Artem chuckled.

"I didn't know that," he said. "But the Atlanteans of the old world, the ones who first fled to the sea—the stories say that they knew ways to... create instinct. Atlanteans are born knowing how to swim."

"And you're saying that they also are born knowing how to fight," she said.

Artem shrugged.

"Merrick has fought beside and against many Atlanteans, and his theory is that it's not by design. That your people tinkered with their genetic memories, and sometimes things latch on. Other memories carried forward. Unintentional benefits."

"I'm basically Neo, downloading fighting styles from the Matrix," Echo said.

"I have no idea what that means. But."

Artem cut himself short to launch another attack at Echo, thrusting with the points of the trident or swinging it in wide arcs. Fear kicked in again, and Echo deflected, dodged, ducked, not thinking, but instead relying purely on innate reactions. She felt a flash of rage, and threw an elbow at Artem. Bone connected with bone as her forearm bashed him under his left eye. The young warrior staggered backward, holding his face. Echo waited, wondering if she'd made him mad. But when he uncovered his face, he was smiling.

"This is good," he said. "The trick we need to figure out is how to make sure you can do this whenever you want to and not when I'm scaring the living hell out of you."

***

On a high dune not far away, Yuri sat watching. He frowned deeply as Artem pressed his attacks, and grimaced whenever Echo attacked back. His whole body shook when they clashed, and tensed with each close call.

"He's going to kill her," Yuri said out loud. "This is stupid."

"You sound jealous," Barnabas said, walking up the dune. Yuri almost jumped out of his skin; he hadn't heard the magician approaching. He covered his non-pierced ear protectively.

"What? No. What?"

"You're sitting here staring at her," Barnabas said. "Look, if you've got a thing for her, I'm not going to judge you for it, but..."

"What?" Yuri said again. "You think I have a thing for Echo?"

"Again, I point to the wistful staring thing you're doing right now."

"That's horrible," Yuri said. "Her mom practically raised me. She's my sister."

"Wouldn't be the first time two teenagers raised in the same house had a thing for each other," Barnabas said.

"I've seen her clip her toenails," Yuri said. "If there were ever a thing to deter some sort of inappropriate reaction, it was that." "Well, if you really are jealous..." Barnabas said.

"I'm not jealous of Artem," Yuri said.

"If you are, just watch for the way Artem and Merrick look at each other," Barnabas said.

"You're really obsessing over this idea I have the hots for her, Barney. Are you projecting? Wait. What?" Yuri said. "Artem and Merrick?"

Barnabas smirked and sat down on the sand next to Yuri.

"First of all, call me Barney again and I'll pierce your other ear while you sleep."

"Noted."

"Second of all, yes," Barnabas said. "I'm glad to see it. Merrick's partner died before his time. I thought he'd never find someone again."

"Kind of a May-December romance going on there, huh?" Yuri said.

Barnabas gave him a befuddled look.

"Two legendary swordsmen living on an island filled with half-breed myths and sea monsters, and you worry about the age difference," Barnabas said. "You continue to become more surprising the longer I know you, Yuri."

"Thank you."

"That wasn't a compliment."

"Anyway," Yuri said. "I'll admit something. I am jealous."

"I knew it."

"But not of her spending time with the walking romance-novel cover model down there," Yuri said. "I'm not Echo's biological big brother, but I'm her big brother, right? I'm supposed to be able to protect her. Look out for her. And she's down there becoming a Sea Jedi or whatever and I'm... I'm feeling a little useless, Barney."

"Do you want another pearl earring, or would you prefer a diamond one next time you nap."

"Sorry."

Barnabas pointed across the dunes. Another figure watched the mock battle below. Merrick.

"Once upon a time, Merrick taught every young creature left on his doorstep here on this island how to fight," Barnabas said. "He did his best with me, even, though I bet if you asked he'd say I'm one of his failures."

"He's jealous that someone else is teaching Echo," Yuri said.

"And I think you should ask him to teach you a few things," Barnabas said.

"That... would be pretty cool," Yuri said. "Thanks."

"Merrick's always loved a lost cause," Barnabas said. "He'll be thrilled."

"Had to get one more insult in under the wire there, huh."

"You'd have been disappointed if I didn't," Barnabas said.

***

They broke mid-morning to eat and rest, but Artem pushed Echo right back into it, this time taking the trident away and giving her what was either a very long knife or a very short sword—Echo couldn't tell and felt foolish asking—and a metal gauntlet that had a smooth, reflective surface on the bottom. She asked Artem what the gauntlet was for.

"Shields are unwieldy in the water," he said. "Virtually useless."

"Oh no," Echo said. "Don't hit me yet."

Artem threw his arms up in the air, mocking exasperation.

"Have I destroyed all sense of trust in me already? Hold your arm up and across, as if you're shielding your face from the sun with your forearm."

Echo complied. Artem reached out with one hand and held her wrist, then whacked her gauntlet with the flat of his own knife several times. The dueling metal surfaces clanged loudly.

"It's not as much protection as a shield, but Atlantean warriors use these often in lieu of a shield to deflect incoming attacks."

"That is terrifying," Echo said.
Artem gave a sympathetic nod.

"I was trained with a buckler," he said. "Even that feels small when you've got someone shooting arrows or throwing spears at you."

"Again, where I come from, I think bullets would be the preferred projectile."

"Well, you'll encounter those too someday, I'm sure," he said. Before releasing her wrist, he turned her hand over, examining it.

"That's pretty creepy, Artem," Echo said.

"Sorry. I'm just wondering… You have super-human strength."

"I can try to throw you if you want," Echo said.

"No, thank you," Artem said. "I'm curious if you've inherited any other abilities."

"You're going to try to drown me, aren't you."

"No. I just wonder if your skin is tougher than an ordinary human's," he said.

"I swear, if you stab my hand to find out I will throw you right out into the ocean, Artem," Echo said.

"Try it."

"What?"

"Try to throw me into the ocean," Artem said.

"… Um. No," Echo said.

"Come on, I can take it," he said.

Echo shrugged, then grabbed hold of his arm and tried to lift him. His feet came off the ground easily enough, but Artem slipped around, somehow ending up behind her, using her own strength to make sure she couldn't throw him. The maneuver was instantly angering. Without thinking, she threw an elbow into his gut, knocking him backward. But he held on, taking her with him. Both ended up on the sand. Artem coughed loudly.

"I think… it's going to be as hard to teach you how not to accidentally kill someone as it will be to teach you not to get killed yourself," he said.

"Are you okay?" she said, mildly embarrassed at how hard she hit him.

He nodded vigorously, though he looked like he might retch.

"I asked for that. That was my fault," he said. "But look."

He pointed, and Echo followed the gesture to see a gash in her pants across one thigh.

"I cut myself when I tried to throw you," she said.

She pulled the rip in her pant leg open to see how bad the injury was, but there was no blood. A vibrant pink line or raised skin where the blade dragged against her flesh, yes, but otherwise, she was unhurt.

"You did that on purpose," she said.

"And if I was wrong, I would've stitched you up myself," Artem said. "But aren't you happier knowing about another of your powers?"

"I'm beginning to think your super power is a malleable sense of right and wrong," she said.

"Get to know me," Artem said. "I'd like to think you'll find the very opposite is true."

Chapter 23: The pack

The were-sharks moved through the water like shadows, sleek hunters riding the currents through distant seas. Their language beneath the waves was one of movement and gesture, subtle signals of fin and eye, tail and back.

They were four now. One dead, quite dead at the hands of the man who named himself after a fish. One left behind, crippled by the crude magic of the sea wizard Barnabas Coy. Coy had a long history with the were-sharks, though not all of it had been violent. He was a fixture, that wanderer, and they'd crossed paths many times, both Maw and his pack, and others of their kind.

Coy was not loved.

The four shadow hunters followed the trail left behind by Coy's ship. It left a taste in the water, a scent of old, forgotten things, not death but some other kind of decay, things forgotten and left to drift.

To many, the were-sharks were forgotten things themselves. The surface world had long let the monsters fade from their memories, even as the lycanthropes of the land, the wolves and other beasts, still haunted their myths, and their nightmares. The same magics that made those land-borne shape-shifters had given birth to these creatures, alike but different, men who swam like sharks and sharks who swam like men. They looked like men, but they were simpler than humans. Their desires less complicated. More easily sated.

His kin were unfazed by the forgetfulness of mankind. Let them have their leviathans, their krakens. Maw's people would simply continue to exist, to hunt, to kill, to live free in a dying sea.

And yet, the pack leader thought, we somehow still find ourselves involved in the affairs of petty creatures. It's the human part of our nature, he pondered in a rare, rare moment of reflection. Our instincts are of the shark, but sometimes the weaknesses of man creep in. Greed overtaking hunger. Want overtaking need.

He led his pack to the edge of an island where nereids had come to gather, along with other things the were-sharks despised. Once—before Maw's time, but if he closed his eyes, if he listened to the eons of memories buried in his brain, passed down through generations—his kind had warred with the merfolk who made the shoals of the island their home. Once upon a time the shark-men had feasted on mermaids, terrorized sea nymphs, made sirens forget their songs. But all of us have faded from history, he thought. There was no sport in it anymore, and the seas were vast, and ever increasingly empty.

They did not set foot on the island of the nereids, but picked up the trail once more. Again, they took to the seas, stopping to devour the rotting carcass of a humpback whale, turning the water pink with blood, yellow with blubber.

They found Coy's ship anchored in the harbor of an island Maw had never seen before, not in all his travels. They watched from a distance, he and his pack, and saw men with weapons of war patrol the coastline. Watched the girl, their prey, learn to fight. She'd be no easy target this time, Maw could see, and she'd fought like a demon when they'd last encountered her.

His brethren showed their teeth, eyes glittering like black pearls in the fading light. They wanted to take her. They wanted revenge for the death of their brother, for the wounds they themselves had suffered. But Maw knew this man Barracuda, and Maw intended to live a long, long life. He held his pack in check and sent one to summon the assassin. If Barracuda wanted to take the girl alive, then Maw would bring him to her. Let the little assassin see for himself that she was no weak little fish.

***

Barracuda came quickly when called. It gave Maw some small satisfaction to see the smug assassin rushed. His voice betrayed nothing but bored patience, but Maw could smell the anxiety on him.

"You've done well," Barracuda said. Maw hated the sound of the man's voice. It was like oil on the surface of the ocean.

"Then our contract is completed," Maw said. He stood in human form on a small outcropping near the hidden island. His men remained in the water, still wearing the skins of their shark-shapes, unwilling to meet with the assassin on land. Were-sharks were simple creatures but their memories were long.

"I have further need of you," Barracuda said.

Maw huffed a short, bitter laugh.

"No," he said.

Barracuda folded his arms across his chest.

"I'll make it worth your time," Barracuda said.

"And if we fail, you'll slaughter us?"

"It's slaughter I need," Barracuda said. "I need a Frenzy."

Maw let the word hang in the air a moment. The Frenzy was not undertaken lightly. A ritual among the were-sharks, word would go out—a message in the water, a hum, a call to arms—inviting all his kind to a berserker hunt, a literal frenzy in the water. There had not been a formal Frenzy in many years. It called too much attention to his people.

"You ask much," Maw said.

"But wouldn't you like to be the man who led the first Frenzy in almost a generation?" Barracuda said. "Think of the honor."

Maw knew he should say no, but he could feel the eyes of his men looking at him from the water. They wanted this. Their kin would come when called. It was something they all wanted in their darkest of hearts.

"How many of your people could you muster?" Barracuda said.

"When," Maw asked.

"As soon as possible, preferably. We can spare a few weeks to gather the forces and plan. But we need to make this happen soon. I want you ready."

Maw lowered his eyes, considering where they were in the world, how far the signal would have to travel.

"A dozen, I think," he said. "We're not what we once were. We're more scattered now."

"A dozen would be a mighty Frenzy, Maw," Barracuda said.

Maw did not respond.

"Bring them," Barracuda said. "Bring them, and you'll go down in history."

Maw sneered and cast his eyes in the direction of the mysterious island.

"What is this place?" he asked.

"It's the Island of Unwanted Things," Barracuda said. "A home for the forgotten. But destroy it, and you'll never be forgotten, Maw. You'll live on forever."

Chapter 24: Man-bull-thing

Yuri knew he was in some sort of trouble the second Barnabas laughed.

Merrick found him early the second morning after their arrival on the Island of Unwanted Things, the bald fighter painfully upbeat and awake while Yuri searched desperately for anything that could be used as a coffee substitute among the island's provisions.

"You said you wanted learn how to defend yourself," Merrick said. Barnabas was with the older fighter, but the magician-pirate-scoundrel hung back a bit, as if he were along for moral support rather than actively helping Merrick talk to Yuri.

"Yeah," Yuri said. "If I'm going to be tagging along this whole time, I should probably know how to fight back."

Yuri felt like in the real world, he knew how to carry himself—no small guy himself, he'd been hauling massive blocks of ice his entire youth, so while he didn't look like much of a brawler, he'd grown up to be a burly young man and he used that size to keep would-be fights at bay when he got into trouble.

Running away from legitimate monsters had changed his mind, though. He needed to know how to do something to keep himself and his friends safe.

Merrick gestured with his head for Yuri to follow. They headed out toward the beach, with Barnabas still hovering in the background.

"What are you doing back there, you sketchy creep," Yuri said.

"I just want see how it goes," Barnabas said, a hint of bemusement in his voice.

"I don't believe you," Yuri said.

Barnabas didn't reply. Finally, Merrick held out a hand and pointed at a figure on the beach.

"Asterion will be your new instructor," Merrick said. "I think you'll have a lot to talk about."

"A lot in common, you might say," Barnabas said.

"What's he wearing?" Yuri said.

The man on the beach sat with his back to them in a meditative pose. His broad shoulders were covered in what looked like a fur shawl, and his head was hidden beneath a massive helmet or mask. From either side of the helmet, a huge horn emerged, made of black, polished bonelike material. Beside him, a pile of weapons rested in the sand, ranging from swords to axes, spears to shields.

"Guy takes his outfits serious," Yuri said. "Okay, I'll give it a..."

Yuri's words caught in his throat as the stranger rose to his feet and turned to greet them. Nearly seven feet tall, but his size was, Yuri realized, the least intimidating thing about him.

"That's not a helmet," Yuri said.

Where a human face should be, the elongated snout of a bull appeared. Those massive horns grew from the creature's head, and the shawl was his own fur. A long tail swished impatiently as he adjusted the long kilt he wore. As he took a stride toward Yuri, hoofed feet kicked up sand and landed with thunderous impact.

Barnabas burst out laughing. Yuri wasted precious seconds to glare at him, and saw even the dignified Merrick had a bit of a grin on his face.

The creature, Asterion, ignored both men and addressed Yuri directly.

"You must be Yuri, son of Rodriguez," the creature said. His voice was deep, his words surprisingly articulate.

"I… yeah, that's me," Yuri said. "I, um. Right. Okay, look, I'm… Like man-shark-things tried to eat me a few days ago. So really, a man-cow-thing shouldn't throw me off even a little bit, but has anyone every told you that you sound like the British actor—"

"Man-*bull*-thing," the creature said. "Call me a cow a second time and I'll crush your skull."

"Man-bull-thing it is," Yuri said.

"Secondly, I'm not a man-bull-thing, I'm a minotaur," the creature said. "And as Merrick, who is not rude or ignorant the way you apparently are, so clearly stated earlier, my given name is Asterion. I would prefer you call me that. But if you must come up with some other term, please pick something that is not insensitive to my heritage."

Yuri looked over his shoulder to Barnabas for help, but the magician was laughing so hard he'd turned his back on them all and took a knee, gasping for breath.

"Asterion it is, then," Yuri said. "You're a…"
"A minotaur," Asterion said.

"Not gonna lie," Yuri said. "Only know what a minotaur is because you're usually a bad guy in videogames."

The creature shrugged.

"Bad publicity," he said. "I blame the Athenians."

"Right," Yuri said. "I have no idea what that means."

Merrick interrupted, putting a reassuring hand on Yuri's shoulder.

"We'll leave you two to it, then," Merrick said.

"Can you take the hyena in the trench coat back there with you?" Yuri said. "He's distracting."

Merrick grabbed Barnabas by the collar and pulled him along, with Barnabas muttering to himself the whole time about the look on Yuri's face.

"I don't really like him," Yuri said.

"Not many people do, I hear," Asterion said. "So: I understand you're useless in the water."

Yuri threw his arms up in the air.

"Well that's a nice way to start our relationship!"

"Can you swim and fight at the same time?" the minotaur asked.

"I can swim and chew bubblegum at the same time."

"Those are not equitable things," Asterion said.

"So, no, I cannot fight and swim at the same time," Yuri said.

"Good," Asterion said. "Neither can I. We man-bull-things not being well-known for our aquatic abilities. What I'd like to do is give you some training on fighting above-water. It's not as diverse a skillset as what your friend Echo is learning, but it will give you a good foundation to not be killed the first time someone swings a sword at you."

"Swings a sword at me," Yuri said. "Great. Yup. Okay. Already off to a great start."

Asterion led Yuri back to the pile of weapons in the sand. He hefted a huge, double-bladed axe with one hand.

"I'm an axe fighter myself," the minotaur said. "I like the weight of it. And I prefer to use weapons that began life as tools. There's something comforting in that."

"I don't know if an axe is my thing," Yuri said, lifting a smaller, single-bladed hatchet from the ground.

"Does anything here strike your fancy at all, then?" Asterion asked.

Yuri spotted something and smiled. Long, like a spear, but heavy, with a wooden shaft, capped on one end in iron, a sharp metal point on the other, adorned with a metal hook.

"I used something like this to drag ice around back home," Yuri said.

"That sounds like a terrible hobby," Asterion said.

"It wasn't a hobby. It was my job," Yuri said.

"Even worse," Asterion said. "But this is familiar to you?"

"Believe it or not, I used something like this to beat one of the man-shark-things away when they attacked us," Yuri said. He picked the weapon up. It was heavy, but better balanced than the tool he'd used before, weighted properly for fighting rather than manual labor.

"It's called a gisarme," Asterion said. "It was designed originally for peasants to fight against armored men."

"Make a peasant joke about me. I dare you."

The minotaur laughed, a deep, throaty noise that sounded like it came from the depths of a cavern.

"No, no," he said. "But a man who works with his hands might find this a good fit for him."

"Then a guy's arm it is for me," Yuri said.

"I believe it's more the French pronunciation. Gis-arm."

"You're a man-bull-thing, what do you know about French?"

"I used to summer on the French Riviera."

"What, what?" Yuri said.

"It's a joke, human. Pick up your gisarme."

"My guy's arm."

"Call it your pointy stick for all I care," Asterion said. "Just be prepared to learn."

***

The pair sparred for hours. Unlike Echo, Yuri noted jealously, combat didn't come to him naturally. The minotaur dumped him on his backside more often than not, and by noon his shoulders and back ached, and he had a growing welt under one eye where Asterion had backhanded him with the hilt of his weapon, though the minotaur had, to be fair, apologized profusely for hitting him so hard.

Asterion knocked him into the sand for the hundredth time—two hundredth?—and Yuri started laughing. He struggled to get back on his feet, but he did, bending his knees to keep from falling over from exhaustion.

"Will you let me in on your joke, Yuri?" Asterion said. The minotaur had barely broken a sweat as they fought.

"A few days ago, I was eating pizza and watching reality TV," he said. "And today I'm getting the bag beaten out of me by a man-bull-thing. I just… I just think it's funny. This isn't a dream. I hurt too much for it to be a dream."

Yuri stabbed his gisarme into the sand and put his hands out to his sides.

"So, boss. What's your assessment? How bad am I at this?"

The minotaur snorted.

"To be blunt, you have no natural aptitude for armed combat," he said. "You're clumsy. You're slow. If this were a real fight you'd be dead several hundred times already."

"I suck, basically," Yuri said.

"Let me finish," Asterion said. "I have knocked you to the ground more times than I can count, and you have, without one word of complaint, pulled yourself back onto your feet to take another beating."

"I might have complained a little," Yuri said. "But I was hoping it came across more as an attempt to lighten the mood."

"Stop talking."

"Yes sir."

"Yuri son of Rodriguez, do you know the one thing you can't teach a fighter?"

"Badassery?"

"Resilience," Asterion said. "And, my strange little human friend, you have more resilience than I've seen in a man in a long time."

"So, I'm not hopeless," Yuri said.

The minotaur snorted again.

"I didn't say that," he said. "But I'm not ready to give up on you yet. Now pick up that weapon and let's go again."

Chapter 25: The Atlantean and the Amazon

Echo could hear almost every time Yuri landed on the ground from where she trained with Artem, on the other side of a large dune.

"They're not going to kill Yuri, are they?" she asked.

"Probably not," the young man said. "Depends on if he makes one too many cow jokes."

They'd begun their own training later in the morning, not to give Echo a chance to rest, but because, Artem explained, there were things she needed to learn that he could not teach her. Thus, he'd sent her to the shore at dawn and told her to swim.

"You need to learn to trust your body to survive in the water," he said. "You, more than any of us, is uniquely created to live beneath the waves. Dive down and see the world you've inherited."

And so, as she did so many mornings at home, she dove in, ignoring the coolness of the water, and began to swim laps along the shore. Once she'd warmed up, she plunged down, opening her eyes, watching the first light of daybreak and shatter against the water.

Take a breath, she told herself. You can breathe underwater. Everyone says you can. Just do it.

She inhaled.

For a split-second it felt as if she were drowning, the water heavy and frigid in her chest. She coughed, bubbles exploding from her mouth and nose, and her limbs reflexively reached for the surface. But she fought off that instinct, remained underwater, told herself to not fight it. Just wait. She thought. What's the worst that could happen? You'd die? Compared to everything she'd been through these past few days, would that be much worse?

A warm, calming sensation ran through her body. She coughed again, but the urge to breathe in had changed—the water flowed in and out of her lungs, but she no longer felt as if she were breathing. The water itself seemed to supply oxygen for her. Do I have gills? She thought? She touched her neck and her clavicle, half-expecting to find slits to breathe through there. I don't know how this is happening, she thought.

But with that thought her fear left her, and she swam deeper, all the way to the bottom, digging her fingers into the mud below. Her eyes adjusted to the deep with ease; she could see small schools of fish in the distance, seaweed tumbling across the ocean floor, could hear sounds in the distance, amplified by the water itself. She twisted through the water, imitating images she'd seen of sea lions, and spurred herself to the bottom again, placing her feet against the muck. I feel like an astronaut, she thought. She picked up a stone the size of a football for weight and tried running, leaving cloudy footprints in her wake.

She dropped the stone and jumped, pushing off the ocean floor, arms held out in front of her like an arrow. She breached the surface like a dolphin, plunging back down again, then rising slower, throwing her head back as she crested the surface to flip her hair back from her eyes. She coughed a few times, mouth filling with water, but with almost alarming ease her lungs readjusted to the surface world once again.

You're uniquely created for this, Artem had told her. I'm uniquely created to live in both worlds, she thought.

She looked toward the island, a momentary panic setting in. She had no idea where she was along the coastline, or how far she'd traveled beneath the waves. With strong, confident strokes, she swam back to shore, the weight of the surface world cold and heavy on her shoulders as she stepped back on land.

***

She found Artem in their usual spot, nearly a mile from where she'd returned to the surface. He sat casually in the sand, oiling his sword. With his anachronistic clothing and weapons, he could have walked out of a period film, she thought. He certainly looked like a movie star.

"How did it go," he asked. He'd brought her weapons with him, so she scooped up the long dagger she had come to prefer and began running a whetstone along its edge.

"I can't believe I've gone my entire life not knowing I can do these things. I carried a thirty-pound rock across the bottom of the sea like it was nothing."

Artem sheathed his sword and leaned back.

"It makes me wonder why they kept these things from you," he said. "It feels like something was stolen from you."

Echo raised an eyebrow.

"Interesting choice of words," she said.

"I can't help thinking the things you could have done, had you known," he said. "But then again, I'm sure they had their reasons."

"What about you," Echo said. "You've known all along who and what you were, right?"

Artem shot her an almost suspicious look, but then sat up straight, brushing sand from his palms.

"The last son of the Amazons," he said. "Last and least wanted, yes."

"Let me get this straight. Amazons are real."

"Yes."

"Warrior women. Like in the myths."

"Whole country of them. Island nation. Hidden away."

"Huh," Echo said. "And they… usually only have daughters?"

"You see a lot of anachronisms here," Artem said. "Men who fight with swords. Ships without engines. My husband prefers to dress like a fighter in the Trojan War."

"You seem to like the look as well," Echo teased.

"It's well ventilated," Artem said, laughing. "But these societies—your people in Atlantis, mine in New Scythia—they are, in their own way, incredibly technologically advanced. There is magic woven in as well, but science and magic together, they make for a very powerful combination. And for some of these societies, that power also means control. It's not so hard for a technologically advanced people to make sure they only have daughters."

Echo half-frowned. Seemed a bit too controlling to her. Although her entire life had apparently been a manipulated lie. Who was she to judge?

"Your mother broke the rules, I'm guessing," Echo said.

"How quick to blame the mother," Artem said. Echo covered her mouth, embarrassed, but Artem laughed again. He sounded like a bell. "No, no, you're right. She broke the rules. She fell in love with someone from the mainland. A land-dweller like your mother, though from what I know of him, he was a bit of a rogue, like our friend Barnabas Coy."

"What happened to them? How did you end up here?"

"That's a long story," Artem said.

"Try me."

Artem smirked.

"How about I give you the short version," he said.

"Fair enough," Echo said.

"They nearly killed my father when he was discovered on their island—men are not allowed by law without special permission, and my father, like any foolhardy explorer, got himself into trouble through too much curiosity and not enough sense," Artem said. "My mother defended him. To this day, I don't know why. My father deserved what he got, wandering into New Scythia like a rodent in the night."

"This sounds like a fairy tale," Echo said.

"Very close to it," Artem said. He looked out over the water wistfully. "Because if it happened six hundred years ago, they would have beheaded my father and drowned me in the sea."

"But they sent you here instead," Echo said.

"Oh, there was so much that happened between my birth and my arrival here," Artem said. "I lived among the Amazons long enough for my mother to teach me how to fight, to learn their ways, to get their viewpoint on the world. I was one of them, for quite a long stretch of my childhood."

"What happened?"

"The situation changed," Artem said. He grew quiet and still. "Echo, nothing good and beautiful, or tragic and terrible, lasts forever. Look at this ocean. Always changing. Always moving. That's the world. That's reality. Never let yourself think the world can become concrete and safe. That is when the tidal wave arrives to wash your little reality way."

Echo picked up a scoop of sand and let it drift from one palm to the other.

"All these places, all these people—the Amazons, the Atlanteans, the nereids like Barnabas' mother. Why don't any of them want us? What do they have against us?"

Artem nodded knowingly.

"That world half of us belongs to," he said. "Your mother, whoever she may have been. My scoundrel father. Barnabas and his lovelorn sailor of a father. They come from a place that scares our people. Humans… they're this unstoppable force. Alone, they're just weak, brutish little creatures. But together? They are gods. And everything the Amazons have built, everything the Atlanteans have created, even the little hideaways where creatures like sea nymphs and mermaids find solace… all those things crumble at the touch of humanity. They terrify these societies. And we remind them of that fear."

"And so, they throw us away," Echo said. She wondered about her father, who never laid eyes on her, not once in her entire life.

Who disappeared to the bottom of the ocean rather than love her mother. She looked at this beautiful, lonely boy, like someone took a slab of stone and chiseled a perfect hero from it, and she could hear the loneliness in his voice. Even Barnabas in his distant mysteriousness, hinted at longing for something he'd never have.

"Well, but that's why we have places like this," Artem said. "For all we unwanted things. A place for the flotsam and jetsam to call home."

Echo almost laughed, then. She drew shapes in the sand.

"What about Merrick?" Echo she said, wanting to turn the conversation to something less depressing. "How'd he end up here? He doesn't seem to be a forgotten thing."

Artem's face lit up when she uttered Merrick's name.

"He's not like us. He and Theo, his partner when he first arrived here, they're just men. And I mean that in both ways," Artem said. "Just men meaning only men, but also just men meaning pure of heart. They were men of the sea, in love at a time when the human world would stand in the way of that love, and they founded a place where all the unwanted things in the world could find a home. They washed up here by accident as young men, and they made it theirs. They became stewards of the unwanted."

"They're not from some land time forgot?" Echo said.

"Oh no," Artem laughed. "Merrick is from London. Theo was American. From Massachusetts."

"Then how did they... Merrick is some sort of master swordsman. And didn't you say Theo could cast spells?"

"Stay here long enough, Echo," Artem said, "And this place will change you. Fate loves an unwanted creature. No one sets foot on this island without fate turning its mighty gaze on them."

Chapter 26: The lair of the serpent

The Island of Unwanted Things was no simple refuge for the displaced. Other unwanted things came to live here as well, unwanted for other reasons, monsters that grew to haunt the darker parts of the island.

These other denizens were what Barnabas Coy listened for as he made his way deeper into the island under cover of darkness, the moon shrouded in heavy clouds. He'd covered his stubbly head in a warm bandana and swapped his loose boots for sturdier hiking shoes, and walked through the brush with his artifact pistol in one hand, a razor-sharp machete in the other.

He hadn't been back to the island in years, even longer since he explored it. But Barnabas still remembered the path to the serpent's lair. He'd been there so many times as a child the route was carved into his memory like a scar.

He paused for a while, crouching down in the darkness, listening to make sure no one followed him. He had come to consider the lair a sacred place; even bringing Echo or Merrick would feel like a violation of the dead creature's sanctuary. And so, he waited until everyone slept and slunk out into the night. It wasn't the first time he'd acted the role of thief, he thought.

Up, up, over a peak and back down into a valley through which a freshwater river ran. Past a waterfall he'd played in as a child, unaware of the dangers around him, unseen, the stalkers and hunters who shared this island with him and his brothers and sisters on the shore. Perhaps I am charmed in a way, Barnabas thought, watching the waterfall glitter in the moonlight. There are many ways I could have died here.

He pressed on, wanting to be at the cave by midnight so he could be back by dawn. No need for anyone to know he'd left, he thought. Best they not know what he was up to.

Beyond the river, the land grew more overgrown, rockier as well, with plant life that felt just slightly misshapen, slightly oversized. Again, he paused to listen, but not for pursuers from the village this time; instead, his ears turned toward the predatory slither and hum of the creatures who lived in the deep hills toward the center of the island. Some had a taste for humans. Others simply had a taste for killing.

Satisfied with the silence, Barnabas moved on. But he took just a few steps before he heard it—a familiar skittering sound, the soft patter of too many feet. Big but not heavy, something that stepped lightly as it stalked its prey.

Barnabas sheathed his machete and reached inside his shirt to pull out an amulet he wore, a circular piece of bone carved with symbols from a language dead for centuries, perhaps millennia. He rested his hand on the machete's hilt again and raised his pistol, whispering a spell, commanding the artifact to be ready.

He could sense them all around him, the size of large dogs, running through the thick underbrush, or clamoring around in the trees above. Looking for a meal. Red eyes, eight at a time, watching him from the shadows. He caught a glimpse of a pair of dripping mandibles, the poison from those fangs hissing at it sizzled against waxy tropical leaves.

Barnabas didn't want to fire his weapon, knowing it would light up the night, a burst of flames visible all the way back at the village. Instead, he spoke. The language he used was not his own though, but an archaic tongue, spoken by an older breed.

"I'll make a poor meal for you, weavers," he said. He could sense the creatures stop moving to listen. They didn't often hear their language spoken by a stranger. "No good will come of it. I'll sicken your bellies, and be sure some of your brothers cook in their own carapaces for the effort. Think wisely."

He heard a tapping sound, the clicking of mandibles clenching and unclenching. They were thinking. Weighing their options. The weavers were ancient, and they did not survive this long by taking chances. Barnabas began walking again, deeper into the jungle, and the creatures remained behind, choosing to end their hunt.

His heart thundered in his throat. Too close, he thought. Too close a bluff, with so many weavers around him. They had him.

Somewhere in the night, not long after, he heard heavy footsteps in the distance. Not nearly as close as the weavers, but too close for comfort. Some beast with a heavy tread pushing its way through the darkness, a leftover from another era. Barnabas never saw the creature, and stood very still until those footsteps were far, far away.

Finally, he came upon the mouth of the cavern that would take him to the serpent's lair. Overgrown with brush and moss, anyone else might have walked right past; but Barnabas knew it even by the light of a dimmed moon. He stepped inside, his own footsteps too loud, echoing into the endless darkness. He muttered more words in a lost language, this one almost new compared to that which he'd used on the weavers, a simple spell that wreathed his hand in flames.

Holding that burning hand aloft, he followed the corkscrew path to the bottom of the cave, where the serpent had once called home. The corpse was still there, fangs longer than his arm sharp and white, empty eye sockets staring out at him.

Barnabas placed a hand gently on the snout of that skull in greeting.

"Good to see you again, old friend," he said to the corpse.

With casual familiarity, Barnabas weaved his way deeper into the cavern. After a few minutes, the silence became comforting;

somehow in all these years, the serpent's lair had remained undisturbed.

Barnabas Coy set himself to work.

He filled several small pouches with gold and gems from the old snake's larder; not a greedy man's sum, but enough to help him with his travels. He found stacks of books and scrolls, old tomes he'd left behind because they were beyond his skill when last left. One in particular, bound in the tanned hide of a blue whale, immediately caught his eye.

"You," he said to the book in a conversational tone. "You I've been looking for."

He slid the spell book into a satchel and carried on.

The serpent had incredible taste in the arcane, Barnabas Coy thought as he loaded his pack up with books of spells and strange magical components. Perhaps I take too much, Barnabas thought as the satchel and a backpack he'd brought grew heavy. But then he remembered how much of this stock was stolen as well, and knew this was the place to find the secrets he needed.

Soon his shoulder ached and his back strained to carry the bags he'd brought with him. Why did the old monster collect so much knowledge? He thought, not for the first time. Was it greed? Was he preparing for something? The snake showed no aptitude for spellcraft; was there some hidden talent, some mystery state of being the snake had hoped to evolve to?

But his musings were derailed when he came upon the part of the cave the old serpent had called "the armory." A pocket in the lair where the old snake had left the weapons and armor of countless explorers and warriors who had come here looking to end his life. Swords and rapiers, axes and lances, whole silvery suits of armor and hand-crafted leather breastplates. Even modern gear like hunting rifles and Kevlar. Nothing protected those who hunted the serpent.

But perhaps, Barnabas thought, curiously looking through the stock, perhaps something in here might protect us.

Chapter 27: Wise words

Atlantis at night glowed with a peculiar beauty. Thousands of lights, from enchanted globes to bioluminescent plants, dotted the cityscape, illuminating sunken streets and thoroughfares, the marketplace that never closed in the center of the city and the tall spires that surrounded it.

Rhegis could see it all from his chambers in the royal tower. Commoners walking through air-filled passageways or swimming the submerged roads, messengers riding massive stingrays as they moved from building to building, schools of little fish that had found a symbiotic relationship with Atlantis, nibbling away at the grime that would, if unattended, eat away at the stone structures built so long ago by Atlantean hands.

It's a beautiful place, Rhegis thought. I want it to always be such a beautiful place.

But the quiet was deceptive, he knew. Reports of altercations in the streets, worse on the outskirts beyond the watchful eye of the city's guards, instigators, a riot in the marketplace last week. Atlantis was a city divided, an explosive keg of frustration.

"You can feel the tension all the way up here," a friendly voice said.

Rhegis turned his gaze away from the window to face his

guests, an old man and a woman still shy of middle-aged, both with hair an almost identical shade of pearlescent green. It was the old man, Brendis Kor, who had spoken.

"If I may be so honest, my lord, your father was a fool," Brendis said.

"Just because my father's dead doesn't mean you get to speak ill of him," Rhegis said.

"I knew your father since we were children together," Brendis said. "I would have said the same to his face, crown or no crown. He was a fool. He should have named an heir."

Rhegis almost laughed. He missed his father terribly, but hearing old Brendis speak of him was a strange comfort.

"And if he'd chosen my sister instead?"

"Well, then, we'd be headed to war with the surface and we'd all die," Brendis said. "But at least we'd know where we were going. This waiting, Rhegis. It's killing us."

"What's the word from the Great Council?" Rhegis said.

"You were there," Brendis said.

"I mean behind closed doors," Rhegis said. "I want to know what they say when my sister and I aren't in the room."

"It's a fair split," the woman, Brendis' daughter Kara, said. She had taken Brendis' seat in the legislature a few years back when the old man retired to teach. "She has her followers who want us to go to war, but you have followers as well. You're not alone in your desire to stay isolated."

"You want to know what I think?" Brendis said. Kara and Rhegis exchanged an amused look. If Brendis wanted to offer his opinion, neither of them could stop him.

"Go on, honored elder," Rhegis said, a bit of sarcasm in his voice.

"I think you're both idiots," Brendis said.

"That is… honest," Rhegis said.

"Father!" Kara said. She'd always had far more tact than her father, and Brendis seemed to be using his advancing age as an excuse to speak his mind.

"No, hear me out," Brendis said. "I think you need to be more aggressive, son."

"I don't want war," Rhegis said.

"Neither do I!" the old man said, scratching his beard. "Do I look like I want to start a war? But this world gets smaller and smaller every moment, my boy. Some day—and that day will come sooner than you want it to, I'm afraid—Atlantis and the men above will come to a head, and how that encounter takes place will define our societies for generations."

"Spoken like the professor of philosophy that you are," Rhegis said.

"If the rumors are to be believed, your sister is trying to hasten that moment along," Kara said.

"This does not leave this room," Rhegis said, "But those rumors are true."

"Gods below, she's going to get us all killed," Brendis said. "Son, Rhegis, my king… you have got to do something about your sister."

Rhegis showed his palms.

"How? I'm not going to kill my sister."

"You could just lock her up," Brendis said.

"Father, you're really pushing tonight," Kara said.

"I can't imprison my twin sister either, Brendis," Rhegis said.

"Are you sure she wouldn't do the same to you?" Kara said. Rhegis was surprised—Kara had never been one to make such a bold statement.

"Have you heard something?" he asked her.

"Not exactly," Kara said. "But if the whispers are to be believed, she's getting desperate. If you don't come to an accord soon, she may make a play for power."

Rhegis shook his head and looked out the window again.

"My own sister wouldn't betray me."

"Now would be the time," Brendis said. "Neither of you have an heir—a damned shame, by the way, since I think of at least one woman who would be very qualified to be queen…"

"Father, behave," Kara said. She grimaced at Rhegis. "I'm sorry."

"Not the first time he's made the suggestion," Rhegis said, smiling.

"Won't be the last, either," Brendis said.

"Besides, how can you be sure neither of us has an heir," Rhegis said.

"Now who's being cheeky," Brendis said.

Rhegis let the comment hang, unsure why he made the joke in the first place. He hadn't heard back from Grimmin for far too long. His daughter and her mother were at the forefront of his mind more than he could afford them to be. They were safe and forgotten, he hoped, removed from the roiling conflict here on the ocean floor. And what would it matter now, if it became known he had a half-human daughter? Would his people let her inherit the throne from him when he died? Would they force him to abdicate, ashamed he'd fallen in love with a surface-dweller?

And why hadn't Grimmin reported back yet? Not for the first time, Rhegis cursed his own aversion to spy games. He had so few people he could trust in his life. The list of people he could send after his spymaster was far too short and even less reliable.

He stared down at his city again. Those lights, the glittering pool of flame, felt far more threatening than they ever had before. And he felt terribly alone.

"Do you have somewhere to go, my old friends," Rhegis said. "If things get bad?"

"We're not abandoning Atlantis, and we're certainly not abandoning you," Kara said.

"I just need to know—tell me you have a contingency plan," he said.

"I have a place," Brendis said. He daughter shot him a dirty look. "What? You know I always wanted to retire to a hermit's life and get away from all this nonsense and political garbage."

"I've been around you my entire life, and I still can never tell when you are utterly full of lies or not," Kara said.

Brendis waved his hand dismissively.

"What about you, Rhegis," Brendis said. "Where can you go, if things go wrong?"

"Wherever fate takes me," Rhegis said. A flock of silver fish flickered past just outside the widow. Below them, life went on, quiet and ominous. "I'll go wherever fate takes me."

Chapter 28: Who we are now

Echo sat on the beach alone, her limbs sore from a day's practice with Artem. He'd left her earlier than usual—the Amazonian warrior boy told her she was learning so quickly he needed time to think about their next lesson—and Echo decided to spend the extra time away from the village. The others there had welcomed her over the past few weeks, and she came to feel a real sense of friendship with all these forgotten beings.

The youngest of them were a great distraction, pulling Echo into games she'd never seen before, little challenges they seemed to have made up themselves here, away from the civilizations that brought each of them into this world. A little boy who couldn't be older than three had taken a particularly strong liking to her, and days went by before she found out he could transform into a seal at will. Barnabas told her he was an orphaned selkie whose mother had been killed by human trappers.

She wondered if perhaps this would become home for her and Yuri. It would be different, she thought; it wasn't an icehouse in a small New England town. It wasn't an ordinary life. But it still felt insufficient. She had things to do. Places to go. She had revenge to seek out.

Echo rubbed her temple absently, fingers brushing the hair on the side of her head. It had started to grow out a bit. She pulled the knife from her belt, which she kept extraordinarily sharp at Artem's urging. He said she'd encounter thick-skinned monsters out at sea and want the keenest blade she could have in her hand, and the knife now possessed a razor's edge.

Slowly and gently, she ran that edge along the side of her skull, shaving her hair down to her scalp and dropping the remnants in the sand. The blade burned a little bit, but the sea air brushed against the now-bare skin like a gentle touch. She turned her attention next to the other side, which she'd previously kept long, and laid the scalp bare there as well, leaving herself with a sloppy, sea-green mohawk. She tidied up the back of her head, carefully guiding the knife until all that remained was a crest of hair on the top of her head. She brushed the stray hairs away, letting the wind take them. The breeze danced across her head as if the air itself wanted to comfort her.

She heard the soft scrape of feet against sand behind her and knew Yuri approached. His distinctively graceless gait was unique on this island.

"You joining a punk rock band?" he asked, sitting down beside her in the sand.

"I can do you too, give us matching haircuts," Echo said. "We'd be twins."

Yuri looked so different now, she thought. He'd lost weight with all the work he'd been doing with Asterion, his face, always given to a bit of pleasant baby fat, hollowing out, his beard growing a little too long. He looked tired, too, though she suspected all the same things could be said about her as well. Her entire frame felt different after weeks of training with Artem. She knew she carried herself differently. Would anyone recognize them back home? Back home. That was an unwelcome thought. Echo had never had many friends, but Yuri had people he'd left behind when they fled. She wondered how the icehouse was doing. If anyone was taking care of it, or if it had been shut down with their disappearance. Would anyone look for them?

"What if we never go home?" Echo said out loud.

"Beginning to feel like we might not," Yuri said.

"How do we go back to normal after all of this?"

"How did you spend your summer vacation?" Yuri said. "Oh, just learning how to kill monsters with a giant axe on a stick from a minotaur."

"I'm sorry I got you into all of this," Echo said. "This is my fault. I ruined your life."

"I think whoever is trying to kill you ruined both of our lives, Echo," Yuri said. "Kinda feels like you had no control over everything that led up to that."

"Still. This happened to me, but you got dragged into it."

"What did you drag me away from, Echo?" Yuri said. "Managing a local business, maybe going to school? I guess you stole my future marrying Ellie Almeida and having a gaggle of little Yuris running around, but…"

"Ellie Almeida was never really into you, Yuri," Echo said.

"I know."

"You were too good for her anyway."

"Oh, I know," he said, laughing. He studied her face. "You sound lonely, Echo."

"How could I be lonely? I'm what, the unwanted princess of Atlantis or something?"

"Well, you look like a warrior queen," Yuri said.

"Drop the 'queen' part and I'll take that as a compliment."

"Viking berserkers would flee in fear of your mighty mohawk, kid."

"Thanks, big guy."

"Any time."

They sighed simultaneously, and then let out laughter tinged heavily with exhaustion.

"I'm glad you came with us, Yuri," Echo said.

"Your mom would have wanted us to stick together," he said.

"Yeah, she would have," Echo said, a familiar pang in her heart. It felt disrespectful how often her mother's death had fled from her mind these past few weeks. It was still a fresh wound, her loss, but running for their lives, and now, learning how to defend those same lives… time for mourning was pushed aside in favor of survival. Maybe when this is all over I'll be able to piece everything together, Echo thought. Maybe I never will.

She glanced over at Yuri, who stared out at the rolling waves, and she found herself smiling at the sparkle of light in his ear where the pearl earring Barnabas had inflicted on Yuri remained.

"Hey, have you had a chance to test out your water-breathing earring yet?" she asked.

"Given that nobody has tried to drown me for a while, no, I have not tried out my water-breathing earring," he said.

"Want to?"

"Not particularly."

"Come on," Echo said. "We can both breathe underwater. We should enjoy it."

"I think this is a terrible idea."

"Don't be a wimp," she said. "I'll show you my favorite underwater spot."

"I want it on record I think this is a bad idea," Yuri said.

"Noted," Echo said. "Let's go."

Chapter 29: The wreck

Yuri learned something new the first time he dove underwater with the "artifact" earring Barnabas made him wear: while it certainly made it impossible for him to drown underwater, it did not magically improve his swimming skills.

Yuri grew up around the water. He considered himself a strong swimmer. But below the surface without a need to come up for air, he found himself struggling, trying to remember different strokes he'd been taught as a kid, fighting both the current and his body's natural tendency to float back to the surface.

Making matters worse: Echo took to the depths as if she were born for it. Her movements changed; she didn't swim so much as drift and dart like a sea lion, graceful and powerful, smiling at him and trying to coax him to go further into the depths with her.

Yuri opened his mouth to speak and nothing happened, other than a couple of oversized bubbles of air emerging. Echo caught his body language though and zipped over to him to grab his wrist. She pulled him along behind her, heading with noticeable purpose toward a specific location.

Great, Yuri thought. She's pulling me along like Peter Pan did with Wendy in the movie. This is cool. I'll just hang back here playing the role of the caboose...

They swam through a ticklish, slimy forest of seaweed, and Yuri half-expected something—a shark, an eel, something—to dart out at them and attack. Instead, they emerged on the other side, and Yuri almost gasped involuntarily.

A shipwreck stretched out before them so perfect it felt more like a movie set then a real thing. It had split in half, cracked like an egg, with its wood and metal guts spilled out onto the ocean floor. One mast had collapsed, but the other still jutted upward like a defiant finger.

Echo dragged him in closer, but Yuri tapped her hand, asking her to let him go. He swam alongside her toward the ship's wheel, long ago crusted over with shelled mollusks resting on the spokes as if the creatures were trying to work together to steer the vessel. Much of the ship looked as if it were covered in a gritty shell of biological matter, shades of rust and green, blue and chalky white. Schools of tiny fish darted around like birds.

Echo grinned widely at him and gestured for him to follow her over the edge of the ship. They swam down to the gun ports along the port side, and Yuri looked inside. So much of the craft remained preserved, shrouded in plant matter. Something big moved inside, and Echo dragged Yuri toward a large gap in the hull so he could watch as giant grouper drifted by, looking at Yuri with an almost human sense of boredom. Echo tapped Yuri on the shoulder, pointed at the grouper, and mouthed the words: "That's Frank!"

She swam toward the enormous fish, and Yuri's stomach twisted into knots. He knew groupers weren't aggressive by nature, but the creature's mouth looked large enough to swallow Echo whole. Yet, astonishingly, the grouper drifted up to Echo and, to Yuri's shock, nudged her outstretched hand like a cat. Echo grinned wickedly over her shoulder at Yuri, ran a comforting palm across the big fish's forehead, and swam back to Yuri's side. He held his hands out to her as if to say: how?

Echo shook her head. Later, she said silently.

The duo left Frank the Grouper to his own devices and swam

to the prow. Echo started to point something out, but Yuri saw exactly what she was looking at without her showing him: an almost perfectly preserved masthead staring proudly ahead. The woman's face had the elegant softness of an old painting, and though the metal had rusted and turned green in places, it was still clear that she'd once worn a Roman-style helmet, her hands were raised up as if they once held a spear or sword. When Yuri turned to look for Echo's reaction, he found her perfectly mimicking the figurehead's posture, complete with empty hands. She bit her lip and laughed at herself then made a "come on" movement with her hands.

Let's head back, she mouthed, and Yuri let her tow him to the surface once again.

***

"So that's where you disappear to," Yuri said as he and Echo dried off on the surface. His whole body felt weighed down, as if gravity worked twice as hard on the surface as it did in the water.

"Sometimes," she said. "Artem and Barnabas want me to be comfortable getting around underwater in case anything ever happens, so I've just… explored. I've been up and down the coast for miles. I'm not sure how large the island is, but I've seen most of it, I think, at least from the shore."

"Do you know the name of the ship?"

"I keep looking for any sign of what it was called, but I think it's all deteriorated," she said. "And there aren't any bodies in the wreckage."

"Thankfully," Yuri said.

"There are bodies out there," Echo said. "I'll bring you to the plane crash I found some time if you'd like."

"There's a body?"

"Two bodies."

"I'll skip the plane wreck, thanks," Yuri said.

"Anyway. Yeah. The ship is my favorite. I think I could build a hideout there. In case ever needed to escape from… y'know. The bad guys."

"And Frank won't mind?" Yuri said.

"How weird is that, right? I think he… Like, I can't talk to him. He's a fish. I never thought there was a lot of thinking going on in fish brains."

"There better not be, given the number of fish sandwiches I've seen you eat in your lifetime," Yuri said.

Echo whacked him on the arm.

"But I was thinking—what if this is one of my powers, right? Maybe I can…"

"Talk to fish," Yuri said.

"Feel empathy towards them," Echo said. "I need to talk to some of the others about it. Maybe Merrick or someone knows."

"That sounds like a ridiculously lame power, Echo," Yuri said.

"You say that now, but what if, y'know, Frank tries to eat you," Echo said. "I can be like, hey Frank, lay off my buddy."

"Exactly like that," Yuri said.
"Exactly."

"I can't believe this is our life now," Yuri said.

Echo flopped down on the sand, her pale green hair still dark with seawater. She brushed it back out of her eyes with the back of one hand.

"Yeah," she said.

And for the first time since all of this began, Yuri saw his best friend looking happy. I hope we can hold onto that for a little bit, he thought to himself. She deserves to be happy for a while.

Chapter 30: The dark council

Atlantis had all the trappings of any city throughout history. It had its wealthy streets, its avenues filled with merchants; it had places where hard working residents met in the evening to unwind and complain about the government; it had schools and houses of worship, police and petty criminals. Atlanteans, for all their arrogance at times, often forgot that they arrived in this world quite human, and their humanity connected them to the surface in ways they'd never admit.

The spires of the city rise high, as if straining to reach the surface; but Atlantis also digs down, getting its mighty hands dirty in the muck, and while grand speeches and great debates happen in the upper levels, the real business is conducted below, when no one is watching.

Tonight, this is where Reina must go.

The Regent traveled in disguise and without an entourage. She had agents along her travel route, ready to scoop her up to safety, and she was not without her own considerable abilities to defend herself, but for this night's business, the less attention she brought upon herself the better. Gone was all her regal finery, her hair hidden behind a hood, face shrouded with a veil. It's not an uncommon look among the Atlanteans in the lower levels. She made her way mostly unnoticed.

Her destination was a nondescript structure on the sea floor, built of smooth stone and the bones of long-dead behemoths. She paused a moment outside, then entered, her body language indicating confidence she did not entirely possess.

The building was sealed inside, like so many structures in Atlantis, with air pumped in from an arcane generator. Reina entered a foyer, a staple of Atlantean buildings, where she could hang her wet cloak and slough off some of the water. Nothing in Atlantis was ever truly dry, but like many of the residents' habits, old behaviors were ingrained in them on an almost instinctual level.

She pulled her hair back tightly into a bun and stepped through the foyer's main doors into the space beyond.

The room was not empty. The chamber was dominated by a large table made of smooth stone. Men and women—all of whom carried themselves with more haughtiness than their clothes would normally predict—milled about, some talking, others simply waiting. When she entered, those who sat stood, and those who stood bowed their heads. It rang a bit false, Reina admitted. These were senators and military commanders, guild leaders and masters of commerce. They did not bow their heads willingly or easily, but they did for her. It wasn't a sign of respect so much as a part of the game, levying for rank and placement.

"My Regent," one man said. He had a singer's voice. Reina recognized it immediately. Senator Cartay.

"Senator," Reina replied. She sat down at the head of the table, and the others joined her, subtly jockeying for position closest to her. Another game, she knew. They're playing a gambling match, betting on me over my brother. It's a risk coming here, but not as big a risk as it would be to oppose her.

"We understand the attacks on the surface are going well," an older woman, said Dame Rois, a baroness of Atlantean industry. One of the voices of reason in these meetings, though Reina knew everything Rois did was for profit.

"We're moving on the final stage now," Reina said. "My agents are preparing for their strikes."

"I heard you're having trouble finding adequate leverage to control your brother," Senator Cartay said. This gave Reina pause. It sounded too much like an accusation.

"I will handle my brother," Reina said. "Are you suggesting otherwise, Cartay?"

The senator held his hands up apologetically.

"No, my Regent," he said. "But we should speak frankly. Neither your brother, nor you, have the full heart of the people."

Reina felt herself beginning to seethe. But she knew she needed these people behind her. With their support, she could more fully manage and control the Atlantean government with her brother removed safely from the equation.

"Our people long for a war with the surface, senator," Reina said. "It's what brought this diverse group of people together in this room, is it not?"

"The isolationist movement is still very significant," a silky voice said. Gormlin, the leader of the merchants' guild. His people grew rich off the isolationist concept, because the less connected Atlantis was with the outside world, the more valuable goods from the outside world became. Gormlin himself thought open trade would be even more prosperous—this was what brought the guild leader to this group in the first place—but the obese old guildmaster had more dealings with the isolationists every day than anyone else at this table.

"And traditionalists outnumber even the isolationists," said a professor named Farris. She was an historian, and felt that the time was ripe for Atlantis to shake up its own future, but she knew well that those who felt Atlantis was almost too superior to be bothered with the surface-dwellers would stand up to a military move against humanity.

"This is why, when the war begins, it will appear as if our people had nothing to do with it," Reina said. "We've watched the land-dwellers for millennia. We know they like nothing better than an excuse to kill each other. Let the plan come to fruition. The people will have no choice but to want us to raise our tridents against the surface world."

"Unless they flock to your brother to keep the peace and keep us uninvolved," Dame Rois said. "We may think Rhegis is weak, but he reminds a lot of the common folk of your father, and your father kept things very stable for a long time."

"But he never made anything better," Reina said.

"Which is why we're all here, and at your disposal," Gormin said.

"But we need assurances," Cartay said.

"My brother will be handled," Reina said. She tried to keep the edge from her voice, and was unsure if she succeeded. She had a reputation for an offensive temper, and she'd long ago realized she couldn't accurately judge how much that temper showed itself on the surface.

"Good," Cartay said. "Because if you can't handle him, we are more than willing to step in."

Reina's eyes turned to blades as she stared the senator down.

"That had best not be a threat, senator," she said.

"What the senator means," Dame Rois stepped in, reconciliatory in tone, "is that we stand ready to help."

"That's not what I said at all," Cartay said. "Regent, we chose you. You are the face of the future of Atlantis. But only if you do not fail. Don't consider yourself irreplaceable."

"I am the heir to Seidon," Reina said, raising her voice like an orator. "I am not replaceable."

"All great monarchies come to an end, Regent," Farris said. "It is not our desire for that to happen now. We simply want to know our plans are not at risk."

Reina took measure of the room. I'm not safe, she realized, looking at the hungry eyes of her co-conspirators. The only way I'll be safe is to make myself irreplaceable. To rule in a way that they are more unsafe without me than with me. Well, then, my backstabbing little friends… you'll see what I'm capable of soon.

"Get back to your roles," Reina said. "You all have jobs to do to ensure the future of Atlantis is safe. Leave me to mine."

Chapter 31: Off the record

Jon Broadstreet got into journalism to change the world.

Ask most of his colleagues at the City's biggest newspaper, and they'd tell you the same thing: they got into newspapers to dig for the truth, to help the oppressed, to bring injustice to light. They got into it, in a way, to be heroes.

Apparently heroes cover the Zoning Board of Appeals, Broadstreet thought. That was his assignment for the night, something about an easement or maybe an expansion for a local, popular restaurant. Still, he was new. He had time. It couldn't all be late night board meetings, right? Something exciting had to happen eventually.

Until then though: I'll become the best Zoning Board of Appeals reporter, he told himself. I'll show this place what I can do.

He sat in the mostly empty and mostly dark newsroom, throwing a baseball up in to the air and catching it over and over again. The ZBA met at seven o'clock, and he hadn't had time to get to his cramped studio on the shadiest end of town and back again, so he stayed at the office and had coffee and a donut for dinner. Eating healthy was a luxury he and most of his colleagues couldn't afford. The office was cluttered and out of date, with broken printers and signs about not stealing pens or blank paper; a big sign announced that the company no longer supplied coffee in the break room. Everything about the place was bleak and tired.

Still, Broadstreet thought. This is what I signed up for.

The only other occupant in the newsroom that night was a veteran reporter named Ike Olson. Ike mostly ignored Broadstreet, but not necessarily in a bad way. The older reporter had the international affairs beat, front page stuff, which kept him busy enough to not have a heck of a lot of time to talk to the new kid covering municipal government meetings on Monday nights. Still, Ike was pleasant enough when they crossed paths, and Broadstreet found himself eavesdropping on him when he conducted interviews sometimes, intrigued by the way he put sources at ease and got so much information out of them.

Tonight, though, Broadstreet heard real tension in Ike's voice as he spoke in hushed tones to a source on the phone. He caught only snippets, like "of course this is off the record," and "there's got to be something you're not telling me." Finally, after a polite goodbye, Ike hung up. He stood, stretching his back, and looked around the office with an expression Broadstreet had never seen on the senior reporter's face: fear.

"Everything okay, Ike?" Broadstreet asked.

The veteran reporter's whole body shook, as if he thought until then he was alone in the office.

"Oh. New kid," he said. "Hey. Yeah, no, I'm fine."

"You look rattled," Broadstreet said. It felt strange, pointing this out, and Ike gave him a bit of side-eye for it, but something turned in Ike's body language and he walked up to Broadstreet's desk, leaning on the low partition.

"Screw it," he said. "I gotta tell someone. Might as well be you. You can keep something off the record, I assume."

"I thought nothing was ever really off the record," Broadstreet said.

"First rule of keeping good sources, kid," Ike said. "Build trust. If they feel like they can be honest with you, when it counts, they'll tell you what you need to know."

"You were talking to a source off the record," Broadstreet said.

"Yeah," Ike said. He turned to stare out the window at the setting sun. "He's a… his job is to know things. I shouldn't tell you more than that."

"That's not vague at all," Broadstreet said.

"Sarcasm will get you nowhere in this business, kid," Ike said. "Anyway. He was rattled. And he's not a guy who gets rattled."

"Because he knows things."

"Look, you're in certain lines of work long enough, you deal with disasters, political shifts, stuff that sends regular people into a tizzy," Ike said. "You get immune to it. Even if it scares you, you have more control over your emotions. You don't show people you're worried."

"And he couldn't keep it together?" Broadstreet said.

"He called me because he wanted a neutral party to talk to," Ike said.

"You're the press."

"We go back almost twenty years," Ike said. "He knows if he asks me to keep something under my hat I will. He wanted me to be prepared in case things escalate."

"Things… escalate?"

Ike rubbed his eyes and exhaled loudly. He looked older than he had even at the beginning of this conversation. Whatever had the source worried had rubbed off on the reporter, as well.

"What is it? I mean, how bad are we talking? Nuclear war?" Broadstreet said, aiming for levity.

Ike turned haunted eyes on him.

"Wait. He thinks we're going to have a nuclear war?" Broadstreet said. "We have to tell someone. We have to get this information out there!"

"It's not at that point yet," Ike said. "But… man, I really shouldn't be telling you this, but if I don't tell someone I'm going to go home and alternate drinking and throwing up."

"Just tell me if I should call my parents and say goodbye, Ike."

"The U.S. has lost a nuclear submarine," Ike said.

"Lost?" Broadstreet said. "Like, misplaced, or sunk, or..."

"Gone," Ike said. "Missing. Disappeared."

"That's... Okay, I'm going to plead ignorance here, Ike. That's a lot of weaponry to lose, right?"

"It's a lot of men and women to lose, too, but yeah," Ike said.

"Covering the ZBA tonight suddenly feels pretty pointless," Broadstreet said.

Ike exhaled again a hand suspiciously on his stomach as if nursing a belly ache.

"What," Broadstreet said.

"Why are you the only one here," Ike said. "I should be running this past the bureau chief, not a... you."

"Ike, what are you not saying? You look like your guts are being dissolved by battery acid."

Ike looked up at the ceiling as if in prayer, then blurted it out in a raspy whisper.

"We're not the only country missing a submarine," Ike said. "That's why I got the call. Because it's not just the United States."

"Who else is missing a submarine?" Broadstreet said. "Who else even has nuclear submarines? I feel like this is a terrible time to realize I don't know this."

"Four of the six countries with nuclear subs are currently missing one of their vessels," Ike said.

"Now *I* think I'm going to throw up," Broadstreet said.

Ike covered is mouth, took deep breath, then stuffed his hands in his pockets.

"Go cover your meeting, kid," he said. "Pretend everything's normal. Everything will be okay. We've survived everything that came before this. We'll be okay."

"Says the guy who looks like he just sat next to the Angel of Death on the bus," Broadstreet said. "You're saying, don't skip the meeting and say goodbye to my parents?"

"Nah," Ike said. "Well. Maybe call them on the drive over. Just to... say hello. If you're inclined."

"What are you going to do?"

"I'm going to go home and call my son," Ike said. "And then I'm going to put a pot of coffee on and I'm going to try like hell to get someone to corroborate this information. And then we're going to warn the whole damned world if we have to."

Broadstreet smiled. Ike looked at him like he was crazy.

"Why are you smiling?"

"Because you just sounded like a hero for a second there, Ike," Broadstreet said.

"Don't go telling anyone," Ike said. "I'm not a hero. I'm a journalist."

Chapter 32: The Frenzy

They gathered in the darkness, below the waves. Shadows made of sandpaper flesh and razor teeth, primordial and dire, deadly mouths like the worst of smiles. Their eyes, jet black, glittered in the darkness like drops of blood.

Maw sensed his brothers all around him like an electrical charge. Muscle and cartilage, rage and hunger, their hearts beat as one in a thrumming, primal dance.

They did not speak. Words were for those creatures who crawled onto the sand and left the sea behind. The were-sharks were born before language, and would live long after language was gone from this world. They were the gods of hunger, the hunters in the night, the tools of death, the instruments of renewal. They were where all things ended, and tonight they gathered in a swirling army of hunger.

So many brotherhoods represented: Great whites and tiger sharks; hammerheads and blacktips; even one stunted little goblin shark, so tiny compared to the others, his face a nightmare of needles beneath a snout like a scythe.

No words were needed. They swam in a vortex, churning the water, letting reason and logic melt away until all that remained was the desire to hunt, to kill, to fill the water with blood and shredded flesh. This is what they were born to do. This is what they would do until the end of time.

Maw felt his thoughts slipping away, the world becoming a faraway place as his rational mind became unnecessary. Instinct took over, the desire to bite and feed, to make the seas run red. His heart felt as though it filled his entire chest cavity, a giant muscle propelling the blood through his veins like fire, his belly gnawing with starvation.

Maw swam toward the island. His brothers followed. And death pursued them in their wake.

***

Echo dreamt of demons in the night, water swirling around her like hurricane winds, massive bodies everywhere, sea monsters with endless rows of teeth. The water churned with bloody pink bubbles. Their hate, their rage, their hunger was palpable, as if the ocean itself conducted their feelings.

It was intoxicating, in a way, to feel their blind fury, to get caught up in it. Her heart raced. She felt strong and relentless. There was a purity to it, this primal sensation, to hunt, to want…

She saw through their eyes. And she saw the Island of Unwanted Things.

Echo bolted upright in her sleep. The thin blankets she'd slept under were soaked with sweat. The air within the small hut she'd taken up as her own felt stifling and murky. She tasted blood in her mouth and spat, wondering if she'd chewed her lip in her sleep. But no, the blood was some sort of phantom holdover from the dream.

The dream. It didn't feel like a dream. It felt like a… premonition. Her heart would not stop pounding in her chest. She slid from her makeshift bed and pulled on her fighting gear. I'm being paranoid, she thought. It was just a dream. A nightmare. A leftover from the night her mother died. Dreaming about shark-creatures in the darkness.

Still, best to check, she told herself. She stepped outside, half-expecting to run directly into one of the shark-men. Instead, Merrick caught her eye, standing by a nearby campfire.

"You look out of sorts," the older warrior said.

"I... I think we're going to be attacked," Echo said.

Merrick rubbed his hands by the fire for a few seconds then walked over to her.

"What makes you say that," he said.

"I had a... okay, this is stupid. I had a dream," she said. "But after everything we've been through, I can't help but feeling like..."

"Like you should be listening to your dreams," Merrick said, his voice low. "You're not wrong. What did you see?"

Echo relayed the images she saw. Merrick's face grew grim.

"We should get Barnabas," Merrick said. As if summoned by magic, the pirate turned around the corner of a nearby hut, a heavy satchel over one shoulder.

Echo and Merrick stared at him in disbelief.

"What?" Barnabas said, wearing a look of feigned innocence.

"What are you doing out there?" Echo said. "I thought you were with the ship."

"What are *you* doing out *here*?" Barnabas repeated back.

"Why are you acting so sketchy?" Echo said. "Wait—are you... are you stealing things?"

"No!" Barnabas said. "Well, not from anyone alive, in any case. It's not stealing if the owner is dead. Right? Right."

"You know what? Never mind. Not important," Echo said. "I think the shark-men have returned."

Barnabas lowered the satchel to the ground and exchanged a long look with Merrick.

"What gives you that impression," Barnabas said.

Merrick spoke up.

"Atlanteans have a tendency toward the Sight, don't they," Merrick said.

Barnabas's expression changed from guilt-ridden to deadly serious.

"You had a vision," Barnabas said, more stating than asking.

"I had a dream. But it felt very real," Echo said, explaining again what she saw.

Barnabas shook his head.

"You have lookouts on the beach, Merrick?" he asked.

"I do," Merrick said.

As if on cue, a bell rang in the distance.

"Please tell me that's just a clock striking midnight," Echo said. Merrick looked shocked. Barnabas, who Echo knew grew up on the island, knew the sound as well. Merrick took Echo by the shoulders.

"We'll protect you," he said.

"No," Echo said. "They're here for me. I'm not letting anyone else die protecting me."

Artem emerged from his hut, buckling his sword belt. Despite the hour, the Amazonian man looked completely alert.

"What's going on, Merrick," he said.

"They've come for me," Echo said.

Artem instinctually put a hand on his sword's hilt.

"Guess it's time to see how well your training has paid off, isn't it, Merrick," Artem said. He sounded both fearful and excited; Echo could tell the warrior part of him was starved for a true fight, but the way he looked at Merrick, she knew Artem didn't want his partner to be a part of that fight.

"No," Echo said.

"We're not leaving you to be murdered by whoever this is," Artem said. "Besides, if you die, I've wasted weeks teaching you how to fight."

Echo tried to smile, but it never touched her eyes. She glanced at Barnabas. The magician nodded.

"They're here for me. We'll lead them away," Echo said. "It's okay. You've done too much for us already. I won't have you risking your lives for us."

"She's right," Barnabas said. "If her vision is true, these are a pack of were-sharks. They're hunters after a specific prey."

"I refuse to—" Artem began.

154

"No, Artem," Merrick said. "Listen to them. We have fighters, but how many children are there among us?"

"Take them up into the hills," Barnabas recommended. "The sharks are too tied to the ocean. They won't pursue you further inland."

All around them, the misfits of the Island of Unwanted Things emerged from their huts and tents. Every single one, even the littlest of them, had some sort of weapon in hand, a spear or knife, a hatchet intended for chopping wood. As when she first arrived on the island, Echo marveled the diversity of them, the way their unique heritage marked them all in some way, even if just in spirit. They're all miracles, Echo thought, seeing the minotaur Asterion standing tall with his massive battle axe; his lover Hesta, whose body became that of a snake below the waist; the ten-year-old triplets, all born without eyes, who could see better and further than anyone gifted with ordinary sight; the woman with wings instead of arms, who Artem had told her fell to the island five years ago and never left. Little girls with fins and hair the color of seaweed. A walrus who walked on legs like a man. So many wonders.

"You have to go," Echo said, more determined than ever to keep these people safe. "We'll head for the *Endless* and lead them away."

Merrick took Artem in his arms, and pressed his forehead against his own.

"Get them to safety, my love," Merrick said. "I'm counting on you."

"Where are you going," Artem said, his tone deadly serious and overflowing with concern.

"I just want a look at our enemy," he said. "I won't be far behind you."

"Merrick," Artem said.

"Trust me," Merrick said. "I didn't get to this age by making stupid decisions. Now get our people up into the hills."

Artem pulled Merrick into an embrace and kissed him. Echo

couldn't look away; it had a terrible finality to it. Her stomach burned with worry. I bring destruction wherever I go, don't I, she thought.

Artem pulled away from Merrick and started shouting orders. The children were like soldiers, attentive, precise, responsive. The older misfits formed a semi-circle around them, a protective shield. Asterion lead the way out of the village, his axe resting on his shoulder, big horned head acting as a banner for the rest of their people to follow. Artem stole a single glance over his shoulder, then disappeared into the darkness of the forest behind the village.

Merrick watched them go, so still Echo thought he had turned to stone. She put a hand on his shoulder.

"Go with them," she said. "We'll be fine."

Merrick favored her with a sad smile.

"I'm just going to make sure our lookout is safe," he said. "Don't you worry."

Barnabas reached out and took Merrick's hand. The grizzled magician's eyes were haunted.

"I'm sorry we brought this upon you," Barnabas said. "I had no idea where else to go."

"This is what we're here for, Barnabas Coy," Merrick said. "Never has this island turned away a lost soul. We weren't going to send any of you away."

Merrick released Barnabas' hand and threw his arms around Echo.

"Stay safe, little one. And come back to us some day, when you've put your troubles behind you. You'll always be welcome here," he said. "Now go on. May the winds be at your back."

Merrick trotted away in the opposite direction of the rest of the villagers. Barnabas picked up his satchel. Echo heard something clink inside. She felt a nagging in the back of her mind. Something didn't feel right.

"Wait," she said. "Where is Yuri?"

***

Yuri grew up in a city. He had very little experience, and even less love, for the outdoors. And the idea of hearing things moving in the dark—even if those things were, say, birds or small rodents or bugs—created a situation he found profoundly unnerving. And so, because Yuri was not the most rational person in the world, he got into the habit of bringing his gisarme with him if he had to go out at night to relieve himself.

Sure, a polearm was a bit of overkill if he were attacked by, say, a large moth, but it made him feel better to be armed. Just in case. He'd heard stories about this island. There was a lot worse out there than rodents or night birds.

Tonight, thought, as he stood facing a shrub with his weapon leaning against the tree next to him, he knew, he absolutely knew he heard something bigger than a night bird.

He tied the waist of the ridiculous pirate-y pants Barnabas had let him keep, picked up his gisarme, and leaned against the tree and to listen. Footsteps, heavy footsteps, growing closer and closer... and a familiar smell, salt water and rot, an animalistic stench he would never forget.

The shark-men, he thought. Not moving quietly, either—the creature was just stomping through the brush, close enough Yuri could hear him breathing. He put his back to the tree, holding his weapon lightly with both hands, waiting, waiting for the shark-man to get close enough...

And then he saw him, that wedge-shaped head, dorsal fin jutting out of the space between his oversized head and his shoulder blades, hunched over like a great ape, a primordial hunter who had no reason to be on dry land. None at all.

Yuri swung his weapon, using the length of it shaft to stay out of range of the monster's teeth. He felt the blade sink into the were-shark's chest, the sickening tearing noise as the hooked blade ripped through muscle and cartilage.

The were-shark let out an unnatural, unholy roar, grabbing hold of Yuri's gisarme and yanking it hard enough that Yuri couldn't let go fast enough. He followed the weapon out of the wooded area onto the sand nearby, rolling in the dirt. The fall knocked the air out of his lungs. Blue stars dotted his vision. And then the stench of the were-shark's skin was upon him, the monster blotting out the night sky as it pounced.

Burning flowers of pain burst through Yuri's shoulder. The proximity of the shark-man was suffocating. The air filled with the coppery tang of blood and he realized that blood was his own—the were-shark had bit him, huge mouth clamped down on Yuri's upper body, engulfing his entire left shoulder. The only thing worse than the pain was the pressure, as if a vice were trying to crush the life out of him. His left arm went numb, and he wondered for a moment if it were even still attached to his body.

I always wondered what it was like to die in a shark attack, he thought, his vision beginning to blur.

Then he felt something bump against his right hand. The haft of his gisarme. Yuri grabbed hold of it and tugged. The shark-man roared in pain—the head of the weapon was still embedded in the monster's chest. Yuri yanked again, harder, twisting, and the were-shark opened its mouth completely, dropping him. Yuri's grip on the polearm was strong enough that the weapon came with him, tearing free of the shark-man's flesh. Both combatants were bloody messes. Yuri couldn't bring himself to stand up. His left arm was useless. The monster circled him, limping and trying without success to staunch the flow of blood from the wound across its chest. There was no reason in its eyes; nothing there that felt like a rational mind. It ran at him, blood-filled maw wide, filled with endless rows of teeth.

Yuri tried to lift the gisarme to defend himself, but the shaft of the weapon got tangled up on something—a root, Yuri's own clothes, he'd never know—and it locked in place, pointing straight out at the oncoming were-shark.

Yuri's entire body shook as the shark-man, blind with blood rage, impaled itself on the polearm. The blade ran through, dead center in the creature's chest, through the heart, bursting out the other side like a fang.

A horrific spasm wracked the monster's body, and it fell to the ground. Yuri lay back on the sand, feeling his life's blood pour from him. He saw the were-shark drag itself away like a wounded animal, then flop to the ground and lay still.

Yuri's eyes grew heavy. He no longer felt pain. Just cold.

And then, he saw nothing at all.

Chapter 33: It didn't have to be this way

Merrick found the lookout lying in a pool of his own blood, terrible wounds inflicted on his entire body as if he'd been mauled. The old warrior knelt beside the boy—the child of a cyclops who had come to the island as a boy, who preferred to be called Bob because it was a simple human name, and despite his heritage, all Bob had ever wanted as to live a simple human life—and gently closed his one, oversized eye.

They had deaths on the island sometimes. Pirates would try to raid their storage caches. Monsters lived on the island as well, and here and there the unwanted things crossed paths with each other to deadly results. But it had been a long time.

I've been here such a long time, Merrick thought. I am this island, and this island is me.

"Where's the girl," a silky voice said behind him. Merrick stood up, hand on his sword, and turned to face the newcomer.

"I know that voice," Merrick said. "I never thought you'd show your face here again."

The man, whip-thin and dark-haired, held a pair of short blades in his hands. He wore form-fitting armor of Atlantean make, designed to blur with the water like camouflage.

"I never planned to come back, old-timer," Barracuda said. "I know where I'm not welcome. But the girl's the thing, you see. I need to bring her home."

"She is home," Merrick said. "This was yours for a little while as well."

"This was never my home," Barracuda said. "I never belonged. But no hard feelings, Merrick. I was never truly lost. Just passing through."

"Go home, boy," Merrick said. "I don't know what monsters you've brought to my island, but they won't be enough to do what you need them to do."

Barracuda made a dismissive noise with his teeth that made Merrick's blood boil.

"I called a Frenzy, Merrick. You know what one of those is?" Barracuda said. "I hope you sent your little charges into hiding, because otherwise, they'll be dinner for a swarm of were-sharks."

"Why would you do this?" Merrick said. "We welcomed you."

"You tolerated me," Barracuda said, examining his blades lazily. "But truthfully, Merrick. I'm just here for the girl. We'll leave if you give me the girl. You can even keep her little friends, the idiot and the sleazy little mage she's traveling with."

Merrick shook his head.

"Don't do this, boy."

"How's Theo these days?" Barracuda said, just the hint of a smile on his face. "Is he well? He was so much weaker than you. He must be gone by now."

Merrick drew his sword.

Barracuda was on him faster than Merrick could believe, a whirling vortex of blades and limbs. Merrick had been a warrior his entire life, though, and he batted away those swords, slipping the shield he wore on his back onto his wrist, using it as much for protection as he did a blunt weapon, bashing back at his attacker.

The men danced as if in a performance, back and forth, blade to blade, sword to shield. Merrick was a force of strength and precision; Barracuda one of elegance and speed. Both were relentless, silent and wordless, the only noise the clash of metal against metal.

Merrick gained the upper hand, smashing Barracuda across the face with his shield, sending the slender man spinning away. But when he stepped forward to press the attack, he almost tipped over. Looking down, he saw a mighty gash across his left thigh, a cut so fast and so fine he'd barely felt it. Blood poured freely from the wound.

Again, the men met blade to blade, but hobbled by his injured leg, Merrick found himself slowing, immobile. It was all he could do to keep up with Barracuda's attacks, to block and defend. A chance swing almost caught Barracuda in the throat, but the younger man moved out of the way just in time. Merrick swore and raised his shield.

But he was too slow.

Barracuda's left blade cut up and under Merrick's arm, piercing his chest, into his lung; before he could even cry out in pain, the assassin's right blade ran him through, piercing his solar plexus.

Merrick fell to his knees. Barracuda placed a foot casually on the older man's chest and pushed him off his blade, letting Merrick land on his back in the sand.

"I wish I could say I regret this," Barracuda said. Merrick stared into the assassin's eyes; and for just a moment he saw a glimmer of something there, guilt or sadness, something that wasn't there before. "It's just the business I've become a part of, Merrick. You understand."

Merrick said nothing, clutching his gut as if he could hold his life in just a little longer. Barracuda began to back away.

"We'll find her, you know," he said. "I'm sorry the last thing you'll know in this life is that you died for nothing."

Merrick looked up at the stars as Barracuda disappeared into the darkness. His thoughts turned to Theo, and to Artem; the love he would see soon, and the love he would leave behind, alone in this cold world.

Chapter 34: The Amazon

Artem led the cadre of unwanted things inland, subconsciously counting and recounting to make sure they hadn't lost anyone. They were all well-trained, even the youngest among them; they moved quickly and sure-footedly through the jungle terrain despite the darkness. They stuck to the shore for the most part, but all of them knew safe places in the forest. It might be an island of forgotten things, but sometimes, people remembered this place, and sometimes, it was best to hide rather than fight.

Once they were well away from the shore, nearing a series of caves they'd long ago set up as a bolt hole in case of an event like this, Artem caught Asterion by the arm. The minotaur looked down at him, head and shoulders taller than the young warrior.

"You lead them the rest of the way," Artem said. "I'm going back."

The beast-man opened his mouth to speak, then shook his mighty head, horns swaying against the night sky like branches.

"I won't stop you," Asterion said. "Help them if you can. We'll keep the little ones safe."

"I thank you," Artem said. He squeezed the minotaur's arm. "You've been a good friend."

"We'll see you soon," Asterion said. "Both of you."

Artem nodded, ruffled the hair one of their nearby charges affectionately, then backed away from the group, letting them disappear into the night.

And then Artem began to run.

There was an unnatural grace and power to his movements, legs swift and powerful as he tore through the forest. His mother named him after the Greek goddess her people held sacred, the huntress Artemis. Artem embodied his namesake, quick and silent and deadly. He danced among the trees, using them for cover to hide his approach.

He could see the glow of the campfires through the trees when he encountered the first of his adversaries. The massive thing, a shark who walked like a man, stomped through the brush, clumsy and out of place on dry land. It sniffed the air like a hound, searching for something, tracking, and Artem, quiet as death himself, used that distraction to slip in close before the creature even realized he was nearby.

Artem's sword nearly cleaved the creature's head in half. He left it twitching and bleeding in the muck and carried on to the village.

He skirted the edge of the tree line until he found another of the were-sharks, this one with the flat, broad skull of a hammerhead. Its mouth hung open, teeth gleaming in the night. The creature's movements were uneven, spasmodic… it looked drugged, or confused, but also aggressive, almost rabid. He could see the monster gasping for air, as if being on the surface was limiting its ability to breathe.

The Amazonian man slipped the small buckler from his back and tapped the flat of his sword against it. The shark-man heard the sound immediately and turned toward the forest, half-running, half-stumbling toward him. Artem waited until the shapeshifter stepped into the shadowy embrace of the trees and jumped, spring-boarding off the trunk of a palm tree, plunging downward to drive the point of the sword deep into the creature's skull. Arms flailing, the shark-man collapsed, muscles twitching as if it were trying to swim in the sand. Artem waited until the twitching stopped and ran for the village.

He made his way stealthily along the edge of the huts, then toward the beach, following tracks he knew well. He always recognized Merrick's footprints, the way he favored his left leg because of an old injury, how he had a tendency to drag his heels a bit when he wasn't paying attention.

Artem loved all of Merrick's imperfections. These are what love is built on, he thought as he followed the tracks. Love is imperfect. Love is imperfection. And that's what makes it real.

And then he saw a shape on the beach and knew exactly what it was.

"No," he said, sprinting toward the body.

Merrick lay in a pool of his own blood in the sand, his sword and shield tossed aside, eyes closed. The older warrior's skin was ashen, his lips blue, the flesh around his eyes bruised and sunken. Those eyes opened as Artem drew near.

"I thought... I wouldn't get to see you one last time," Merrick said.

"You hush," Artem said, quickly assessing Merrick's wounds. Not one but two killing blows, and precise, not the sort of ragged mess he'd expect from one of the shark-men.

"We'll get you help," Artem said, cradling Merrick's head in his hands. "You'll be fine."

"I won't be fine," Merrick said. He smiled. Blood stained his teeth. "I can't feel anything but cold, Artem. It's over."

"It's not over yet. Don't you dare leave me," Artem said. "We have so much more to do together. Who did this to you, Merrick? Who did this?"

Merrick made a clicking noise that might've almost been a laugh.

"An old pupil of mine," he said. "Would you believe that? Such a ridiculous... he's called... Barracuda. What a stupid name. What a stupid way to die."

"You're not going to die," Artem. "I won't let you."

Merrick tried to speak, but nothing came out. Instead, a single tear fell from the corner of his eye. Artem hushed him.

"You were my rising sun," Merrick said, his voice barely a whisper. "Every day, I lived for you."

"I can't do this without you, Merrick," Artem said. He tried to keep the panic from his voice.

"Yes, you can," Merrick said. The older warrior suddenly grasped Artem's hand. The grip was weak, his flesh icy. "I had a good life, right?"

"Don't leave me," Artem said.

"Tell me, my love," Merrick said, his eyes growing glassy. "Did I leave the world better than I found it?"

"You made this world better every moment I've known you," Artem said. "Every day. Every hour. Every minute."

"That's all I wanted to do," Merrick said. "I…"

Merrick's lips moved wordlessly, but Artem caught the words, and held them in his mind and memory like a butterfly, like something infinitely breakable, and impossible to replace.

"I love you too," Artem said.

And Merrick was gone.

Artem hunched over Merrick's body, his frame wracked with sobs, a pain tearing through his insides worse than any injury battle could inflict on him. His jaw hurt from clenching, his teeth grinding together with grief and loss. He kissed his one true love for the last time, and then he sat up.

Artem muttered an Amazonian prayer to a god he didn't believe in. He strapped his buckler onto his back, and picked up his own sword as well as Merrick's, tucking both into his belt. He gently closed Merrick's eyes with his thumb and forefinger.

"Goodbye, my setting sun," he said.

And then Artem, the only living son of the Amazons, ran into the night, his heart heavy with grief and vengeance.

Chapter 35: Run for your life

Echo felt like she was living a scene from an Indiana Jones film. Y'know the one, she thought, the one where there's a giant boulder chasing Indy and he's running like back end is on fire to get away from it. This is exactly like that.

Except instead of a boulder, she and Barnabas were running from a massive were-shark determined to rip them apart.

"Good thing they aren't great on land, huh?" she yelled over to Barnabas, who looked like he might keel over and die at any moment.

"Can't... talk... must... run..." he said. The magician was fiddling with one of the pendants around his neck, a wooden medallion. He caught Echo staring at him and waived her off, too out of breath to explain what he he it was for.

And then she heard a familiar voice screaming in pain.

"Yuri!" she yelled.

Barnabas shrugged at her as if to say, so? And Echo fired him a furious glare. She planted her heels and came to a stop, righting the trident she'd taken with her from the village, preparing to take on the shark-man who closed in on them like a car with its brake line cut. She hefted the weapon up above her shoulder and threw it just like Artem had taught her, launching it with her superhuman strength at the shark-man's head.

With the grace of a prima ballerina, the were-shark side-stepped the projectile and kept on charging at them without missing a beat.

"Are you kidding me," Echo said.

"Ekk," Barnabas barked out, so out of breath he couldn't even form her entire name. His message was clear though—he tossed her his flintlock pistol-shaped magic wand and pointed at their oncoming attacker. She caught it one-handed and aimed, pulling the trigger.

A massive burst of flames erupted from the artifact and a basketball-sized fireball spurted forth, slamming into the shark-man's chest with perfect aim. The monster launched backward as if kicked by an invisible giant, bounced several times in the sand, then lay still.

"If you could have done that the whole time why were we running?" Echo said.

Barnabas waved his hands around as he gasped for air, then held up one finger.

"You could only do that spell once," Echo translated.

Barnabas nodded.

Echo tossed the gun back to him and picked up her trident, heading into the brush toward the sound of Yuri's scream.

They were never after him, she thought. Just me. Why Yuri? Please don't be dead. There's no reason for them to hurt him. He's just been dragged into this because of me. None of this is fair to him.

"We need... to move," Barnabas said, his breathing almost returning to normal.

"We just fried the one that was chasing us," Echo said.

"Yeah, and because we did that, the rest of them know where we are," Barnabas snapped. "That's why I didn't shoot the first one."

"I thought..." Echo said, but she stopped herself when she heard Yuri moaning. She raced into the shadows until she found him, covered in blood and lying next to a barely breathing body of another were-shark. She ran to Yuri, dropping to her knees beside him.

"Oh, no," she said, brushing dirt from her friend's face. His chest and shoulder had been pierced in a perfect semicircle, the shark's teeth marks clear as day. The blood covering his body wasn't entirely his—she could see the pool of dark fluid gathering under the monster's body as well—but checking his pulse, she knew her friend didn't have much time left.

She almost jumped out of her skin as Barnabas' gun went off again. She looked up to see him standing over the were-shark, his weapon outstretched.

"These things never stay down," he said. "Relentless."

"Barnabas," she said, shocked at the calmness of her own tone. "Yuri's dying."

Barnabas started down at the boy, his eyes focusing very intently on the bite.

"Huh," he said.

"Huh? That's all you have? My best friend is dying! Help me!"

Barnabas moved swiftly, fingers roughly probing the wounds on Yuri's chest.

"No, he's not," he said. "It's worse than that. We've got to get out of here."

"I'm not leaving him to die here alone," Echo said.

"He's not—okay, okay," Barnabas said. Let's get him up and back to the ship before the other…"

Barnabas and Echo simultaneously turned their attention in the direction of the village. The distinctly heavy, dragging footsteps of were-sharks grew closer, and fast.

"Let's move it," Barnabas said. Echo looked at him questioningly and the magician gestured violently at Yuri's body. "You have super-human strength! Pick him up!"

Echo's jaw dropped for a moment, but then she slid her arms under Yuri's prone body and scooped him up easily with both arms. Barnabas picked up her trident adjusted the satchel across his back, which he'd somehow managed to retain through the entire escape.

"You're going to have to keep them off us," Echo said.

"I have an idea," Barnabas said. "But we need to get closer to the water. Come on."

They skirted the edge of the trees for as long as they could, hoping to stay out of sight, but the were-sharks were hot on their trail, so close Echo could hear their labored breathing.

Then she saw their goal: the dinghy that would carry them to the ghost ship. She wondered for just a split second how Barnabas knew it would be here, but then she remembered the charm he whispered to—clearly sending some sort of spell or signal to the undead crew of the vessel.

The shark-men crested the top of a nearby dune in a cloud of muscle and sand and the rank scent of blood and death. There had to be almost a dozen of them, all shapes and sizes, massive brutes shaped like Great Whites and little horrors like something that crawled up from the very bottom of the sea. They ran toward them, an array of goblins, rabid and frothing.

Echo was so caught up in the approaching horde she almost collapsed into the raft, banging her knees and dropping Yuri with a thump into the boat. Even carrying a grown man in her arms, she'd outpaced Barnabas, who tugged the satchel from his shoulders as he threw her trident into the little boat as well.

"Get in, get in, get in!" he yelled. "We need them in the water!"

"They're faster in the water!" Echo said, pushing the dinghy away from the sand easily, still marveling at her own strength. Barnabas sloshed beside her and climbed in, letting Echo pull herself aboard as he rummaged through his bag.

"What are you doing?" Echo said.

Barnabas pulled out a rolled-up paper tube from the satchel and held it above his head. He gasped for air as he unrolled it, waving his free hand at some invisible presence that started rowing them away from the shore.

"Need a minute," Barnabas said, eyeballing the scroll. "Oh, hell…"

Shark-men were close enough to splash their way into the foamy water, grunting and roaring, their breath hot and rank. Echo scooped up her trident and prepared to fight.

And then the air filled with arcs of blood.

Artem looked as if he could fly. The Amazon used the shark-men's own bodies for leverage, leaping from their shoulders and heads, a sword in each of his hands as he spun like a dervish. His mouth was a howl of silent rage and grief; his eyes filled with blind battle fury. He twisted like a tornado in the air and landed with a thump in the dinghy, the craft sinking low in the water as his weight slammed down.

Echo and Artem traded the briefest of glances. Neither spoke.

The were-sharks were a chaotic mess, still worked up into a mindless rage, but that rage was now tinged with pain, their own blood filling the air like a mist. The unwounded pushed past the injured, their bodies taking to the water with a grace that was completely counter to their clumsiness on land. The ghost-rowers paddled faster, but the sharks were on them, the water surrounding the little craft a collage of scythe-like fins. The ghost ship drew nearer—Echo stole a quick look and saw ropes dropping from invisible hands in preparation to pull the dinghy out of the water—but they needed something to buy them more time.

Artem stepped to the stern of the little boat, preparing to dive into the water.

"I've got this," he said. "Go."

"No," Echo said.

"Shut up and sit down," Barnabas said. "Sit! Down!"

Echo found herself complying unwillingly with the magician's command, and even Artem took a knee.

Barnabas held the scroll he'd been reading aloft like a protest sign. He began speaking in a language that sounded like water falling softly over smooth stones.

It sounded like a prayer.

The water beneath them began to churn, and the sea level rose, as if a hill were growing beneath the surface. They swooped forward, their craft carried by gravity toward the ghost ship.

"By all the gods," Artem said.

Echo said nothing. There was nothing to say. What could she say about the thing that rose out of the water before her? Shaped like a man, but made of pure water, a face made waves, arms made of tides, a great golem whose flesh was carved from the ocean itself...

The giant picked up the dinghy in one hand and callously tossed the little craft and all its occupants onto the deck of the ghost ship. Echo heard wood snap and splinter. Artem acrobatically rolled with the fall, twisting as he fell from the sky; the others were not so lucky. Yuri flopped down like a stunned fish. Barnabas swore in three languages, banging his head against the deck, but holding onto something desperately with both hands —another scroll? Echo's Atlantean physiognomy let her weather the landing better than the others, but the shock still rattled her to her bones as she struggled back to her feet.

What she saw was something she would never forget.

The sky filled with rain, but not true rain—the massive creature cast off sprays of water like a downpour with each movement. And move it did; huge, blunt-fingered fists scooped up rabid were-sharks and threw them out into the water like skipping stones. It stomped its approximation of feet down onto unseen assailants, kicked others so hard they went flying back onto the beach. The creature roared, and its voice was that of a hurricane, Mother Nature's own anger.

But it couldn't catch them all—relentlessly, the were-sharks who evaded the giant's attacks swam toward the ghost ship, tails whipping furiously.

"They're still coming!" Echo said.

Barnabas opened what she thought was a tube containing another scroll. A single sheet of paper, it glowed blue and white in his hand, and Barnabas yelled three more words in a language Echo had never heard before. The paper burned up, disappearing into nothing; the magician collapsed as if struck down by an unseen blow, crumpling to the deck.

The space in front of the ghost ship opened like a window. Beyond it, a different sky, slate gray, waited for them, with waters black and frigid. Cold air blasted through that window, sending chills across Echo's skin.

They sailed through that window. It closed behind them.

And they were gone.

Chapter 36: Magic has a cost

Echo couldn't believe the temperature shift.

They'd gone from the warm, almost tropical air of the Island of Unwanted Things to icy, near-arctic chill. The air was a cloudy, neutral gray; she almost gasped as an iceberg drifted past them on the left.

"Where are we," she said.

She climbed to her feet, but the deck had already grown slick—she took a knee and surveyed the damage. The dinghy had been smashed to bits by the impact, boards scattered across the deck like broken bones. Artem sat against the rail, holding his head, looking otherwise no worse for wear. The other men were in far worse shape.

Yuri lay prone on his belly, arms listlessly at his sides. Echo staggered over to him, but caught sight of Barnabas even further away, curled up in fetal position on the floor. She watched as he unfurled himself and began coughing violently. Blood sprayed from his mouth, which the magician wiped away with the back of his hand. He held his stomach as if keeping his guts from falling out. He saw the look on Echo's face and waved her off.

"Check the boy," he said, coughing up more blood.

Echo rolled Yuri over. The teeth marks on his chest and

shoulder were healing at a terrifying rate. She pulled a shark tooth out of one hole and she could see the flesh beneath it seal up.

"What's happening to him," Echo said. "Where are we?"

Barnabas groaned as he tried to speak, then wiped his mouth again.

"Let's get him below deck and I'll explain," Barnabas said. He turned his attention to Artem. "If you came with us…"

"Merrick's dead," Artem said, rising. "And whoever killed him is after you, so my best chance of cutting this Barracuda's head off is by your side."

He changed the focus of his attention from Barnabas to Echo.

"You have my sword, until his death, or mine," the Amazon said.

"I'm sorry this happened," Echo said, her voice barely above a whisper. Everything I touch is destroyed, she thought. I'm not worth the trouble I bring.

"We're glad to have—" Barnabas said.

"Shut up," Artem said. "You led them to us. The girl's not to blame. But you are. Merrick had such faith in your heart, Barnabas Coy, but the rest of us knew you. You've never cared about the consequences of your actions."

Barnabas took the verbal beating in silence, only moving to wipe a dribble of blood that fell from the corner of his eye like a tear. Snowflakes gathered in his ragged beard.

Echo put a hand on Artem's shoulder, but he pulled away gently, bending down to pick up Yuri as easily as Echo herself had.

"Come. Let's get you both below deck," Artem said. "You're probably freezing."

***

Artem found an empty bunk below and tucked the still-unconscious Yuri in. Echo lit a lamp, which gave off a flame-like light but seemed to be powered by some sort of spell instead of actual fire.

"I don't understand what's happening with him," Echo said, pulling the blanket Artem had just pulled over Yuri away to look at the bite again.

"Well, for starters, he won't need the water-breathing earring I gave him," Barnabas said, clomping down the wooden steps slowly, gripping the handrail tight. "Both of you should check the chests in the store room. There's warm clothes that will fit you."

"What do you mean, he won't need the earring?" Echo said.

"He's been infected with the were-shark curse," Barnabas said.

"I thought infectious bites from shape-shifters were old wives' tales," Artem said. He stepped into the next room but left the door open so he could listen. Echo heard a scraping noise as Artem dragged a chest of clothes closer.

"It's not an infection," Barnabas said, sitting down slowly. And what happened to *him*, Echo thought. He looks like he's dying. "Lycanthropy is magic-based. It's a curse. And under certain circumstances, they can share that curse. Pass it along."

"What circumstance made tonight special?" Artem said. He tossed Echo a deep gray, hand-knitted sweater, which she pulled over her head. It nearly fell to her knees, but it was warm, and smelled like old wood.

"The were-sharks have a ritual called the Frenzy," Barnabas said. His eyes rolled back into his head for a split second, and Echo thought he was going to pass out. Instead, he shook his head and continued. "They get worked up into an almost religious state of bloodlust before a great hunt. Like tonight. Did you see how mindless they were when they chased us? There was no logic there. No grace. They were running on pure animal instinct."

"It was different from when we fought them at my mother's house," Echo said. Again, that pang of loss. With so much going on, it was hard to remember just how much she'd lost in just a few weeks. I can't lose Yuri too, she thought. "I think they spoke to each other there. None of the shark-men talked tonight."

"Well, all shapeshifters have rituals like this. It often centers around the hunt. Brings them back to their baser instincts. It's tradition," Barnabas said. "And sometimes it's used for recruitment."

"Will the boy die?" Artem said. He found a pair of long pants and a sort of oversized tunic to pull on over his island clothes.

"No," Barnabas said. "He won't be happy, though."

"Will he be... like them?" Echo said.

"You mean will he be a monster?" Barnabas said. "I don't know. I can take us to someone who can tell us more about it. But from what I understand, he'll keep his personality. He may have trouble controlling his rage when he transforms. He'll be hungrier. More primal. But he won't turn on us. I've never met someone infected exactly this way, but I've known my share of shapeshifters in my day."

"How long will he be unconscious?" Echo said.

Barnabas shrugged. He reached into a cabinet near enough he didn't have to leave his seat to pull open and withdrew a dark knit cap, which he pulled won over his stubbly scalp.

"I have a question," Artem said. Barnabas nodded at him without speaking. "I've always heard you were just a petty dabbler in magic. A hedge mage. What we saw on that shoreline was not the work of a half-trained wizard."

Barnabas nodded, holding his belly again.

"I had some help with those spells," Barnabas said. "The scrolls I used. It's possible to write a single spell on a scroll like that. A one-time use. What do they say on the mainland? 'Break glass in case of emergency.'"

"You didn't have those before," Echo said. "They came from that bag of things you took from the island."

"What did you steal, Barnabas," Artem said, his tone deadly.

"I didn't steal them," Barnabas said defensively. "I left them there. They were no use to me when I found them the first time I left, but I thought they might come in handy. A thank you might be polite."

Echo shook her head.

"What did they do to you," she said, indicating with her eyes his damaged health.

"Every spell has a cost, Echo," Barnabas said. "Even borrowed ones on enchanted scrolls. I summoned a powerful water elemental to fight for us and then opened a portal to travel through. Even with the barrier of casting spells like that through a scroll… they were out of my league. I'll be throwing up blood for days."

"It's not permanent, what's happened to you," Echo verified.

"Everything leaves a scar, my dear," Barnabas said. "But I'm not dying yet. There's too much work to do."

"A portal," Artem said. "To where?"

Barnabas laughed, coughing up more blood as he did.

"I have no idea," he said. "I pulled the second scroll at random. But don't worry, I can get us home."

"The last teleportation spell almost killed you," Echo said. "You're going to do it again this soon?"

Barnabas waved a hand drunkenly. Echo could see how tired he was in his eyes. Using the scrolls had taken an incredible toll on him.

"No need. There's little…" Barnabas drew something in the air with his forefinger. "Tears in the sea. Gaps where things come and go across great distances. We'll find one of those and head somewhere warmer, before this ship hits an iceberg and sinks."

"Comforting thought," Echo said.

"We're heading back," Artem said.

"We can't run forever, can we?" Barnabas said.

Artem nodded and headed back up onto the deck. Barnabas watched him go.

"That's why I never get attached to anyone," Barnabas said. "Love is dangerous. It makes you irrational."

Echo crossed her arms, watching a Barnabas closed his eyes.

"Merrick was my friend," Barnabas said. "Your mother was my friend. I don't have many friends, Echo. I can't afford to lose any more."

"Then what are we going to do about it," Echo said.

Barnabas opened his eyes.

"What do you want to do about it?"

"I want to stop running, Barnabas."

He nodded. The tiniest of smiles appeared behind his messy beard.

"That can be arranged," he said. "I know a place where we can have Yuri looked at. And maybe, just maybe, we can find out who's chasing us and what we can do to stop them."

Chapter 37: A more aggressive approach

"I'm beginning to think you're deliberately sabotaging me," Reina said.

It was an active struggle to contain her rage as she received Barracuda's report in her private study. The man was known through the darkest circles of Atlantis as a consummate professional and deadly assassin, but capturing a teenaged surface girl appeared to be beyond his skillset.

"She's acquired powerful allies," Barracuda said. "If you wanted her dead it would be done by now. Taking her alive when she's gathered warriors and magicians around her is another story."

"Outcasts and smugglers," Reina said. "These nomads she runs with can't be so dangerous as to be impossible for you to circumvent."

Barracuda shrugged in such a dismissive way Reina wanted to have him murdered on the spot. But now was not the time. When his services were no longer needed that would be a different story.

"We need to prepare for the inevitable," Reina said. "Have our men ready the surface weapons for attack."

"Consider it done."

"Your thoughts?" Reina said.

"Their missiles are crude by our standards, but they'll do the job," Barracuda said. "We have the stolen craft in place as discussed."

"Good," she said.

"The men who captured the submarines are skilled and loyal," Barracuda said. "I wish you'd let me use them to capture the girl."

"I won't use Atlanteans directly against my brother," Reina said. "I'll only test their loyalty so far."

"I think you'd be pleasantly surprised at how ruthless they can be," Barracuda said. "You should have seen them against the whalers, or the diggers."

Reina waved him off.

"Go. Be ready," she said. "I may have further need of you here in Atlantis."

"Of course," the assassin said, backing away and slipping into the shadows in the recesses of the study.

As if on cue, one of her personal guards knocked on the door and entered.

"Your appointment is here," the guard said.

Reina nodded for him to let the guest in. Senator Cartay entered, smiling broadly and confidently, as if this were just a normal meeting about the winter food stores or upkeep of the public meeting center.

"My Regent," the senator said, bowing deeply. The door closed, leaving them alone, and Cartay's demeanor changed quickly.

"I understand you've had another disappointment," he said.

"Remember your tone, Cartay," Reina said.

"A simple statement of fact," he said. "We don't have any more time to wait. Your brother has to be dealt with."

"And I will deal with him," Reina said. "Our plan is moving forward as intended. We will launch the surface-dwellers' own weapons against them, creating suspicion and war. They'll cull themselves and their militaries for us through attrition, and then, we make our presence known as a world power."

Senator Cartay grinned pleasantly, but unconvincingly.

"Before we move against the surface, we need to know we have

Atlantis itself well in hand," he said. "Rhegis must be handled."

"Do not presume to—"

"I presume nothing, your highness," Cartay said. "But I cannot guarantee the backing of the guilds and my cadre of senators without assurances that we have one, distinct ruler. You must act."

"Don't put me on a deadline, senator," Reina said.

"You put yourself on a deadline, your highness," Cartay said. "I'm simply holding us to the plan. My sincerest apologies if I seem… pushy."

"Enough," Reina said, unable to keep the anger from her voice. "Enough. Get out. I'll deal with my brother. I don't want to see you again until I've done so."

The senator bowed again, backing out of the room.

"As you wish, my Regent," he said. "I live to serve."

Cartay left, and he wasn't gone but a few seconds before Reina threw the empty glass of wine she'd had in front of her across the room. Her bodyguard at the door reentered.

"Regent?" he said, hesitantly.

"Find out where my brother is," Reina said. "Have an escort prepared for me. I need to have a conversation with him. Now."

Chapter 38: Stand up and face it

He dreamed of deep water and freedom, of a dark world where creatures fled in fear from him. He dreamed of power, real power; strength in his arms, in his back. He dreamed of senses that could help him know things miles and miles away; a sixth sense, like telepathy. He felt part of something greater, something ancient, something inhuman.

All of these things whispered in his veins like a promise. The ocean could be his, if he wanted it.

And then he woke up on Barnabas' ship.

"Well this is disappointing," Yuri said out loud. He twisted a bit to see Echo scooting her chair closer to him. She ran a cool hand across his forehead. Her touch hurt just enough to tell him he was running a pretty vicious fever. His whole body ached, especially his left shoulder, which burned like an infection.

"Welcome back," Echo said, smiling at him. The smile didn't touch her eyes though.

Something is really wrong, Yuri thought to himself. There were days he wished Echo had learned how to be a better liar. She had no poker face.

"I'm pretty sure I should be dead," Yuri said.

"You're going to be fine," Echo said.

Yuri heard a soft shuffling behind her, and Artem drifted into view, steadfastly trying not to look like he was watching them both.

"Hey, Artem," Yuri said. "You decided to join our merry band?"

Artem didn't respond, but rather returned to sharpening his sword. The rasping of blade on stone made Yuri's ears itch.

He sat up tentatively, hugging the blankets around him, and cried out in a high-pitched yelp when he saw the state of his torso. Bruised in a cloud of yellow, purple, and blue, with red welts where teeth marks were healing with remarkable, almost horrifying speed.

"I got eaten alive!" he said. "I knew it! What is all this?"

"Yuri," Echo said.

"Don't Yuri me. I should be one hundred percent dead!" he said. "And don't think I don't recognize that look on your face, Echo. I know you. What are you thinking about not telling me?"

"I need to you promise to not freak out for at least five minutes," Echo said.

"And now I'm freaking out already," Yuri said. "Just say it before I have a meltdown."

Echo took a deep breath, then blurted it out.

"You've been infected with the were-shark curse," she said.

Yuri stared at her blankly for a long couple of seconds. Then he started laughing.

"That's the most ridiculous thing I've ever heard," he said.

"Yuri…"

"I get it, I get it—I got bit by the were-shark back there and you and Barnabas were like, this is the perfect opportunity for a prank, right? I mean I'd play a prank on you if you survived a near death experience but I knew you were going to pull through. No offense," he said.

"Yuri, I'm not kidding."

"I'd tell you I wasn't kidding too! I only look gullible, Echo. C'mon."

Yuri caught a look on Artem's face that turned his stomach. The Amazon fighter had been quick to smile back on the island, but he hadn't seemed much of a prankster, and his expression was grim, with a hint of pity.

"Oh no," Yuri said.

"It's going to be fine," Echo said.

"I'm a were-shark," Yuri said.

"Maybe… it could be cool?" Echo offered.

"No, no, you're right," Yuri said. "You get super powers and you're all like, awesome and cute and normal. I get super powers and I look like a Katy Perry backup dancer."

"You won't look like a Katy Perry backup dancer all the time," Echo said. "Just when you… y'know."

"Shark out," Yuri said.

"That's good. You should go with that. That's a good way of putting it," Echo said.

"Why can't I just turn green and start talking about myself in the third person instead?" Yuri said. "Why this? I mean… what happens, I turn into a shark under a full moon?"

Echo rubbed her forehead, fighting off the ghost of a headache.

"Okay," Echo said. "Barnabas says he knows someone who can explain it all better. But it's not a full moon thing. It's like a control thing. You can get good at it. The things chasing us change back and forth all the time."

"Where are my glasses?" Yuri said.

"We… I'm sorry, we lost them," Echo said. "When we found you on the beach…"

"But they're not on my face?"

"Nope. What. Wait. What?"

"I found a side effect," Yuri said.

"You're not nearsighted anymore?" Echo said. "Didn't see that coming."

"Not worth turning into a cross between Jaws and a Ninja Turtle villain, but there's one upside," Yuri said.

"And you can breathe underwater. No more stupid earring," Echo said.

"I was kind of into the earring," Yuri said.

"I'm sorry. I think you can probably keep it if you want."
Yuri shrugged.

"I'm also starving," Yuri said.

"I think that... might be another side effect," Echo said.

Yuri sank back into the bed a bit and looked at his hands.

"I'm a monster," he said.

"You're not a monster," Echo said. "You're still here. Listen to me, Yuri Rodriguez. You are my friend, and I love you, and you're still here. That's all that matters."

"Even if I transform into a kaiju?" he said.

"Especially if you turn into a kaiju," Echo said.

Yuri laid back and fixed his eyes on the ceiling.

"You okay?" Echo said.

"I think... I think I just need some time alone to process it," Yuri said. He felt a lump at the back of his throat. This all feels so unfair, he thought. I was just getting used to everything being wrong, and different, and scary, and now... I'm wrong, and different, and scary. I don't want to be a monster.

"Are you sure?" Echo said.

"Yeah," Yuri said. He turned his back to her, feeling his eyes well up. I could be dead, he thought. She's right. I'm still here. But I don't want to be a creature. I want to be me.

He felt Echo's hand rub his back for a few seconds, a gentle reminder that she was here for him, and then she slowly, hesitantly walked up the stairs onto the deck. It wasn't until Artem spoke that Yuri realized he was still in the room.

"The love of my life died in that battle," Artem said.

Yuri rolled over so he could face the Amazon.
"Merrick's gone?"

"Someone murdered him," Artem said. "Not one of the shark-men. A man, like us, with a sword. Stabbed him in the heart. Might as well have stabbed me in mine. I've never lost someone I loved before, Yuri. I don't know what to do with all this anger. The sadness feels like it's going to drown me."

"I'm sorry, Artem," Yuri said. "Merrick... he was a good guy."

"He was the best man I'll ever meet," Artem said. "And the world is a darker place without him."

Artem looked at the floor for a long, silent moment. Yuri couldn't tell if he were crying or just thinking. When he spoke, his voice was strong and clear.

"My people. The people who made me and abandoned me. The Amazons," Artem said. "They believe in a pantheon of gods."

"Do you?" Yuri said.

"I don't know," Artem said. "I've never met these gods. I've never seen a reason to believe they're anything more than stories. But they're not like modern gods. They're quite human. Quite fallible. And they are very, very cruel."

"Sounds like a lot of other gods I've read about," Yuri said. Artem nodded.

"And in their myths, the heroes do not walk an easy path. They suffer. Oh, do the heroes in their stories suffer. Murder and chaos. Their families are slaughtered. Their lovers. Their friends."

Yuri just listened, unsure where Artem was going.

"This is a terrible world, Yuri. It will break your heart, and it will test your will," Artem said. "I do believe this. But I also believe that the only thing we can do is stare it in the eyes and dare it to hurt us. We need to scream in its face, and raise our swords, and say: not today. Not tomorrow. I am stronger than you think I am. And I will not break."

"I…" Yuri began.

"You're stronger than you think you are, Yuri," Artem said. "Now stand up and scream your battle cry. Because we have a war to fight, and we need you by our sides."

Artem didn't let Yuri respond. The Amazon simply stood up, taking his swords with him, and went deeper into the bowls of the ship.

"Good pep talk, coach," Yuri said to the empty room. He pulled the covers back over himself and tried to sleep.

Chapter 39: Don't get attached

Echo found Barnabas alone, leaning in the crook of the prow of the ship. For a moment, he painted a sad and solitary figure; with his strange clothes, the tattoos on his hands and neck, the unkempt beard, he might have been a figure from a Melville novel.

Then he spotted her, and the moment of silent reverie was broken.

"How is he," Barnabas said.

"He's Yuri," Echo said. "He's not as tough as he pretends he is. He's upset."

"There's worse things," Barnabas said. "There are as many shapeshifter heroes in the old stories as there are villains."

"He thinks he's a monster," Echo said.

Barnabas nodded. On the starboard side of the ship, a snow-capped, green and stony coastline made for an almost picturesque scene.

"We're making good time, I take it," Echo said. "I feel like yesterday we were surrounded by icebergs, and now we're seeing dry land."

"Like I said before—we're not traveling ordinary routes," Barnabas said in that mysterious tone he always used when he tried to make magic sound more mysterious than it actually was. "There are paths in the ocean where time and distance work differently.

We're taking the faerie lanes."

"We'll be... wherever you're taking us soon."

"I'll do my best," Barnabas said.

"Or your ghost crew will do their best, you mean," Echo said. Barnabas laughed and nodded.

"Can I ask you something?" Echo said. Her stomach felt filled with icy fluid. Her hands were slightly numb.

"Of course."

"Will it... will it always be like this?" Echo said.

"It'll always be weird, Echo," Barnabas said.

"No," Echo said. "Not weird. I mean... My mother. And Merrick. They both died because of me."

"That wasn't your fault," Barnabas said.

"And now Yuri—Yuri's maimed. Or whatever. None of this would have happened if they weren't trying to protect me," Echo said. "I can't do this forever, Barnabas. I can't feel this responsible for other people."

Barnabas almost rolled his eyes. Echo felt a flicker of rage in the center of her chest.

"None of this is on you, Echo," Barnabas said. "You were born into this. This is a situation you could only have avoided by literally not existing. It's happening to you, not because of you."

"Because of me. Even if I didn't cause it, it still revolves around me," Echo said. "And people keep dying because of me. And it's making me sick."

"You're going to have to let that go," Barnabas said. "You're fighting to make it better. You're not giving up."

"And how many more people have to die before I realize I can't fix it?" Echo said. "Does Yuri have to die next time? Artem? You?"

"You don't even like me."

"I like you, kind of," Echo said. "I'd feel bad if you died, at least."

"That's comforting," Barnabas said. "You're the first person in a long time who isn't outright disgusted by me. It's an improvement to my usual situation."

"Oh, shut up," she said. "Now you're trying to out-do me with self-pity, and it's…"

"Unflattering?" Barnabas said. "It's funny how unflattering self-pity is."

Echo fought the urge to take a swing at him.

"I came up here hoping you'd have something to say that might help me," Echo said.

"Came to the wrong place," Barnabas said.

"You're a jackass," Echo said.

"Told you. You won't miss me if something happens to me," Barnabas said. "At least you can take comfort in knowing one of us is expendable."

"You're awful," Echo said. "You're not expendable, you jerk. I don't want anything to happen to anyone else. Including you."

"Caring must be exhausting," Barnabas said.

Echo almost laughed. Barnabas' face twitched into a smile.

"It really is," she said, exhaling heavily.

"This is why I don't get attached," Barnabas said.

"That's a ridiculous thing to say," Echo said. "And you are attached."

"I'm seeing something through to the end," Barnabas said. "But Artem's right about me. I'm selfish. I do what best benefits me."

"I don't think helping a couple of fugitives is in your best interest," Echo said.

"Maybe I'm hoping for a handsome reward from the Atlantean royal family for keeping you safe."

"Maybe you're actually my friend," Echo said.

Barnabas smirked.

"Maybe you," Barnabas said. "The other two I could take or leave."

"They grow on you," Echo said.

"Says you," Barnabas said.

"You really don't have friends?" Echo said. "All the traveling you do. There's nobody you care about?"

Barnabas gave a noncommittal shrug.

"People in my line of work tend to die a lot," he said. "And I won't lie—magicians are shadier than you could even imagine. We might work together, but I don't think magicians ever trust each other, not really."

"You cared about my mom," Echo said.

"I did," Barnabas said. "Watching over you was a job, but your mother made me feel welcome. And I…"

"You blame yourself," Echo said. "That's why you're still helping us."

"This is why I don't get attached," Barnabas repeated.

"How long?" Echo asked. "How long were you there?"

"Not your whole life," Barnabas said. "There were other protectors before me. I was hired… maybe eight years ago? Ten? I don't remember. Time moves differently the way I travel."

"You're not as old as you look, are you," Echo said.

"I prefer to think I'm not as young as I look," Barnabas said.

The sun grew low in the sky; mist formed on the surface of the water as the warmth of day gave way to the chill of evening. In the distance, Echo heard a whale singing. If she closed her eyes, she could sense where it was, drifting in slow motion below the surface, timeless, immense, beautiful.

"I think I can read the minds of sea creatures," Echo said.

"That sounds incredibly useful," Barnabas said.

"You're being sarcastic," Echo said.

"Just a little bit," Barnabas said. "What's it like?"

Echo listened again for the whale. If she was very still, she could feel its mighty heartbeat in her chest.

"It makes me feel like I'm connected to the world," Echo said.

Barnabas let out a soft, hissing laugh.

"Let me guess," Echo said. "Don't get attached."

"See," Barnabas said. "You're learning."

Chapter 40: The coup

The Throne of Atlantis was a literal thing; a massive seat carved of ancient coral, adorned with pearls the size of fists and inlaid with gold, silver, and metals the surface world had never even heard of. It sat in a massive chamber, oft left empty these days, the polished floor slightly damp, the way everything in Atlantis is.

Behind the throne, an enormous pane of glass looked out over the hidden city. Its shimmering lights created a glowing painting behind the ruler, a constant reminder that everything done in this chamber was not for the aggrandizement of the king or queen, but for the good of the people of Atlantis.

It was a sacred place as much as it was a political one. And this was why Rhegis was so infuriated to find his sister sitting casually in their father's chair, waiting for him to arrive to the meeting she'd called.

"Your games are getting tiresome, Reina," Rhegis said. His twin crossed her legs, hands resting on their armrest. She looked like she was posing, playing ruler; but Rhegis had to admit he could see enough of their father's regal demeanor in her to think she felt like a natural fit there.

"Just keeping it warm," she said. "One of us should."

She stood up and walked down the short flight of stairs that led up to the throne. Reina wasn't alone; she'd brought a group of her personal guards with her, dressed in mourning black, as they all would for months after their king's death. Rhegis had done the same; he didn't think his sister was capable of violence against him, but he didn't trust her allies. Not in the least.

"We've got to resolve this, Reina," Rhegis said. He tried to keep his tone professional, but he'd never had a good game face—he loved his sister, and he was afraid for her and the path she was going down, and he felt this rift between them in his heart, in his soul. His voice betrayed him. "We need to work together, or Atlantis will fall apart."

"I agree that we need to resolve this," Reina said. She was playing a character, Rhegis sensed; they came into this world together, and he knew her intonations, her body language. She was putting on a show to give herself confidence, but she was up to something else as well. "But brother, your passivity will get us killed. The time has come for us to stop letting them poison our world. We need to change the course of human history before it terminates the path of Atlantean history."

"Then let's end our isolationist laws," Rhegis said. Oh, sister, if you only knew the things I gave up in my life to follow Father's wishes, he thought. I let him keep us from the surface. I failed us. I failed our entire world by not changing his mind. "Have I not always said I wanted us to work with the men and women of the surface? I know father wanted us to remain secret, to remain private, but why not talk with them? Why not make allies instead of enemies?"

"Because you know they won't accept us," Reina said. "Everything is an enemy to them. Everything is an adversary. And the only way to make sure our people are safe is to make sure the surface dwellers fear us."

Rhegis' heart sank. War was the only thing worse than isolationism, he thought. At least their father's policies kept them away from the humans above. It ensured they would never turn their eyes toward Atlantis. But this solitary life, this law of hiding...

all it did was put their people at risk.

"Let me go to them," Rhegis said. "I'll stake my life on it. If I go to them and they don't believe me, if they kill me, take me hostage… then you rule. You win. You do what you need to do. But let me try to make peace with them first. Please. I'm begging you."

Reina folded her arms across her chest. The movement made her look even more severe, like a high priestess in her black mourning dress.

"Rhegis, the most wonderful thing about you is your optimism," Reina said. "I appreciate your faith in the goodness of others. But if we send you to the surface as an emissary, you reveal our existence to them. You put us in harm's way. You destroy our element of surprise. You put our entire operation at risk. I can't allow you to do that."

Rhegis felt a flash of anger like an electric shock through his ribcage.

"*Allow* me?" he said. "When did I require your permission to act on behalf of our people? How dare you think you can oppose me? I've done nothing to stop the foolish and dangerous behavior you've engaged in for months, Reina. You'll not stop me from doing what I know, in my heart, is best for Atlantis."

He turned to leave, waving a dismissive hand over his shoulder.

"You've overstepped yourself for the last time, sister," Rhegis said. "Your games are over."

"I thought you might say that," Reina said. "Men, take them into custody."

Her men moved instantly, but not to disarm or capture Rhegis' guards. Without warning, her soldiers acted with lethal brutality, slitting the throats of the nearest members of Rhegis' entourage, or jabbing a blade beneath their armor into kidneys or hearts. In the space of a breath, his entire entourage lay dead or dying on the throne room floor.

Rhegis froze, his limbs growing cold. He made no sound. But his sister did. She gasped at the butchering act, a sharp intake of air the first indication that this was not her plan.

"What have you done!" Rhegis said, but Reina spoke over him.

"I said take them! Why did you do that!" Reina said. "Why! I demand to know why! You'll all be—"

And then Rhegis felt a sharp pain in his side. He dropped to one knee. His eyes blurred. Looking down at his gut, he saw not a knife or spear but a simple dart. Poison, he thought, his heart racing in reaction to whatever toxin had just entered his system.

"There'll be no repercussions at all for them," a new voice said. "But there will be for you."

Rhegis blinked, trying to identify it. Dame Rois, one of the great industrialists of Atlantis. Nobility by way of money and power. He'd known her for years. One of his sister's supporters. She stepped from a side passage, flanked by a man dressed as a mercenary. It must've been him who threw the dart, Rhegis thought. His mind became cloudy, hazy. He began to wonder if the poison were lethal or not.

"You had no right," Reina said.

"What are you complaining about?" Rois said. "You'll get what you wanted. You'll have your throne, and your war, and your meddling brother will be out of the way."

Rois turned to Rhegis, her slender, aggressive frame like a statue come to life in front of him.

"Don't worry, your majesty. That's not a lethal dose. Just enough for us to put you away for a while," Rois said.

Rhegis felt hands on his shoulders, helping him stay upright. His sister's hands.

"You can't do this," Reina said.

"Oh, I think we just did. And don't worry," Rois said. "We'll put your brother away somewhere safe, and you'll ascend the throne as the one true ruler of Atlantis, and you'll lead us to war against the surface."

"Why would you do this," Reina said.

"To help you!" Rois said. "To build the future Atlantis deserves. To do away with the air-breathing vermin. To make sure we have a future to look forward to."

Rhegis, his vision fading fast, felt strong arms lift him and carry him away. His sister clung to his shirt.

"Don't," Reina said.

"Come now, my Regent," Rois said. "Ascend the throne. Let us help you. Build our future, Queen Reina."

"You didn't do this for me," Reina said. Her voice echoed in Rhegis' head. He didn't think he had much more time before the drugs would put him to sleep. Or kill him.

"Of course not," Rois said. "We did it for Atlantis. Now let us put your wisdom into action. Take the throne. Take the crown. And lead Atlantis back to the supremacy it so richly deserves."

Rhegis hit the depths of his strength. The room swam, and then, darkness.

Chapter 41: New Tortuga

The trip passed in a strange sense of timelessness. Echo often sat on the deck, watching the sun move across the sky with almost hallucinatory swiftness; she couldn't tell if time moved faster or if the sun simply wanted to be rid of them.

The waters below melted swiftly from frigid black to pale, crystal blue, and every shade of blue and green in between. The air stopped biting at her skin far too soon, and became warm enough to sweat long before it should have.

The entire way, they never saw another vessel, or came within shouting distance of any land masses. Islands sometimes appeared in the distance, like optical illusions.

Echo wanted to know more about this, but Barnabas was preoccupied. The grumpy magician passed the time checking maps and consulting with orbs made of glass; sometimes someone would answer him back, but those conversations were hushed and secretive.

Artem kept mostly to himself. He paced the deck, or climbed to the crow's nest, watching vigilantly for pursuers. None ever came, but the young man was determined to make sure they were not caught unaware. He'd sit with Echo for short periods, maybe to share a meal, but mostly the warrior watched and waited, as if convinced the enemy could strike at any moment. Barnabas, in a rare chatty mood, said the Amazon was being paranoid.

"We're not moving through real space and time," he said. "The people who are after us would need more than shark-men to catch us."

Yuri, meanwhile, pouted incessantly. He'd have occasional flashes of his old personality, but a cloud hung over him, a shadow of self-pity that he could not shake. Echo would catch him staring at his own skin, watching for his flesh to change into the rough epidermis of a shark, or checking his eyes in reflective surfaces to make sure he still had irises.

It all became too much for Echo, tired of the worry and the silence. She caught Barnabas in his quarters and kicked the door open.

"Where are we going, and how soon will we get there," she said.

Barnabas dropped a bottle of liquor he had in his hand. The cork stayed in place and the glass held, though, and so the bottle just rattled across the floor rather than shattering.

"Don't they teach you to knock on the mainland?"

"We're clearly going somewhere," she said. "Answer my questions."

"We're going to Tortuga," Barnabas said.

"Tortuga's in Haiti," Yuri said. Echo hadn't realized he'd followed her down to confront Barnabas, and was as startled by the sound of his voice as Barnabas had been by hers. "Why would we go to Haiti?"

"Not that Tortuga," Barnabas said. "There's another one. New Tortuga. It's Pirate Island."

"Wasn't the original Tortuga like a pirate's paradise?" Yuri said. Echo let him talk over her; it was the first time since he started getting out of bed that he seemed to show even the slightest interest in real conversation.

"Tortuga, the real place, yes, was known as a pirate's den historically," Barnabas said. "But the world moved on from that sort of piracy. And the folks who couldn't let go... they built New

Tortuga."

"For when you're feeling nostalgic for the days of pillaging and stuff," Yuri said.

Barnabas shrugged.

"It was a culture," he said.

"Of pillaging," Yuri said.

"And theft," Echo said.

"Murder and death," Yuri said.

"And a surprising amount of socially accepted maiming," Echo said.

"Whatever," Barnabas said. "Anyway. A group of pirates found an unused island and, using a combination of luck, magic, good old-fashioned refusal to believe in the laws of physics, and a whole bunch of found materials, built a pirate town. And that's where we're headed."

"To meet your friend," Echo said.

"Who can help me," Yuri said.

"Nobody can help you," Barnabas said. "And she's not a friend exactly. But she might have some advice for making your life easier."

"This sounds wonderfully promising," Yuri said. "Between you and Artem I feel like I've got an Olympic-level pep talk team on this boat."

"Ship," Barnabas said.

"Whatever."

"How is it—your father was a fisherman, right?" Barnabas said.

"Died at sea. Thanks for bringing it up," Yuri said.

"How is it you know almost nothing about ships?"

"Died. At. Sea," Yuri said. "Do you know the lengths my momma went to in order to make sure I never followed my father's career path? I'm lucky she let me in the water long enough to learn how to swim!"

"But you worked in a building with a dock!" Barnabas said.

"You're making fun of me, when you don't know a single thing about how to sail your own boat," Yuri said.

"Ship, it's a ship, and that's what the ghosts are for," Barnabas said.

"What if the ghosts quit?" Yuri said.

"Ghost don't just quit a job," Barnabas said.

"Oh, what, do they give you two weeks' notice?" Yuri said.

Echo backed out of the room and left the men bickering. While Yuri had been quiet lately, the banter was something they'd started back on the Island of Unwanted Things, a way of connecting without admitting they were trying to get to know each other. From the outside, you'd think they couldn't stand each other, but Echo could hear an underlying tone of affection.

Still, it got tiresome. She headed up to the deck and found Artem watching something in the distance.

"Whatcha got," Echo said.

"I believe we've reached our destination," Artem said.

Directly ahead of them, an island jutted out of the ocean like a broken bone. The waters surrounding it were peppered with vessels of all kinds; tall ships and yachts, strange, steampunk-inspired monstrosities, Viking ships and submarines, all anchored and waiting for their crews. But beyond this cacophony of ships lay an even more patchwork sight: New Tortuga itself.

It looked like the sort of city a child would build, not understanding the constraints of physics. Tall towers rose like daggers from its rocky shores, massive and illogical, like something out of a Mervyn Peake novel, buttressed with wooden buildings made from whatever material could be scrounged from shipwrecks or debris. In fact, at least one building appeared to be made entirely out of a ship, hauled from the ocean and cemented in place, forever landlocked and tilted at a disconcerting angle.

Along the western edge, buildings literally hung off the surface of the island, propped up with old masts, looking dangerously off-balance, as if they could slough off into the sea at any moment.

Echo could see smoke billowing up—whether from cooking fires or arson, she couldn't tell—and from the chaotic skin of the island, she couldn't rule out either.

The entire sight gave her vertigo. Her stomach roiled at the thought of trying to navigate those streets.

"I think I've seen this place in a nightmare once," Artem said. "After eating bad mushrooms."

"I don't even know where to look," Echo said.

"Look everywhere," Barnabas said, joining them on the deck. Echo heard Yuri groan with nausea as he spotted the island. "And nowhere. New Tortuga is unlike anywhere you've ever been or you'll ever be. But keep one hand on your wallet at all times. It's full of thieves and miscreants."

"Like you," Echo said.

"The folks here will make me look like the Patron Saint of Virtue," Barnabas said. "But you'll find no better place for hearing rumors about what's going on across the seven seas. We'll get what we need here."

"I'll stay with the ship," Artem said.

"Are you kidding?" Barnabas said. "I guarantee you Yuri will look at someone the wrong way ten minutes into our trip. I need you there to kill people for me."

Artem scowled at Barnabas, as if looking for a wink or smirk to indicate he'd been joking. Finding none, the Amazon sighed.

"I'll get my swords," he said.

Chapter 42: The Lady

If the island appeared chaotic from the water, setting foot on it felt like a fever dream.

As on the Island of Unwanted Things, they'd left the ghost ship anchored in the harbor. Artem questioned whether leaving the ship unmanned was safe, but Barnabas told them that if there was one thing this place honored, it was the sanctity of a person's ship— harm done to another man's vessel brought the righteous fury of the entire populace down on the offender. No one would risk it.

"Besides," Barnabas said. "The ghosts are protective of their ship."

They rowed in together in a single dinghy, everyone but Barnabas dressed specifically for the foray. The magician had made Echo put on a drab, hooded shirt to hide her face and hair— claiming that she "looked too Atlantean," which Echo was getting tired of hearing since she still had no idea what that even meant— and made sure Yuri wasn't particularly recognizable either.

He was taking on a slightly more shark-like countenance, Echo thought, not wanting to admit it. Not monstrous, not ugly, but there was a darkness in his eyes that hadn't been there before, and his features seemed leaner, his skin almost shiny. She couldn't tell if Yuri was willfully ignoring the transformation or if he really hadn't noticed.

Artem, meanwhile, simply put on pants and boots. The fighting kilt and sandals he'd worn on his home island might not look entirely out of place, Barnabas said—they'd see all kinds here—but anything to throw onlookers off about their origins would help them blend in.

"Anonymity is the key," he said sagely.

Once ashore, Echo had no idea why Barnabas had even bothered.

It felt like the cantina in *Star Wars*, she thought. While the bulk of the people walking around were, at least on the surface, human, the crowds were peppered with other things—a walrus-man, carrying a spear that had to be nine feet long; willowy, silver-skinned fish men who didn't speak, but rather communicated through looks and subtle gestures; talking apes with patches of their fur shaved away to display vibrant tattoos.

But the humans were just as bizarre. Facial tattoos were so common as to almost be boring. She saw characters walking around like they'd stepped out of old Hollywood movies or ancient myths; turbans and tricorn hats, bandanas and bone-masks. Everyone crushed together so tightly that collisions were common. She saw no fewer than two stabbings before they'd even left the docks.

"Nice place you brought us to," Echo said.

"Home sweet home," Barnabas said.

"This place is a cesspool," Artem said.

"I won't argue with the accuracy of that statement," Barnabas said.

Yuri was uncharacteristically quiet.

"You okay, kid?" Echo asked him.

"All these people, Echo," Yuri said. "I feel… like something at the back of my mind is trying to get me to fight. I feel irrationally angry."

Artem and Barnabas shared a worried glance.

"Looks like we got here just in time," Barnabas said, putting an arm around Yuri's shoulder.

The magician led them deeper into the island, toward a tower that had snapped off at some point, sending the top half of the spire tumbling into the sea. It had been clumsily rebuilt, with a sign bearing a pictogram of a book on it.

"The New Tortuga Public Library," Barnabas said.

"You guys don't look like you read much," Echo said.

Barnabas lowered his voice.

"The literacy level among pirates is notoriously low," he said. "Suffice it to say nobody really seemed to care when half the library literally fell into the ocean."

"That's tragic," Artem said. "All those books. Gone."

"Oh, no," Barnabas said. "The library was in such dire financial straits they'd taken to renting out the upper levels to a brothel."

Echo, Yuri, and Artem all stopped walking at that comment. Barnabas kept going, oblivious. He noticed he was leaving them behind, and spun around.

"What?"

"Were there people in there when it collapsed?" Echo said, incredulous.

"Just the proprietor," he said. "Don't worry. Nobody liked him anyway. Come on."

Barnabas opened the front door to the library with a flourish and disappeared inside. Echo followed, hesitant.

The scent of books hit her instantly, that comforting smell of paper and leather she'd come to associate with reading. It took a moment for her eyes to adjust. The library was dark—too dark to read, certainly, she thought—but blinking a few times, she saw the walls lined with books, others scattered on long tables or stacked on chairs. A handful of electric lanterns cast a bit of luminescence, but made the library feel more like a storage room than a place of learning.

She saw only one occupant, but that occupant more than filled the room.

Echo had never been inclined to cherish beauty; she considered herself fairly plain at best, and was happy with that status, though people often told her otherwise. She certainly didn't admire beauty in others. But the woman reading in an oversized velvet chair next to one of the library's tall, thin windows was astoundingly beautiful. Her face had a sort of unearthly refinement to it, as if carved from marble. Her hair, cut into a bob that looked like it might fit in a 1920's gangster movie, framed that face perfectly. Her clothing was entirely inappropriate for this pirate's paradise as well, looking more like an executive headed to a business lunch in Manhattan than down among the ruffians of New Tortuga—a pristine white dress shirt, black pencil skirt, alarmingly high heels.

She raised her eyes from the book she'd been reading and smiled.

Her eyes glowed like orbs of flame. Echo almost gasped. Yuri swore. Artem muttered something in another language.

"Barnabas Coy," the woman said. "What have you got yourself into now?"

"Natasha," Barnabas said, crossing the room to shake the woman's hand. She took his hand, but inclined in to kiss both his cheeks. Her accent was strange—light and subtle, but unlike anything Echo had ever heard before.

"Look at the menagerie you've brought with you," Natasha said. "You always did have a tendency to attract strays."

"It comes from being a stray myself," Barnabas said. "This is Echo, Yuri, and Artem. Everyone, this is the Lady Natasha Grey."

Natasha bowed her head in greeting.

"You *do* have the little Atlantean I've been hearing whispers about," the Lady said. "Oh, Coy. That's a hilariously volatile situation. Tell me you're not caught up in that mess."

"You asking me to lie to you?" Barnabas said.

"How do you know about me?" Echo said. "What have you heard? Are you going to rat us out?"

Natasha waved a hand dismissively.

"Darling, I try to stay as far away from Atlantean politics as I can," she said. "I take it you didn't grow up there?"

Echo remained silent. The Lady shrugged.

"Your people have wonderful magical artifacts to trade, but they are collectively deranged sometimes," she said. "Trust me. The last thing I want to do is involve myself in that mess."

"How generous of you," Artem said, an edge in his voice.

"Oh, I know what you are," Natasha said. "I thought the Amazons threw their sons off cliffs onto rocks? How'd you get so lucky?"

Artem remained silent, just as Echo had.

"Ah," she said. "Sensitive point. Right. But neither of you are why Barnabas called me here. You must be the poor unfortunate creature he reached out to me about."

Yuri pulled back his hood and threw his hands up in defeat.

"That's me. I'm the monster," he said. "Don't suppose you know a cure for were-shark disease."

"I'm afraid there's no cure," she said. "But I can make your transition easier, I think. If…"

She looked at Barnabas, who reached into his coat and pulled out a small book, its over made of exquisitely hand-tooled leather.

Natasha accepted the book and thumbed through a few pages.

"Barnabas Coy," she said. "Where on Earth did you get this? This book is so far beyond your abilities as a magician. I'm surprised you didn't kill yourself with it."

"I didn't kill myself with it because I'm not stupid enough to try to cast the spells in it," Barnabas said. "But I'm betting they're worth something to you though."

Natasha nodded almost imperceptibly.

"I know most of the spells in this book already," she said. Barnabas opened his mouth to argue, but she cut him off. "No, no, hold your tongue before you say something you'll regret, Barnabas. You know I trade in information. Just because I know the spells doesn't mean I can't turn a profit on this little tome."

"It'll serve as payment," Barnabas said.

"Coy, this book is worth far more than teaching a fledgling lycanthrope how not to eat his friends," she said. "I'm going to have to ask you to request something else from me before we leave here today, because I refuse to be in your debt."

"I won't hold you to it. Consider it a tip," Barnabas said.

"Not," Natasha said. "I balance my ledgers. Now think about what else I can do while I talk to our little friend here."

"Little friend," Yuri said. "You know how to make a guy feel special, lady."

Natasha smirked as if holding back a dirty joke, but said nothing. Instead, she grabbed Yuri buy the head, pressing her palms into his temples.

"They were-sharks are more primal than a lot of the other shapeshifters," she said, closing her eyes. Echo watched as Yuri's expression seemed to fade into a blank calmness. "All lycanthropes are given to uncontrolled rage and hunger, but you'll need to be especially careful of that."

"So probably I should see my psychiatrist more often?" Yuri said.

Natasha laughed. Echo found it to be both terrifying and enthralling. A silver bell in a dark night.

"Don't stray far from the sea. It will call you back. Let it," she said. "It's where you belong now. The ocean is your home. If you fight that, you'll never be happy. The transformations will be worse."

"I haven't… transformed yet," Yuri said. "Will it hurt?"

"It will if you fight it," Natasha said. "You need to accept the two parts of yourself. You, and the monster inside you, you'll either work together to survive, or you'll drive each other mad."

"I like option A," Yuri said. "Why are you holding my head?"

"I'm casting a spell," she said. She kissed him on the forehead, then traced a symbol with her fingertip on the skin where her lips touched him. "There. That might help you a bit."

"What did you just do to me," Yuri said.

"I gave you the magic equivalent of a mood stabilizer," she said. Again, Yuri searched her face to see if he was being made fun of. Clearly he couldn't tell, and Echo couldn't figure it out either.

Natasha reached into her pocket and pulled out a slip of parchment. She handed it to Yuri, but addressed her statement to Barnabas.

"Those are a list of mystic wards he should have tattooed on himself as soon as possible," she said. "There are calming techniques other shapeshifters use, but it's... different for were-sharks. Do you know how wolves or tigers or bears can be trained to comply with human wishes? They can be taught to be an ally or a friend?"

"I really don't like where this is going," Yuri said.

"Sharks can't be trained," Echo said.

Natasha favored her with a radiant smile.

"Exactly," she said. She turned to Yuri. "The sad state of you is that your monster can't be reasoned with in the same ways that other shapeshifters can master their inner demons. But with the right spells, you can harness the creature you'll become rather than be devoured by it."

"This sounds absolutely horrible, and I want to thank you for explaining how horrible my life will be from now on in such clear and concise terms," Yuri said.

"I'm always happy to help," she said.

"I've fought were-sharks before," Artem chimed in. "They don't seem out of control, at least outside of their Frenzy ritual. Why would Yuri be different?"

"They're never truly in control," Barnabas said. "It's like anything. They're accustomed to it. But there's a reason were-sharks don't usually live among other men and women. They keep to themselves because they know to do otherwise puts them at risk."

"Why don't they do what you're telling me to do?" Yuri said. "Are you saying my people suffer for no reason?"

"Your people?" Echo said. "That was quick."

"Acceptance, Echo," Yuri said. "I'm on the 'acceptance' stage of grief."

"They don't want to, for one," Natasha said. "Why should they?

They're free men. Wild creatures. They live on the edge of the world. It's where they belong. But they're born to it. You weren't. You'd have to give up everything you've ever known. They simply... live in the way they always have."

"Also, they don't have someone like Natasha Grey to help them," Barnabas said.

"For a fee," she said. "Speaking of. I'm not leaving here without settling our debt, Coy."

Barnabas nodded. He leaned in and whispered something into Natasha's ear. She grinned wickedly.

"Well, I'll have to get back to you on that," she said.

"I assumed you don't just carry those sorts of things around," Barnabas said.

"You are a crafty little man, despite your shortcomings as a wizard," Natasha said.
She smoothed her skirt and stepped away from Yuri. Clearly, Echo sensed, the session was over.

"Get those tattoos soon, darling. Better to not risk him having an episode," she said.

"We'll take him to an artist right here on New Tortuga," Barnabas said.

"I never, ever wanted a tattoo in my life," Yuri said. "And now I'm going to have a bunch of magical tattoos. I'm going to look like the painted man over there."

"Mine are mostly spells and wards as well, Yuri," Barnabas said. "I'll take you to someone I trust."

"See, that doesn't mean much when I don't actually trust you," Yuri said.

"I'll leave you to it," the Lady said. She made a strange gesture with her hand, and a doorway of light appeared behind her. She walked toward it, then spoke over her shoulder.

"I'll have those items delivered for you, Barnabas," she said. "Then our scales are balanced."

"Of course," Barnabas said. "Thank you. And hello to our mutual friend if you see him."

"The Doctor's been quiet for some time," Natasha said. "But I suspect I'll see him soon. I'll give him your regards."

And with that, she disappeared through the doorway. The room went dark again. No one spoke for a long moment.

"Well, that was bizarre," Echo said.

"That woman was at least half-demon," Artem said.

"More than half at this point," Barnabas said.

"Do tattoos hurt?" Yuri said.

'Depends on where you get them," Barnabas said.

"Where do I have to get mine?" Yuri said.

"Where they hurt," Barnabas said.

"I hate you so much," Yuri said.

Chapter 43: A royal prison

Rhegis awoke in pain, a deep throbbing in his muscles, his vision blurred. All, he assumed, the after-effects of poisoning. But I'm alive, the king thought. I'm alive, and my men are all dead.

My sister's soldiers killed them.

He rolled onto his side, groaning as sharp spikes of discomfort shot through his torso. He struggled to sit up. The room was dark, but that didn't make it any harder to tell right away it was a cell. He'd been imprisoned. He placed his feet on the floor—softly carpeted, he noted, far nicer than any ordinary prisoner might expect—and his fingertips told him the bedding he'd been wrapped in was also of fine material. Clearly they think it's important to keep me comfortable, if caged.

"Is that you I hear moaning, Regent?" a friendly voice called out in the darkness.

"Brendis," Rhegis said. His father's friend, the retired senator. His ally. Why would he be here, unless... "They've imprisoned you too."

"Aye, they have," Brendis said. He sounded tired, but not unwell. "And most of your supporters in the government. At least the ringleaders."

Rhegis laughed.

"We must be a very small group then," he said bitterly. "I didn't know I had many allies."

"More than you know, son," Brendis said. "A coup. Can you believe that? There hasn't been a coup in Atlantis since the city fell into the sea."

"A first time for everything," Rhegis said.

"Better if there weren't," Brendis said. "You sound hurt."

"Some kind of poison dart," Rhegis said. "A paralytic. I'll be fine."

Brendis sighed.

"Well, they want us alive," he said. "Hopefully that means they hope to change our minds and not intend to publicly execute us."

"I can't imagine the people will stand for that," Rhegis said. "A change in leadership, fine, but public executions?"

"We're in a dark time, my liege," Brendis said. "Never put your faith in the common man during dark times."

"You never struck me as a pessimist, old friend," Rhegis.

"My cheery disposition has been somewhat muddied by the fact that I'm in a cage," Brendis said.

Rhegis' stomach turned as he realized there was a voice missing in this conversation.

"Where's Kara?" Rhegis asked.

Brendis laughed.

"Hopefully giving them a run for their money," Brendis said. "When they came for me, she escaped. She's gone into hiding."

"Your daughter, the politician, has gone into hiding," Rhegis said.

"Let it not be said that the Kor family lacks ancillary talents," Brendis said. He sighed. "I really didn't think your sister had it in her, Regent."

"You can dispense with the honorariums, Brendis. I'm a prisoner just like you. Call me by my first name," Rhegis said. "And I don't know if this was entirely my sister's plan. She seemed shocked when her soldiers used lethal force on mine."

"Her cabal, then," Brendis said. "The warmongers are a ruthless lot. Most of them came into power by making the hard choices. Maybe they toughened her up. Maybe the turned her into one of them."

"Or maybe they're using her," Rhegis said.

"She's been the biggest critic of your father's isolationist policies of her generation," Brendis said. "If they're using her, she's using them as well."

Rhegis pressed his face into the bars of his cell. The metal was damp—the prisons were capable of being vented with water to keep prisoners who need contact with the ocean to survive. That included Atlanteans too, unfortunately.

"What are we going to do, Rhegis?" Brendis said. The tone of the statement was like a needle in the king's heart—his old friend's voice sounded lost and fearful, and it had been years since anyone other than Reina had called him by his given name.

He felt very alone, and had failed all of those who put their trust in him.

"We'll find a way through this," Rhegis said, but he was unable to convince himself this was true.

Chapter 44: The pirate and the spy

Echo was entertained to know they'd finally found something that could make Artem smile after his loss. That something was Yuri whining in pain as he squirmed in a tattoo artist's chair, but still, it was good to see the Amazon happy.

"These tattoos couldn't go somewhere with fewer nerves?" Yuri said. The artist, a man the size of a small hill with a gleaming bald head and a black beard intricately braided like sculpture, had Yuri pinned into an ancient wooden chair as he worked, drawing an arcane symbol onto Yuri's ribcage.

"Would you rather it on your face?" Barnabas said.

Yuri had quite an audience. Apparently most of the customers at this tattoo parlor—a weirdly ordinary place in the market district of New Tortuga, looking more like a barber shop than a pirate's haven—had never seen someone less willing to go under the needle and many of the regulars, painted in garish tattoos themselves, were watching the spectacle with great amusement.

"Where does the next one go?" Yuri said.

"Armpit," the artist muttered. Yuri's face faded into a ghastly green-white hue.

"What?"

"He's kidding," Barnabas said. "Next one's on your back."

"Oh good," Yuri said.

"Right on the spine," Barnabas said, smirking. "It's going to hurt like hell. Tattooing over the spine makes you think you're going to pee yourself."

Yuri started to complain, but the artist pushed him back into the chair with such force he couldn't get the words out.

"Please tell me there's more tattoos," Artem said to Echo. "I could watch this all day."

"Don't be mean," Echo said.

"I'm not being mean," Artem said. "He's so dramatic. I've been stabbed and complained less than this."

"He's adjusting,' Echo said.

"Very slowly," Artem said, smiling radiantly. He's a radiant being, Echo thought. She wondered if all Amazons looked like walking, talking art the way Artem did.

Barnabas, on the other hand, had clearly tired of listening to Yuri's complaining. He put a hand on Echo's shoulder. "I'm stepping outside before I feel the need to put him out of his misery," Barnabas said.

"I'll come with you," Echo said. Yuri was her best friend, but he dealt with fear and pain by talking, and she had her limits.

"I'll keep an eye on him, make sure he doesn't get out of line," Artem said.

Barnabas raised an eyebrow at him.

"You sure?"

"I'm sorry," he said. "I think this is hysterical."

Barnabas shook his head and left the salon. Echo trailed behind him.

"More than half my body is covered in tattoos, and I never complained like that," Barnabas said.

"Well, everyone has a different tolerance for pain," Echo said. Barnabas rolled his eyes. "Will those really help him?"

Barnabas nodded and leaned against the side of the building.

"Mystical tattoos are an ancient tradition," Barnabas said. "Magicians have used them forever. They work."

He tapped a mazelike pattern on his neck.

"This wards off evil spirits," he said. "Not all of them. But the kind that want to steal your essence."

He showed her the back of his hand, where a colorful, stylized sun adorned his skin.

"This steadies my hands when I cast spells. Not every magician needs this, but it's a cheat. A trick."

"What are the words on your chest," Echo said. She could see fine black script peeking out from the collar of his Henley-style shirt. Barnabas pulled the fabric back a bit, laughing.

"That's just poetry. That one's for me."

"What is it?" Echo asked.

"From Tennyson's 'Ulysses,'" Barnabas said. "It says: 'Come my friends, 'Tis not too late to seek a newer world.'"

"My mom loved Tennyson," Echo said. "Wasn't that one about sailing?"

Barnabas chuckled.

"It's about an aged king who wants to explore and adventure again," Barnabas said. "'To strive, to seek, to find, and not to yield.'"

Echo smirked at him.

"You don't strike me as the poetry type," she said. "Or as someone who sees himself in an old Greek king."

"Ulysses was a wise trickster," Barnabas said. "If I'm lucky enough to live long enough to grow old, I'd like to be like him some day."

"Before all this began, I thought growing old was something we could count on," Echo said.

"We live a dangerous life," Barnabas said. "But none of us are guaranteed a long life, Echo. You do what you can with the time you're given, and you fight like hell for as much time as you can."

"Spoken like a man who has more honor than he likes the world to think he has," a stranger's voice said.

Barnabas reached for his pistol; Echo drew the long knife she'd kept sheathed at her back. The stranger, a thick-bodied, hooded figure, made a calming gesture with one hand. Echo watched the other, half-expecting a weapon, but she saw instead that his arm was in a sling.

"Now, now, Barnabas Coy," he said. "You know me. No need for dramatics."

Barnabas took his hand off his holster and took a hesitant step forward.

"Is that really you?" he said. The figure drew his hood back, revealing an older man, something vaguely alien about him. He had a full white beard, bald on the top of his head, the rest gathered into a ponytail in the back. His face was covered in recently healed cuts. Despite his wounded arm, the stranger clearly carried himself like a fighter.

"You're a hard one to find, Coy," the man said. "I thought if I waited here on New Tortuga long enough, you'd show."

"I've been busy," Barnabas said. His eyes darted to Echo. "Doing the job you hired me to do."

The old man let out a hissing, pained laugh.

"Bet you never bargained you'd actually have to earn that money," he said. "I'm surprised you haven't cut your losses."

"It... became personal," Barnabas said.

"It often does, doesn't it," the man said. "And this must be the one."

"The one would like to be spoken to as if she's a person and not a package," Echo said.

The old man's face burst into a wide, white grin.

"Oh, little one, you have your father's eyes," the man said. "It's a strange thing seeing you. I've known about you your whole life, but I've never set eyes on you."

"Are either of you going to tell me who this is?" Echo said.

"Echo, this is..." Barnabas started.

"My name is Grimmin," the man said. "And I've stood by your father's side for longer than you've been alive."

"What are you doing here, Grimmin?" Barnabas said. Echo caught a tone in his voice she hadn't heard before. For someone as sly as Barnabas, she realized, she'd never heard true suspicion in his tone. Not like this.

"Tell you the truth, son, I came looking to make sure Echo here was safe," Grimmin said. He gestured at his battered body. "Clearly someone else wanted to make sure I didn't find you."

"What happened?" Echo said.

"I was ambushed," Grimmin said. "A trained attack beast of some kind. I didn't get a good look. Barely got away alive."

"But you did," Barnabas said. "You have to understand, Grimmin, we've been on the run for weeks. You showing up here…"

"I'm not going to almost rip my own arm off just to make sure you think I'm on your side, boy," the old man said. "And I found you because finding things is what I do."

"So, you've found us," Echo said. She eyed the street, watching for anyone who might be listening. *When did I become so paranoid?* She thought. *When did I start looking for enemies in every shadow?* "Now what?"

Grimmin raised one white, bushy eyebrow.

"When I came looking for you, I expected to find a helpless girl and a barely trustworthy thief," he said. "But I see someone who can hold a knife like a killer, and a man who has finally accepted that he's better than he ever expected of himself. And if I'm not mistaken, you're traveling with the last son of the Amazons, as well as a shapeshifter."

"The shapeshifter's not exactly reliable," Barnabas said.

"What are you saying?" Echo said. "I'm getting tired of having clandestine conversations in the street."

"I'm saying," Grimmin said, "That your father's life is in danger, and I think you might be able to help me rescue him."

Chapter 45: All for one

"This sounds like something out of *Game of Thrones*," Yuri said.

They'd retrieved Yuri from the tattoo parlor and, along with Artem, retired to a room in a nearby inn where Grimmin had been hiding out, waiting and hoping to catch Barnabas here. The old soldier tried to explain the infighting in Atlantis, but none of it felt real to Echo, and clearly Yuri thought it had a fictional vibe to it.

"I don't understand," Echo said. "Why would... my aunt? She's my aunt, right? Why would my aunt betray her own brother? IS this some sort of right of Atlantean passage? Do I come from a long line of backstabbers?"

"That's not entirely inaccurate," Barnabas said.

"Our people have always played against each other for power and influence," Grimmin said. "But humans aren't all that different, right? Your history is littered with betrayal."

"It just feels so... personal," Echo said.

"The different stances on the surface world are personal. To all Atlanteans," Grimmin said. "You outnumber us immensely. But your people are killing the oceans, and by default, killing our way of life. Killing us, really. Many thought your grandfather was too weak-willed for not warring with the surface."

"And now my aunt wants to start that war," Echo said.

"Worse. She wants to start humanity fighting against itself," Grimmin said. "She wants to instigate a war to weaken the surface world so she can then move in and claim victory."

"Humans are really good at fighting each other," Yuri said. "Gotta give us credit for that."

"But—okay. But. What can we do?" Echo said. "We're not an army. We're not from Atlantis. Why would anyone listen to us?"

"I just want your help getting Rhegis out of Atlantis," Grimmin said. "If he's free, he can lead the opposition. And there will be an opposition. This is not a cut and dry issue for Atlanteans. Many, many live in justifiable fear of humanity."

"There's something you're not saying," Echo said. She caught Barnabas' eye. He nodded. "What is it you're not saying?"

"You're... in the end, you're the heir to the throne," he said. "Should Reina and Rhegis die in this quite little civil war, you are the last of the line. You're the only one left."

"So, she's the *King Ralph* of Atlantis, basically," Yuri said.

"You think Atlanteans will respect the line?" Artem chimed in. The Amazon had remained stoically quiet through the entire discussion, but she could see him strategizing, thinking their position through.

"I know they will," Grimmin said. "Well, enough of them."

"Enough to sway things in Rhegis' favor?" Artem said.

"Enough to get them to hesitate to betray their entire system of government," Barnabas said. "That's why she sent her people after us, isn't it?"

"I don't think she wanted you dead," Grimmin said. "I've found out who she had directing the attacks on you and your family, Echo. The man she sent is an agent and assassin named Barracuda. If she wanted you snuffed out, he would have done it easily that first night. Capturing you is important to her somehow. My guess would be leverage over her brother."

"Say that name again," Artem said. His tone had changed— gone was the cool, analytical calmness he'd had moments before, replaced instantly with a hot, deadly anger.

"Barracuda," Grimmin said. "Not his birth name, of course, but…"

"I'll help you," Artem said. He glanced at Echo apologetically. "I'll help you, old man. Barracuda murdered my husband. If helping you puts me close enough to him to cut his heart out, I'll join you."

"So much for sticking with us to the end, huh," Yuri said.

"You know why I came along," Artem said. "And for what it's worth, I think we should all go. Aren't you tired of running? At best, you'll be hunted the rest of your days. At worst, this half-queen of Atlantis unleashes war on the surface and gets everyone killed anyway. At least we'll die with a sword in our hands."

Echo rubbed her eyes. The way Grimmin said "we" earlier, including her in the ranks of the Atlanteans… this was not what she was expecting. He seemed to consider her one of them. Was it that easy for him? Would others be so easily swayed? Or would she be a pariah, some half-breed mutant from the surface, their king's child of shame? And now she had Artem making a ferocious, but not illogical, case to go.

Even if they failed, even if she died trying… would it be worth it? Just to see this city at the bottom of the sea? Her ancestral home? My father is king of Atlantis, she thought. I should see the place before it's gone.

"He never came to see me," Echo said.

Artem bowed his eyes and crossed his arms across his chest. Yuri looked at her with a worried expression. Barnabas was unreadable behind his rough beard, but stared intently.

"Princess," Grimmin said.

"Don't call me that. If I were your princess of Atlantis my father would have come for us. He would have… he would have taken better care of us. Not sent his manservant to pay some drifter to keep an eye on us to make sure we still existed."

She shrugged at Barnabas.

"Sorry," she said.

"If the name fits," he said, not looking the least bit offended.

"Where was he? Was this guy so important he couldn't show up at a birthday party, or, like, my junior prom, or a swim meet or something? And my mom. Do you know how much she loved him? She never stopped loving him. I knew. I *knew*. I always knew. She looked out at the ocean like someday he'd rise up out of it and everything would be right with the world."

"Echo," Yuri said.

"And now she's dead. She'd dead because of him, and my best friend will never be the same again, and I'm homeless and hunted and afraid, I'm so tired of being afraid, do you know that?" Echo said. "And now you want me to go rescue this father I never met? Maybe I should let his sister burn the world to the ground. Maybe that's what we all deserve."

Grimmin exhaled. His body shook, and it took Echo a moment to realize it wasn't anger, but pain. The man had been standing up through sheer force of will for how long, she couldn't tell. And now he was being scolded by another man's daughter for things he could do nothing about.

But when he spoke, his voice was tight with sadness, and soft with understanding.

"We live at the bottom of the sea," Grimmin said. "Some of us never see the sun. I don't think a lot of Atlanteans know what they're missing, never coming to the surface. Humans, Atlanteans, Amazons… it doesn't matter who you are. You get caught up in your place in the universe and you don't leave it and then one day you wake up and realize… you never saw the sun."

The old spy smiled at Echo. There was real pain in it.

"Your father loved the sun. Do you know how strange a thing that is, for an Atlantean? He would sneak away to the surface as a boy. I only knew him as the king's willful child then, not as the king I would come to serve, not even as the man I know and respect. He knew this world was bigger than his people would admit it was. He knew his father was afraid of acknowledging how big this world is. Your father fell in love with the surface. He fell in love with your mother. But duty is a terrible thing to carry, Princ—Echo. No man or woman has ever been true to their duty without making sacrifices that broke their heart."

"Did he miss her?" Echo said. "Did he ever wonder about me?"

Grimmin rubbed at his eyes with his good hand.

"On a clear day, we can see light from the surface trickle down to the city," he said. Fractured beams of light. Sun storms, we call them. And I would catch him staring out the window, watching those glittering beams of light falling, and I'd know what he was thinking about."

"I don't know if I believe you," Echo said.

"You don't have to," Grimmin said. "That's okay. But Echo, your father never wanted to rule. He never wanted to be king. He wanted to be free. If he were a lesser man, he would have walked away and left Atlantis behind. But he knew he was the only thing keeping his people safe. He gave up the life he should have had to hold everyone's world together. And now I'm afraid they'll kill him for it. I wish to all the gods he'd been able to walk away all those years ago. But heavy hangs the head, Echo. He broke his back holding Atlantis together."

Echo sighed, biting her lip. She found herself more afraid to meet her father than she was of dying. But mom would want me to meet him, she thought. Maybe just once. Just to know where I came from. Maybe to understand why her parents did what they did. Or to understand myself just a little more.

"I'll go," she said. "I don't know how much help I can be, but I'll go."

Artem put a hand on her shoulder. She grasped that hand and squeezed. The Amazon smiled at her.

"By your side," he said.

"Don't give me that," Echo said. "You were going to leave us five minutes ago."

"I knew you'd go," Artem said. "You're too much of a hero to refuse."

"I'll go too," Yuri said.

"No, you won't," Echo said.

"What am I going to do, stay here on Treasure Island?" he said. "These people killed Meredith, and Merrick, and they want to kill you. I'm not going to stay behind while you risk your life. You're all I have left, Echo. You're it. Wherever you go, I go."

"I love you, Yuri," Echo said.

"Love you too, kid," he said, smirking. "And besides, I'm a were-shark now. Don't we want to see what I can do with these powers in a real fight? I think it'll be pretty amazing."

Everyone turned their attention to Barnabas, who sat on the armrest of a chair, flexing his fingers nervously.

"Your work's done, Coy," Grimmin said. "Whatever you've been paid, you've earned it ten times over. This isn't your fight."

"It's not," Barnabas said. "I don't owe Atlantis a damned thing."

"This is it, then," Echo said.

"If I were smart, it would be," Barnabas said.

"You're not as smart as you think you are," Echo said.

"I'm really not," Barnabas said. "And I don't want to be remembered as a thief and a drifter."

"You're in?" Yuri said.

"What can I say," Barnabas said. "Echo brings out the best in me."

Echo and Barnabas exchanged knowing grins.

"I can see your tombstone now," Yuri interrupted. "Barnabas Coy: A thief and a drifter, but he died a hero."

"Oh, who are you kidding," Barnabas said. "If we all die down there none of us is getting a tombstone."

"Looks like you've got us," Echo said to Grimmin, whose smile finally reached his eyes. "So: what's next?"

Chapter 46: One last look at the sky

Grimmin left the group to go find a vessel that could safely take them to Atlantis, the ghost ship lacking, of course, submersible abilities. Barnabas sent Echo, Yuri, and Artem back to the ship while he accompanied the old spy on his shopping trip, ostensibly to help by calling upon his long-term contacts in New Tortuga, but he pulled Echo aside on the docks.

"I think we can trust him, but I'm not letting him out of my sight," Barnabas said. "If we're not back in a few hours, take the ship and run."

"Take the ship how?" she said. "None of us know how to sail."

"Neither do I," he said. "No excuses. Just go."

"I'm not abandoning you here," Echo said.

"Trust me, if there's any place in the seven seas I should be safe, it's New Tortuga," Barnabas said. "But with who we're up against, I don't want to take that chance. The spirits know you now. They'll listen to you if you tell them to set sail. Don't risk it. If you have a bad feeling, run."

And so, the spy and the magician disappeared into the crush of people on the New Tortuga docks, and Echo and her crew rowed the dinghy back out to their own ship.

The day was strangely still, the sky flat and blue, the harbor calm and quiet. She saw Artem tilt his head back, feeling the sun on his face.

"Are you okay?" she asked.

The Amazon smiled.

"We may never return," he said. "For all we know, we'll die in Atlantis. I want to feel the sun on my face one more time. I want to remember this."

"That is unbelievably morbid," Yuri said, nursing the patches covering his new tattoos. Blood and ink seeped through the protective cloth.

"You should enjoy the time we have here," Artem said. "There's no promise of victory, and you never know the last time you'll see something you love."

Yuri nodded silently. Echo followed Artem's lead, truly feeling the warmth of the sun on her skin. The soft touch of the sea breeze. The smell of salt and brine and oil and sweat, the smells of the harbor, the living, breathing organism this place was. I've missed so many things, she thought. I'm too young to regret the things I missed.

Yuri caught her melancholy expression. He seemed incapable of taking a moment for himself, Echo thought.

"This'll all be over soon," Yuri said. "Win or lose. At least it'll be over."

"But we'll never be the same," Echo said. "And I'm sorry for that. I'm sorry for what I've put you through. Both of you."

"You're not to blame, Echo," Artem said. "Life is a series of tests. You break, or you carry on. You can't change what's happened. You can only focus on what is to come."

"Are you really going to kill this man, the Barracuda?" Echo said.

"If, gods willing, we find him," Artem said.

"Will it make things better?" Echo asked. "It won't undo the things he's done."

"No," Artem said. "And I know revenge is a selfish act. The dead are gone. Their cares are not of this world. The people we lost are unconcerned if we avenge them or not. But we will, because…"

"Because it'll make us feel better," Yuri offered.

"Nothing will put my heart back together again, Yuri," Artem said. "But I will know this man is no longer traveling this Earth, and cannot break someone else's heart the way mine has been broken. It's a small, petty comfort. But it's the only thing I know how to do."

Echo remembered swimming in the waters outside her house, and how moving through the ocean felt like what she'd been born to do. But she hadn't had a purpose then, had she? She was aimless. Pointless. Just another bored human being, passing time quietly and without complaint, no mission, no use, no destiny.

I have a destiny now, she thought. I have a reason to be.

"This won't be our last look at the sky, Artem," she said. "We're going to succeed. And we're going to be able to come home again."

"But Echo," Artem said, without cruelty, without dramatic effect. "Do any of us have a home to return to?"

"Then let's plan on creating one when we get back," Echo said. "I don't intend to stay forever at the bottom of the sea."

"Still, best to be prepared," Artem said. "Speaking of which—Yuri?"

"Oh no," Yuri said. "What?"

"Your new powers allow you to breathe underwater, I understand," Artem said.

"So I've been told."

"Good," Artem said. "I'm going to need your earring."

Chapter 47: That's not a submarine

Neither Barnabas nor Grimmin returned looking particularly pleased with themselves. The Atlantean's body language was resigned, but what worried Yuri, looking at both men, was the mischievousness in Barnabas' eyes.

"What," Yuri said. "What did you do?"

Barnabas helped Grimmin up over the rail and onto the deck of the ghost ship. Grimmin grunted, showing his age and just how much his injuries slowed him down.

"We found transport," he said. "It's not ideal, but it'll get the five of us to Atlantis faster and safer than swimming."

"What is it," Echo asked. "I mean, you can't just go buy a submarine, right? You must need a permit for a submarine."

"Whatever it takes to get us there," Artem said. He now sported Yuri's pearl earring in the lobe of his left ear. The Amazon had taken it from Yuri, sanitized it in a bottle of rum—which Yuri firmly believed was not the right way to sanitize something—and unhesitatingly pierced his own ear with the earring's post in one shot. The ease with which Artem did this legitimately turned Yuri's stomach.

And now the earring looks better on him than it does on me, Yuri thought. I really can't win.

"It's not a submarine," Barnabas said. "It's better."

"It's not better," Grimmin said. "It's too exotic for my tastes. But as we said. It'll work."

"Define 'exotic,'" Yuri said.

***

"That is not a submarine," Yuri said.

The next morning they'd headed back to shore, Barnabas leading them to a series of caves on the far side of New Tortuga where submersible craft often docked. Barnabas felt, he said, that he should prepare them ahead of time before heading out.

No good ever comes from saying they need to "prepare" you, Yuri knew. It was the same as "maybe you should have at a seat," or "please don't get upset."

He was unquestionably upset.

The "transport" Grimmin and Barnabas had secured was not a vehicle at all, but rather a creature that looked like an enormous jelly fish, bigger than a van, and completely transparent, its skin a sort of blueish-purple gel.

"Is it alive?" Echo said.

"That's, um… yes, yes it's alive," Barnabas said.

"Does it have a name?" Echo said.

"You're worried about its name?" Yuri said. "How do we get inside? Wait, don't answer that, I already know the answer to that, don't say it…"

"Relax," Barnabas said. "It's bioengineered for this job. It's made for people to ride inside."

"Bio-engineered by *who*?" Yuri said.

"Can we not call it an it?" Echo said. "Is it a he or a she?"

"I've heard of these before, but never seen one," Artem said. "They're grindylow-made, aren't they?"

"What-made now?" Echo said.

"Wait, wait, wait, wait," Yuri said. "Grindylow are real?"

"We don't see them much on the surface, but yes," Artem said.

"Mostly to trade," Barnabas said. "Though this jellyfish was bought second-hand from a smuggler who trades with Lemuria."

"Grindylows," Yuri said.

"I think he's having an episode," Barnabas said.

"No—serious question. Are they more J.K. Rowling type grindylows, or China Mieville grindylows?" Yuri said.

"I have no idea what you're talking about," Artem said.

"Mieville," Barnabas said. Echo, Yuri, Artem, and Grimmin all turned to stare at him in shock. "What? You look at me like I don't know how to read. It gets lonely on that ghost ship. I go through a lot of books."

"We're riding in a genetically engineered jellyfish created by psychotic underwater demon creatures," Yuri said.

"I wouldn't call them demons," Barnabas said. "Psychotic isn't completely inaccurate though."

"I hate my life. I hate everything about my life," Yuri said. "I'm never going to enjoy my life again, am I?"

"Relax," Barnabas said. "What's the worst that could happen?"

"The jellyfish gets a stomach ache?" Yuri said.

"I think we should call her Jem," Echo said.

"Her?" Yuri said.

"You can't tell?" Echo said.

"I used to like my life," Yuri said. "I really did."

Chapter 48: The dead never answer back

Barnabas Coy walked the deck of his ghost ship alone, his bags packed, his spells prepared. Grimmin and Artem were gathering supplies in New Tortuga together; Echo and Yuri packing up their meager belongings and preparing to leave.

Barnabas squinted so he could watch the ghosts who inhabited this vessel move about. Testing lines, patching sails, scrubbing the deck; day to day life on sailboat, things Barnabas had never had to worry about, because the dead took better care of this ship than any living crew could. He'd never been an even remotely competent sailor. Before discovering the ghost ship, he'd been a ship's magician with several crews, making up for his lack of nautical skills by using spells to call the wind on still days, or set fire to an enemy's sails with a word, or leading them to hidden treasures through the mystical art of scrying.

But this had been his home for a long time. He felt like he knew every inch of the ghost ship, even if he had no idea how to sail it himself.

The roster of spirits had not remained constant over the years. Some, like the peg-legged buccaneer he could see in the crow's nest right now, or the French naval officer with his powdered wig, had been here when he found the ship. Others—the ghost of the teenaged girl in rich kid's polo and white shorts, the heavyset fisherman in the waterproof jumpsuit—were new additions, sailors who lost their lives recently and hadn't found their way to the afterlife yet. Sometimes the ghost-sailors just disappeared, and Barnabas knew that those souls had found their way to whatever afterlife they expected to go to, that they'd finally made peace with being dead and were willing to give up this world. He missed some of the familiar faces, but none of the spirits ever left voluntarily. They simply moved on. And always, always, always, new spirits would find their way here. The ghost ship was a way station, a haven for those who had lived their lives on the ocean and were not ready to leave it. All were welcome, for as long as they wanted to stay.

A place for lost souls. Sort of like Barnabas himself.

"Hey, guys," Barnabas said.

Some of the ghosts took notice of him talking, looking up from their tasks; others simply continued with what they were doing. Barnabas had, over the years, taken to talking to himself frequently. To hear him speaking out loud was nothing new.

"You should probably listen to this," he said. "Well, some of you, at least. Someone should know. We're leaving for a bit."

More of the ghosts paid attention now. The French naval officer folded his arms and listened intently from the ship's wheel.

"We might not come back. I might not come back," Barnabas said. "I mean I plan to. I want to. I don't intend to die out there. But I just wanted to let you know that there's a chance something might happen."

Now most of the crew had begun listening. Most still puttered at their tasks, but their attention was on him.

"If I don't come back, you should move on," he said. "I know you need a living captain to give you direction, but I think you can leave New Tortuga if you'd like. Someone will replace me just like I replaced the man before me. The ghost ship always has a captain. Fate makes sure of that."

Now everyone had stopped working. Barnabas had an audience,

a semi-circle of ghosts, all listening in eerie silence to his words.

"And I want you to know," he said. "It's been an honor. You deserved a better captain than me, but I hope I've done my best to take you to interesting places, to let you see the seas you so loved in life, to make sure your talents, your art, was not wasted. That's all I wanted for you. I hope I haven't let you down."

The dead cast their eyes upon him, hundreds, maybe thousands of years of history among them. His silent crew, the caretakers of a vessel that would sail the seven seas long after Barnabas Coy was gone and forgotten.

"Who knows," he said. "If I die down below, maybe I'll return here anyway. Someone can teach me how to tie a proper knot. Or maybe I'll just swab the deck."

He'd swear, later, that he saw a few smiles among the ghostly faces, but he'd never be completely sure.

And as always, the dead never answered back. It was simply the way of things.

Chapter 49: Eyes on Atlantis

Someday, if I survive this, Echo thought, I'm going to have a lot of trouble reconciling my sense of wonder with my sense of repulsion.

The jellyfish—which she forcefully convinced everyone to refer to by name, persistently correcting everyone relentlessly during the first few hours of their journey—was surprisingly spacious. For the most part, they sprawled out on the "floor"—what part of the jellyfish's anatomy Echo didn't know and didn't want to know either—while Grimmin used patterns along one of the walls like some sort of steering device.

Artem sat lotus style, sometimes meditating, sometimes sleeping, once attempting to sharpen his swords, but Echo snapped at him for possibly leaving metal shavings in Jem's belly. Barnabas studied a set of laminated scrolls, which he said were potentially useful spells for the upcoming battle. He seemed more lost than she'd ever seen him, and wondered if he regretted his decision not to stay on the surface.

Yuri mostly looked uncomfortable and panicked.

As for Echo herself… she listened to the sea.

Ever since the dreams started, she realized she could sense things in the water. Not telepathy, really, but something like it. She could feel a pod of dolphins miles away, playing in the waves. She felt the stabbing pain of fear in a school of fish and knew they were being hunted, rounded up in a vortex by sailfish. It seemed the more complex the animals, the better she could sense them—the dolphins all but spoke to her, while the fish were waves of instinct and emotion. She tried to read Jem's mind, but the jellyfish was such a simple organism, her thoughts so uncomplicated, that there was little there to sense but basic instincts.

For most of the journey, they stayed close enough to the surface that Echo could see the sky through the duel filters of water and jellyfish skin. The vastness of the water around her, the way the blue went on forever, blurred out by the fog of war, it all felt endless. She felt incredibly small. Inconsequential. The way everyone should around nature, she thought. We are such tiny parts in the great machine.

"How long will we have to wait to get there?" Yuri said, breaking the silence.

"In a rush to battle, Yuri?" Artem said.

"I'm bored to death," Yuri said.

"It won't take as long as it should, given how far we are from Atlantis proper," Grimmin said. "But we're following the old paths."

"Oh, we know all about the old paths," Yuri said. "We have spent some time on the old paths, we have."

Echo tuned them out, letting her mind stretch across the miles of the ocean. She sensed something—distant, enormous, ancient, its thoughts only on hunting, as it lazily drifted in search of prey...

Hours stretched on. She dreamed; she traveled; she slept.

And then she felt a hand on her shoulder.

"Echo," Artem whispered.

It was night; the ocean a deep an impenetrable blue. On the horizon, something glowed gold and white and pale, pale green, a crystal dropped at the bottom of the ocean. She stood up, pressed her hands against the clear wall of the jellyfish's belly, her eyes widening in disbelief.

"It's a city," she said.

"It's your city," Grimmin said. "Welcome to Atlantis."

It was hard to make out the full dimensions of the place at this distance—a sprawling skyline at the bottom of the ocean, with squat, rounded buildings below and tall, twisting spires shooting up like daggers. She could make out small crafts rocketing about like underwater scooters, and creatures, manta rays and giant eels and massive groupers used like horses and pack animals. Even in the night, Atlantis seemed to bustle with urban life. A living, breathing city beneath the waves.

"It doesn't seem possible," she said.

"It shouldn't be possible," Barnabas said. "But Atlantis exists anyway."

"Bringing civilization to a place that should be wild and untamed," Artem said. "Even in the circles I've traveled in, no one knows of any place like Atlantis."

"In another lifetime, I could've been born here," Echo said.

"In another lifetime," Grimmin said. "I'm sorry this is your first introduction to your city. The daughter of Rhegis should have been welcomed with fanfare, not smuggled in under the cover of darkness."

"They're not going to welcome me, are they," Echo said.

"Why wouldn't they welcome you? You're awesome. You have a fantastic fauxhawk," Yuri said.

"I don't envy you," Artem said. "I've always wondered what it would be like to go home, but I've been too convinced I'd be barred at the gates."

"Under normal circumstances," Grimmin said, pausing to take a deep breath. "I think they might be afraid of you. Atlanteans are distrustful of the surface, even those who don't want a war with humanity. But if you can stop that war from starting…"

"Rock star status," Yuri said.

"I'd be happy with simply not being thrown out on my backside," Echo said.

"You're going to save their kingdom, Echo," Barnabas said, no humor or levity in his tone. "If these snobs reject you after you save their little world... they can go to hell."

"How do you really feel, Barnabas," Yuri said.

"What happens next, Atlantean," Artem asked Grimmin. "Do we walk up to the royal palace and knock?"

"We'll meet with some of Rhegis' supporters first, too get ourselves situated and find out what has changed since I last checked in."

"And then we rescue my father, stop my aunt, and prevent a war," Echo said.

"That's it?" Yuri said. "This'll be super easy."

Chapter 50: Bombs will fall

I have a war council, Reina thought, looking around the table at those who had followed her down this path. Her cadre of influencers—Senator Cartay and Dame Rois, the merchant Gormlin and the historian Farris—sat around her in one of the Atlantean palace's grand meeting rooms. With them, one of the city's most powerful generals, a battle-scarred veteran called Pol. General Pol had remained quietly neutral throughout the subtle power play between Reina and her brother, but in the final hours, Rois and Cartay had wooed him to their side.

Somewhere in the shadows, Barracuda skulked, on the pretense of acting as her bodyguard. But his role was so much more now. He was her triggerman. He would be the one who would activate the land-dwellers' weapons.

"We're in agreement then," Reina said.

"It will be done as you command," Cartay said, his face blank.

"I didn't bring you hear to simply agree with me," Reina said. "I want real input. Speak freely."

"Launching the human weapons from two of their war machines makes sense," Rois said. "Holding the remaining submersibles for either future attacks or as collateral in negotiations leaves us in a position of strength."

"And the choice of targets will maximize the destruction above," Farris said. "It will set two of their greatest powers against each other, using weapons of their own design. Holding the other machines in our pockets also allow us to start a secondary war between next-tier nations to sow more chaos if the initial attack does not whittle down their numbers sufficiently."

"You don't think they'll try to retaliate against us first," Reina said.

"By all indications, your highness, they still consider us nothing more than a myth," Farris said. "One wonders how they ever evolved to be the dominant species on the surface."

"But if they do, our forces stand ready," the general said. "They have numbers, but they also have no experience fighting a real war beneath the surface. And our intelligence shows that while they have great weapons of war and superior numbers, they have absolutely no affinity for magic. Our arcane defenses will be something they've never encountered before."

Reina's mouth tightened.

"How is morale, General Pol," Reina said. "I know my brother was not without his supporters."

"Your troops will follow orders," Pol said. "At the end of the day, they are soldiers of Atlantis, not private citizens who can choose their actions based on their own personal whims."

"And the people? We feared there might be insurrection," Reina said. "Things remain quiet?"

"Indeed, they do," Gormlin said in his weirdly silky voice. "There are those who grumble, but Atlantis is still well-fed and secure. They won't rise in greater numbers as long as there is stability. And if you can bring them a victory against those who are poisoning their waters and causing such devastation... I think you'll be pleasantly surprised how quickly they fall in love with your reign, Majesty."

"And we'll monitor the surface reaction closely," Reina said.

"We've trained and deployed every available magician with an inclination toward scrying," Farris said. She, like Reina, was an adept with magic herself, if not fully trained as a sorcerer. "We've also backwards-engineered much of the communications equipment on the stolen submersibles. Their technology is not as complicated as we'd expect from such a powerful people. It gives us hope that much of their technology is subpar compared to Atlantean tech."

"Good," Reina said. "If they turn their attention toward us, I want Atlantis to be ready. And if they don't, I want a front row seat to their destruction."

She felt a gnawing in her gut the more specific the discussion got. The more real it became. Was this why Father never went to war? She thought. Did he know how terrifying it is? Was he pushed to inaction not by his own philosophies, but because he knew the weight of the things it would take to bring Atlantis into this new era? What it would take to save their people?

Because, she thought, Atlantis was so much worse than she even knew before the coup. The information she had access to now, the threats of the surface world, they were exponentially greater than what she'd suspected. This was a war they not only needed to fight—it was one they couldn't afford not to start.

But still. They'd looked at the risks. They saw the dangers. They knew the cost. And that cost would be so very, very high if anything went wrong in the slightest.

"Are you alright, my queen," Dame Rois said. The baroness had a distinct tone of worry in her voice. Reina knew the change of power had a profound effect on her own health—the bags under her eyes, the weight in her shoulders and back as if she carried a body everywhere she went.

"I'm just worried about our people," Reina said. "As always. Nothing more."

Rois nodded, though her expression hinted at silent disbelief.

"Shall we issue the commands, then, my liege," Cartay said.

Reina took a deep breath. Her throat hurt as she swallowed.

"I'd like to take the night," she said. Cartay and Pol looked frustrated; Rois concerned; Farris unreadable, and Gormlin creepily approving. "Give Atlantis one more night's peace before we thrust a war upon them."

"As you wish, my queen," General Pol said.

She dismissed the committee, telling them all to get a good night's sleep, for tomorrow everything changes. Once they were gone, the door closed behind them, she beckoned Barracuda out of hiding.

"Yes, my queen," he said.

"Double the guards on the human weapons tonight," she said.

"Of course," He said. "Is there a reason why, if I might ask?"

"Just a gut feeling," Reina said. She hadn't liked Cartay's tone. Pol was too agreeable, as was Gormlin. Rois' concern felt forced. They're waiting for me to make a mistake, she knew. They're hoping I fail. And then they'll go to war with each other to fill the power vacuum.

"It will be done," Barracuda said. "Any further instructions?"

"Make sure my brother is treated well," Reina said. It ate at her, knowing her twin was imprisoned. For all their differences, for everything they believed so divergently about. He is my brother, she said to herself. He is my responsibility.

"I'll check in on him myself," Barracuda said.

"If anyone has abused him, I'll have them killed."

"I can do that myself as well, if you'd like," Barracuda said.

"No," Reina said. "Just make sure he's safe."

The assassin bowed and made his way out of the meeting chamber, leaving Reina alone.

I was never meant to rule this place without him, she thought to herself. Rhegis, why did you have to be so wrong?

Reina sat alone in the large chamber for a long time. She thought of her past, and she wondered, with no certainty or clarity, what the future held for all of them.

Chapter 51: Gifts

The path they took into Atlantis was one reserved for spies and thieves.

Grimmin left their jellyfish transport on the outskirts of Atlantis itself, saying they'd have to approach on their own to avoid attention. Echo, sorry to see the creature go, tried to reach out to her with her mind, sending thoughts of appreciation and affection to the simple, elegant beast. The jellyfish's iridescent skin rippled as Echo attempted to connect with her thoughts, and somehow, she hoped, the message got through to the silent animal.

I don't know if she understands, Echo thought, but I'll miss her. The ocean feels so vast. We might never see this beautiful thing again.

Before they disembarked, Barnabas pulled open a waterproof bag he'd carried with him from the ghost ship.

"I brought you some surprises," he said, the closest thing he'd had to a smile on his face since they'd left the surface. He removed what looked like a half-sized trident from the bag.

"What is that, a toy?" Echo said.

"Watch," Barnabas said, and he snapped the trident with his wrist. The weapon extended full length. He tossed it to Echo.

"Little something I picked up along the way," he said. "Thought it might be convenient. Also, this."

Barnabas drew a long-bladed dagger from the bag as well. The blade was hidden by a sheath of coppery scales. This he handed to Echo.

"That's an Atlantean blade," Grimmin remarked. "And an old one too. Where did you find that?"

"In a cave on the Island of Unwanted Things," Barnabas said. "There was a corpse there, hundreds of years' dead. He carried that blade, and…"

Once again, Barnabas reached into the bag. This time, he pulled out covered in green-gold scales like armor. He handed it to Echo gently.

"Looked about your size," he said, offering it to her.

"This is…" Echo began.

"Atlantean scale to go with your Atlantean dagger," Grimmin said. "We may be sneaking you in like a bandit, but you'll be attired like a true Atlantean, girl."

Echo pulled the armor over her head, not thinking about where it had been or who wore it before. The scales draped perfectly across her shoulders, falling to just below her hips, covering her vital organs.

"I really raided the cave like a greedy thief," Barnabas said. He gave Echo a pair of gauntlets carved to look like seashells to go with the scale shirt. She slid these onto her wrists, and admired herself, fighting back a smile.

"You look like a warrior queen," Artem said. "You'd fit right in among the Amazons."

Echo laughed.

"How about just a warrior," she said.

"Got anything in there for the rest of us, Coy?" Yuri said. He had brought his own poleaxe from the ship, but the gisarme felt unwieldy in the face of fighting underwater.

"For you, I have this," Barnabas said. He unwrapped a bundled cloth and removed a leather wrist cuff. This he carried over to Yuri and strapped on his left wrist for him.

"Now I can be in a rock band," Yuri said. "We'll call ourselves Fish Food."

Barnabas ignored the quip and lifted a flap on the leather band. Inside was a small compass.

"I asked for a few artifacts from the Lady when we parted—you remember her demanding I make sure our scales were balanced," he said.

"This came from the creepy demon lady," Yuri said.

"From her personal collection, I'm sure," Barnabas said. "I was thinking—there may be a time when you lose control. When the shark inside you takes over."

"I love this line of conversation," Yuri said. "The idea of me becoming a mindless monster is so much fun."

"Listen," Barnabas said. "If you're like any other lycanthrope I've ever met, you may black out. You may run off—well, swim off. And when you wake up, since you're you and you don't know anything about sailing or navigation or the ocean…"

"You! You don't know anything about sailing or navigation either! Why do you always paint the picture that I'm the most useless person on this adventure," Yuri said.

"Because you *are* the least useful person on this adventure?" Artem offered.

Yuri pointed at the Amazon defiantly.

"Et tu, Brutus?"

"I thought inverting the statement was less offensive," Artem said.

"Yuri! Focus, Yuri. Stay with me," Barnabas said, "This is a compass. It will guide you home. Wherever you go, however far you roam listen to this compass. It will tell you where to go."

"But… where is home?" Yuri said. "We don't have a home anymore. Any of us."

Barnabas pointed at Echo. Her eyes widened.

"I didn't know where else to tell her," Barnabas said. "The Lady manipulated the compass so that Echo is your home."

"No matter where I go, this thing… will lead me back to you,"

Yuri said to Echo.

"Feels like the way it should always be, doesn't it," Echo said.

"Yeah," Yuri said. "Yeah, it does."

"I realize I'm new to the equation here, but—" Artem began to say, but before he could finish, Barnabas flipped something metal to him like a coin, flicking it with his thumb so it created a bell-like ring of nail on metal. Artem caught it easily and held it aloft.

It was a ring, carved in pale blue metal. Artem examined it for a moment, then slipped it on his left hand.

"I didn't know you cared," Artem said.

"I saw you took Yuri's earring," Barnabas said. "That'll make sure you don't drown down here. But that doesn't mean you'll swim and move easily. You're still a land-dweller at heart."

"It's a funny thing hearing that from you," Artem said. "I forget that you're half-nereid yourself."

"I know, with my dashing good looks it's easy to forget my mother was an immortal sea nymph," Barnabas said. "But that ring, it's an artifact for freedom of movement underwater. It's not perfect, but you'll be much more adept when you swim. And it'll keep you safe from the added pressure at this depth."

"He gave you a scuba ring," Yuri said. "I think that means you're officially part of our... scuba gang."

"I have other things," Barnabas said. "An oil that will keep your swords from rusting too fast underwater. A breastplate I found in the cave that... well."

Barnabas pulled the plate out of the bag, which, Echo realized, was clearly bigger on the inside than the out. It was a simple metal chest piece, molded with an eagle.

"That shouldn't exist," Artem said, his voice very soft.

"I know," Barnabas said.

"What is it?" Yuri asked.

"That's an Amazonian eagle," Grimmin said.

"Why shouldn't it exist?" Echo asked.

Artem turned the breastplate over and over in his hands.

"Because it's shaped for a man," Artem said. "There is no

reason on this blue Earth anyone should have put the Amazonian eagle on a piece of armor designed for a man's frame."

"But someone did," Echo said.

"How long have you had this?" Artem asked Barnabas. The magician shook his head.

"Not long," he said. "I went to the cave—this cave, it's a place I found as a boy, I never really went through everything that was there—but as I was searching, I found it. It's not new, Artem. It's got to be generations old."

"And it is hand-made," Artem said. "Someone spent years tooling this."

"I don't get it," Yuri said. "Who made the armor?"

"Someone like me," Artem said. "Someone who… Someone who lived. A son of the Amazons. I'm not the only one. I always thought I was the only one."

"Are you okay?" Echo said. She put a hand on Artem's shoulder. He didn't react to her touch.

"He must have been very lonely," Artem said, but Echo knew he was speaking as much about himself as about the man who made the breastplate.

"What else do you have in there, Barney," Yuri said. Barnabas pointed an angry finger at Yuri, then stopped himself.

"I've got some surprises up my sleeves yet," Barnabas said.

"Then let's get moving," Echo said. "Let's go be heroes."

Chapter 52: The resistance

Grimmin led them through the back roads and alleys of
Atlantis, water-filled passageways sculpted and scalloped like the
inside of shells. The walls ranged from volcanic stone to glassy,
glistening material like pearl, often lit by glowing globes of mystical
light, and sometimes occupied by creatures that gave off
bioluminescence in blues and greens and pinks.

They traveled in silence. Echo wasn't sure if they could even
speak, here below. Yuri and Artem swam awkwardly, unfamiliar
with the sensation, while Barnabas and Grimmin moved with the
ease of people who had done this their entire lives. Echo felt like
she should have been more like Yuri, struggling and
uncomfortable, but the fact remained that she truly felt at home
here—that same biological, shared memory that Artem had
triggered to teach her how to fight carried over to a life aquatic, it
seemed. In some ways, she felt more at home here below than she
did on the surface.

Finally, Grimmin paused at a circular door. He spun the
oversized wheel that acted as its doorknob, and entered first, alone.
A moment later, he stuck his head back out and beckoned them
inside.

Once everyone entered, Grimmin closed the door once again.

Automatically, the water level began to drop and the chamber filled with air. It a few moments, but soon they stood chamber filled with breathable oxygen, though the floor remained puddled with seawater.

"That was one of the most alarming experiences in my entire life," Artem said, holding his chest as if amazed he were still breathing.

"Oh, y'know, Echo and I have done this sort of thing before. Underwater casual strolls. We're good at it," Yuri said. "You get used to it."

Grimmin held up a hand for silence. Barnabas drew his artifact pistol, and Echo snapped her new trident to its full extension. They turned their attention to a darkened corridor, which Grimmin watched with uncomfortable anticipation.

"There's a face I never thought I'd see again," a middle-aged woman said, stepping into the light. She had what looked like a high-tech crossbow in her hand, but aimed at the floor, way from them. "We got your message, Grimmin. Didn't figure you'd be able to make it back."

"I know every back alley in this city," Grimmin said. "I'd hope I could at least sneak into it when my enemies think I'm dead."

"I hope these are allies," the woman said.

"We are," Artem said. "We're here to help."

"Got some bad news for you, then," the woman said. "I don't know if four more fighters, no matter how special you are, will be enough to make a difference."

"Well, we're here to try," Echo said.

The woman turned her full attention on Echo for the first time. Her face softened from grim to almost tearful. A smile briefly lit up her expression.

"You're her," she said. "By all the gods, you look like your father."

Echo had no answer. She lowered her weapon, but offered nothing else.

"I'm Kara," the woman said. "Kara Kor. I am—I was a senator, before Reina took control. And I was a friend of your father's. I am. I have been my whole life."

"If you've known him your whole life, I must ask," Echo said. "Did he ever talk about me?"

The woman, Kara, lowered her eyes to the floor and said nothing. He never talked to her about me. Not a lifelong friend. Just an old spy and a sketchy magician. Oh, dad, if we ever to meet, you're going to have so much to explain to me.

"It doesn't matter," Echo said. "We're not here to debate the merits of my father's parenting techniques. Tell us what we can do to help."

***

The resistance, Kara explained, had taken to moving throughout the city via ancient tunnels and abandoned sections of Atlantis.

"This city is millennia old," Grimmin explained. "We've built on top and around and through whole sections of Atlantis. No one really knows every inch of this place."

"You seem to come close," Barnabas said.

"I know enough," the old Atlantean said. "And I'm sure Reina's people know enough as well. It'll be like playing chase through a coral reef down here. Hidden cubbies, secret passageways. It won't last forever, but it'll buy us time."

"So how is this resistance going to handle... us?" Yuri said.

"You don't seem particularly warm to outsiders," Echo said. "And, well, I'm..."

"I wouldn't worry about that too much," Kara said.

"I would," Grimmin corrected her. "You're right to have concerns. We can be a xenophobic lot. We don't have a blanket rule about preventing outsiders from entering the city—we trade with other aquatic cultures in fact—but you are outsiders at a dangerous time. And then there's your heritage."

"Because I'm an accident," Echo said.

"There will be..."

"Racists," Yuri said.

Grimmin opened his mouth to speak, but closed it.

"Racist Atlanteans," Barnabas said. "I always knew you guys were kinda bigots."

"And I thought *my* people were bad," Artem said. "She's come to help and your people would turn her away because she's not a through and through, full-blooded Atlantean?"

"You aren't allowed back into your home country because of your gender," Grimmin snapped back. "Don't dare lecture me on acceptance."

"Enough," Barnabas said. "We'll cross the whole bigot path when we get there. Right now, we're here to help. Right?"

"The pirate is being the voice of reason, guys," Yuri said. "I want everyone to take note of the fact that the thieving pirate is the voice of reason."

"Thanks, Yuri," Barnabas said.

"Any time, Barney."

Kara led them to a larger space deeper in the tunnels where maybe a dozen members of the resistance were waiting. All were armed, and none of them looked particularly trusting.

"Oh hey, guys!" Yuri said. "We were just looking for the bathroom."

Several of the more brutal-looking Atlanteans trained weapons on them, while another, a burly figure with his hair braided tightly to his scalp, spoke.

"We're taking a chance letting outsiders get involved," he said. His eyes flickered between Grimmin, Kara, and Echo. "And you know she'll never be considered a true potential heir."

"That's so far beyond what we should be concerned with right now as to be a non-issue," Kara said.

"Heir to what?" Yuri said.

"I didn't come here to be an heir to anything," Echo said.

"I don't think you have a choice in the matter," Artem said.

"I suspect they're going to decide that for you," Barnabas said.

"None of it matters," Kara said. "Not if Reina's plans are followed through on. Arguing over whether we want help from a handful of outsiders when she's about to set us on a path of annihilation is worrying about the future while the seas boil."

"Enough," Echo said.

Everyone—friends, allies, and strangers alike—all turned their attention to her. She felt suddenly both very self-conscious, and very powerful.

"I don't care about where I fit into the family line. I don't care about your opinions. We're here to help, and if you want me gone when it's over, I'll leave. Maybe I don't want to stay here. Maybe I find Atlantis as distasteful as it finds me," she said. "But right now, you're telling me we can stop a war, and I can save my father. I'd suggest we discuss how we can make those things happen. Because as far as I know, we don't have a hell of a lot of time."

"Whoa," Yuri said.

"Well done," Artem whispered, so softly only Echo heard him.

Barnabas burst out laughing.

"I am so glad I came on this suicide mission," he said, clapping his hands.

Grimmin and Kara exchanged a long, knowing look.

"All right then," Kara said, opening her arms wide in a gesture of welcome. "Echo of the above, let's talk about how we can save Atlantis."

Chapter 53: Chance your arm

Echo found it hard to believe the people who sat around the great stone table with her had been so easily defeated. They knew their enemies' moves and plans; they seemed competent and dangerous; they felt ready for war.

And yet they were hiding underground, as if waiting for a savior.

What's worse, though, she thought, was the information they did have about her aunt's plants.

"They're going to launch missiles from military submarines at two different countries to set off a war," Echo said, repeating back what had just been told to her by Kara's people.

"They have more than two of your submarines, too," Kara said. "As backup plans."

"Our submarines," Yuri said, almost laughing. There was a hint of crazy in his tone Echo wasn't happy with. "Ours. Right? All humans, we own those subs."

"We've got to stop those missiles," Echo said.

"We have a lock on where one of the submarines is hidden, thanks to spies we have in Reina's ranks," Kara said. "We have Grimmin's soldiers to thank for that."

"Glad to see my espionage machine didn't fall apart in the

weeks I was gone," the spy said.

"Your attack is threefold," Artem said. "The missiles should take first priority. They cannot be allowed to launch. But you also need this king Rhegis free—if he's locked away, he's not available to help calm the panic that will inevitably erupt if your country goes to war with a foreign—an alien empire, really."

"You said threefold," Yuri said. "What's the third?"

"You've got to eliminate the queen," Artem said.

"That is cold, dude," Yuri said.

"We can't murder her," Kara said. Grimmin began to protest, but the woman silenced him with a calming gesture. "No, we need both siblings alive. They both have massive supporters among the Atlanteans. We don't know what one side will do if the other is dead. The common folk who support Rhegis remain quiet for fear he'll be executed if they revolt."

"I don't see why or how you can let her live," Artem said. "She's a danger to all of you, and to the surface world as well."

"Maybe she can be turned," Barnabas suggested. "She didn't kill you, Echo. She didn't kill your father. Her minions have killed people we care about, but those were—I hate saying this, but those were collateral damage. They were victims of circumstance. If she were truly irredeemable..."

"Merrick was not a victim of circumstance. Neither was your mother," Artem said. "You can't trust this woman."

"We need something to slow her plans," Kara said. "Something to derail her long enough for us to make sure the missile attack doesn't take place."

"I'll go to her," Echo said.

All chatter in the room went quiet.

"You'll what?" Yuri said.

"I'll walk up to her door and knock," Echo said. "She's been looking for me. I'm her flesh and blood. Even if she means to eliminate me, I must be a distraction to her, right? She'll want to at least get a look at me."

"You'll just... chance your arm," Barnabas said. "Go say hello, auntie, fancy a cuppa?"

"Got a better idea? Charge in there with all our forces and kick the door in?" Echo said.

"Sounds like a fine plan to me," Artem said.

"Fine," Barnabas said. "Let's go get this over with."

"No," Echo said. "I'll take care of my aunt I never knew I had; you will go get my father."

"Me?" Barnabas said.

"He's in the royal prisons," Grimmin said. "Locked tight behind mundane and magical defenses."

"Good thing Barnabas Coy here is a legendary magic-using thief," Echo said. "It's like we brought you on purpose."

"You're not contractually obligated to call me a thief every time you reference me, Echo," Barnabas said. "But I may... have some experience breaking out of prisons. Okay, I'll go."

"Our people have the location of the first sub. We'll send a team to the location to retake it," Kara said.

"That doesn't exactly help if we don't know where the other one will be launching from, does it," Yuri said.

"Maybe Echo will be able to tease that information out of the queen," Barnabas said.

"We also know that the queen's agent, an assassin named Barracuda, is her go-between," Kara said.

Artem stood up quickly at the sound of that name.

"Do you know here he is?" Artem said, his voice deadly calm.

"He spends most of his time in the palace currently, our sources say," Kara said. "He's her most trusted agent. We know he's also the one she trusts to make sure her brother is well cared for in the prison."

Artem's eyes darted back and forth between Echo and Barnabas.

"Go with Barnabas," Echo told him. "You'll be spotted as a threat the minute we walk in the room. I can get closer without you there."

"If you find him, you know what to do," Artem said.

"I understand," Echo said.

"What's this all about," Kara said.

"Shakespearean tragedy," Yuri said. "Just... better not to ask."

"Then we have our missions," Kara said. "Echo, your forces will be given encrypted communications devices and any intelligence we have on the palace and the prison. Good luck."

Yuri raised his hand.

"Um," he said.

"Oh," Barnabas said, looking sheepish.

"Oh, he says," Yuri muttered. "You were going to forget about me, weren't you?"

"I was hoping maybe you'd stay behind where it's safe," Echo said.

"Like hell," Yuri said. "I'm coming with you."

"That sounds like a terrible, terrible idea," Barnabas said.

"No," Artem said. "It's the perfect idea. Echo, say he's your... servant or something."

"Servant?" Yuri said, indignant.

"Whatever you need to call him to keep him with you. Because if things go wrong and you need backup, you've brought a bomb with you," Artem said.

"I don't understand," Kara said.

"Welcome to my world," Yuri said to her. Then to Echo: "If we get in trouble, I'll shark out."

"Shark out?" Echo repeated, smirking.

"I'll unleash the beast," Yuri said, flexing his bicep.

"As bad ideas go..." Barnabas said.

"It's not the worst one we've had," Echo said.

"I was going to say it is literally the worst one we've had," Barnabas said. "But it sure beats you walking into the viper's den alone."

Chapter 54: Manta Express

Echo had some concerns about finding her way to the Atlantean royal palace, but her concerns doubled when she saw how the Atlantean resistance would get her there without a guide.

"I'm not doing this," Yuri said, speaking out loud the words running through Echo's own head.

One of the Atlanteans had wrangled a giant manta, it's wingspan at least twelve feet, and lead it up to the tunnel entrance Kara had led Echo and Yuri to, far from the meeting room where the others waited.

"It's trained as transport," Kara said. "Just hold on and it'll deliver you to where you need to go."

"How will we know when we get there?" Echo said.

Kara pointed at the glittering spire in the distance, standing watch over the sleepy underwater city.

"You'll be standing in front of that," she said.

Echo swam up onto the creature's back and held on lightly near its mouth as instructed, She reached out with her mind, once again testing the strange, almost telepathic sensations she'd had with other sea creatures. To her surprise, the creatures seemed to immediately realize her connection. She felt waves of panic turn to calm, as though the creature were glad to be close to her.

"What did you just do?" Kara said.

"She talks to fish," Yuri said, joining Echo on the manta's back.

"I can't tell if you're kidding or not," Kara said. "Are you sure you're up for this?"

"Meeting my megalomaniacal aunt? I don't think I'll ever be up for it, but I'll do what I have to do to keep us safe," Echo said. "So just hang on 'til we're at the tall, pointy building."

"Simple as that," Kara said. "Good luck."

The handler released the manta, and the massive creature sailed gracefully down the exterior corridor and into a sunken courtyard that might have looked at home in ancient Greece. It swam up and over a greening stone wall, swooping through a school of tiny yellow fish.

This feels like flying, Echo thought. Her hair pulled back from her face as the manta picked up speed, taking them through a district lit entirely with golden spheres, and then through the alchemy district, where Echo could taste dangerous chemicals in the water. The streets here were painted in abstract art, beautiful and profane, subversive and a little obscene. Some of this she subconsciously understood, though the writing was in Atlantean—it was as if that institutional memory, the same that taught her how to fight, also gave her a glimpse into the language and culture here.

They passed through an underground tunnel, too dark to see, though she felt as if they were being watched the whole time, and then emerged on higher ground, over a bridge—how unnecessary a bridge felt underwater she thought, where swimming felt like flying—passing a huge, open theater, empty at this hour, its backdrop painstakingly painted like the surface world. Echo wondered if Atlanteans had the world above imprinted in their memories the way she had their language imprinted in hers. Do they long for the surface? She thought. Do they remember a time when they weren't lost at the bottom of the ocean?

The manta flew over a merchant district, little stalls carved out of rock and tents made of the skins of great ocean beasts or knitted with long fronds of seaweed. The art district was alive with statues, with the hum of distant music, muted by the water but still rippling in her ears. She heard someone singing, and though the words were muffled in this subsurface world, the melody drifted through, and though she could not understand the words, there was something profoundly moving and sad to the music, as if it were written at the end of the world.

And then the palace drew closer, more massive than she'd even imagined seeing it in the distance, its walls greenish stone, great columns reminiscent of ancient Greece like soldiers guarding its perimeter.

The manta took a long, lazy turn above the palace. Strange, Echo thought, that she could see guards, men with tridents in armor, but they did not seem particularly afraid. Perhaps a civilization on the bottom of the sea did not see violence the way the surface world did. Maybe there just weren't enough of them to properly terrorize each other the way humans do.

Echo pressed her palm against the manta's skin, and she thought thankful thoughts, unsure how else to repay the creature for its service. It drifted lower, close enough for Echo and Yuri to let go and float to the ground. As the manta swam away, Yuri watched, his face full of wonder.

"Every day," he said. The words felt strangely distorted; their Atlanteans had given them a crash course in speaking underwater, but they were both still getting used to how different it felt. "Every day since all this happened, I've seen something I never knew existed."

The front gates of the palace rose before them, massive doors built with some sort of smooth, gleaming material Echo couldn't identify. No guards stood watch outside. Echo and Yuri looked at each other and shrugged.

"I guess we knock," Echo said.

And she did just that, rapping her knuckles on the door three times, then stepping back to wait. The door creaked open, and an armored guard stepped out, his trident ready. Several of his fellows watched behind him.

"Who are you?" the guard said.

"I'm the daughter of Rhegis," she said. It felt strange saying her father's name out loud, the alien, inhuman name with all its loaded linguistic meaning. "And I'm here to talk with my aunt Reina, if you please."

"And who is that," the guard asked, gesturing at Yuri.

"This is my manservant," Echo said.

"Manservant?" Yuri said, offended.

"Very well," the guard said. "We were told you might be coming. Come along."

Chapter 55: I thought you'd look more human

The guards never spoke, and yet, Echo realized she never felt threatened. They seemed to be more confused about how she got there than whether or not she and Yuri posed some sort of danger to their queen. And there was something else, too—a hesitancy. They didn't grab her or try to put handcuffs on her, or whatever the Atlantean equivalent of handcuffs were. Instead, the palace guards were almost afraid of her, staying a few feet further away than she'd expect them to, refusing to make eye contact, signaling to each other in a way that seemed to hint that they didn't actually agree on how to handle Echo's presence.

Only the foyer of the palace was submerged. The guards led them to a set of stairs, and everyone walked slowly into the air, Yuri looking over his shoulder suspiciously at the guards more often than he faced forward.

"I think they're afraid of you," he whispered once they were out of the water.

Echo stretched, the sensation of leaving the water, as always, creating a strange sense of weight on her shoulders.

"Something's not right," Echo agreed. "Hey. Where are you taking us?"

"To see me," a woman's voice said. Her voice was deep with a hint of commanding presence, though, Echo noticed, not as much presence as the woman herself wanted it to have.

She stood above them on a landing at the top of the stairs, flanked by two more guards in anonymous armor. The newcomer wore a long blue dress that moved around her legs like water. Her feet were bare except for rings on several of her toes. She had long hair so dark it seemed like shadows cascaded down her back, held back by a demure gold and emerald tiara.

But it was her face that struck Echo most of all. That is what royalty looks like, Echo thought. Cheekbones and brow carved from glossy stone. Eyes like burning beacons that studied Echo and Yuri like prey.

"You look like my brother," Reina said, in a tone that told Echo the statement was more to herself than anyone else. "I thought you'd look more human."

"Is it me, or do the Atlanteans look like humans too?" Yuri said. Echo shot him a dirty look. "What? Someone had to say it."

Echo shook her head at Yuri and spoke instead directly to Reina.

"People keep saying that. That I look Atlantean. That I look like my father," she said. "But I've seen your people. And I don't understand. Atlanteans look just like us. Why do you insist that we're so different?"

The corners of Reina's mouth quirked into a smile but offered no answer.

"Your aunt seems nice," Yuri said quietly.

"You sound like your father, too," Reina said. "He had such a soft spot for the surface world. It made him weak."

Reina seemed to regard Echo in a different way just then. Appraising her, looking her up and down, lingering briefly on the clearly Atlantean armor she wore, the trident strapped to her back.

"So, you're my niece," she said, finally.

"And you're my aunt," Echo said, defiant. She tilted her chin up at her tormentor.

Reina paused, pursing her lips.

"It's not exactly a warm and longed-for family reunion, is it?" she said. "Why are you here, little girl?"

"Because I had nowhere else to go," Echo said. "Because your goons have chased me across the seven seas and I got tired of being the pursued. Because you stole my life."

"A flare for the dramatic like your father as well," Reina said. "It's one of the things I love about my brother. Everything is either poetic or life and death."

"You talk about him like he's still alive," Echo said. "Should I take that as a good sign?"

"A good sign?" Reina said, and burst out laughing. "You've never met him. Why would his whereabouts be anything to you, good or bad?"

"Because I know what you're planning to do," Echo said. "And I'm here to stop you."

"Oh really," Reina said. "And what, please tell me, am I planning to do."

"You want to start a war on the surface," Echo said.

Reina bowed her head.

"True enough," she said. "But do you know why?"

"Does it matter? You're starting a war!"

"What kind of monster starts a war without a reason?" Reina said. "Do you think I'm some kind of half-crazed nihilist?"

Echo paused, her heart pounding in her chest. This had to be a trick, she thought. It had to be. And yet—I want to know why, right? She thought. I should understand her.

Reina sensed her hesitation.

"Come with me," the queen of Atlantis said. "I want to show you something."

"Oh, this is such a bad idea," Yuri said.

"Tell your man-pet to be quiet," Reina said. "And follow me."

"What if I say no?" Echo said.

"You're not going to say no," Reina said. "You're too curious. I can see it in your eyes. You have your father's tells. Come along."

Echo waited, every muscle in her body tense. And then she

started walking up the dais.

"Where are you going," Yuri said.

"To see this through," Echo said. "Come on."

The queen turned her back on them and walked through a set of double doors into a grand corridor. One of the guards stopped her with a polite gesture.

"Your highness. She's armed," the guard said.

"A month ago, this girl had no idea she was one of us," Reina said. "I seriously doubt she's become some sort of legendary warrior with a trident since then. Let her keep her toy."

Echo didn't take the bait, letting the comment go unchallenged.

Reina led them down into a lower level, through a tunnel that seemed to sweat seawater, and through a set of gates. Guards watched them along the way, but soon, the armored warriors were joined by others, men and women in loose-fitting, monochromatic garments that reminded Echo of something quite the opposite of military garb—hospital scrubs. Beyond the passageway, the space opened into a massive chamber, lit with brilliant strips of arcane luminescence, the walls pale, the air antiseptic.

Reina asked them to follow her to a railing overlooking the room below, with stairs twisting down on either side, leading to the chamber floor.

"This is why I was angry when my brother wouldn't fight. This is why so many Atlanteans agree that the surface-dwellers should die. This is what I fight for. This is the reason why we cannot stand idly by any longer. Look, little niece," Reina said. "This is what your 'people' have done."

Echo couldn't help herself—she gasped audibly at the sight below. Yuri cursed and shook his head.

"No way," he said.

"Is this what I think it is?" Echo said softly.

"It is exactly what it looks like, my dear," Reina said.

The entire length of the room, longer than a football field, was lined with beds. Every bed was filled. Hundreds of beds, the occupants of which were wasting away. Dying. Sick.

They were children, almost all of them. An adult stood out here or there, or the occasional elderly patient. But the rest were younger than Echo, some barely old enough to walk. A vast room full of dying children.

"Why is this happening," Echo said, her voice raspy with fear.

"Humanity poisons the oceans, Echo," Reina said. "Oh, I know some of your kind want to stop it. But hundreds of years. Centuries. That's how long your people have been poisoning mine. We didn't understand what it was at first, of course. Does any epidemic present itself with perfect clarity right away? No, no. It started slowly. Took a generation for the first signs of sickness to appear. My grandparents saw the first victims, but no one knew the cause."

Reina walked down one of the spiral staircases. Echo followed her, only vaguely aware that Yuri was behind her. Reina stopped at one of the first beds they passed. The child looked up at her with massive, bleary eyes of indigo. Reina took the child's hand in both of hers.

"You're so strong, little one," Reina said softly, kissing the girl on the forehead, brushing her sweaty hair back from her brow.

The queen moved on to the next bed, and the next bed after that, touching hands and cheeks, whispering words of comfort.

"What is it," Echo asked. "What's happening to them all?"

"You have a word for something humanity very much like it humanity faces, Echo," Reina said. "Your people call your scourge cancer. We have our own unique illness, not unlike your cancer, from breathing in water filled with the refuse and sludge and excrement and chemical waste the surface world had nowhere else to dump. Every generation it gets worse."

"We... we didn't know," Echo said. "Most humans don't even know you exist."

"Does that really matter?" Reina said. "Is that truly an excuse? It's your world too. Your people eat the beasts of the oceans, just like us. They swim in these waters, they absorb it through their skin. But your kind also poison the air they breathe. Why should they care about the water we inhale?"

"Why didn't you reach out to us? You could have tried to stop us!" Echo said.

"Would humanity have listened?" Reina said. "We're not savages, Echo. We've studied your people. We know their fears, and their xenophobia, and their uncaringness. We know their greed. There is nothing we could have done to stop them. Not at this point, anyway. A hundred years ago, we might have stopped this. I blame my father and grandfather for not taking action. And I'll be damned if I stand by and let my brother follow in their footsteps."

Echo caught Yuri out of the corner of her eye, sitting with one of the dying children, talking to him softly. She saw the little boy laugh at some joke Yuri said. Yuri looked up for just a second to lock eyes with Echo, waiting for her signal. She shook her head.

"Do you understand now?" Reina said. "You came to stop me. Do you still think you should?"

Chapter 56: Not my first jailbreak

Having a royal spy among their allies was proving to be extremely beneficial.

Barnabas wished he had the sort of behind-the-curtain information Grimmin provided them about the prison for every other heist he'd ever pulled in his life. The old man had offered to come along, but given his injuries and age, Artem suggested the old spy would've slowed them down.

Barnabas was somewhat disappointed to not have the mental maps Grimmin had in his head of the prison layout, but the details he did provide—like the old, hidden hatch leading to a tunnel in the back of the building, used for interrogators to come and go from the prison for ages—were more than sufficient for Artem and Barnabas to get into the building.

Of course, someone had sealed the hatch from the inside, and Barnabas felt more than a little exposed as he crouched beside it, trying to remember the right spell that would unlock the door.

"Can't you move any faster?" Artem said. The Amazon's voice had a strange, metallic echo to it, the result of yet another spell Barnabas had cast, allowing the two of them to speak to each other by mouthing the words rather than talking out loud. Artem found speaking underwater particularly jarring, having never done so before, and Barnabas, despite being born to a mother who could converse underwater as naturally as breathing, had never been able to become comfortable with the concept. The spell helped. Except it sounded like the Amazon was yelling at Barnabas over his shoulder, disturbing his work.

"I'm doing the best I can," Barnabas said. Wizards had been using magic to unlock doors they shouldn't open since the dawn of time. Barnabas knew more than his fair share of unlocking spells, but, like a thief rummaging through his toolkit, he needed to find the magical equivalent of the right hex wrench to get the job done.

"Even their prison is pretty, though, isn't it?" Artem said. The comment was strangely sentimental from the young man, who had, in Barnabas' short time knowing him, proved himself to be profoundly unsentimental.

He looked up from his work on the hatch to see Artem looking at the structure. It looked like a giant conch shell rising out of the sea floor. Fronds of seaweed drifted like fields of grain, tall enough to provide the men the cover they needed to fiddle with the entrance without being spotted.

"How much do you remember of your homeland?" Barnabas said.

"What does this have to do with opening that door," Artem said.

"Nothing," Barnabas said. "Just curious."

Artem looked at Barnabas sideways, but answered anyway.

"Like a dream," Artem said. I was so young the things I do remember I doubt. They could just be a childhood fantasy."

"You should see it someday," Barnabas said.

Artem stared at Barnabas as if he had something weighty to say, but just shook his head.

"Open the door," he said instead.

Barnabas muttered the words to the spell he thought would do the trick and twisted the rusty handle on the hatch. It creaked open.

"Got it," he said.

But Artem was gone.

Barnabas bolted upright, scanning the field of seaweed for his companion.

"Where'd you go," he said, trying to keep the panic from his voice. "This isn't funny, Artem."

And then he saw Artem rise into the open water above the seaweed, and not under his own power—he was held tight in the grasp of a giant tentacle. And the Amazon was angry.

"Kill it!" Artem yelled. Barnabas saw him struggling to move his arms, pinned to his side by the coils of the tentacle. And then the rest of the creature rose out of the weeds—a giant octopus, skin shifting and changing to match the environment around it, eyes alien and intelligent staring at Barnabas like a threat.

"Of course. It's a guard octopus. Why wouldn't an Atlantean prison have a guard octopus?" Barnabas said.

"Just bloody kill it!" Artem said.

"I'm not going to kill it," Barnabas said calmly. "If you were breaking into a building on land and it had a guard dog, would you kill the dog?"

"If it were throwing me around like chew toy, yes I would!" Artem yelled.

"It's just doing its job," Barnabas said, reaching into one of his many pockets for spell components.

"Shoot it!" Artem said, the octopus swinging the warrior around like a conductor in front of his orchestra.

Barnabas raised his hands and released a pinch of sand, which glowed pale blue as it drifted away. The octopus started to charge toward him, but then became lethargic, its eyes glassy, limbs languid. Finally, it dropped Artem entirely and sunk beneath the seaweed line, disappearing.

Artem swam furiously toward Barnabas, cursing him out the entire way.

"You put it to sleep?" he said.

"Like I said. He was just doing his job. I'm not going to murder a guard animal for doing something people put him up to doing,"

Barnabas said.

"And you just happened to have a spell in your arsenal for putting an octopus to sleep," Artem said, incredulous.

"What can I say?" Barnabas said, shrugging. "This is not my first jailbreak."

***

The tunnel they had to crawl through was the stuff of nightmares. Artem, not one inclined to claustrophobia, felt the walls closing in on him as he swam down the corridor in the dark, a tiny crevice of light in the distance his only guide.
The tunnel was designed for swimming rather than crawling or walking, and it took a moment for Artem to adjust to that sensation. This world is so alien, he thought—up and down make less sense. Gravity works differently. I have to think about the world with an entire additional parameter. Like the monstrous octopus outside; the creature dropped him, fifteen feet from the ocean floor, and he just floated there. On the surface, that drop would've potentially broken a limb on impact. Not here.

Behind him, he heard Barnabas cursing, his long coat catching on rough corners of stone.

"I told you to leave that behind," Artem whispered.

"It has all my things in it," Barnabas said. "Do you know how hard it is to cast spells without things?"

"I don't know, and I don't want to," Artem said.

"Just keep going."

"I am."

"Hurry."

"You told me to be patient when you worked on the door," Artem said.

"Now you're just being vindictive."

After a long, painful crawl, they climbed out of the tunnel and into a wider pool. Artem swam to the surface, allowing only his eyes and the top of his head to breach. They were in a small room.

A cell. Artem saw a cot, a small table, and one barred door. He climbed from the water stealthily. Barnabas did the same.

"Why would there be a pool in a cell?" Artem said.

"Some of their prisoners, I suspect, can't survive out of the water for long periods of time," Barnabas said. "A cell like this would let an amphibious creature be submerged as often as it needed to. I bet a lot of their cells are like this."

Artem crossed the cell and placed a hand on the metal door. He pushed. It was unlocked.

"Good sign, or bad?" he asked.

"You ask me that like I know," Barnabas said, pushing past him into the hallway. "Let's keep moving."

The duo moved swiftly through the halls, passing empty cell after empty cell.

"Not many captives, it seems," Artem said. "This prison is virtually empty."

"The Atlanteans have truly kept to themselves for a few generations, as far as I know," Barnabas said. "If you have no enemies…"

"The human world is full of prisons, isn't it?" Artem said. "I've never been among them, but Merrick used to talk about…"

"Mainland humanity? They love taking away peoples' freedom," Barnabas said. "It's a matter of pride."

"Are they particularly criminally-minded?" Artem asked.

"Depends on who you talk to," Barnabas said. "I learned early on the less time I spend with regular people the better. Maybe they're all crooks. But I think I'd have liked the ones I've met better if they were."

"I used to think people like us were unfortunate to have been born among our 'other' side," Artem said. "And wondered if our human parents would have treated us better."

"As far as I can tell, Artem, we were doomed either way," Barnabas said. "You make the most of what you've got. I think we both have."

"That's debatable," Artem said, then held up a hand for silence.

He pressed his back to a wall and listened to two guards talking.

"He's here," one of the guards said.

"He makes me uncomfortable," the other guard said.

"He should," the first said. "That's his job."

"I feel like—he's not one of us, for sure."

"He's on our side, though."

"Are we sure, really?"

"You're sounding dangerously close to subversion," the first said.

"Our... She's employing a known assassin. A non-Atlantean."

"Desperate times, mate," the first said.

"We're on the right side, right? In all of this?" the second said.

Artem and Barnabas exchanged a knowing look. Artem mouthed the word "Barracuda?" Barnabas nodded. Artem indicated they should take out the guards, and Barnabas responded with a gesture basically saying: "be my guest."

Artem unslung the shield strapped to his back, turned around the corner with lightning quickness, and hurled it at the guards. The shield struck the first guard square in the chest, knocking him to the ground. Before the other could raise a weapon, Artem had crossed the distance between them, drawing both of his swords. He swatted the guard's trident from his hand and then spun swiftly, using the flat of his blade to knock the guard unconscious.

Then he heard the sharp clang of metal on metal. He ducked and felt the air move as a weapon breezed past his head. When he righted himself, he saw Barnabas, sword in hand, taking on a third guard neither of them had spotted. Deftly, Barnabas parried the guard's strikes, then uttered three words in a language Artem had never heard before. The guard collapsed like a puppet whose strings had been cut.

"You actually know how to use that thing?" Artem said, nodding at Barnabas' sword.

"What?"

"You've been carrying it since I met you and I've never seen you use it," Artem said.

"That's because I have a magic flintlock pistol that shoots spells," Barnabas said. "It's a lot more fun."

"I'm just surprised," Artem said.

"Hey, Merrick at least tried to make a fighter out of me," Barnabas said. "I might have been his worst student, but he could work wonders with the most hopeless of specimens."

"He really could," Artem said. He picked up one of the guards by the collar and slapped him. The guard gasped and struggled, but Artem pressed him against a wall and held him there.

"Who are you?" the guard asked.

"Where is the Barracuda," Artem said.

"What?"

"Where is he?"

"I can't—you can't..."

Artem leveled his sword at the guard's throat.

"I have two more of you to question if you won't answer. Tell me what I need to hear and you'll live through this."

"Um," Barnabas said, but the guard started talking, cutting him off.

"He's arriving any minute. Here to check on the prisoners," the guard said. Artem realized this was the one who had been voicing concerns about the assassin. The weak link.

"Where?"

"He always uses the servant's entrance, upstairs," the guard said. "That way. Up two stories."

"See, that wasn't so bad," Barnabas said. "Now don't kill the nice guard, Artem, like you promised."

"Thank you," Artem said, and then reversed his grip on his blade and walloped the guard on the side of the head, knocking him out.

"Hey!" Barnabas yelled.

"He'll live," Artem said. "You go to the cells. I'll find Barracuda."

"You can't kill the assassin yet," Barnabas said. "He knows where the second submarine is."

Artem smiled wickedly.

"Oh, I'll get him to talk first," he said. "It'll be my pleasure."

Barnabas frowned.

"Just… be careful, huh?" Barnabas said. "Don't have too much fun."

Artem shook his head.

"Revenge will never be fun, magician," he said, and held his hand out to Barnabas. The smuggler took it. "Good luck."

"You too," Barnabas said.

Artem released his hand and ran for the nearest stairwell and wondered, not for the first time, if he could defeat the killer who murdered the man taught him everything he knew.

Chapter 57: Your daughter looks just like you

Barnabas had broken out of prisons before. He'd broken into prisons too. He'd broken into prisons to break people out of prisons. But he'd never broken into a prison to rescue an imprisoned member of a royal family.

First time for everything, he thought, as he found himself in the more luxurious part of the facility, obviously intended for captives who required a more delicate touch.

He'd left the three guards unconscious, using the same sleeping spell he'd used on the octopus to make sure they stayed that way, and dragging them into a nearby cell, using their own keys to lock them in. Must be getting soft, he thought. Despite his protestations to Artem to leave the guards alive, there was a time he wouldn't have hesitated to kill them himself if it meant staying safe. Life among pirates and other unfortunate folk had pushed upon him a ruthlessness that even he felt uncomfortable with sometimes.

Add to that the fact that everyone on his ship until a few weeks ago was undead, and there was little doubt why he was so poorly socialized.

The luxury cells—what do you call these? Barnabas thought. Luxury cells sounded funny, but there must be a name. VIP cells? The surface world has some name for them, something about the

color of the collars worn by the criminals, blue or white?—
sprawled out in front of him, most empty, and long unused by the
look of them.

"If my last stint in a jail looked like this, I might not have
escaped," Barnabas said.

"Who said that?" a voice called out. Barnabas followed it row
by row until he found them, perhaps a dozen prisoners, all looking
tired and worried but otherwise no worse for wear. Some sported a
black eye or a few scratches—the ones who fought capture,
Barnabas thought, and good for them—but for prisoners of the
state, they could look a lot worse.

"You look like you escaped from the lower dungeons," one
captive said, an elderly man who smiled as he said it, his tone more
humorous than insulting.

"Keep it up and I'll leave you here," Barnabas said. "I'm really
only here for…"

And then Barnabas saw him. The resemblance was uncanny.

"You," Barnabas said. Rhegis watched him from behind the
bars of his cell. The king, unlike the other captives, did look like
he'd been mistreated. His side was bandaged, blood from an injury
showing through. His face was gaunt and pained, though his eyes
were clear and bright.

"Leave him be," another prisoner said, this one younger,
angrier.

"Let him speak," Rhegis said. "Do you know who I am,
stranger?"

"I know who you are," Barnabas said. "Your daughter looks just
like you."

This seemed to startle all the captives. A rumble of hushed
whispers worked its way through the cells.

"That means one of two things," Rhegis said. "Either you're here
to do me harm, or…"

"Your daughter sent me," Barnabas here. "I guess I'm here to
rescue you."

Rhegis' face broke, his expression that agonizing space between

275

joy and tears.

"You know my little girl," he said. "I think I know who you are now. You must be Grimmin's agent. The magician."

"Magician is stretching it, but close enough," Barnabas said.

"Thank you for watching over her," Rhegis said. He sounded nostalgic, almost delirious.

"If you'd done a better job than hiring some half-arsed smuggler who knows a few spells to watch her, we wouldn't be here," Barnabas said, surprised at his own anger. "If you'd been better, her mother would still be alive."

Rhegis's face withered at those words. Her eyes widened. His mouth tightened.

"Meredith is gone," he said.

"My king, a daughter?" the older prisoner said. "Who is this woman? What is going on?"

"Not now, Brendis," Rhegis said. "Later, if we survive. I'll explain everything. But you, magician. You've kept her safe? My little girl?"

"She's kept herself safe," Barnabas said. "She's remarkable. And powerful. And heroic. And brave. Braver than you lot, I suspect. Braver than me, certainly. She deserved better than what she's been through."

"Where is she now?" the king asked.

"With your sister," Barnabas said. "Buying us time."

"No," Rhegis said. He grasped the bars desperately. "We have to go her. She's not safe."

"Nobody is, thanks to all of you," Barnabas said. He pointed at the lock on the king's cell and uttered a quick and rough unlocking spell. The door snapped open.

"What about us?" said one of the prisoners, a middle-aged woman with a split lip still healing.

Barnabas glared at Rhegis as the king exited his cell. The king looked at him with an expression that was almost pleading.

"Please," he said. "They're good people."

Barnabas sighed. With a vicious hand gesture, he repeated the unlocking spell again and all the doors collectively disengaged.

"Come on," Barnabas said. "Let's go put a stop to all of this."

As the prisoners quickly pushed their cell doors open and gathered in the hallway, Rhegis touched Barnabas' arm.

"What's she like," he said softly. "My daughter. Is she really what you say?"

"Echo is worth more than all of us combined," Barnabas said. "And I think she's wasting her life trying to save this place for what you've done. But maybe that's why she's better than me. Maybe that's why she's better than you."

"Watch your tone," the one called Brendis said.

"No," Rhegis said. "No, he's right. I've made mistakes, sir. Thank you for standing by my daughter when… when I didn't."

Barnabas bit his tongue, quite sure whatever words bubbled beneath the surface in his mouth would be the sort he couldn't take back. Instead, he led the ragtag group of prisoners out of the cell block and back toward the escape tunnel. But before they got very far, a squadron of prison guards turned the corner, ready to stop them.

"Halt! All of you!" the lead guard shouted. He raised what looked like an over-complicated crossbow, taking aim at Barnabas. "Everyone back to your cells. No one's going anywhere."

Barnabas twisted his wrist. A small scroll slipped from within his sleeve and into the palm of his hand.

"Everyone here can breathe water, yeah?" Barnabas said.

"That's a strange question to ask," Rhegis said. "All of us are true Atlanteans. We can breathe air and water."

"Good," Barnabas said. "Be ready."

"Why? What are you doing?" Brendis said.

"I said back to your cells," The guard captain said. "And you— whatever you are, in the coat. Don't do anything stupid."

"Oh, I'm about to do something really stupid," he whispered.

"Whatever you're thinking of doing, now's the time," Rhegis said.

"The last time I cast this spell it almost killed me," Barnabas said. "I'm not sure I'll survive a second casting. If I end up bleeding to death through my eyes, do me a favor."

"Anything," Rhegis said.

"Tell Echo I went out doing something brave and stupid, okay?"

Without giving anyone time to respond, Barnabas unfurled the scroll and began shouting the words to a spell. The scroll began to glow, then caught fire, the flames blue and bright. The hall grew cold, and suddenly very damp, as if the ocean itself were permeating in through the stonework. And then something roared, some great, angry beast. The water coalesced into a shape, like a man's shape, and that body grew, and grew, and grew...

The water elemental raged under Barnabas' command, but complied with them, growing massive, shattering walls, battering the guards aside like dolls. The creature kept expanding, ten feet, twelve feet tall, bigger, wider. Seawater came crashing in as it grew to such enormity it destroyed the entire ceiling, ripping through stone and metal, tearing the prison itself apart. The sounds of the creature's rage could not be distinguished from the squeals and rumbles of the prison's destruction. All around him, the water came to claim this space, abhorring a vacuum, washing away the sins of incarceration, a storm of chaos and pain.

Barnabas felt his body grow cold and numb. He did not fight as the ocean came to claim him. His mouth tasted like blood, but his heart was light. Then darkness came to wash him away.

Chapter 58: The day love died

It didn't take long for Artem to find an area that resembled a hangar bay, a wide-open space dominated by a large pool where Atlanteans could enter the air-filled prison. He watched from hiding for a moment as guards came and left, often arriving on the backs of manta rays or other sea creatures acting as mounts. Once, a giant octopus like the one he'd fought outside lifted a tentacle above the surface, and one guardsman tossed it some sort of fish carcass as a treat.

It didn't feel like a main gateway, though—this was a service entrance, the guards moving supplies or heading out to patrol the perimeter. He heard one of them mention that a guard octopus hadn't checked in, his partner complaining that the octopi were as smart as people and could be stubborn like that.

And then a man rose out of the pool, astride the back of a giant seahorse, which surfaced only long enough to let the newcomer dismount before disappearing below again. The guards' tone changed as he arrived—they seemed put off by him, perhaps even a little bit afraid.

Everything about him seemed sharp—cheekbones and eyes, wide, thin shoulders like a clothes hanger, body built like a snake. He carried a pair of long knives, one on each hip, and moved like a killer. Artem recognized the body language—Artem himself moved the same way.

And then Artem heard the words he wanted to hear:

"Barracuda, sir," one of the guards said. "We weren't expecting you."

"The queen wants me to check on her brother," the newcomer said. "I'm just here to fulfill her wishes. No need to panic, boys."

He thought about sneaking after him, catching him in a less open space. But Barnabas was still down there. There was no way of knowing if he'd found Rhegis yet, or if they'd escaped. He couldn't risk Barnabas being caught unaware.

He drew both swords and stepped into the chamber, revealing himself.

"I've been looking for you," Artem announced, twisting his wrists to loosen them, his swords whistling.

Barracuda seemed surprised for just a second, his eyebrows frozen, forehead wrinkled in shock. Then he laughed.

"Look at you," Barracuda said. "You're a long way from home."

"You destroyed my home," Artem said. He walked slowly closer, watching the guards, prepared to kill them swiftly if they got in his way. Both guards put hands on their own weapons, but didn't draw, hesitating as they tried to parse out what this strange land-dweller meant, or where he came from.

"I've destroyed a lot of homes," Barracuda said. "You're going to have to be more specific. I will say I'm wholeheartedly impressed you found me here. Unless… Unless you're here because of all of this. Who do you work for, boy? You don't look like a typical human. You'd be wearing some nation's flag and carrying a useless firearm."

Artem's heart pounded in his ears. He took a breath to calm himself, to pull back. This was not a fight that would be won in anger, he knew. This Barracuda was too skilled. He killed Merrick in single combat. No one should have been able to do that. No one but me, Artem thought. I was the only one Merrick couldn't beat.

"I'm from the Island of Unwanted Things, murderer," Artem said. He exhaled. His limbs went loose and cold. Fear left him. Anger subsided. Something else crept in. Confidence. Not confidence, he suddenly realized. Acceptance. Life ends here, either way, he thought. I'm going to die in a few minutes. But this is how I choose to end my life. This is how I want it to end.

"Oh, don't tell me," Barracuda said. "You've come all this way for... Oh, you poor little lovelorn creature. You were his partner, weren't you?"

"He was the best man who ever lived," Artem said. "And you took him away from this world. You took him from me."

"Sir," one of the guards said. "Should we...?"

Barracuda held up a hand for silence.

"Why don't you two go on and check on the prisoners," he said with icy calm. "There's no way this lunatic got here on his own. Bring a full squadron. Someone may be trying to free the rebels."

"Are you certain, sir?"

Barracuda smiled slowly, showing his teeth.

"I'll be just fine," he said in a singsong voice. "This is nothing I can't handle. Go look in on the prisoners."

The guardsmen hesitated a moment, then ran toward a doorway behind them, away from Artem's approach. Barracuda drew his knives with a soft hiss. His stillness was that of a predator.

"You came all this way to die," Barracuda said. "Do you know how tragic that is? This isn't a fairy tale, boy. There's no one better in the world at killing people. You've wasted your life on vengeance you won't be able to fulfill."

"I owe it to him to try," Artem said. The calm in his own voice mystified him. He felt very far away from his body, as if he'd already left it behind. "The day you killed Merrick was the day love died. And I died with it."

"So melodramatic," Barracuda said. "This is so sad. I can see your potential. You might have lived to become something great someday. It'll be a shame putting you down."

"Still," Artem said, a smile creeping across his face. "Best to get it over with."

Barracuda laughed, a frigid, empty chuckle that echoed throughout the chamber.

And then they both attacked.

It was a blinding cacophony of blades, the clang of metal on metal, their blows ringing a staccato rhythm of violence. Parry and attack, duck and jump, the men moved with superhuman speed. An onlooker might not have even seen the fight happening, but rather witnessed a blur of metal and flesh.

Barracuda drew first blood, raking a knife across Artem's shoulder, but Artem used the momentary victory of his opponent to pierce Barracuda's thigh, sliding three inches of his blade in and out of the man's quadriceps and withdrawing it immediately. Blood spurted out from the wound. Neither warrior made a sound though, as the fight became bloody and brutal.

Artem barely dodged a slash to his throat, feeling the hot wetness of his own blood running down to his clavicle. He caught Barracuda across the back of one of his hands, and the assassin cried out, less in pain than at the way his own blood made the handle of his long knife slippery and harder to hold.

Neither man gave any ground to the other. Both were covered in nicks and slashes, bleeding from dozens of small wounds. Artem broke Barracuda's nose by smashing his forehead down on the bridge; he was rewarded for it by a blade digging into the flesh above his hip.

The battle slowed. Their moves were still precise and elegant, but the whirlwind pace began to flag, transitioning from art form to street fight. Artem nearly lost an eye as Barracuda's knife tore a bloody line through his cheek and forehead; Barracuda spit out gobs of blood from his mouth after Artem smashed his jaw with the butt a sword.

And then Artem slipped.

The floor was slick with blood and seawater. He stumbled, falling onto his backside, miraculously holding onto his swords. The assassin used the fall to his advantage, rising over Artem for the killing blow.

Desperately, the Amazon thrust forward with both blades as Barracuda slashed downward. Blood sprayed in a quick explosion of red.

Barracuda's right knife had pierced through Artem's armor, into the meat of Artem's trapezius muscle. But his other knife clattered to the ground, useless.

Barracuda's face was filled with shock more than pain. Artem's swords, thrusted upward, had slipped through Barracuda's chest, each blade cutting through the crevice where pectoral met shoulder, the tips of his swords emerging out his back, covered in blood. Barracuda's hands twitched reflexively, as if the fingers had forgotten their job. Artem kicked upward, sending Barracuda flying. The Amazon jumped to his feet and pushed the assassin to the ground, using his swords to pin him there. He knelt on Barracuda's chest, convinced that the assassin could somehow still fight; certain that he was faking the extent of his injuries.

But Barracuda just lay there, his eyes glassy. He smiled softly.

"This isn't the fairy tale I signed on for," the assassin said. "This is wrong."

Artem gritted his teeth and prepared to yank one blade out of the man's chest to finish the job by slitting his throat. But then he remembered his mission. His damned, terrible mission.

"Where is the other submarine?" he demanded. Barracuda looked at him as if lost.

"What?"

"The other war machine. Where is it?"

Barracuda started laughing.

"Is that really what you care about?" the assassin said. "This isn't right. This isn't how it ends."

"Where?" Artem said, twisting the blade. Barracuda didn't cry out in pain, though he gritted his teeth.

"It's in the trench," Barracuda said. "The volcanic trench to the north. But it's too late. Gods, what a stupid way this is to die."

Artem stood up, yanking both swords out of Barracuda's body.

He reared back one hand to strike.

"I lived on the Island of Unwanted Things, you know," Barracuda blurted out. "I knew him. I knew Merrick. I was an unwanted thing like you. Like him."

"Not like us," Artem said softly.

"I suppose not," Barracuda said, smiling. "I suppose not."

"This is for Merrick," Artem said.

But before he could deal the killing blow, the building rumbled and shook. The walls around them cracked and split. Seawater began pouring in through gaps in the ceiling above, through the walls. Barracuda roared laughing.

"Of course," Barracuda said.

And then the prison collapsed around them like an exploding bomb.

Chapter 59: The reason I can't

Reina led them out of the infirmary, closing the doors behind her as if a great weight landed on her shoulders.

"It's not a simple thing, Echo," Reina said. "You've come here to stop a war you know nothing about. And I'm sorry that you don't know more. If my brother had brought you here..."

"But he couldn't, could he," Echo said. "That's what I keep coming back to. You're afraid of us. You're afraid of me. I'm an abomination. Part of the problem. My father had a child with one of those monsters who poisoned your people."

Reina remained silent, her mouth a tight, unreadable line.

"And that's why he told almost no one," Echo said. "What would have happened? Would they have thought he was a traitor? A sympathizer? For falling in love? For seeing past everything else? Would he have been banished? Or would it have forced your people to look in the mirror and realize we're not so different?"

"You're not the first of your kind," Reina said. "Above and below, we've always had a fascination with each other. The only thing special about you is your father."

"Whoa," Yuri said. "So much for the loving aunt act."

"All of this," Echo said, ignoring the jab at Reina. "It just perpetuates the cycle. Of fear and distrust. Yes, humanity is ignorant and dangerous. But look at what you're about to do. And what do you think will happen when the surface world finds out who started this war? All you're doing is ensuring more death, more suffering."

"It's too late to forgive, little one," Reina said. "Too much has been done that can't be undone. There's no fixing the wounds that have been inflicted."

Echo could feel her pulse in her eyes. The rage building up inside her caused her heart to race. Forgiveness. The things that can't be undone.

I'm done trying to forgive, she thought.

"The reason I can't... I can't let this go, Reina," Echo said. "I can't see your reason, or your logic, or your worldview. Because of you my mother is dead. You killed my mom. And I came here to try to put the world back together again, or stop you from taking it apart, but you... my mother is dead because of what you've done. Don't talk to me about forgiveness for things that can't be undone."

Echo slid the trident from its loop on her back and snapped it open to full extension. She pointed it at Reina.

"Now we're going to stop that submarine," she said. "And you're going to let us. No one else is going to die because of you."

Reina sighed, her expression conflicted and tired.

"I meant you no harm," she said. "Unfortunately, I can't let you interfere. So…"

The Atlantean soldiers within earshot lifted their weapons and approached slowly, surrounding Echo and Yuri on all sides.

"Take them," Reina said. "Put them with the others. Don't injure her, if you can avoid it. She is family, after all."

The guards drew close, tridents outstretched, forming a semi-circle around Echo and Yuri.

"What are we thinking?" Yuri said. "This is a lot of pointy things to deal with."

"I think you should back off," Echo said. She reached out to grab one of the men's tridents, and the guard jerked it away reflexively, sending one of the sharp points up into Echo's hand. But where it should have cut through flesh and bone, Echo automatically caught the blade. She cried out, expecting her fingers to fall from her hand.

But no pain came. Instead, the point gave way to her grip, bending instead of cutting.

"Huh," Echo said, confused shock in her voice as she felt the metal edge of the trident dull against her skin. She tested it further, yanking the weapon from the guard's hand easily and bending it in half.

"You can add unbreakable skin to super strength to your list of positive features?" Yuri said.

"Looks like," she said, dropping the ruined trident to the floor. Curious, she pushed herself onto another trident, letting the three points curve and bend away from her as Echo forced her chest against the weapon, right where her heart would be.

"You guys see this?" Yuri asked, laughing. "This is my best friend. She's a super hero and she's going to kick all of your—"

Yuri looked down at his own torso, and then up at the guard closest to him. The Atlantean warrior's eyes weren't on Yuri, though, but rather on the point of his own trident, which had sunk several inches into Yuri's chest.

"Oh, you suck," Yuri said.

"Yuri," Echo said. "No. No, no, no."

Yuri reached down and pulled the trident out of his own body. Blood spurted out, spraying onto the hands of the Atlantean soldier. Echo looked back and forth from Yuri to Reina to the soldiers, holding her own weapon but unsure what to do. She grabbed Yuri's arm to steady him, but he felt stronger than ever. The muscles of his arm seemed to expand before her eyes.

"Yuri?" she said.

And then he turned to look at her.

His face had gone grayish white. His neck thickened unnaturally. His shoulders visibly expanded, tearing the fabric of his shirt with harsh ripping noises. He gazed at her with eyes that had gone pure black, reflective onyx spheres like those of a shark. When he opened his mouth, which widened monstrously, he revealed teeth that were transforming into sharp wedges. Each second, Yuri looked less and less human. The wounds on his chest sealed as if watching a video in reverse.

He put a hand on Echo's wrist. His fingers were long and silvery gray, ending in pointed claws.

"Echo," he said, his voice no longer sounding human at all. "Run."

And then chaos erupted.

Yuri's body exploded in size, nearly doubling in mass. He sprouted a tail with a sickle-shaped fin, which he used to toss the guards around like toys. He lashed out with oversized clawed hands, rending armor. The smell of fear and blood filled the room.

He turned his now-completely transformed head toward Echo. She saw nothing of the boy she knew there behind those dark eyes and the wide grin of razor teeth. He huffed at her, an alien, unreadable sound.

Echo ran.

She heard the men screaming, heard Yuri roaring in pain and rage, a terrifying pounding noise as he followed her, thick, clawed feet slamming against the floor gracelessly and powerfully. She threw a shoulder at a closed door and smashed it from its hinges, trying to remember the route Reina and her guards had led her along to get to the infirmary. I need to keep him away from the infirmary, Echo thought, I need him to follow me, he's going to kill those guards and I need to make sure he doesn't hurt the patients as well...

She saved one guard's life by knocking him silly with the butt of her trident as he tried to stop her, the trooper spinning and falling to the floor and under Yuri's outstretched claws.

They fled toward the entranceway to the palace, toward freedom and escape. There was a heavy, violent bang, almost like an explosion, and Echo felt a strange anxiety creeping up her spine.

She looked over her shoulder.

Yuri was gone.

Prone bodies of Atlantean soldiers lay sprawled all around. One wall—not a doorway, a full-fledged, reinforced wall—had been smashed open. Water poured in on the floor at an alarming rate. Some of that water was red with blood.

"Stop this now!" Reina cried, running to catch up, lifting her skirts to keep from tripping. She began yelling commands to the few soldiers who remained standing. "Get the engineers! That creature has breached the wall! Plug the leak before the entire palace floods. Hurry! Kill him if you must, or let him leave if he's already outside. No, don't pursue him, it's not worth the risk of life."

"Don't you dare kill him!" Echo said. "You did this! This is on your head."

"You," Reina said. "Don't you move another step."

"I think you've proven you can't stop me," Echo said. "And I still have a war to stop."

And then Echo felt herself hit with something like a giant fist, knocking her from her feet. She tried to stand up, but a great weight pushed down on her, keeping her on one knee.

"It's not your war to stop," a new voice said.

The newcomer was an older woman, dressed in rich, highly detailed robes. Beside her was a younger woman, wearing simple, almost drab clothing, her hand outstretched and glowing with arcane energy. A man entered with them, his gray robes like some sort of uniform of office. He was flanked by more Atlantean guards.

"What is this, Dame Rois?" Reina said.

"You've made a mess of things, my queen," the woman called Rois said. Echo strained against the magical restraints holding her down, her muscles bulging and burning as she pushed. "We're here to make sure the plan comes to fruition."

"What are you doing?" Reina said. She looked at the other two new arrivals with furious disdain. "You've overstepped yourself,

Dame. Senator Cartay, Professor Farris, you are interfering in royal family business."

"Perhaps it's time your royal family is answerable to the people they rule over," yet another new voice said, this one silky and soft. The latecomer walked with a cane supporting his heavy frame. He had a wonderfully welcoming face, Echo thought, but everything else about him oozed untrustworthiness.

"Gormlin," Reina said. "You were all together in this. For what? For power? For control?"

Dame Rois laughed. The sound cut through Echo's heart like a blade.

"For the same reason you were on our side, my queen," she said. "You think we simply thought you'd be a better ruler than your brother?"

"I lost my wife," the man beside Rois said. The senator, Echo realized. "My wife. Dame Rois lost her only daughter. Professor Farris her beloved nephews, who meant the world to her."

"My brother," Gormlin said. "He was my best friend. Do you know what it's like to lose the person you care about the most, my queen? Do you care about anyone at all as much as you care about yourself?"

"What do you mean?" Reina said. 'What are you talking about?"

"They lost people to the wasting sickness. To the poisons," Echo said, her jaw tight and clenched. "Haven't you. This revenge, this war, it's personal for all of you."

Dame Rois smiled at her. It was not a cruel smile. It seemed, in Echo's mind, to be one of sympathy and understanding.

"Rhegis' daughter," Rois said. "Oh, you poor little accident. I pity you. Born into this family, who cared for no one person as much as they cared for the kingdom they ruled over."

"This is the human girl?" Gormlin said.

"The abomination," Cartay said.

"No. She's not an abomination," Farris said. The professor was the one maintaining the spell holding Echo down. She walked closer her hand controlling the spell held perfectly still. "She's a miracle. And a tragedy. Little girl, if only our people weren't so afraid of beings like you. We're assured our mutual destruction, when we have always had the ability to bring women like you into the world."

"I'm not an abomination," Echo said. "And I'm not a miracle. I'm just a person, trying to stop you from ruining everything."

Gormlin, the soft-spoken one, knelt beside her so he could look her in the eyes.

"Too little too late," he said. "I can see in your eyes you've lost more than your father or aunt ever have. In another lifetime, little one, maybe you might have been the sympathetic voice our dying world needed. I'm sorry we had to meet like this."

"You're all crazy," Echo said.

"A broken heart will drive you a little mad," Gormlin said.

And then they heard the sound like a mountain tumbling down.

Chapter 60: Feral

Yuri witnessed the entire thing as if an audience member in a horror movie.

The blood, the violence, the looks of terror on the faces of the Atlantean soldiers as they looked at him. It felt like it happened to someone else, another person's body, even as their weapons pierced his skin. He remembered seeing Echo, not fear in her eyes, but rather worry, trying to calm him down, trying to make him stop.

But it's not me, Yuri thought. It's... him. The other one. The monster. I thought this would be different. I thought I'd be in control. But I'm not. I'm a passenger, and the shark is in control.

And yet, when he told the monster to flee, it fled. They—Or us? Am I still alone on my own body? Yuri wondered—found an armored window and destroyed it, ignoring the reinforced glass as it tore his snout and head, his arms and shoulders.

There was a rush of water, and then they were free, pushing through the fountain now leaking into the palace and into the open ocean. The tail he had never had before propelled him forward with incredible speed. It all felt so natural, so easy. As if this is what he was meant to be his entire life.

It's like I'm watching *Jaws* from the shark's perspective, he thought.

The rage and fear carried him forward, away from Atlantis. His new body moved with superhuman speed. Miles passed so quickly. Soon, he found himself surrounded by nothing but blue ocean, murky and vast. He felt as alone as he ever had in his entire life.

He didn't stop moving, but instead continued to swim relentlessly away, putting more miles between himself and the city at the bottom of the sea. I should go back, he thought. Echo needs me. I left her alone.

But if I go back, will I be able to control myself? He thought. Or will I go on another rampage? The terror in the eyes of those men haunted him. He could still feel their flesh rip beneath his claws. I'm a monster. I'm the thing that crawls out of the ocean in the night. And I don't know if I can stop from doing it again.

He looked down at his wrist, where the leather cuff Barnabas gave him remained. That felt like years ago, Yuri thought. When was that, a few days past? Everything feels blurry. I feel blurry. Like I'm losing my mind.

He reached down with a massive, clawed hand and flipped the cuff's cover open. The compass inside remained safe and intact. The arrow did not point north, but rather back where he'd come from.

It's set to lead me back to Echo, Yuri thought. And if it's still pointing that way, she must be okay.

He closed the cuff and clumsily re-fastened the cover. No, he thought. I'm not ready to go back yet. I can't go back. Not like this. Not when I'm this thing.

The shark inside of him, the monster he was becoming, demanded that he keep swimming. Do not stop, the creature said, if not with words, through emotions. We must never stop. To stop is to die. Keep going. Keep going. Keep going.

Yuri stared into the distance toward Atlantis, his heart full of questions and doubt.

And then he turned away and kept swimming toward the emptiness.

It's for the best, he thought. I don't belong with them anymore.

Chapter 61: I leave you alone for one hour

Chaos erupted in the palace foyer as the ground shook beneath them. Echo pushed against her magic bindings, but somehow the woman maintaining the spell kept her concentration, immobilizing her. The shouting began immediately, with all the conspirators throwing questions and accusations at each other while their bodyguards and soldiers regained their footing. No one seemed to know where to look or who to point their weapons at.

"What did you do?" Reina demanded, pointing an accusatory finger at Dame Rois and Senator Cartay.

"This is not my doing," Rois said. "This must be your brother's people."

"Guards! I want to know what that was," Reina shouted as the building stopped shaking. "Get a report immediately."

One of the guards began running toward the pool leading to the foyer exit, but he stopped in his tracks by a splash of light exploding from beneath the surface. Before the guard's body had even stopped bouncing, another flash of light exploded. Echo felt the weight of the spell lift off her shoulder before she saw the woman Reina had called the professor on the ground, looking uninjured but rattled, shaking her head as if to try to stay conscious.

"Hey, everyone," a familiar voice said. "I might have broken your prison."

Barnabas Coy climbed out of the pool, but not completely under his own power. He was flanked by a group of Atlanteans wearing prisoners' garb, and was supported by a man Echo had never seen before. He had Barnabas' arm draped over his shoulder as if the magician might collapse at any second. Barnabas looked terrible, with bruises under bloodshot eyes. He smiled, and Echo saw blood on his teeth.

Before she could ask what had happened to her friend, the other man's features sunk in. He had a mop of graying curls, and a well-kept beard.

Something about his face reminded Echo of herself.

"This needs to stop, Reina," the man said, setting Barnabas down at the edge of the pool. "This has gone too far."

"It's too late to change it now, Rhegis," Reina said. "What's done is done. The order has been given. The attack is eminent. And no matter how many of these oddities you suddenly find at your disposal to help you, we can't stop it."

"You're my father," Echo said. Everything else faded away in that moment, seeing this man she'd only ever met in her dreams. A stranger without whom she wouldn't exist. The man who left her on another world.

Rhegis stared back at her with haunted eyes. *He looks so tired,* Echo thought. *Not old. Tired. Worn down. But there was a strength to him, too. We are all a mixture of courage and cowardice,* she thought. *It's just a matter of which way the scales tip.*

"And you're Echo," he said. "We have so much to talk about."

"When this is over," Barnabas said. "Can that wait 'til this is over? Maybe prevent the entire surface world from going to war with itself and then coming after Atlantis?"

"I told you—the commands have been sent. We're launching two sets of missiles at surface targets from their own weapons," Reina said. "This is the right thing to do, brother."

"There's no right thing to do anymore," he said. "We've done all the wrong things, Reina, and we keep doing all the wrong things. We need to put an end to this."

"We know where the first submarine is," Echo said, loosening her shoulders and shaking off the weight of the spell she'd been under. "We can stop that attack."

"Where is the other one," Rhegis demanded. "Reina. All of you. Don't do this. Don't set us on this path. We won't survive it!"

Reina hesitated. Dame Rois spoke instead.

"What does it matter?" she said. "We're a dying species! And we've done nothing. Nothing. What tragedies have you faced? Who have you lost, either of you? Protected here in this tower. You've never known pain, even as your subjects suffered. You've let this happen. And we will not let you stop us."

"One of you," Echo said. "One of you has to have some shred of regret. Reina. You—I can see it in your eyes. You know this is wrong."

Reina shook her head, her eyes betraying her doubt. But she remained silent, as if trapped, unable to decide what to do.

"We can't stop the other attack if we don't know where they've hidden the vessel," Rhegis said.

"Good thing we know where it is now," another familiar voice said. Artem, a bloody, battered mess, clawed his way out of the entranceway pool. He waved at Echo, then shot Barnabas the filthiest look Echo had ever seen. "You the one that leveled the prison?"

"Leveling is a strong word," Barnabas said.

"You nearly killed me," Artem said.

"I thought that assassin was going to kill you anyway," Barnabas said, smirking. "Glad to see you're still standing."

Echo looked back and forth between the two men, her jaw hanging open.

"What happened to the two of you?" she said. "I leave you alone for one hour and you come back looking half-dead!"

"That's what you get for letting us out of your sight," Barnabas said. "You found the other sub?"

"It's in something called the trench," Artem said, scanning the room. "Anyone feel like pointing us in the right direction so we can save the world?"

"Are you okay?" Barnabas said. "You're showing more personality than usual."

Artem waved a hand at his head. He really doesn't look right, Echo thought. Though his spirits seemed to be brighter than she'd ever seen them.

"I think I'm concussed," he said. "Someone dropped a building on me."

"The trench? Poseidon's Scar?" Rhegis said. "We can't send you to the trench."

"Why not?"

"It's at a dangerous depth," an older man standing next to Rhegis said. "Even Atlanteans struggle at that level. Why on earth would you put it in the trench?"

"What is it about this trench that's dangerous?" Echo said.

"It's the pressure," Rhegis said. "And the heat. There are vents at that depth where lava sometimes erupts. It's not safe. Reina, what were you thinking?"

"What would someone need to swim into the trench?" Echo said. "Would, say, unbreakable skin and super-human strength be enough?"

Rhegis raised is eyebrows at her in disbelief.

"Yeah, your daughter is a superhuman," Echo said. "Maybe if you'd ever introduced yourself we both could have figured that out a long time ago. Now—Barnabas, Artem, can you take out the first sub?"

The men shrugged at each other.

"I've got a couple spells left in the tank," Barnabas said.

"I feel fantastic," Artem said, wiping away blood trickling down from his temple. "But I need a seahorse."

"What?" Echo said.

"A seahorse. I saw one earlier. I want to ride a giant seahorse into battle," Artem said.

"He's completely concussed," Barnabas said. "I think I like him better concussed."

"We have stables," Rhegis said. He gestured at one of his followers to fetch the creature.

"And you just need to tell me how to get to the trench," Echo said.

"I can't let you do this," Rhegis said. "Not alone."

"Fine," Echo said. "Then you're my guide. Saddle up. We don't have much time."

Chapter 62: Unwanted Things

I'm on a seahorse, Barnabas thought to himself. I'm astride a giant seahorse, riding off to stop a war, and I'm riding a seahorse because of my friend the Amazon.

"How you feeling, Artem?" Barnabas said. He'd renewed the minor spell he cast earlier allowing them to talk to each other clearly underwater.

The Amazonian's sense of humor—or rather his customary lack thereof, seemed to be returning to normal. He rode his seahorse like a warrior out of an old fairytale. He really does look the part, Barnabas had to admit—if you were going to cast a hero in a legend, Artem, with his sword and long hair and angelic face, he'd be the guy you'd choose.

"Like I've been stabbed multiple times and I'm not sure I'm going to survive the night," he said. "But I have a giant seahorse, so it could be worse."

"What happened with you and the assassin?" Barnabas asked cautiously. "Did you…"

"I was going to kill him, and then you dropped a prison on top of us," Artem said sharply. "I did not have a chance to finish him off. For all I know he's out here waiting for us."

"So that's definitely my fault," Barnabas said. He almost felt guilty about it. Except… "Were you really going to kill him? I mean. He deserved it. I don't deny he deserved to die. But Artem—you're not… It's not what Merrick would have wanted."

Artem didn't make eye contact, riding on as fast as his seahorse would carry him. Barnabas' steed seemed to see it as a competition.

"Look, Artem. I'm sorry. I wasn't thinking about that. I was just trying to get the rest of us out of there."

"Thank you," Artem said softly.

"What?"

"Thank you, Barnabas Coy," Artem said. "I would have killed him. I would have murdered a man out of vengeance. And there are worse reasons to kill a man. He took away the one person I loved most in this world. He would have deserved it."

"I hear a but in there."

"But you knew Merrick," Artem said. "You might have even been friends, in the odd way you are almost friends with people. And you understood what he believed. You're right. He would not have wanted me to seek out his killer and murder him myself. He would have wanted me to… do what a hero would do."

"You're not mad at me, then," Barnabas said.

"That's really what you're concerned about," Artem said, deadpan.

"I'm just making sure you aren't going to try to kill me for stopping you from killing Barracuda."

"You saved me from myself, as unintentional as it was," Artem said. "I not only forgive you for that. I thank you for it."

"You're welcome," Barnabas said.

"You did drop a prison on my head though," Artem said. "I'm mad at you for that."

"I completely understand," Barnabas said.

Artem reined his seahorse in and pointed into the distance.

"There," he said.

Drifting like a great beast in the murky ocean water was the submarine, slowly working its way to the surface. It was guarded on all sides by Atlantean warriors, flanking the vessel.

"Okay," Barnabas said. "All we have to do is take over the ship and…"

"It's too late," Artem said. "Do you hear that?"

Barnabas had never heard a noise like it in his life, but he was certain the rumbling noise he heard was the sound of some sort of propulsion device.

"They're launching the missile," Barnabas said. He remembered what Reina said back at the palace in a moment of guilt as they were leaving—the missiles were not what the land-dwelling societies called nuclear weapons, because the Atlanteans did not want to poison the air above the way humanity had poisoned the water below. They wanted to start a war, not destroy the very planet itself. Which mean, he thought, that this was basically a very big, very powerful bomb…

"I have an idea," he said. As he spoke, the Atlantean warriors spotted them. A squadron detached from the sub and started making their way toward them.

"Your ideas always go so well," Artem said.

"Just… keep them off me for a few minutes, okay?" Barnabas said. He pulled out his artifact, the magic wand disguised as a flintlock pistol, and began recalling the words to a spell he'd learned years ago among the books in the great serpent's tomb. I don't know if this will work underwater, he thought. But that's what magic is, right? Magic is defiance against reality. It is making the impossible possible. It is chaos and art.

And I am a magician, Barnabas thought. This is going to blow up in my face.

"I'll do what I can," Artem said, drawing one of his swords, sliding his shield onto the other arm, and looping the reins to his seahorse to his shield hand. He spurred the mount forward, and together they charged at the approaching Atlanteans.

Barnabas pulled one of the many charms he wore around his neck, snapping the hemp cord, and whispered an ancient phrase. The charm, a pink-white stone, turned to dust in his hand, the powder swirling around and entering the muzzle of his pistol. He turned his own seahorse to give himself a clear shot at the sub and raised his arm, taking aim.

This is going to hurt, he thought.

As he waited, he saw Artem meet the Atlantean troops on the field of battle. It should have been one-sided—Artem was no sea creature, just a man surviving underwater through parlor magic and relentless will. And yet he met the Atlanteans blow for blow, whirling and slashing, and the water ran red with blood, too much blood to be Artem's alone. It was a magnificent sight to behold. Not a fairy tale, Barnabas thought. A Greek tragedy, one of sacrifice and folly, brave men dying in a distant land for decisions made by leaders who would not pick up the sword themselves.

The missile erupted from the surface of the submarine, exploding in a jet of flame and foam. Time slowed. Barnabas let his spells alter reality for a split second. And he pulled the trigger.

A ball of light exploded from the muzzle of his pistol, a fireball that trailed not smoke but arcane symbols behind it like a tail, a spell incarnate, stronger than anything Barnabas could cast on its own. It did not travel in a straight line. No matter how accurately Barnabas shot, no natural projectile could move fast enough to match the speed of the missile. The mystic bolt arced upward, faster than anything man or Atlantean could build.

The spell struck the missile just below the warhead. The entire weapon lit from within as though its guts were aflame. And then it exploded.

Barnabas felt his pistol shatter in his grip, the artifact unable to sustain its form after casting the spell. The force of that transformation pounded into his hand, and Barnabas felt the deep, gut-wrenching pain as bones fractured and broke. He didn't have any time to truly assess the pain as a shockwave from the exploding missile washed over him, knocking him from his seahorse, sending him spiraling down deeper into the water.

He saw the submarine shudder and tilt so close to the explosion it lost all control. The ship began to sink, slowly at first, then dropping like a stone, disappearing into the dark waters below.

We did it, Barnabas thought, letting himself drift into the darkness as well. A couple of unwanted things, abandoned and unimportant. I wonder if anyone will ever know. I suppose it's just as well. Forgotten in death as well as life.

And then he felt a strong hand grab his wrist and pull.

"You could have warned me you were going to blow the damned missile up," Artem said. Somehow, the Amazon was still astride his seahorse—he'd even found Barnabas' poor, forgotten mount, and held both sets of reins in his other hand, steering his seahorse with his legs. Artem lifted Barnabas up pushed him onto his steed.

"Didn't know if it would work," Barnabas said. "I really figured we were going to have to fight our way onto the sub."

"I never want to do that again," Artem said.

"You don't have to worry about that," Barnabas said, cradling his broken hand. "I destroyed my magic gun. That was a one-time trick."

"Good," Artem said, smiling. "Guns are for savages anyway."

"Says the greatest swordsman who ever lived," Barnabas said. "You're biased, my friend."

"Whatever it takes to make sure you stop trying to kill me with collateral damage from your spells," Artem said. "You're a terrible magician."

"I know," Barnabas said. "But it gets the job done."

Chapter 63: Poseidon's Scar

No one had wanted to let Rhegis go with Echo to the trench called Poseidon's Scar. It was almost funny, Echo thought as they were preparing to leave, how the same people who locked him up refused to let him risk his life like this. Her father was adamant, though. He did calm down a bit when reinforcements showed up, including the old spy Grimmin, who insisted on joining them at least as far as the edge of the trench to make sure they found the submarine faster.

Echo needed to physically move people who both supported and opposed Rhegis from their path as they left, shoving their way out of the palace by force.

"They don't want to see you die," she said as the three of them rode individual manta rays away from Atlantis toward the glowing crack in the ocean floor Grimmin identified as the trench.

"I know you've seen the worst of us," Rhegis said. "But the Atlanteans—your people—they're not bad people, at heart."

"Forgive me for not believing that," Echo said. Every sentence she exchanged with Rhegis made her feel squeamish and conflicted. She wanted to hate him. She wanted to know him. She wanted to never speak to him again. She wanted to ask him about his life. It made no sense.

Or maybe it made all the sense in the world, she thought. He's the other half of my origin story. I should know where I came from.

The water above Poseidon's Scar was thick, almost foggy. Clouds of heat bubbled up from below like a storm.

"The submarine is hidden somewhere down there," Grimmin said. "These damned fools. What if something went wrong? What if it malfunctioned or sank?"

"And now I've got to, what, swim down there sabotage it?" Echo said. "How deep does the trench go?"

"Further than you can swim, even with the powers you have," Rhegis said. "I have to believe they didn't send the submersible much further than the ledge itself, otherwise they risked losing it for ever…"

Rhegis' voice trailed off. Echo followed his wide-eyed gaze and saw what had stolen the words from his mouth. Rising from the Scar like a leviathan was the submarine they sought, already heading for the surface.

"We're too late," Rhegis said.

"It's still too deep," Grimmin said. "If we can stop it from getting closer to the surface, we can prevent the launch."

"I can do that," Echo said.

"No," Rhegis said. "You're not going to do this alone."

"I realize we're new to each other here, but I don't think you understand," Echo said. "I'm not asking permission. And you're only going to get in my way."

"Echo," her father began.

"No," she said. "You can't help me. And if I fail, someone needs to be ready to try to save Atlantis from the surface world when they find out how this happened. Is your sister up to that task?"

"But we just met," Rhegis said. "I can't… I've done so much wrong, Echo. We need more time."

"Then you better hope I succeed," Echo said. "Because I don't plan on dying until I've had a chance to tell you how angry I am with you."

Rhegis gave her the softest, saddest smile she'd ever seen. Why does it have to be so complicated? She thought. Why can't I hate him more easily?

Because life is not simple, she knew. Because it's not easy. Because there's no right way to get through this world in one piece.

"Hey dad, watch me do this thing," Echo said, a half-hearted smile on her face.

"Echo," Grimmin said, interrupting the moment. Echo turned her attention back to the submarine and felt her stomach twist.

"Is that a second sub?" she said. Something moved alongside the vessel, long, and fast, with six fins, an unnatural shape moving with predatory grace.

"I know that thing," Grimmin said. "It's the creature that attacked me."

"An afanc," Rhegis said.

"I thought the afanc were gone from this world," Grimmin said.

"Okay, I'm going to need you guys to fill me in on…" Echo started. But before she could finish, the creature materialized in greater clarity, swimming out of the vent's murky waters. It was huge, large as a whale, with a head like a crocodile, three heavy fins on either side of its thick, scaly body, its hide scarred and muscled.

The afanc turned its yellow eyes on them. And as if sensing a threat, the creature headed straight for them.

"Run," Echo said.

"What?" Rhegis said.

"Go, just go," Echo said. She hefted her trident and prepared to charge. It had to be twenty or thirty tons, like a ship with teeth, forty or fifty feet of monster swimming at her with unearthly speed, its mouth large enough to swallow her whole.

But the creature never reached them. Out of nowhere, a man-sized storm of teeth and claws rocketed down, planting itself on the afanc's snout, ripping and biting like a rabid animal. The afanc bellowed, its deep, unearthly voice a wail of pain, and Echo realized what she was witnessing.

"Yuri," she said.

Her best friend was still in his were-shark form, a primal, powerful thing, rending and tearing, an uncontrolled mass of silvery skin and white, sharp teeth. The afanc tried to snap him in half with its jaws, but Yuri proved too fast, darting out of the way, circling his enemy so quickly he dove into its underbelly before it could stop him. The water became cloudy with blackish blood as the great beast and the were-shark battled.

"I've never seen anything like this," Grimmin said.

"I'm about to make it even more interesting," Echo said. "If Yuri fails, just keep the monster off me for a little longer."

She didn't wait for a response. Instead, she shot through the water, swimming faster than she ever thought possible, propelling herself with ferocious kicks like a dolphin. She closed in on the submarine fast, and slipped her trident into its holster on her back. The weapon would only get in the way, she knew.

She leveled her shoulder and with all the strength she had— human, Atlantean, super-human—she slammed into the hull of the sub, knocking it off course.

The metal skin of the vehicle dented beneath her, caving in. It listed to one side like a losing boxer, tilting.

Echo went to work, pounding her fists into the hull, feeling her fingers go numb, her shoulders aching with the impact. She grabbed hold of the armored exterior and pulled, peeling away the sub's outer layer like a banana skin. She felt suction pulling against her as she breached the hull and water went flooding in. She knew only Atlanteans were on board, and that they would survive, if they evacuated; but this ship would not.

Echo changed angles, pushing the submersible down toward the ocean floor. She put her shoulder into it, shoving it way from the trench, worried what would happen if the explosives within came into contact with the lava springs at the bottom of the ravine. I won't be the one to detonate the Earth's core, she imagined, picturing some nightmarish apocalyptic end of the world.

The nose of the sub pierced the sea floor, crumpling like a crushed cigarette. The rest of the vessel followed suit, tearing up the mud and muck, crashing to a final resting place. Atlantean fighters darted out of missile tubes and cracks in in the hull, but they didn't stay to fight, instead fleeing back toward Atlantis proper.

The afanc roared again, its voice carried so strongly by the water she felt it in her bones. She swam higher, ready for a fight, only to see the great monster swimming way, trailing blood, abandoning the battle.

She looked around for Yuri, but her friend was nowhere to be seen.

"Yuri!" she yelled. She searched for any sign of him—even his body, though the way the afanc fled, she thought the creature had given up a losing battle—but there was nothing. For the second time, her best friend was gone.

"Echo," Rhegis called out, steering his manta ray toward her. Grimmin flanked him, circling the area, watching for stragglers from the submarine.

Echo stared at Rhegis as if she didn't recognize him. Her whole body hurt; her shoulder, her back screamed with the realization of what she'd just done to herself. But more than anything else, her heart ached.

Another thing in my life that will never be the same, she thought. With Yuri gone, she had nothing left.

"I hope this was worth it," she said to her father.

"I don't know if I can tell you that," Rhegis said.

She could read the look on his face easily—empathy, guilt. Fear. I'm looking at a man who thinks everything he's ever done is a mistake, she realized. He failed his world. He failed his family. He failed me.

And he doesn't know how to make things right again.

Well, Echo thought, her eyes welling up with tears the sea would wash away. That makes two of us.

Chapter 64: Breaking news

Jon Broadstreet once again found himself cooling his heels in the office, waiting for an early evening meeting at City Hall. Not the zoning board this time—nope, school committee, voting on this year's budget. Which, he noted as he bit into the sad, world-weary peanut butter sandwich he'd brought with him from home, was actually kind of fun to cover, watching people argue about school budget. It wasn't covering some sort of cataclysmic disaster, but it was an improvement to his usual gigs.

Speaking of covering cataclysmic events though, Ike Olson, the international affairs lead reporter, was once again the only other occupant in the office at this hour. He'd taken a cell phone call in one of the fishbowl-style conference rooms littering the office, and, from the body language and hand gestures Broadstreet made extra effort to not get caught staring at, something big was happening.

Ike hung up his phone and stormed out into the bullpen, walking around in circles a few times, heading for his desk, then reversing direction and storming over to Broadstreet's desk.

"I need to tell another human being something," Ike said. "You're close enough. You'll do."

"Thanks. I guess."

"A ballistic missile detonated in the middle of the Atlantic

Ocean," Ike said.

"Okay," Broadstreet said out loud. Internally, he ran through most of the obscenities he knew but felt like he should hold in right now, because of professionalism.

"Nobody's taking credit for it. No nation, no terrorist group. Satellite footage shows what looks like one of the missing subs at the source of the explosion, but the missile never reached the surface. Detonated underwater."

"Do they know which missing sub?" Broadstreet said.
Ike shook his head.

"They might. They're not talking. The U.N. is going to get involved. This is…" Ike trailed off, sounding mystified. "This is an international incident involving no nations. It's a complete mystery."
"Doesn't it make sense that no one would want to take credit for, like, carjacking nuclear submarines?"

"It could go either way. Someone might want bragging rights, or to use it as a threat," Ike said. "Alternately, isn't it scarier not knowing who has them or where?"

"Who do you think it is?" Broadstreet said.

"Damned if I know," Ike said. "I'm just hearing off-the-record information—which, if you repeat, will ensure that I have to destroy your career, by the way."

"Understood."

"Just because I needed someone to rant to doesn't mean I like you or trust you."

"You got it, Ike," Broadstreet said. "Do you think it's terrorists?"

"I mean, that's where everyone goes immediately, y'know," Ike said. "It's not an unreasonable first assumption, but everyone is proceeding with understandable caution. There's also a lot, a lot of distrust between nations that have reasons to not trust each other already."

Ike held his stomach with his hand as if in pain.

"I'm going to need to get my doctor to up my prescription for

311

antacids," he said. "This job is going to kill me."

"It's either an act of war no one's claiming, or it's terrorists, or it's... what, the lost city of Atlantis?" Broadstreet said.

"My money is on the Loch Ness Monster if we're going to start crediting mythology for stolen nuclear submarines," Ike said.

"Did you know that every time you and I have a conversation I don't sleep well for like a week?"

"I used to be so much healthier before I started covering this beat," Ike said. "I need a new job."

"Then who would tell us all the terrifying things happening in the world?" Broadstreet said.

"Someone who doesn't care about a dramatically shortened life span through stress," Ike said.

"So... what happens next, then?" Broadstreet said. "Should we be preparing to cover World War III? Practicing drills hiding under our desks? Doomsday prepping?"

"I guess we wait and hope it's the Loch Ness Monster and not a foreign adversary," Ike said.

"I still think it'll turn out to be the lost city of Atlantis," Broadstreet said.

"I'll take that bet," Ike said.

"A week's worth of coffee at Apollo's. I win if it's the fictional city of Atlantis, you win if it's a sea monster. I'll even sport you the mulligan that it doesn't have to be Nessie," Broadstreet said.

They shook on it.

"You're on," Ike said. "Now if you'll excuse me, I'm going to go buy industrial strength antacid and try to find some reason to not live in fear."

Chapter 65: Fathers and daughters

The return to quiet in Atlantis happened with disconcerting ease, Echo noted. The soldiers who had fought on behalf of Reina and her conspirators quickly returned to their posts, as did the men who sided with Rhegis and his supporters. The city itself seemed to be almost unaware of what had happened just beyond their borders, or within the palace walls, though they looked at the damaged prison—not completely leveled as Barnabas had been claiming, but certainly close enough—with a sort of fearfulness that seemed out of character for the people of Atlantis.

Rhegis walked, or rather swam, with Echo, showing her the neighborhoods, the residential areas, the marketplaces. People stared, as much at the king being out and about as they did at this stranger in their midst who seemed to look so much like their king.

I don't belong here, Echo kept thinking to herself. I'll never belong here. She felt not like a stranger in a strange land but truly alien, an oddity, an experiment. This is not my home.

Back at the palace, she stood beside her father in a room high above the city, looking out over the glittering beauty below. She knew those streets now, not just by meandering with Rhegis, but her own adventures, the manta-ride she'd never forget on her way to confront Reina. She had a map of this city at the bottom of the sea burned into her mind now.

"I can't stay here," she said out of nowhere.

"You don't have to leave," Rhegis said. "We can make you comfortable here."

"I don't think you can," she said. She studied his face. I don't look that much like him, she concluded. It's all an illusion. People see what they want to see. "I think I understand why you never came for us."

"I wanted to," Rhegis said. He looked older than he should, and tired, like the events of the coup had taken years off his life. "Not a day went by I didn't think of you."

"But you never came to visit. You didn't have to… you didn't have to stay, you know that? All my life I wondered who you were," she said. "And I only got to meet you because of all of this."

"I had a duty to my people," Rhegis said.

"You had a duty to your kid, too," Echo said. "But I'm not mad for me. I'm mad for her. I don't think mom ever loved anyone else. I don't think she wanted to. There was just the memory of you."

"Was she unhappy?" Rhegis said.

"I don't think she was," Echo said. "But I'll never know now, will I? Because of your stupid city and your stupid politics and your stupid wars. You took her away. From me. And from yourself."

"I know this isn't a comfort," Rhegis said. "But if I'd done what I wanted to do—and Echo, I wish I could make you understand, if I had been an ordinary person and not heir to this throne, I could have done what I wanted to do—I would have never come back to Atlantis. I met your mother on a beach in a place far from here and far from her own home. She was surfing, and she was the most beautiful thing I'd ever seen in my life, above the waves, or below."

Echo said nothing, watching as her father seemed to lose control of his words.

"I loved her," he said. "But I always knew this was coming. Do you understand? This conflict has been building since before I was born, and I knew the breaking point would happen when my father died. It was always there, looming in the distance. And if I'd stayed on the surface with her? With you? Would there be bombs raining down on humanity right now? Would there be an unstoppable, unwinnable war started by my sister and her people?"

"We'll never know, will we," Echo said.

"There's a lot of things we'll never know," Rhegis said. "I never thought I'd get to meet you, Echo."

"I suppose you're disappointed," she said. "Maybe you wished your daughter would be someone who was a little different."

"Echo, you're exactly who you should be," Rhegis said. He placed a hand on the window, framing the city between his fingers. "You're perfect. And I have nothing to do with that."

The silence between them hummed like electric lights.

"I know I'm a disappointment to you," Rhegis said. "I don't say that out of self-pity. I just can't imagine in any of the visions you might have had for your father, I'd be what you hoped for."

"You could be worse," Echo said. "You... you're better than a lot of your own people in some ways, aren't you."

"I've seen the world above," Rhegis said. "Most of them haven't. You can't love what you've never encountered. You can't understand where you've never been."

"It's time for you to change that," Echo said.

"I know," Rhegis said. "Gods below, Echo, I've wanted to change that my whole life. We need to come out of the shadows."

"And you need to deal with your sister," Echo said.

"I do," Rhegis said.

She rubbed her eyes, exhaustion crashing over her like a wave.

"But Atlantis needs you both, doesn't it," she said. "You're the yin and yang. Without both of you, the balance is off. Things will fall apart."

"My father knew that much," Rhegis said. "I wish he'd been better at predicting other things."

"Would I have liked him? My grandfather?"

"He was a fascinating man," Rhegis said. "I loved him with my whole heart. I think you would have enjoyed him. He would have enjoyed you."

"Even if I'm half-human?" Echo said.

"Echo, we're all human," Rhegis said. "Atlantis didn't start at the bottom of the sea. We like to deny it, or to think we're better than humanity, but we all came from the same place. We're not nearly as special as we think we are."

"I think you're wrong," Echo said. "I think everyone is as special as they think they are."

Father and daughter smiled together, realizing, if nothing else, they were both optimists at heart. Some small thread to share, to bind them together. This is what they saw in each other, wasn't it, Echo thought. My father and mother. They saw hope. They had hope. And they never let it go.

"What will happen to Reina and the others?" Echo said.

"We'll make peace," Rhegis said. "She's my sister, Echo. She's not evil. She just made mistakes. Terrible, costly, tragic mistakes. But when people are afraid and angry and sad, they do awful things."

"My mother is dead because of her," Echo said. "I can't forgive her for that."

"I wish I could do the same," Rhegis said. "But to keep this city together, I need to make peace with her. I can't execute people for wanting to avenge their children and families."

"We all came here for revenge," Echo said. She almost called him 'dad.' She almost called him 'Rhegis.' Instead, she chose nothing at all. "What a waste of passion."

"Maybe we should put you in charge," Rhegis said.

Echo's head jerked up. Rhegis wore the slightest of smiles.

"That's not funny," Echo said.

"I'm not really kidding," he said. "You're the only heir to the throne now."

"You or Reina better get to work on fixing that pronto," Echo said.

"Maybe it should be you though. You've from above. You're from below. You could be the one who leads us into the sun,"

Rhegis said.

"You need to cut the crazy talk right now," Echo said.

Rhegis laughed. He has such a kind laugh, Echo thought. She pictured him talking with her mother, the two of them laughing and in love, in a time before all of this, before a life of tragedy and loss.

"Or maybe it truly is the end of the line," Rhegis said. "Dame Rois might be right. Perhaps our time is over."

"Well, don't keep the seat warm for me," Echo said.

"You might well change your mind someday," Rhegis said. "You have time."

He took her hand. She let him. The hand of a stranger. The hand of her father. A king. A flawed man. Someone she might never have known, had her life gone differently. None of this is worth what I lost, she thought. It will never be enough. But I will make the best of the life I have before me.

"I am so glad we met, regardless of how it happened," Rhegis said. "I don't know how else to say it."

"I think… I'm better for having met you too," Echo said. "I wish it happened another way."

He squeezed her hand. Outside the window, Atlantis bustled with activity, like any city, seemingly unaware of how close it had come to disaster.

This is not my home, Echo thought. But maybe someday, just maybe, I could care about this place too.

Chapter 66: Sort it out yourselves

Echo attempted to sit in on negotiations between Rhegis' people and Reina's, but Atlantean politics proved simultaneously too polite and too rude for her to handle. She sat between her father and aunt at first, but watching them try to determine what to do was more irritating than scary.

The room full of people—senators and barristers, generals and spymasters, left her feeling sick. The passive-aggressive tone many of them took was bad enough, but the way more than a few looked at her as if she were some sort of stain on the table infuriated her. The room went deadly quiet when someone—the former senator who had introduced himself to her as Brendis Kor—referred to Echo as "the heir-apparent," and that was nearly all she could handle from them. They bickered about whether to send a delegation to the surface or wait for an envoy, to hold off to find out if the surface had discovered Atlantis yet, to build up additional protections using arcane magic even stronger than that which currently masked the city from the surface.

"Y'know, I think you can sort it out yourselves," Echo said, standing up. "Someone can fetch me if you need me."

She walked away and the table erupted into more negotiations, much of which involved laws and precedents that meant nothing to her at all.

Grimmin, her father's spymaster, walked with her to the chamber's great glass door and followed her out into the hall.

"Not much of a politician, are you," he said.

"And I hope I never become one," she said.

"There's not many of us left, we Atlanteans," the spy said. "We've mastered the art of bickering because it keeps us from... well, doing what just happened. It's been a long time since we've had outright warfare in Atlantis. Sure, we've had our share of poisonings or mysterious deaths or the occasional stiletto to the throat, but most of our bloodshed is spilled through words. It's, well I can't say it's better, but it benefits the survival of our people."

"The surface world isn't much different, to be honest," Echo said. "Maybe I'm just not cut out for civilization anymore."

"You have the right to an uncivilized life, ma'am," Grimmin said. He raised an eyebrow as he spotted Barnabas and Artem approaching, both men patched up from the infirmary. Artem's arm was in a sling, his visible flesh a mess of bandages and stitches. Barnabas' hand was in a cast, his fingers immobilized so they could heal from all the damage he'd sustained.

"You'll keep my father safe?" Echo said before her friends joined them.

"That has been the one thing I've always tried to do," Grimmin said. "And you, princess."

"Really, you're going to use a term of endearment like that on me?" Echo said.

"I use it literally," Grimmin said, his white teeth breaking into a wide smile. "You are, without a hint of irony, the princess of Atlantis. What you choose to do with that title is up to you, but it's yours by birth."

"I would prefer you call me Echo," she said.

"Your wish is my command," Grimmin said. "I should return to your father. I suspect you might leave soon."

"We might," she said.

"Well then, your 'Jem' is in the stables," Grimmin said. "She'll take you wherever you need to go, and you can simply tell her to return here when you're done. We'll keep her safe for you."

She took the old spy's hand.

"I think you're probably one of the good ones, huh," she said.

"Shush," Grimmin said. "I'm an intelligence agent. We're not supposed to develop a reputation for being nice."

Grimmin shook her hand and returned to the conference stealthily. Her father, mid-conversation, looked through the glass door and caught her eye. He looked like the most lost man she'd ever seen.

"Did I hear him call you princess?" Barnabas said.

"Shut up, Barnabas Coy," Echo said.

"Princess Echo. Sounds like a fairy tale character," Barnabas said.

"It's a bit flouncy a title for you though," Artem said.

"Are you saying I'm not flouncy?" Echo said.

"You lack certain upscale attributes one usually attributes to princesses," Artem said.

"If I wanted to be a princess, I'd be as not-flouncy as I want to be, thank you very much," Echo said.

"We should just call you Echo,' Barnabas said. "For now."

"That'll do, guys," Echo said. "Let's go home."

Chapter 67: Where we go from here

Barnabas was legitimately surprised the ghost ship was still unoccupied when they climbed back on board.

"I really thought someone would've stolen it. The *Endless* is not a ship that likes to be captain-less," he said, waving at the ghost crew as they made ready to set sail again. He laughed at the spirits' eagerness—they were as ready to move on to the next journey as the living were.

"Who steals a ghost ship?" Echo said, setting aside her trident and sitting on the rail with a casual comfort Barnabas almost laughed it.

"In a way, I sort of stole a ghost ship," he said.

"But you're a lunatic," Artem said.

"Have you met many pirates?" Barnabas said. "Mental health isn't exactly high on their most common attributes. Once we left New Tortuga, it was up for grabs."

"It's good to be back, though," Echo said. "I don't know if I could ever live there. Never truly feeling the sun on your skin."

"Some of them wanted you to stay," Artem said. "I overheard them talking. There were quite a few who thought you might be the solution to some of their problems."

"All the more reason to get out of there," Echo said.

"But now that we're back," Barnabas said. "It begs the question: where do we go from here?"

"We need to find Yuri," Echo said. "That's my one and only goal."

Barnabas took off his long coat and tossed it on a hook never intended to hold a coat. One of the ghosts shot him a dirty look for his disrespect. He looked over his heavily tattooed arms, noticing scratches and burn marks he hadn't seen before.

"That compass I gave him will help him find his way back you," Barnabas said. "I don't know if finding a man who doesn't want to be found is the right thing to do. Echo, he may not be ready to come home yet. Yuri might not want to be found, and it might not be our right to find him."

"He's out there, alone, and probably afraid and ashamed," Echo said. "He's my oldest friend. I can't leave him to suffer through this by himself."

"Then we'll look for him," Artem said forcefully.

"Does that mean you're staying with us?" Echo asked.

Artem folded his arms across his chest and looked at the deck.

"I should go back to the Island of Unwanted Things. To say the goodbye I didn't get to say to Merrick," he said. "And to make sure everyone is okay. I abandoned them in my rush to vengeance. That was unfair. It was unkind."

"We'll go with you," Echo said. "Together."

Artem smiled. Again, Barnabas almost laughed—the Amazon, now that he'd made some peace with himself, had returned to being irritatingly grim, to the point where a smile on his ridiculously good-looking face seemed almost funny.

"Thank you," Artem said.

"I assume I'm welcome to come back as well," Barnabas said.

"I spoke to you in anger before, Barnabas Coy," Artem said. "We've faced enemies together. We've fought side by side. I hope…"

"I gotcha," Barnabas said. "And same to you."

The two men nodded at each other and Echo threw her hands up in disgust.

"Could you two stop acting like dudes for two seconds and hug it out or something?" she said.

"Maybe later," Barnabas said.

"We'll consider it," Artem said simultaneously.

"You're not planning on staying there though, picking up where Merrick left off?" Echo asked.

"I'll return, but I can't stay there forever," Artem said. "I've seen too much of the world. Hiding on an island, even one that does such good for the lost and abandoned... there are others who can carry on his work. This world needs heroes to fight for it, like you and me. I can't do what needs to be done by never leaving my island."

"You or me, he says," Barnabas said. "You catch that? See how he left me out of that sentence? We bury the hatchet but he has to throw in that little insult..."

"What about you, though," Echo said to Barnabas. "You don't have to look out for me anymore. You could go anywhere."

"I've spent my life living on the fringes of the world," Barnabas said. "I've done a lot of things I'm not proud of. But what we've done together... You got to me, Echo. I'll watch your back, wherever you go. You've got me."

Echo beamed a smile at him. She put a hand on each man's shoulder.

"Then we know where we're headed," she said. "Now if you don't mind, I'm going to go pass out for an hour. I feel like I haven't slept in days."

"Go on," Barnabas said, watching her disappear below deck, a fading smile on his face. "We'll set sail for the Island of Forgotten things."

When she was out of sight, Artem punched Barnabas in the shoulder.

"Stop that," the Amazon said.

"Stop what?" Barnabas said.

"She's too young for you," Artem said.

"I was thinking no thoughts even remotely related to that statement," Barnabas said in his most scandalized tone. "And wasn't Merrick like, thirty years older than you?"

"She's also too good for you," Artem said.

"Now that's an inarguable truth," Barnabas said. "I won't dispute that one bit. Go get some rest, tough guy. I'll get us where we need to go."

Artem headed below deck as well, shaking his head at the magician.

Barnabas Coy headed up to the captain's wheel, leaning on it casually, looking out over a blue see painted below a golden sky. His had been a very solitary life. He'd had few allies, and fewer friends. He'd been a liar, a thief, a mage, and a con man. And yet here he was. Sailing into the future among heroes.

"This funny old world," he said to himself. "You never cease to surprise me."

Chapter 68: In every story, you can choose

Yuri pulled himself to shore on some forgotten rock in the Atlantic, his body shaking as the transformation back to his human form finished. He gagged at the air in his throat. It felt alien, poisonous, made his head swim. But the pain subsided, and the confusion, and he rolled over onto his back to stare up at the clear blue sky.

My life is over, he thought. I've become a monster.

He flipped open the cuff on his wrist again and watched the needle spin until it found Echo, somewhere to the East. That's where I should go, he thought. That's where it's telling me to go. But how can I return to them? What if I transform again and can't control myself? What if I hurt Echo, or Artem, or Barnabas? Well, I could hurt Barnabas, that'd probably be fine. But still.

He laid there in the sand for hours, letting the sun burn his skin. Maybe I'll dry up and die, he thought. Isn't that what would happen if a shark ran aground? Do sharks run aground? No, they beach themselves, like whales, right? Is that what they do?

"This is not how I expected my life to end," he said out loud.

"Then stop being a coward and don't let it end that way," a gravelly voice said.

Yuri jumped to his feet, holding up his fists as if to fight. The newcomer didn't seem interested in fighting, Yuri thought, though he certainly didn't look friendly. Brawny and homely, he had a wide jaw, thick neck, and near-white hair he'd cut into a mohawk and slicked back, not unlike the style Echo favored. The man carried a net with him containing several large silver fish.

"Who are you?" Yuri said.

"Didn't figure you'd recognize me," the man said. "This wasn't planned, what happened to you. It never is. Our history is a long list of wrongs unintended."

"What wasn't planned," Yuri said, but the pieces were already starting to come together.

"One of my brothers bit you," he said. "We feel stupid. We were used. We should be better than we are. Most of us are just brainless thugs, hunting machines, barbarians looking for a good fight to die in. We were once kings of the oceans, and now we're little more than a rabid pack of monsters."

"You're like me," Yuri said. "You're a were-shark."

"One of the last who still walks around on land like he belongs there, too," the man said. "That's something else our brothers forget. We're as much men and women as we are sharks. We're two halves made whole, not beasts wearing the skin of men like a disguise. But the world hates us, so we play our part. Our nature inclines us to be the villain in stories. Sometimes it's easier to perform the role the world expects of you."

"You don't seem like the others," Yuri said.

"I'm not," he said. "But the others don't have to be like that. Neither do you."

"I don't have to be a monster?" Yuri said.

"Son, in every story, you can choose to be the monster, or you can choose to be the hero," the man said. He slid an oiled bag off his shoulder and pulled out flint and steel, and began gathering dried debris from the beach to make a fire. "You look hungry. Help me out here."

Yuri climbed to his feet and started picking up dry seaweed, bits of flotsam. The stranger drew out a boning knife and got to work preparing the fish.

"Some of the others, they'd just eat these raw. Still alive," the man said. He held up a finger and pointed at Yuri for emphasis. "You don't have to forget where you came from. You don't have to forget who you are."

"I... don't know your name," Yuri said.

"Call me Whitetip," the man said. "You've met my brother Maw and his bruisers. I'd like to help make amends for that."

"I'm Yuri," he said, holding out his hand. Whitetip took it and shook.

"Your world's about to get very strange," Whitetip said.

"That's okay," Yuri said. "It's been getting weirder by the minute for a long time now."

Chapter 69: Tis not too late to seek a newer world

They kept moving, as if they still felt as though they were being hunted. The journey to the Island of Unwanted Things passed quickly. They spoke little, but it was a companionable silence, the three heroes turning recent events over and over in their minds like stones picked up on the beach.

Artem healed with remarkable speed, something about his Amazonian heritage making this possible. Even still, his reception on the island was one of shock—old friends looking over his mostly-healed wounds, asking where he'd been, if he'd caught the man who killed Merrick, where they'd gone.

The other Unwanted Things kept Echo and Barnabas as arm's length at first. If Artem had forgiven them, the islanders had not had enough time to process that forgiveness yet. Echo spent the first day on the island, but slept on the ship after that. She felt the weight of their accusations in her heart.

She missed Yuri. Yuri might have helped win the unwanted back to their side.

A service was held for Merrick at the grave the islanders had dug. Artem stayed there long after the others had gone back to the village. He wept for hours, and spoke openly and out loud to the grave, telling Merrick everything he'd seen and done. Echo and Barnabas stayed with him for a while, and then left him to his grief. When they saw him later, he looked a changed man, ready for the future.

Barnabas disappeared often, for hours, returning with bags of mysterious items he wouldn't talk about. He told Echo he was emptying the last of his cache, because he felt he'd never be welcome here again. Echo said that the Unwanted Things would forgive him some day, as Artem had.

Barnabas just shook his head and gave he a sad smile.

"I brought death here," he said. "They'll never trust me again."

The minotaur, Asterion, asked about his former pupil. Echo thought about lying, saying he had gone back to the mainland safe and sound, but she looked into those huge eyes of watching her beneath his massive horns, and she knew he'd sense her lie. She told him the truth, that he'd been transformed, and run away, and that they were going to look for him.

"He has the heart of a warrior," Asterion said. "No one with such an unbreakable spirit will truly give up. Find him. Let him know that no matter what he's become, he is always welcome here at our table."

"I don't know if that goes for all of us," Echo said.

"They're scared," Asterion said. "Find your friend. Bring him back. Things will change. The island is nothing if not a place of forgiveness. Sometimes it just takes longer than others."

The ghost ship set sail the next day. They chased the horizon, heading east, then south. Echo asked Barnabas to bring them back to the isle of nereids to ask his mother for another favor, to find Yuri's hiding place.

"The sea is too big," Echo said. "Well never find him on our own."

Barnabas protested, but finally acquiesced. They set sail for the isle once more. Every mile they traveled she worried they were putting more distance between themselves and her best friend.

Barnabas and Artem found her in the prow of the ship,

watching the sun set, just the hint of coastline visible. She'd been thinking of her mother, of their home, of pizza on Friday nights, of swimming each morning, of the icehouse, of a simple life, before she knew so many terrible and beautiful things, before everything she'd loved was taken from her.

"I'm the girl with no home," Echo said.

"Homes are overrated," Barnabas said.

"And homes can be found again," Artem said.

"I can't take my eyes off the horizon," she said. "I feel like whatever we need, it's there, just out of reach."

"Then we'll keep going," Barnabas said.

"Like the poem," Echo said. "'Tis not too late to seek a newer world."

And with eyes on the horizon, they sailed on.

Epilogue: Once, on a shore

"I don't know why we have to meet this guy," Echo said, throwing a grumpy expression at Barnabas.

They waited on a beach somewhere in New England, depressingly close to where Echo grew up. She didn't like sailing this close to her old home; it brought back memories, and with most of the people she knew in her past life believing her dead, the possibility of running into someone who would recognize her filled her with anxiety.

"Look," Barnabas said. "A friend asked for a meeting. I'm just... Doing a favor."

"Why does this feel like a setup," Artem said, hands on the hilts of both swords.

"Because you're paranoid," Barnabas said.

"And you're eternally sketchy," Echo said. "It's not like you've never given either of us a reason to doubt you."

"I really resent that," Barnabas said.

Echo was about to throw a possibly hurtful barb back at Barnabas, but realizing a man was falling out of the sky stopped her.

"He's flying," Echo said.

"He is," Barnabas said.

"The things we've seen, this shouldn't be at all alarming, but somehow… a flying man is really disconcerting," Artem said.

The man landed softly in the sand a hundred feet away as if the wind itself deposited him gently on his feet. He wore a long black coat over jeans and a college tee shirt, his steel-toed boots looking ridiculous stomping along the beach as he trudged toward them. While his clothes looked out of place, it was his face that truly set him apart. His hair and neatly cropped goatee were pale blue, almost white, and he wore a pair of red-lensed glasses, hiding his eyes completely.

"Let me guess," Echo said. "One of your magician friends."

"I wouldn't call Barnabas Coy a friend," the man said. "Colleague maybe. Friends don't steal artifacts from other friends' collections."

"That was one time," Barnabas said.

"Three times, and you still owe me for the parts you needed for your pistol," the man in red glasses said.

"Yeah, that pistol's gone," Barnabas said. "Long story. It exploded."

The newcomer looked at Barnabas with an expression of profound disappointment, but then turned his focus on Echo—and, surprisingly, on Artem as well.

"I'm not really here to talk to him, though," he said. "My name is Doc Silence."

"How dramatic," Echo said. "Do all magicians have dramatic names and wear long coats?"

Doc Silence laughed.

"It's the pockets," he said.

"Lots of pockets," Barnabas said.

"Magicians need lots of pockets," Doc Silence said. "Anyway. I'm not here to talk about magic with you. You've drawn the attention of a lot of people out there in the world."

Echo started to protest, but Doc held up a hand.

"Not Barnabas' fault. You're a half-Atlantean with super-human strength sailing around stopping wars," he said. "People notice."

"I don't know how people could notice," Artem said. "The surface world doesn't care about the things we're doing."

"And you," Doc Silence said. "The last son of the Amazons. An extraordinary warrior. Both of you are unique in this world, and the sort of people who watch for strange and amazing things to happen... they know you're out there."

"Is this a threat?" Echo said.

"It's an offer," Doc Silence said. "I'm gathering a group. A team. It's made of remarkable young people. Wonders and miracles. And they're going to make the world a better place."

"You have always been so melodramatic," Barnabas said.

"Quiet, you," Doc said. "I'm talking to your friends."

"I thought we were friends," Barnabas said.

"Colleagues," Doc Silence said. "So. What say you?"

Echo grinned, but shook her head.

"You want me to become a super hero," she said.

"You might call it that," Doc said.

"I... I can't," Echo said. "There's so much I can do here at sea. So much I've left undone. My place is here. My work isn't finished."

Doc Silence nodded his head, an understanding smile on his face.

"Fair enough. I understand," he said. He turned to Artem. "What about you?"

"I go where she goes," the Amazon said. "Though maybe someday, we might reconsider."

"That's all I wanted to hear," Doc Silence said. He turned up the collar on his coat. "You're doing good work. You're heroes. All of you. Even you, Barnabas."

The pirate flipped an obscene gesture at Doc Silence in response.

"If you change your minds, you know where to find me," Doc said. "And if you ever need help—we'll be there if you call."

With a gesture, he lifted off the ground and alighted into the sky, disappearing among the low gray clouds.

"Well, that was a waste of time," Echo said.

"You never know," Artem said. "Some day we may need a real magician in our corner."

"You never stop with the insults, do you," Barnabas said.

"Come on, guys," Echo said. "We have work to do."

Also by Matthew Phillion

Novels in the Indestructibles Series – in print and e-book formats

The Indestructibles (Book 1)
The Indestructibles: Breakout (Book 2)
The Entropy of Everything (the Indestructibles Book 3)
Like a Comet (the Indestructibles Book 4)

Tales from the Indestructiverse

Echo and the Sea

The Indestructibles One-Shots (digital shorts)

The Soloist
Gifted
Blood & Bone
The Monsters We Make
Krampus in the City
Roll for Initiative (an Indestructibles Story) – also available in print

The Dungeon Crawlers Novella Series

The Player's Guide to Dungeon Crawling (The Dungeon Crawlers Book 1)
The Dungeoneer's Bestiary (The Dungeon Crawlers Book 2)
The Ghoul Slayer's Guidebook (The Dungeon Crawlers Book 3)

ABOUT THE AUTHOR

Matthew Phillion is a writer, actor, and film director based in Salem, Massachusetts. He is the author of the Indestructibles YA superhero novel series, the spinoff Echo and the Sea, and the Dungeon Crawlers series of novellas. A recovering journalist, Phillion has written about healthcare, cybersecurity, mental health, pop culture, and more. He can usually be found in the company of his sidekick, Watson the Wonder Dog, or acting as manservant to his belligerent cat Harley.